ANGUS DONALD

TEMPLAR ASSASSIN

canelo

First published in the United Kingdom in 2026 by

Canelo, an imprint of
Canelo Digital Publishing Limited,
20 Vauxhall Bridge Road,
London SW1V 2SA
United Kingdom

A Penguin Random House Company
The authorised representative in the EEA is Dorling Kindersley Verlag GmbH. Arnulfstr. 124, 80636 Munich, Germany

A CIP catalogue record for this book is available from the British Library.

ISBN 978 1 83598 092 7

Maps © Dave Slaney 2026

Cover design by Black Sheep Design Ltd

Cover images © Depositphotos Inc

Printed and bound in Great Britain by Clays Ltd, Elcograf S.p.A.

Look for more great books at
www.canelo.co | www.dk.com

1

MIX
Paper
FSC™ C018179

Templar Assassin

Angus Donald is the author of the bestselling Outlaw Chronicles, a series of ten novels set in the 12th/13th centuries and featuring a gangster-ish Robin Hood. Angus has also published the Holcroft Blood trilogy about a mildly autistic 17th-century English artillery officer, son of notorious Crown Jewels thief Colonel Thomas Blood. Before becoming an author, Angus worked as a fruit-picker in Greece, a waiter in New York City and as an anthropologist studying magic and witchcraft in Indonesia. For fifteen years he was a journalist working in Hong Kong, India, Afghanistan and London. He now writes full time from a medieval farmhouse in Kent.

www.angusdonaldbooks.com

Also by Angus Donald

Fire Born

The Last Berserker
The Saxon Wolf
The Loki Sword
King of the North
Blood of the Bear

The Mongol Knight

Templar Traitor
Templar Assassin

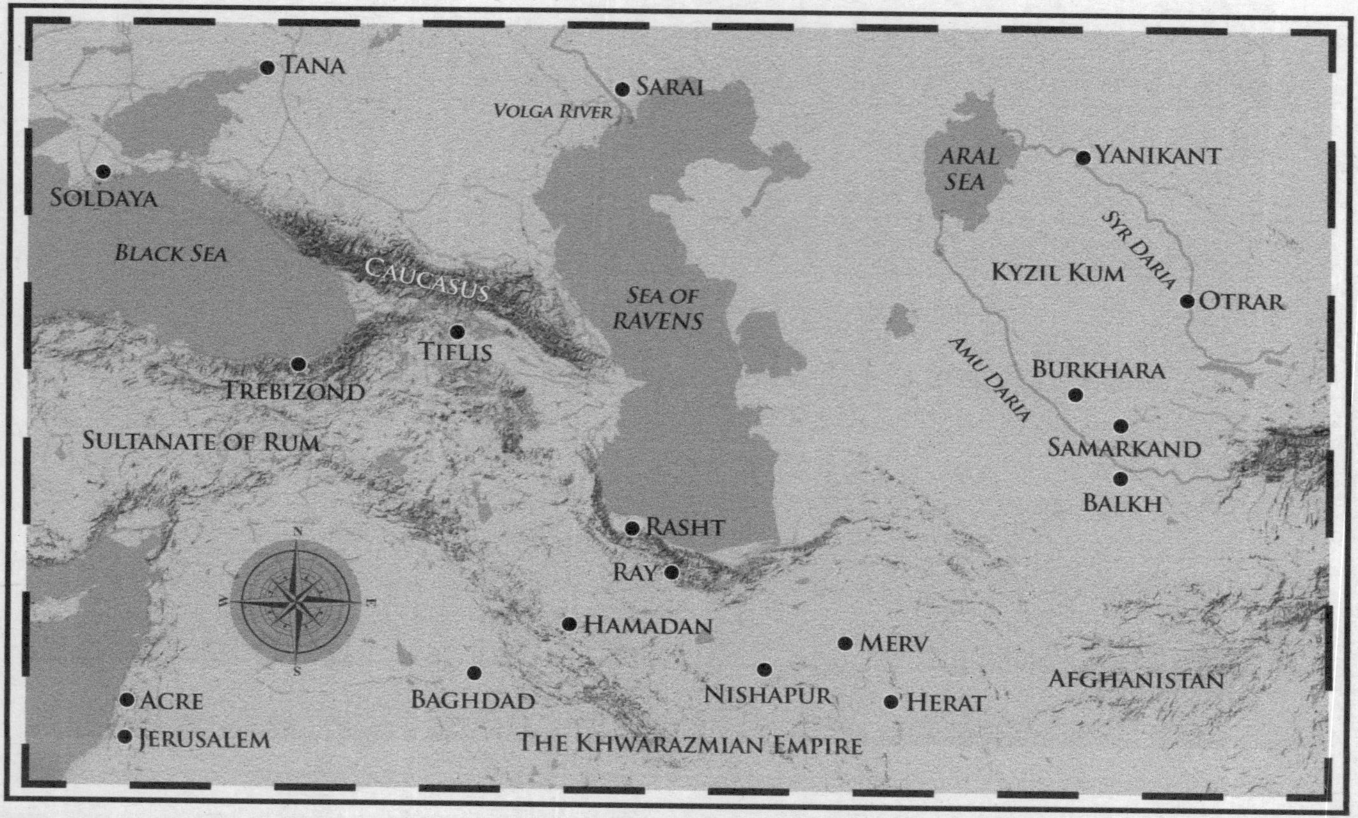
Tana
Sarai
Volga River
Soldaya
Black Sea
Caucasus
Sea of Ravens
Aral Sea
Yanikant
Syr Daria
Kyzil Kum
Otrar
Tiflis
Trebizond
Amu Daria
Burkhara
Samarkand
Balkh
Sultanate of Rum
Rasht
Ray
N
W
E
S
Hamadan
Merv
Afghanistan
Baghdad
Nishapur
Herat
Acre
Jerusalem
The Khwarazmian Empire

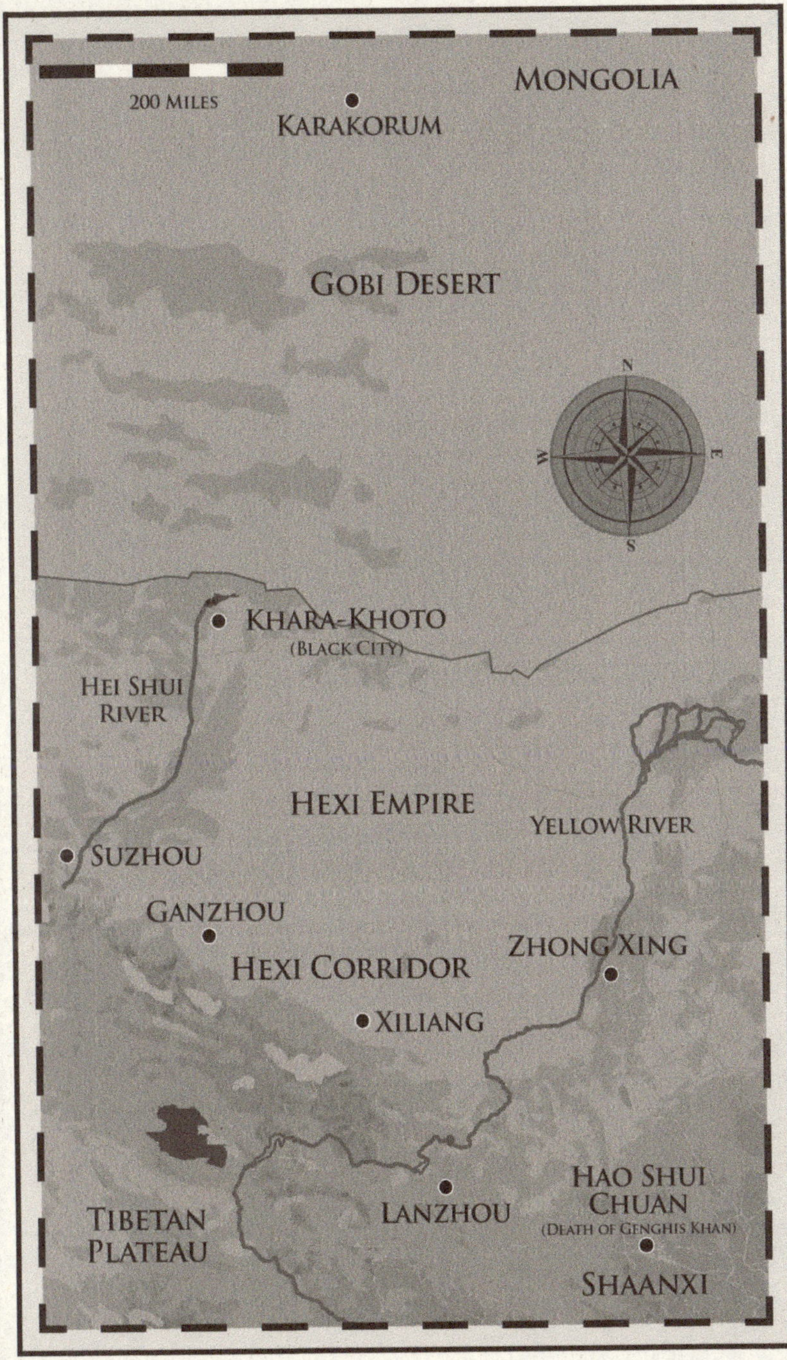

200 Miles
Mongolia
Karakorum
Gobi Desert
N
W
E
S
Khara-Khoto
(Black City)
Hei Shui
River
Hexi Empire
Yellow River
Suzhou
Ganzhou
Zhong Xing
Hexi Corridor
Xiliang
Hao Shui
Chuan
(Death of Genghis Khan)
Lanzhou
Tibetan
Plateau
Shaanxi

Chapter One

It was the smells that struck him first, all familiar yet somehow half-forgotten during his captivity. Robert kept his eyes closed and breathed in greedily through his nose.

The shutters of the hall had been thrown wide and the Englishman sucked in a great lungful of the dusty, peppery essence of stubbled fields, shorn of their barley and slowly baking in the late August heat. He scented the river, too, the mighty Danube, which flowed slowly outside the walls of the castle – a sour, rotten-vegetable smell.

Someone in the castle courtyard, just outside the hall's open shutters, was frying sausages and onions – a bold, bullying smell – and Robert's pinched belly grumbled like a distant summer thunderstorm. His gaolers, who were in truth no crueller than any ordinary men, had given him a heel of dry rye bread and a mug of good ale to break his fast when they brought him up blinking into the light, but it had not been enough to sate his hunger. He truly believed he would be hungry the rest of his life.

Which was unlikely to be a lengthy period. A few days at most.

The gaolers had allowed him to wash his emaciated, sore-marked body, too, in the sluice-house. With a bucket of chilly well water, he had attempted to scrub away the accumulated filth of nearly seven weeks of solitary captivity in that dank, black cell in the lowest depths of the stone keep. They had even given him a clean white chemise of rough linen, the usual garb of the penitent, to cover his skeletal nakedness.

Robert opened his eyes and received the second shock: a surfeit of light and colour. There were two hundred people sitting on rows of benches and stools along the sides of the hall, wearing scarlet and sky blue, moss green and creamy white.

Hard sunlight streamed in through the shutters, illuminating the painted plaster walls, which were adorned with scenes from the scriptures. To his right, St Matthew was depicted in all his dazzling glory, reading from a huge golden Bible, splendidly clad in a magnificent crimson robe and a gold-bordered cerulean over-mantle.

It was also troublingly noisy to Robert's cell-numbed ears: the crowd chittering like magpies, a mixture of German nobles in fur-trimmed gowns and knights in long robes with arming swords belted at their waists, their ladies in elaborate starched white headdresses and coloured veils. There were solemn prelates in their churchly pomp and monks in austere fustian, and wealthy merchants residing here in Vienna and from other towns in the Duke of Austria's domain, flaunting their wealth with elaborate plumed headwear. And a scatter of the poorer folk, too; travellers of all kinds, smiths and farriers, chapmen, rowdy apprentices and raggedy mendicant friars.

Some folk had come from as far as Prague up in Bohemia or Munich in Bavaria, or so he had been told by the excited gaolers. A few had travelled all the way from Paris, from the lands of Louis IX, the saintly King of France. They had all come here to Vienna Castle see him in the flesh: Robert of Hadlow. They had come to see the famous Englishman, the traitor to Christendom, meet his judgement and his doom.

Some in the crowded hall gawped openly at him as he sat there on a stool in the dock, tall, skinny and meek in his white penitent's chemise, confined in a waist-high square wooden box, rather like a pulpit, but at ground level, with the head gaoler Gutto standing proudly beside him outside the dock on the left, and Father Ivo of Narbonne, the inquisitor and his confessor, in a mirrored position on his right.

There were a trio of burly men-at-arms standing behind them, too, the castle constable Heinrich von Leitzdorf's men, grim in mail and armed with swords and steel-tipped spears, lest he should try to escape or require to be restrained by force.

Yet for the assembled worthies who ogled him from the benches, the spectacle was, so far, a disappointing one: Robert was a painfully thin man in his fifties with a clotted mass of grey-blond locks. He did not appear to be the epitome of traitorous evil. He was a once-broad-shouldered fellow, strong and long limbed, but now much reduced. His long face gaunt and angular from hunger and years of hard riding, but still bearing the faint yellowish traces of weathering by many harsh Eastern suns.

Robert engaged with none of these curious onlookers. He sat there stone-faced and silent, his blue eyes lowered. Then, just once, he glanced up at Ivo of Narbonne, the priest who had induced him, during several lengthy visits to his underground cell, into making a confession of his crimes. He seemed to be silently seeking reassurance.

Father Ivo, a large, hairy, round-faced man, smiled and nodded at him.

'Simply tell them the truth, my son,' Ivo said, reaching down to pat the prisoner's skeletal shoulder. 'God's holy truth shall be your shield.'

Robert looked away. There was a stir at the side of the hall and he saw that three men were now entering the chamber. The first to come in was a broad-chested, short-legged man in a green velvet gown with a golden chain bearing a huge ornamental key around his bull neck. This fellow strutted into the centre of the hall and, after loudly and unnecessarily clearing his throat, he proclaimed in French, 'My lords and ladies, clergy and commoners, I pray you all to be upstanding now for His Grace, Frederick of House Babenberg, second of that glorious name, the Duke of Austria and Styria.'

'Who is that proud little cockerel?' whispered Robert, as he rose to his feet.

Father Ivo replied, 'Wilhelm von Eslarn, the Provost of Vienna. He has been charged by the duke with conducting this trial.'

The next man to enter was known to Robert. It was the duke himself: a man of about thirty years, powerful and eager. He bounded forward into the space and strode up to a trio of heavy oak chairs placed at the far end of the hall on a raised dais. Without the slightest ceremony, he hurled himself into the middle chair, the grandest one, and immediately began scratching at his ribs through his fine blue robe and scanning the crowd of worthies on the benches, looking for faces that he recognised.

The older man who followed the duke also possessed a face that Robert recognised: it was lined, lean and watchful under a thatch of grey hair. He looked like a gnarled hunter from the deep Alpine forests except for the red-and-white surcoat he wore and the arming sword belted at his waist. He stalked, long-legged, after the duke and took his place, fittingly, at the right hand of his master. This, Robert knew, was Heinrich von Leitzdorf, constable of Vienna Castle and the duke's trusted counsellor.

The last man to enter the crowded hall was the most diffident of them all: a tonsured friar in the long black robe and knotted rope belt of a Dominican.

He was a slight fellow, small, thin and nervous as a fawn in a sunlit glade. He paused in the middle of the hall, glanced all around at the assembled people, then looked directly at Robert, offering the prisoner a tiny, almost conspiratorial smile, and nodding his head in cordial greeting as he did so. Robert nodded back, perplexed. He was certain he had never seen this delicate Dominican friar before in his entire life.

'And this little one?' he whispered, turning to look at Ivo.

'Geoffrey of Beaulieu, he is a Norman, personal adviser to the King of France on legal matters. His royal master petitioned the duke to allow Brother Geoffrey to sit on the panel of judges.

This is a great honour for you, Robert; the Dominican is said to possess the sharpest legal mind in Europe.'

With all three judges seated in their thrones on the dais, the Provost of Vienna stepped forward, his chin held high, and began the proceedings.

'You may all be seated,' he began. Then he waited impatiently, tapping a foot, for the multitude to settle on the benches and all their murmuring chatter to subside.

'We are gathered here this day,' Wilhelm von Eslarn said, 'to try the case of the prisoner arraigned before this court, one Robert of Hadlow, an English knight, and a former member of the Order of the Poor Fellow-Soldiers of Christ and of the Temple of Solomon, who stands accused of being a traitor to Christendom, a murderer of fellow Christians, a despoiler of goods and lands, a heretic condemned by the Holy Roman Church, who consorted with the foul armies of the Antichrist…'

There were hisses, boos and catcalls from the crowd, and one man called out, 'Burn him now! Forget the trial! Burn him at the stake this very day!'

Wilhelm von Eslarn held up his small right hand, and scowled at the crowd. 'I will have silence in this court – out of respect for our beloved duke. Where was I? Yes… who consorted with the foul armies of the Antichrist and betrayed all good and decent Christian folk by his actions.'

The Provost of Vienna paused, pleased with himself. He glanced across at the duke, who gave his minion a brisk, approving nod. 'Who then speaks for this Devil-worshipping traitor to Christendom?' asked Wilhelm.

Ivo of Narbonne rose to his feet. But before he could say a word, the Dominican, seated on the duke's left, raised his hand. Then, without waiting for permission, he said, 'You ought not to speak of the prisoner thus.'

There was an instant of appalled silence in the court.

'What!' said Frederick. 'Why not? Why can he not speak like that?'

'You may not yet have been fully appraised, Your Grace, of recent changes to the royal law in the Kingdom of France,' said the Dominican. 'But my master has decreed that all his prisoners are henceforth to be considered innocent until they have been proven guilty. In France, it is deemed to be the function of the court to demonstrate publicly in its proceedings an accused man's guilt or his innocence. But, until such a time as the court has deliberated and come to its decision, King Louis has decreed that a prisoner should always be treated as an innocent man.'

Duke Frederick was scratching at his blond scalp and frowning.

'I am aware that Austria is not France,' continued this odd, fawn-like friar, 'but when Your Grace invited me to join this tribunal, with King Louis's blessing, it was agreed that the laws of France would be observed during the entire proceedings. All Christendom is watching, Your Grace, and it is vital that justice is seen to be done in this matter. Therefore the provost will kindly *not* refer to the prisoner as a "Devil-worshipping traitor to Christendom" until he has been found guilty – if he *is* found guilty – prior to that he must be referred to as "the prisoner" – or by his own name.'

'God-damned lawyers,' muttered Frederick under his breath, then much louder, 'Very well, do as he says, Provost. Call him "prisoner". Carry on now, if you please.'

Wilhelm von Eslarn turned to the dock once more. 'Who then speaks for… for the prisoner?' he asked. But Father Ivo was already on his feet.

'I have that honour,' he said, making a bow to the dais. 'I am Father Ivo of Narbonne, loyal servant of His Grace Géraud de Malemort, Bishop of Bordeaux. I am the prisoner's friend, his counsellor and his confessor, and the only man to whom he has given any kind of account of his long and various travels in the East.

'However, I, too, have a quibble with the court which I seek to address. You mentioned earlier, my lord provost, that

Robert of Hadlow is a *former* member of the Order of the Knights Templar. This is not the case. My friend maintains that he *remains* a member of the Templar Order in good standing and a devout Christian. He insists that all his actions in the East were at the behest of his Templar masters. That is, in essence, his defence against these accusations. Robert of Hadlow insists that he cannot be a traitor to Christendom because he has always *served* and *continues to serve* Christendom, in his role as a Brother-Knight of the Templars.'

There was a murmur of conversation in the ranks on the benches, and Duke Frederick conferred briefly with his elderly constable. Geoffrey of Beaulieu stared up dreamily into the rafters, a tiny smile playing over his lips.

The duke beckoned the provost over. They spoke together, for a while, their conversations inaudible in the dock. Then the provost nodded, bowed and strutted away from the thrones on the dais, and back into the centre of the hall.

He addressed the whole hall, turning frequently to aim his remarks both at the dais and to the dock, and the packed benches of onlookers on both sides.

'This is the court of His Grace, Frederick, Duke of Austria, just as this is *his* hall, in *his* castle of Vienna, and my lord has determined the shape and form that this trial will take. This is not France, this is not England, nor any of the kingdoms of Outremer, and His Grace has no overlord but the Holy Roman Emperor and therefore the duke himself shall prescribe the proceedings of the trial *in his own court*.'

The provost paused to let that sink in.

'Duke Frederick has sagely decided that the court officer, in the person of myself, Wilhelm von Eslarn, shall adumbrate the charges against the prisoner, and state the evidence we have gathered of his crimes. Then the prisoner's friend and counsellor shall make a statement explaining the prisoner's current situation and his past actions and movements. Then the prisoner himself shall be questioned by the members of the court, including the duke himself, and he will be allowed to answer freely. And when we are satisfied that our questions have been answered, to the best of the prisoner's ability, then the prisoner's counsellor shall make a final statement in his defence and the court will adjourn while the three judges consider their verdict. Once the verdict is given –' and here the provost looked at the Dominican – '*if* the prisoner is found to be guilty, the court's sentence will be pronounced immediately and carried out forthwith.'

'On behalf of the prisoner, I accept this form of trial,' said Ivo.

'It is not for you to accept or refuse,' snapped Wilhelm. 'This is the shape that the trial will take. His Grace has decided. This is what will happen.'

Father Ivo bowed his head. Robert did not appear to be listening. He was gazing at the ceiling. He even seemed to be smiling. Remembering something pleasant.

'Therefore, I shall now state the charges and present the overwhelming evidence we have gathered,' said Wilhelm. And he took in a large breath and began.

'The prisoner was captured on the third day of July, the day of the Feast of St Thomas the Apostle, in the Year of Our Lord Twelve Hundred and Forty-one outside the village of Korneuburg on the north bank of the River Danube, no more than eleven miles from this hall. His capture was personally witnessed by His Grace the duke himself and by his constable Heinrich von Leitzdorf.'

The provost waved a small hand towards the dais. 'When the prisoner was captured, he was riding and fighting with a large party of those barbarian horsemen we call the Tartars. He gave every impression of being their leader.

'As every Christian knows, these Tartars are a race of inhuman beings, part-centaur, part-Satanic imp, who feast on the corpses of their enemies and mutilate captive women for their pleasure. These Satanic legions erupted in their thousands of thousands from the Eastern wastes; they smashed the princes of Russia, then cowed the King of Hungary and destroyed the massed Christian knighthood of Poland in the catastrophic battle at the town of Leignitz, which took place in April of this year. And I must repeat that the prisoner appeared to be the leader of the company of these fiends.'

There were gasps from the benches at this.

'If any further proof were required that Robert of Hadlow is a chieftain of these diabolic horse people, this plague upon mankind, this curse upon Christendom, it is the testimony of His Grace the duke and Constable von Leitzdorf that this very same Englishman presented himself an envoy or ambassador from the Khan of the Tartars in the Hungarian city of Pest in the spring of this year, threatening King Béla with total destruction of his land if he did not immediately surrender to the invaders.'

There were now loud growls of anger from the benches. Duke Frederick stood. 'I will have silence in my court. This is no common entertainment, no bull- or bear-baiting,' he said. 'Anyone who creates a disturbance will be expelled from my hall.'

The duke made a gesture at the provost. 'Continue, Wilhelm, if you please.'

'This is the essence of the case against the prisoner: that he was not only a member of this foul army from Hell but one of the commanders. And that these Tartars did make unholy war on Christendom, wreak destruction on our lands and kill countless thousands of innocent souls. Therefore, since he claims to be a Christian, he must have betrayed his own folk. In short, Robert of Hadlow is a traitor to Christendom.'

Apart from a few murmurs, the crowd more or less kept their silence.

'I now invite you, Father Ivo,' said the provost, 'to make your statement.'

Ivo stood up from his stool and cleared his throat. 'The first thing you must all understand,' he said, 'is that the horse-borne invaders you call Tartars, are, in fact, a diverse people called the Mongols. One tribe among them is indeed known as Tartars, but these many peoples, unified by their great leader, Genghis Khan, two generations ago, is called the Mongol nation. The second thing you must grasp is they are *not* fiends from Hell but mortal men just like you or I – fierce in war, yes, ruthless, certainly – but no more Satanic than any common enemy faced in battle.'

'Get on with it, priest,' said the duke. 'Who cares who these foes are or what their true name? Tell us why the prisoner was riding with them.'

'Very well, Your Grace,' said Ivo. 'This is the tale the prisoner related to me during his captivity. Robert and I were together in his cell for many days, and I believe it to be a true account of his actions. The tale begins in Acre in the Year of Our Lord Twelve Hundred and Eighteen, when Robert of Hadlow was a respected brother-knight of that Templar stronghold in that great city in the Holy Land…'

Chapter Two

Robert closed his eyes again and listened as Father Ivo recounted his story to the court. He heard the priest describe his recruitment for a vital years-long mission, by his friend and mentor Jean de Malemort, the Seneschal of the Templar Order. The mission was to bring military aid to the beleaguered Christians of Outremer. Robert could hear, in his mind, the Seneschal telling him never to speak of the mission, on pain of death.

'You can never tell a soul, Robert,' Jean de Malemort had said. 'You must take this secret knowledge to your grave. No man can ever know the part you played.'

Robert had sworn an oath to his mentor that he would never reveal the truth. And he had broken it. Ivo of Narbonne had wormed it out of him in that black and stinking cell, using Robert's ever-gnawing hunger as well as soft persuasions and unanswerable arguments. Robert had been broken. He was ashamed of that – but, at the same time, what did it really matter? What did it matter if these Austrians knew that he had been sent east by Malemort more than twenty years ago? Malemort was dead. His mission had been a failure. Now he was doomed to die a traitor's death when this farce of a trial was done. He did not want to die but knew he deserved it: there were several black crimes on his conscience that fully merited a sentence of death.

He listened to Ivo describe another farcical trial in Acre, in which Robert had also been in the dock. It had all been arranged by Malemort with Robert's agreement: the

Englishman had been tried and found guilty and, ostensibly, publicly expelled from the ranks of the Templars for gambling. Stripped of his prized Templar cloak and arms, he had been sent penniless in rags to wander in the wastes of Syria.

Malemort had told him to make for an oasis deep in the baking Syrian desert and, after an attack by a gang of bandits, he had only just made it there alive. He had been found half-dead of thirst and heat by the Habbani, a tribe of Jewish merchants, led by a man called Aaron, a friend of Malemort's, who shared with the Seneschal a hatred of the Ayyubid Sultanate, the enemy of the Latin kingdoms, which ruled the Muslim lands around the tiny Christian redoubt on the Mediterranean coast. Aaron and his camel train had borne Robert north, over the Caucasus Mountains, to Tana, a remote Venetian settlement on the Sea of Azov, on the lip of the steppe.

At Tana, Robert had been received by Niccolò Ziani, a wealthy Venetian merchant, who was an ally of Jean de Malemort's but who was motivated by lust for gold rather than hatred of the enemies of Christ. And it was at Tana that Robert had learned of the fate of his younger brother Gilbert, a fellow Templar Knight, who had become a prisoner of the Saracens at the siege of Damietta and… But that was far too painful a thought, and Robert pushed it down into a deeper part of his mind.

Robert opened his eyes and looked up at Ivo of Narbonne. The priest was in full flow. He was recounting how Robert, equipped by Ziani, had been dispatched east from Tana. His mission was to seek out a great Eastern potentate – the legendary Prester John, a Christian monarch, who some said was the King of India. The overt reason for this long and dangerous journey was to make a trade treaty between Venice and this great king. But, the covert mission, his true intent, was to bring this puissant monarch and his army to the aid of the beleaguered Christians in Outremer.

'Imagine the triumph of our cause, the cause of Christ, my lords,' said Ivo, 'if the prisoner had brought the numberless armies of Prester John to battle in the Holy Land. A surprise attack from the east, springing out of the trackless deserts… It would surely have routed our Saracen enemies and brought a great and noble victory to the failing lords of Outremer. This was the secret mission on which the prisoner here, Robert of Hadlow, was dispatched by his Templar masters. Think of the glory if Robert had but succeeded – the Holy City of Jerusalem recovered for Christendom. The Saracens all scattered or dispatched to Hell. The ground made sacred by the footsteps of Our Saviour finally in the hands of true Christians.'

Ivo paused. Robert could see the crowd was impressed with this glorious vision. For a moment, Robert allowed himself a sliver of hope. Maybe they would come to understand why he had done what he did, maybe they would even forgive him his actions.

'Alas, Robert of Hadlow never found Prester John,' said Ivo. 'This Eastern monarch does not exist, and perhaps never has existed. What the prisoner found after many weeks of travel in the unknown was an even more powerful lord, the ruler of the Mongol nation, the Great Khan, the one called Genghis Khan. And he was every inch the mighty ruler that Prester John was rumoured to be.

'Genghis Khan was also sympathetic to our cause – indeed, members of his family are Christians – admittedly of the Nestorian heresy – but devout, if misguided, followers of Our Lord Jesus Christ nonetheless.

'So Robert was not daunted by his initial failure. He set about trying to fulfil his two missions, both overt and covert, and he managed, after gaining the Great Khan's trust, to secure a lucrative trade treaty for the city of Venice. Then he began the work of persuading this great Asian king to ride to the aid of Christendom. In his mission to persuade Genghis Khan to come west, he was also, at first, apparently successful.'

Ivo stopped again. Robert, watching the faces on the benches as they listened, could see that they were confused by the notion that Prester John did not exist. He knew that confused men soon become angry ones. His faint hope that the court could be swayed in his favour began to fade away.

'I did not have time to fully interrogate the prisoner,' said Father Ivo. 'Your Grace was eager to bring Robert of Hadlow before your court and I had to curtail my investigations. But Robert did vouchsafe to me that, by the spring of the year Twelve Thousand and Twenty-one, he had managed to bring a Mongol army, some twenty thousand horsemen, to within just a few weeks' march of the Holy Land.

'Robert of Hadlow did not complete the tale he related to me in his cell. But I have learned several truths about this prisoner. Firstly, his intentions were noble. He went eastwards to try to persuade a great king to come to Christendom's aid. Secondly, he undertook this most hazardous mission at the behest of his masters, the lords of the Knights Templar, and more specifically Jean de Malemort, Seneschal of that Order.

'Therefore, my lords, I beseech the court to release Robert of Hadlow to his freedom, or if it deems a punishment is appropriate, impose the lightest possible. Now, of your kindness and mercy, I beg you to set my poor friend Robert free.'

A long silence fell over the court.

'You are far too hasty, Father Ivo,' said the duke. 'You say you have not heard the prisoner's full story. Neither have we. You have not explained to the court *at all* why he was riding against Austrian knights, against his fellow Christians earlier this summer. Nor have you explained why he appeared as an envoy of the Tartar invaders before King Béla of Hungary in Pest in the spring, uttering threats of annihilation. There is much more we must learn before we may determine his guilt or innocence.

'Why,' continued the duke, 'if he persuaded a Tartar army of twenty thousand to come within a few weeks' ride of the Holy Land, did he not persuade them to come yet further? I've heard of no tidings of an Eastern army fighting against the Saracens.'

'I cannot answer that,' said Father Ivo. 'There is only one man who can.'

The provost, the duke and the other two judges convened for a few moments, then Wilhelm went back to the middle of the hall, every eye on him.

'The prisoner will stand,' he said, and Robert got slowly to his feet.

'His Grace the Duke of Austria invites the prisoner Robert of Hadlow to give an account of his actions from the spring of the year Twelve Thousand and Twenty-one until the present time. He asks the prisoner to swear before Almighty God that he will give a true and honest telling of his actions. The duke specifically asks the prisoner to explain why he took up arms with the enemies of Christendom. His Grace also insists that the prisoner deliver his account as briefly as possible.'

Robert felt dizzy. He was horribly weak from lack of food, and so many weeks without sunlight or exercise had transformed him into a feeble old man. But he summoned all his remaining strength, straightened his spine and began to speak.

Three hundred miles north of the Caucasus Mountains

They had been riding all day, save for brief breaks at midmorning and in the late afternoon to water the horses and change their sopping saddle blankets, yet Robert's mount was still as spritely as a colt.

It was a steppe pony, one of a string of a dozen he owned. The pony was called Samson and he was strong though far from beautiful, with a broad, brutish head, wide shoulders like an ox and stubby, muscular legs, but brave Samson could carry him all day without complaint – and so Robert loved him. The Englishman reined in on a small rise and held up a hand to halt his companions.

The *arban* took a few moments to gather beside him, their ponies snorting and stamping. Robert glanced left and right to see they were all there: ten Mongol riders under a leader called Arslan, an ugly, quarrelsome fellow, but a good man in a fight and the second best shot with a recurved bow Robert had ever seen.

Robert did not care for Arslan much, but he was respected by the other nine men of the *arban* – as these small Mongol squads were called – and that was what mattered. He counted only eight riders and Arslan, and remembered that Hasar's pony had been discovered lame at the afternoon break and Hasar had been left behind to tend to his mount and catch up when he might. Robert had given him detailed directions to their destination.

They were travelling, most unusually, with only one pony per man. The rest of the *arban* horse herd was with the Mongol army on the far side of the Caucasus Mountains, along with the other ninety members of Robert's company, his *jagghun*, as the Mongols called it. He was the captain of this *jagghun*, the *akhmad*, and that honour had been granted to him by the Genghis Khan himself. Travelling with only one pony each meant that a mount with a painful stone wedged in its hoof might cost him a fighting man, but it also meant they could travel fast without raising too much visible dust, and thus pass more unobtrusively through enemy territory.

Ten men – well, nine now – was enough strength to make most of the Cuman and Kipchak bandits who infested this part of the world keep their distance. And if they met any force larger than a dozen men, they would run for it. They had made the journey here, after crossing the Caucasus range, in just eight days, and so far had met no trouble at all.

The sun was low in the west and Robert shaded his eyes with his hand and looked out at the expanse of shimmering blue, touched with streaks of gold from the slanting rays, that stretched to his left all the way to the horizon. This was the Sea of Azov, a body of water north-east of the Black Sea – or the Euxine, as the ancients had called it – which was fed by the mighty River Don.

When Robert turned in the saddle and looked north, he thought he could just make out the low form of the town of

Tana on the marshy north bank of that river, squatting on the barren, windswept shores of this golden sheet of sea.

Tana – he had not set eyes on the Venetian trading town for more than two years. He had ridden away from it with a single companion, a Cuman rogue called Altan, in the last days of winter, heading due east into the unknown. He had hope in his heart then – and fear – mingled with excitement at the great adventure that lay before him.

He was returning to Tana, if not quite in triumph, then certainly with the spoils of his great adventure in his saddlebags. Tana was a homecoming, of sorts. He had so much to tell his friend Niccolò Ziani – doyen of Tana's merchants and the wealthiest – when he reached Tana, and yet another difficult and dangerous task to accomplish.

'Shall we push on, *ezen*?' asked Arslan in Mongolian. 'There is an hour yet of daylight. If we ride hard, we will reach the town before midnight.'

'No. We camp down there by the stream. Tana can wait till morning.'

'*Ezen*, the ponies are not done. They have strength in their legs yet. We can ride three more hours and have wine with our supper – and hot food.'

Robert looked over at Arslan frowning with irritation. The older man called him *ezen* – a term of respect which meant lord or sir – but Arslan also seemed to question orders at every turn. 'I said no,' Robert snapped. 'We camp here tonight.'

Robert began to give instructions to the *arban* and was gratified to see them all leaping to obey his commands. Yet Arslan was not finished with him.

'Better we ride on, *ezen*,' he said. 'I have seen the sign earlier today of other horsemen. Maybe bandits. We would sleep safe in that town yonder by the shore.'

It was on the tip of his tongue to tell Arslan that Tana would surely lock and bar its gates at nightfall, and would certainly refuse to open them to armed strangers in the dead of night.

But he restrained himself. He was not about to start explaining his every order to his subordinates.

'Go and scout our back trail,' he said brusquely, 'if your pony still has strength in his legs. Be back here before nightfall and report to me.'

Then he called down to the two nearest members of the dismounting *arban*, 'Saka and Taka – you are on wood duty. Let us have a good blazing fire for once and a hot pot of *shulen*. We are near our journey's end – let us celebrate a little.'

His words were greeted with grins from the two squat, powerful men, twin brothers, both of whom were adept at the popular Mongolian pastime of wrestling. They had not had a fire since they had come down from the cold mountains, and since then they had endured only leathery dried mutton strips for their rations.

Arslan opened his mouth and seemed about to argue. But Robert quickly said, 'Go on, man! Scout our back trail. Now. Do not make me tell you again.'

The leader of the *arban* saluted, turned his pony and cantered away.

Two hours later, wrapped in his warm blanket by the crackling fire and sipping a steaming bowl of *shulen*, the ubiquitous boiled mutton stew of the Mongols, Robert wondered if he had been too hasty in dismissing the threat of Kipchak bandits. He carried a precious cargo in his saddlebags. Arslan had returned after a scant hour of scouting their back trail to report grumpily that he had seen nothing of any particular interest, but it would be an agonising irony to have come so close to achieving this part of his mission only to be murdered in his sleep ten miles from safety.

Therefore, he put down his half-finished stew bowl, shed the warm blanket, got up and walked out into the darkness outside the fire-lit camp.

Away from the fire, he allowed his eyes to become accustomed to the darkness, and soon made out a small, crouched shape about twenty yards from him. He walked slowly towards it and, as he approached, the shape rose and turned to face him. In the gloom, Robert recognised Khuchar, the *arban* scout he had posted as a sentry.

'Anything?' he asked, as they stood together and looked out into the darkness.

Khuchar said nothing for a moment, then replied. 'I don't know, *ezen*.'

'What is it?' said Robert.

'Maybe nothing. I did not like to trouble you, *ezen*. But I heard a sound like a vixen. You know the sound – like the cries of desert demons we heard in the Kyzil Kum. But it was not quite right. Very close to the true sound but a little off. Maybe the foxes here are of a different breed.'

Robert knew the sound: an eldritch shrieking that made the bravest man shiver. He also knew Khuchar well, since long before the burning crossing they had made of the Red Desert between the Syr Daria and Amu Daria rivers. He was not a man easily frightened by a noise in the darkness.

He listened hard. And thought he heard a click of stone on stone.

He turned quickly back to the fire, put cupped hands to his mouth and bellowed as loudly as he could, 'To arms, *arban*, to arms!'

He saw in the flickering light the men all leaping to their feet, reaching for their bows and blades. He drew his own Mongol sword, a fine, light, slightly curved weapon, as keen as a razor; another magnificent gift from Genghis Khan.

For a moment, he thought he had made a mistake. His men were tired. Maybe it *had* been a vixen in the dark, a mating call from a lonely female.

Then the night erupted with a cacophony of yells and shouts. A dozen demonic figures were charging at him out of the blackness. Men in shaggy coats and animal skin hats; fierce faces, distorted horribly by their screaming rage.

A big man in a leather skull-cap was running at him, a long, double-handed sword lofted over his head. And there were more men coming behind him. The warrior was shouting something – Robert realised it was in the Cuman tongue. His original companion, Altan, had been a Cuman and had taught him the language during the time they had ridden together.

Robert waited till the very last moment, then sidestepped – avoiding the massive blow that would have carved him from collar bone to thigh – and dancing smoothly past the big man he swept his own sword sideways and down, cutting his opponent deeply through the waist and out of his back, the razor-sharp Mongol blade ripping through his fur-wrapped body with ease.

Robert had spent thousands of hours training with sword and shield, dagger and lance, learning from an early age to fight with all manner of weapons and none. He was once reckoned to be one of the finest men-at-arms in the Templar Order, which was partly why he had been chosen for this dangerous mission into the unknown east.

The man whose waist he had opened like a fish belly stumbled on past him, pissing blood, moaning, staggering and falling to his knees. He was mewling with pain. Yet there were now enemies all around Robert, yelling and striking at him with steel weapons. He was aware that Khuchar off to his left was shooting his recurved bow with extraordinary speed, skewering the oncoming bandits one after another. Robert blocked a sword blow, ducked under another swipe, then found himself exchanging cuts with yet another bandit. He blocked the first strike, high, reposted with a lunge and pierced his roaring, red-faced opponent deeply through the belly.

His enemy reeled away, cursing. Robert felt an arrow hiss past his left cheek, which made him jerk his head back. He heard a yell to his right and saw a dim shape coming at him. He blocked an axe blow, his Mongol blade cutting a white sliver off the axe's wooden handle, then rotated past his enemy, slashed low and half-severed his opponent's left leg. His foe fell to the earth, howling like a stricken wolf.

Another man was now beside him, yelling and waving a long, curved dagger. Robert dodged a lateral slice from the blade, stepped back, then lashed the sword's tip across the man's eyes, then shoved the blood-blinded bandit away.

There seemed no end of them. Arrows were coming in thick and fast from the *arban*. When Robert took a split instant to look towards the fire, he saw his men had all dispersed into the night – just as they should. They were well trained. A small man ran at him out of the dark night, and Robert took his ready position, sword high, weight balanced on both feet. But instead of attacking, the little fellow veered away south and disappeared.

An arrow swished past his face. He could hear piteous cries of pain. The sounds of dying men. He saw a line of shadowy figures, then a thick group of running men, and one man falling to the ground. He looked round for an enemy to fight, but the bandit attack seemed to be faltering.

The arrows were still flying like horizontal rain, but the Mongols shooting them were invisible. The results, however, were plain to see.

There were three men down around Robert's feet, all stuck with shafts.

He suddenly found himself facing a huge spearman, with an arrow jutting from his beefy forearm, who jabbed at Robert's face with the iron spear tip, once, twice, making him side-step quickly, then duck. But when Robert came at him, step-stepping forward and slicing first at his thighs, then his head, the big man hurled the long spear at the Englishman as if it were no more than a quarterstaff. But Robert batted the pole-arm away easily and came forward again. And the big man simply turned on his heel and ran off into the night.

Robert paused, panting, looking around. He could see Arslan over on the left loosing a final arrow at the departing bandits. But they were gone.

He looked for Khuchar, and saw him on one knee, a cut across his forehead, a sword slice most likely. His face was bloody but the Englishman could see that, beneath the gore, he was grinning. When Robert called his name, he got slowly to his feet and replied with reasonable good cheer.

They had killed or badly wounded eleven bandits and, as the twins Saka and Taka went round each of the wounded man and slit his throat, Robert made a head count of his own people. They had lost one man – a fellow called Tuyuk – who had a black enemy arrow lodged deep in his throat.

The Mongol was lying on his back staring up into the black sky just in front of their campfire – the beacon that had drawn the bandits to them like moths, and which Robert had allowed out of weakness, merely for the sake of a bowl of mutton stew.

Robert knelt beside Tuyuk and saw that the lethal arrow strike was his only wound. One well-aimed arrow from a bandit bow and Tuyuk had gone into the void. Robert gently closed the dead man's eyes and began to mutter a prayer begging Almighty God to receive the immortal soul of this heathen trooper into His grace.

When he had finished praying, he looked up to see Arslan, standing two paces away, staring down at him. The *arban* leader said no words to which the Englishman could object, but his contempt for Robert was clearly visible in his dark Mongol eyes.

Chapter Three

Niccolò Ziani opened his arms and enfolded Robert in a hug. The Englishman felt all his long-contained emotions, fear and love, sorrow and hope, churning in his breast. He felt weak, tired, happy and relieved at the same time. He realised he was in danger of weeping. Ziani seemed to recognise this and remained silent as they embraced.

They were in the hall of the Venetian merchant's grand house in Tana, and it was late afternoon of the day after the attack by Cuman bandits on their fire-lit camp. The *arban* had reached Tana well before noon and Robert had lodged his men and stabled their horses at an inn just inside the settlement's walls – at the same place he had overwintered more than two years before when he was travelling with a large clan of Jewish merchants, the tribe of Aaron of Sana'a – a friend of both Robert and Jean de Malemort.

Once his Mongols were settled and the inn's cooking pots were set to bubbling, he went to Ziani's house, with a pair of heavy saddlebags draped over his shoulder.

His host took him to his long table, poured him some excellent wine, and issued a string of instructions to his many servants to prepare a meal.

'So,' said Ziani, speaking to Robert for the first time since he had entered the house, 'you are returned to me in glorious triumph. I heartily congratulate you, Roberto. I had begun to believe I'd never see your English face again. Welcome!'

'Not in glorious triumph,' said Robert. 'Not yet. There is the matter of my brother Gilbert yet to resolve.'

'Yes, indeed. We shall speak of your brother in due course. Now drink up your wine and tell me all about your magnificent treaty. You have it on you, I trust?'

Robert looked at his host. Ziani was a tall man with a narrow wedge of a face and a long, aquiline nose. He was smiling affectionately at him.

For one mad moment, Robert considered denying he had secured the treaty – a document that outlined a solemn and binding agreement between the Great Khan of the Mongols and the Doge and the Great Council of Republic of Venice. It was a full, comprehensive treaty that granted the Venetians rights to trade in all manner of goods with Genghis Khan's people in all the diverse lands between the Sea of Azov and the far kingdoms of Cathay; to trade under the protection of the Great Khan and with his knowledge and sanction. It was an extremely valuable document to Venice, yet it was Robert, rather than Ziani or any Venetian, who had paid the high price for it in blood, toil and frustration to wrest its priceless concessions from the khan.

That moment passed. And Robert pulled out a copy of the treaty from his saddlebags and showed it to Ziani, pointing out the large, heavy crimson wax seal of the Great Khan at the bottom, and his own green wax imprint beside it. The treaty was written in Persian, with a Uighur transliteration of the Mongol tongue, which was incomprehensible to both Robert and Ziani, with an accompanying translation in Latin, too, penned by Robert himself, on the reverse side of the thick, kidskin vellum.

'Wonderful,' said Ziani, taking the scroll, examining the seal and turning the vellum over to scan the Latin. 'Quite wonderful! This is truly superb work, Roberto.'

He gazed at the document a little longer, holding it carefully, almost reverently, in just his fingertips as if it were some precious relic.

He looked up at Robert then, smiled and said, 'Now tell me about the House of Karacha and your partner in this venture, this Lord Karacha of Otrar.'

'Karacha is a young man, not yet thirty but a successful Persian merchant of great charm, skill and knowledge. He is my agent in Samarkand – indeed, he is our agent, since we three are all the co-owners of the House of Karacha, through which all our trading must be done in the Mongol domain. I hold two shares in the House, and you also hold two – and Karacha has one. However, I think the best way to explain the initial workings of our new joint business is to show you this.'

Robert delved into the saddlebags once more and produced a leather folder containing dozens of sheets of vellum, once again covered with Latin and Persian script. 'This is the accounts of the last two quarters of trading of the House of Karacha in Samarkand last year. You will see here the items we bought; in this column those we sold. And here, see, is the total profit, minus the House expenses and the tax demanded by the Mongol authorities, which are listed here…'

Robert left Ziani to pore over the accounts and went back to delving into his saddlebags.

'This is your share, a two-fifths share, of the profit of the first two quarters,' said Robert, as he dumped three large, heavy linen bags on the table. As they hit the wood, they made a delightful metallic chinking sound.

'This is just under one thousand gold dinars, minted by the late Emperor of Khwarazmia. It belongs to you and the Republic of Venice.'

Ziani stared at him. 'A thousand gold dinars for half a year's trading?'

Robert smiled, and he could not help but allow himself a touch of smugness. 'You said yourself a river of gold would flow west from this venture, Niccolò. You were right. This, my friend, is the first trickle of that golden flood.'

The Venetian came over to him and embraced him once again. 'You have done supremely well, Roberto,' he said. 'I am so very proud of your accomplishment.'

At which point, a gaggle of servants came bustling into the hall with trays bearing platters of steaming food. Fried pork chops and onions, a pair of golden roasted capons, fresh wheaten bread, cheese, figs and more wine. And they both seated themselves at the table and began to help themselves eagerly to the fare.

After Robert had given him a brief account of what had happened in the many months since he left Tana, Ziani sat back in awe; indeed, he seemed utterly amazed.

'The risks you took, Roberto,' he exclaimed. 'The bloody battles, the terrible perils. I can feel my hair turning white just to think of you enduring them. And Father Pietro was a spy for Genoa, all along. I am glad you settled with him. I cannot believe I ever trusted that vile man.'

Father Pietro had been a corrupt priest, who had followed Robert eastwards and had tried to kill him several times. He was in the pay of the trading city of Genoa, Venice's bitter rival, which also wished to secure a lucrative treaty with the Great Khan.

Robert had killed Father Pietro in single combat during the Battle of Ray, after the priest stood in the battle line with the doomed Khwarazmian shah.

The death of that corrupt priest was a memory the Englishman relished.

Then Ziani told Robert what had been happening in Europe since his departure. He spoke of the dazzling coronation of a new Holy Roman Emperor, Frederick. The wonder of the world, *Stupor Mundi*, he was called, a great monarch who ruled from Sicily to Saxony, from Bohemia to Burgundy. 'Like you, Roberto,' said Ziani, 'the emperor has linguistic talent – he speaks Latin, French, Italian, German, Greek and Arabic; he is a scholar and a mathematician, and architect and a poet. I believe he will bring Europe into a new and glorious age. An age of wealth and plenty with a demand for the luxuries of the East, which the House of Karacha shall provide.

'Do you plan to return to Samarkand soon? We need to conjure a way to bring goods from Khwarazmia and beyond safely here to Europe – Chinese silk, of course, and delicate pottery, silk carpets, too, Persian gold and silver items, jewellery. I know that I can find many eager distributers in Europe for all these fine, luxurious goods.'

'I do not plan to travel east soon, Niccolò. And perhaps never again. But I have a notion as to how we can bring goods safely here from Asia and send fine European products back to the House of Karacha in Samarkand. Have you heard of the House of Oktay, a merchant named Suleiman Oktay, from the Sultanate of Rum?'

'I know him by reputation, no more than that. He runs trains of packhorses east from Antioch and Constantinople to Trebizond along the Silk Roads. Do you plan to employ this Suleiman Oktay to transport our precious goods into the Mongol lands?'

'It was in my mind to do so, but we can discuss this another time. I would hear your news, Niccolò, the news of Christendom. Tell me of the progress in Damietta, if you please. How goes the fight with the Saracens?'

'Poorly,' said Ziani, putting a large, grease-dripping portion of roasted capon on Robert's platter. 'I confess I have only bad tidings of Damietta to share with you.'

'Tell me anyway,' said Robert.

'You heard William de Chartres, Grand Master of the Templars died?'

'I heard. I grieve for him. But the Army of God *did* capture Damietta?'

'They did take it, eventually, at a great cost in Christian lives – and the neighbouring city of Tinnis, too, and they hold both still. However, they have made no further progress into Egypt. Our army is only holding on to the edge of the Ayyubid Empire – but they cannot advance and cannot defeat the Sultan. His counterattacks have kept them penned by the sea for months. Many are dying of disease and John of Brienne, King of Jerusalem, has returned to his palace in Jaffa.

'A new man, Cardinal Pelagius has taken charge of the army,' Ziani continued. 'The Sultan offered him a truce, earlier this year, if they would leave Egypt; he even offered to give them Jerusalem. But the cardinal refused. He has vowed to possess all the Holy Land or nothing, and the Hospitallers and your people, the Templars, support him in this. Now the tide has turned in the Sultan's favour. Our army is weak and sick, exhausted after three years of fighting. Soon, I fear, they may be forced to retreat to Outremer with nothing of value to show for their efforts.'

Robert bowed his head, absorbing this blow. 'Therefore,' he said, 'it is all the more vital that I bring the Mongols to battle against the Ayyubid.'

'Yes, I meant to ask. I know the nine riders who came here with you are at my inn, but where are the rest? You hoped to bring a mighty army. Where is it?'

'In the south. Beyond the Caucasus. Encamped at a town called Gandza in the Kura Valley. There are some twenty thousand Mongol riders. Their leader is a man called Subutai, a clever Mongol general, a seasoned campaigner. He is waiting for me to lead his army over the Caucasus. They mean to come north to quell a rebellion of Cumans who defied their rule in the east and attacked several Mongol garrisons.'

The Venetian stirred uneasily in his chair. 'Twenty thousand Mongol warriors are coming north?' he said. 'Coming up here? I thought you meant to lead this great heathen army against the Ayyubid. Was that not your design with Jean de Malemort?'

'I have made an arrangement with General Subutai. He has promised that if I will guide him and his men over the mountains and help him put down this rebellion, then in turn he would turn his army south afterwards and capture Baghdad for the Great Khan. Yet I do not entirely trust him. I am minded to tell them that crossing the high Caucasus barrier cannot be done. I will say the passes are still closed by snow, even now. That they must remain south of the mountains. Then I will push the general more strongly to advance on Baghdad. Once the Mongols hold the city of Baghdad, it should be fairly simple to make them take that final step to the gates of Jerusalem.'

'Have a care, Roberto,' said Ziani. 'If you lie to this Mongol general, and he discovers it, the consequences could be dire. He may have others who will tell him the passes are clear. I think it is best if you adhere strictly to the truth.'

'Do not lecture me about my dealing with the Mongols,' snapped Robert, in a sudden rush of anger. 'I have walked the knife edge with these people for two long years, careful every moment to say the right thing. I have only survived at their whim.'

Ziani looked compassionately at his friend, then poured him some more wine.

Robert slowly regained his composure and ate a bite of capon. 'I am sorry for my outburst,' he said after a while. 'I am very tired. I beg you to forgive me.'

He was, in truth, not angry with Ziani. He was anxious about another matter.

'I forgive you. You have struggled long and striven hard, Roberto, you have brought me this marvellous treaty and covered yourself in glory. And you are quite safe here now. This Mongol general who holds your life in his hands is five hundred miles away, and if you never wish to see this man again – or his twenty thousand riders – you could take ship from Tana and be gone. I will lend you a ship. You would have no want of money, I can guarantee that. I would give you all this gold here on the table, and send you your fair share of the riches of the House of Karachi every quarter without fail. I would dispatch it by trusted courier to wherever you wished to live in the world. So I repeat to you, Roberto, you are safe – and you are free.'

'I am not free. You know that, Niccolò. I am not free; I can never be easy while my brother lies in chains. I cannot be truly free until Gilbert is free.'

'Ah yes, Gilbert. Your brother. We must speak of his fate, now, I think.'

Ziani made a brisk gesture and one of his attendants came to the table. As the tall serving man bent towards him, the Venetian spoke softly in his ear. The fellow was a Circassian; Robert could see that from his willowy height, pale skin, blue eyes and pitch-black hair. A handsome man, too, as were all their race, but also a warrior. It was unmistakable from his posture, quite apart from the long, slim, ivory-handled dagger stuck in his belt.

The tall Circassian bowed and padded away, and the other household servants came to the table and began to clear away the dishes.

Looking around the large room, Robert spotted three more of these tall, pale Circassian creatures leaning against the walls, watching him and their lord with their unblinking blue eyes. He said, 'You have taken on new retainers, I see, Niccolò – a few more trained men-at-arms.'

'Yes,' said Ziani, 'it is this rebellion you mentioned. Outside the walls of Tana, I dare not travel these days without a strong force of men-at-arms. Bandits roam unchecked, both Cumans and their equally rascally Kipchak cousins. There is a man called Köten, the most ruthless bandit of them all, who is their elected leader, their *khan*, they call him. But, Heavens above, why am I telling *you* of all people this?'

'We also encountered Cuman bandits on the road,' said Robert. 'But do please tell me, my friend, I am burning to know. What news is there of Gilbert?'

'I have sent one of my Circassians to fetch a letter – a missive from the Podestà of Genoa, from that wobbling great turd Barisone Adorno himself.'

'Where is Gilbert? Is he still a captive of the Genoese in Soldaya?'

Robert's younger brother Gilbert, who was also a Templar knight, had been captured during the early fighting at Damietta, and had been bought out from the Sultan's stinking gaol by Barisone Adorno, the richest merchant of Genoa, and its elected ruler, known as the Podestà.

Gilbert had been imprisoned along with Adorno's son, Lanfranco. But instead of immediately freeing Gilbert, the Genoese merchant had demanded a huge ransom for Gilbert's release. A hundred thousand marks of silver. An impossibly large sum.

A sum that a Poor Fellow-Knight such as Robert could never hope to pay.

Father Pietro had told Robert that Gilbert had been moved to Soldaya, a remote Genoese trading outpost on the Black Sea, where he was being held far beyond the reach of rescue. Robert had also intercepted a message from Father Pietro to Barisone Adorno, advising the Podestà to murder his captive brother since he was of no value to them.

'Your brother Gilbert is still alive, as far as I can tell, and still held in Soldaya,' said Ziani. 'The letter from Adorno will prove it to you. The Podestà also makes a financial proposal, which I will share with you – ah, here we are…'

The Circassian was returning and, gripped in his long, pale right hand was a square of thick paper, with a broken wax seal in the centre of the square.

Robert looked once again at the Circassian: not only was this fellow a trained warrior, he was also, apparently, an educated man, one who was trusted to go through his master's private papers and select one particular letter from among all the rest.

'I thank you, Idar,' said Ziani, taking the letter from his tall servant's hand.

The Venetian opened the folded paper and quickly scanned the written contents. Then he passed the letter over to Robert.

'As you will see, Adorno has had good intelligence about our plans and he knows you have returned from the East with a treaty…'

But Robert was deep in the letter. The silence lengthened, Ziani held his peace. Robert glanced up once, very quickly, at his host, then he shook his head and went back to the page to re-read the entire letter once again.

'There is no date on this,' he said eventually.

'I received it one week ago.'

'You have not replied?' said Robert.

'I, too, have my intelligencers. I heard a rumour that a Mongol army was encamped somewhere in Georgia below the Caucasus range; I even heard that there was a big blond foreigner with blue eyes who commanded one of the companies of their scouts, and who was a trusted adviser to their general. So I waited for you to come to me at Tana before replying to this. Besides, what possible answer could I make to Barisone Adorno but no?'

Robert looked down at the opened letter on the table in front of him. In essence, the Podestà of Genoa was offering Ziani a chance to meet and discuss, under the conditions of a formal truce and safe conduct, a binding alliance between Genoa and Venice to trade jointly with the Great Khan in the East. His eye caught one Latin phrase on the paper: '*...together, Venice and Genoa are stronger than we are apart; and there is enough wealth in the golden ruins of the Khwarazmian Empire to satisfy both our cities, I'm sure. Why should we not share this bounty...*'

To sweeten the deal, Adorno offered to lower the price of Gilbert's ransom by half – he would accept fifty thousand silver marks for Robert's imprisoned brother – in exchange for a half share of their business with the Mongols.

'You cannot trust Barisone Adorno, nor any of those Janus-faced Genoese whoresons,' said Ziani at last, breaking into Robert's thoughts.

Robert looked up at him. He suddenly felt completely exhausted.

'I know what you are thinking, my friend,' said Ziani. 'You are pondering giving your share of the House of Karacha to Adorno in order to extract your brother from his chains. You cannot do this. I could never allow it.'

Still Robert did not speak. He took a meditative sip of his wine.

'Adorno is a treacherous snake,' said Ziani. 'If we allowed him to meddle in our joint business, even a little, we would both come to regret—'

Robert held up his hand to silence his friend. 'I know this, Niccolò,' he said. 'I know we cannot give away any part of our venture to Genoa. Have no fear, my friend, on that score. Yet I *must* find a way to free my poor brother.'

Ziani had the wit to remain silent. He took a draught of his own wine.

'Before I left for Asia,' said Robert, 'you said that if I achieved this feat you would give me the money to free Gilbert. You said you were willing and able to pay the hundred thousand marks to free him. You remember?'

'I said, Roberto, I would *advance* you a sum large enough to free your brother – and from the Sultan – after I had negotiated to lower the ransom to a reasonable price. Adorno is a different matter. However, I *am* willing to make you a sizeable advance, at a generous rate of interest, too, with your income from the House of Karacha as collateral. However, a hundred thousand is far too much. It would take you ten years or more to repay me.'

Robert cast his mind back to the long conversations they'd had before his departure. Had Ziani said *advance*, rather than *give*? It did not matter. The money would have to come from Ziani, anyway. Robert possessed only a fraction of that sum. And, the Venetian was right, a hundred thousand was far too much.

'If you wish, I will write to Adorno and suggest a smaller amount,' said Ziani. 'I could begin negotiations. I am sure we could get him to come down to a more reasonable figure. What good is a prisoner if no one will pay the ransom for him?'

Robert frowned. 'That will not be necessary. I'll speak to Adorno myself. I shall look him in the eye and tell him the sum I am prepared to pay. I shall also ascertain that Gilbert is alive and well, and has not been maltreated, and God help Adorno if my brother has been harmed.'

'You cannot be serious,' said Ziani.

'But I am,' said Robert. 'I will ride to Soldaya and, with God's grace, I shall return very soon to Tana with my brother Gilbert.'

Chapter Four

Robert rested his nine men for three days at the inn in Tana, ensuring that they all ate well, slept long and were able to care properly for their horses. On the fourth day, in the soft, milky light of dawn, Robert saddled Samson, and they all rode out on to the wide empty grasslands to the west of the Venetian settlement.

Niccolò Ziani had given Robert the letter from Adorno, which contained the written promise of truce and safe conduct. It was a physical signifier of his honest intent to negotiate the ransom with the Podestà, and the great man's seal on the back of the missive would allow him to pass should he meet any Genoese patrols on the roads near Soldaya, and it should also gain him admittance to the fortified port itself.

The Genoese town was some five hundred miles distant from Tana, beyond the far western side of the Sea of Azov, on the south-eastern coast of a large diamond-shaped peninsula that jutted into the Black Sea. The ancient Greeks who first colonised this near-island called it Tauris, and it had long been known as the Tauric Peninsula. The Genoese had built their trading settlement at Soldaya, only half a dozen years before, absorbing a tiny Khazar fishing village on the coast. Then they had set about their principal business in the North: the trade in human flesh.

For, while the knights of Christendom struggled with the Ayyubid warriors and shed their blood for mastery of the Holy Land, the venal merchants of Christendom, most prominently the Genoese, traded with these same Saracen lords of Egypt in the bodies of young men, women and children, rounded up from villages on the steppe, or captured in battle, or simply purchased from the gangs of leather-tough Rus' hunters, who also brought them animal furs, timber, gold and amber from the North.

When Robert and his *arban* rode west, along the shore, with the light of the rising sun bouncing blindingly from the shimmering waters of the Sea of Azov, they were accompanied on their mission by a guide provided by Ziani – the Circassian warrior Idar. He rode beside the Englishman, his back as straight as an arrow, on a cream-coloured, high-stepping horse with a flowing brown mane. They had left most of their baggage in Tana, and rode only with their weapons, bedding and essential kit.

Robert aimed to travel fast and light and to reach Soldaya within five days – a feat of horsemanship all in itself. But he was concerned with two things far more important to him than a swift journey. First – was Gilly still alive? He hated to admit it but it would be so much simpler – and cheaper – if his younger brother had already been called unto God. He pushed that thought aside as unworthy of him: Adorno had written to Ziani proposing his deal for Gilbert a handful of days before Robert and his men left Tana; he would be unlikely to do that if he had no living man to exchange.

The second thing on Robert's mind was whether Adorno would accept his new offer. He was minded to offer only ten thousand silver marks for Gilbert. He could just about amass that sum, if he accepted a sizeable loan from Ziani, a loan he could afford that would not hobble him for a decade. He planned to say to Adorno that ten thousand was the figure he would pay and not a penny more. The Genoese was a trader, a man of business, after all, for all his titles and wealth. He would make a deal.

Robert might, if necessary, make a further arrangement, a side deal, perhaps, to sell his personal share of all the silks that the

House of Karacha acquired to Adorno at a substantial discount. But his main argument would be that he could not afford to pay any more than ten thousand, which also had the additional merit of being true.

There was another option deeper in his mind, lurking like a cut-purse in a dark alley. But he would not contemplate that strategy unless all negotiations failed.

They made camp the first night by a stream that flowed into the Sea of Azov, tying their horses to scrubby, wind-bent gorse bushes, and eschewing a fire and hot food, since the ghost of poor Tuyuk seemed to hover over the circle of bedrolls.

As the sun sank, Robert, as was his daily custom, turned his back to it and, facing east, knelt down beside his bedroll and pressed his two palms together.

He had resumed this childhood practice since leaving the Mongol army, praying once in the morning and once before sleep, and he found the ritual comforting. He allowed his mind to play over events of the day and contemplate the struggles ahead.

He sorely wished his friend Altan were with him. That ugly old steppe warrior, who had died at the Battle of Ray, would inevitably have had a wry joke, or a bit of shrewish scolding for him. That had been comforting too. When Robert asked Altan for foolish certainties or predictions, the old man would just shrug his skinny shoulders and say, 'The steppe is wide.'

Robert had often told his *arban* stories about Altan, and had even tried out the old man's favourite phrase with them, but they just stared at him in incomprehension.

Which was odd. The steppe *was* wide – even at this western end of it, the flat grasslands seemed to stretch into infinity northwards beyond the shores of this sea. And who could say what might happen to a man during his life on the steppe? Who could say what might happen in this endless expanse of pastoral emptiness? Anything at all. Life was unknowable, that was what Altan had been saying all those times. The steppe is wide. Like Christians, the old warrior recognised the ineffability of God.

Robert prayed for Altan's heathen soul but soon his mind jumped to another beloved figure from his past. Someone he had tried hard to wipe from his mind.

Sarantuya was her name. Which meant moonlight in the Mongol tongue. He called her Saran and loved her with all his heart and soul. But, alas, Sarantuya was the wife of another, a Mongol chieftain called Khuyag, a brute of a fellow, who blustered and boasted and beat her, and drank himself insensible whenever he had the opportunity.

Yet Khuyag was also Robert's friend and comrade, a man who had welcomed the Englishman into his tent; and this made Robert's betrayal of his host with his beautiful wife all the more shameful. Robert felt the burn of his guilt even now, at the memory of their lovemaking. And then, for added measure, there was his broken vow of chastity. He had made that solemn oath when he was inducted into the Templar ranks. He had sworn that he would eschew the company of women and all their fleshly snares. And he had broken that oath – joyfully, and often, with his Mongol beloved. He had left Saran behind in Samarkand, and he knew he must never set eyes on her again. But he did not leave her there because he feared Khuyag's wrath. He left her because he knew Sarantuya was a woman of the East, a soul of the steppe. His future, and his heart, lay in the West, in the true and faithful service of Jesus Christ.

They could never be together. Both had recognised this truth. So he had turned his face from her and ridden west with the Mongol army, leaving Sarantuya behind.

And yet… when he was apart from her, he felt he was missing a vital piece of himself. As if there were now a cold and echoing void in the centre of his soul.

Robert heard a tiny noise and opened his eyes. He saw that Idar the Circassian was now kneeling beside him, his pale, long-fingered hands also pressed together in the attitude of prayer. Robert stared into the Circassian's face – his eyes, he noticed were a light blue colour, and very striking with his black hair and dead-white skin.

'You object?' asked Idar. 'My people pray together with fellow Christians.'

'I do not,' said Robert, astonished that this warrior should share his faith. 'Shall we say the Lord's Prayer together, as Our Saviour taught us?'

They were speaking in Italian, in the dialect of Venice, yet when Idar began intoning the prayer – '*Pater Noster, qui es in caelis, sanctificetur nomen tuum…*' – Robert realised they were both speaking in Latin.

Who is this man? he thought. *No ordinary servant, that is for sure.*

When the prayer was over both men continued kneeling in silence for a while, side by side, eyes closed. But Robert's whirling mind was too full of questions to allow him to commune with the Almighty for much longer.

He got to his feet and walked over to where Arslan was grooming his pony.

'Sentries?' he said.

'I have given Saka and Taka the first watch,' said the leader of the *arban*. 'Begter and Chankai will take the second spell at moonrise.'

'Good. Have them wake me at midnight, and I will take the middle watch with Khuchar. No, wait. How is his head wound?'

'He does not complain,' said Arslan. 'But it has surely weakened him.'

'Let him sleep. I will watch alone. You and Hasar take the watch before dawn.'

'As you command, *ezen*,' said Arslan, and continued his long brush strokes.

Robert looked at the man for a moment. It was in his mind to say something about the death of Tuyuk and the stupid mistake he had made in allowing them a campfire. But, even as the words of apology rose in his throat, he decided against it.

He nodded briskly at Arslan, turned and walked back to his bedroll. He took off the sword belt that held his *deel* together, allowing the heavy, yak-wool Mongol robe to flap free. He pulled off his big, reindeer-hide boots by the up-curled toe and dragged his warm blanket over his body. A few moments later, Robert was asleep.

–

It took them seven days to reach the walls of Soldaya, since most of the third day was wasted finding a crossing place for a mighty river, swollen by spring rainfall, that he had been told by that knowledgeable servant Idar was called the River Kalka.

Yet Robert was still proud of his men and of their speed of travel. Five hundred miles in seven days was excellent going. The Mongols had a system of elite travelling couriers, known as the Arrow Riders, who galloped as swiftly as shafts from a bow, or so it was said. The Mongols set up stations every fifteen to forty miles in the territory they occupied, and the Arrow Riders galloped from station to station and at each they received food and fresh horses. These riders could go days without sleep.

Robert was sure the men of his *arban* could hold their heads high beside even the swiftest Arrow Riders – and they only had one pony apiece. Even Idar had done well. His cream-coloured horse might be pretty to look upon, but it had stamina, too.

They had seen very few people on the week-long journey. Some villages on the long Azov shore had supplied them with fresh bread and flapping, silvery fish, but the inhabitants were a sullen, uncommunicative breed, offering their food grudgingly for the copper coins Robert offered them. They reminded the Englishman of whipped dogs, resentful but too frightened to bite. They saw a band of Rus' hunters outlined on the skyline on the fifth day, a file of three mounted men with fur coats and fur hats, leading a string of packhorses. However, when Robert trotted towards them on Samson, calling a greeting, they turned their mounts and galloped away.

Men feared each other in this wilderness. And they were right to do so.

On the morning of the seventh day after their departure, Robert halted his small cavalcade on a low bluff that overlooked the town of Soldaya and gazed down at the collection of huts and halls, forges and warehouses, that were enclosed by a high wooden palisade. There was one large square brick house in the centre of the town, with a spacious, stone-paved courtyard set before it, but the rest of Soldaya was packed in tightly, the houses and workshops jostling each other on both sides of narrow streets.

Outside the town, on the western side, was a much smaller palisade, lower in height and cruder in its construction, the walls more like an animal enclosure than a battlement, and encircling a dark-coloured, gently moving mass of living creatures. There were several men carrying crossbows and wearing yellow surcoats patrolling the outside of the palisade on foot. It took Robert a few moments to recognise what it was. A stock pen – and a couple more moments to realise with shock that the moving objects inside the palisade were hundreds of human beings.

There was a long quay on the shoreline and a pair of jetties that lanced out into the blue waters of the Black Sea, and Robert could see three large trading cogs moored there, each one flying the red-and-white St George's cross of Genoa. There was a gatehouse at the entrance to the town on the north side, and Robert could see several dozen more men-at-arms with crossbows and yellow surcoats manning the battlements, the sun reflecting off their polished steel helms. Above the gatehouse fluttered a standard, a buttercup yellow flag crossed diagonally with a bold, black-and-white chequered pattern, the proud blazon of the House of Adorno.

Good, Robert thought. For that jaunty flag indicated that Barisone Adorno, the Podestà of Genoa, was in residence in Soldaya.

Just then Robert noticed a party of horsemen approaching the gate, along the road that coiled east along the shore of the

Black Sea. They were dressed in short green jupons and greasy leathers; about twenty men, most on foot, a few mounted, and a pair of footmen were slogging along with the carcass of a deer slung beneath a pole. A returning hunting party, no doubt.

The gates were swung open and the hunting party was admitted to the town without delay. Robert turned to look at his own men, at their sunburnt faces, dark eyes squinting from long days in the harsh sun. Tough men, armed with short bows, and lances in sockets on their horses' withers, men festooned with swords, daggers and axes. They looked exactly what they were: a band of swift-riding, iron-hard killers. He had never felt more proud of them.

He had a difficult choice to make. And, as usual, he made it swiftly.

'Idar, Begter and Chankai, you will accompany me. Arslan you take the rest of the *arban* and make camp yonder in that copse there.'

Robert pointed at a small hill a mile behind them with a sparse stand of alder trees visible on its bald summit.

'If I do not emerge from the town to rejoin you within three days, and you do not receive any word or message from me, you are ordered to ride back to Tana and report my demise to Lord Ziani. He will then tell you what to do next. Understood?'

'*Ezen*, it is not safe,' said Arslan. 'These people down there are your enemies, evil men who hold one of your kin as their captive, is this not so?'

Robert, who had never discussed his brother with Arslan or any member of his *arban*, was astonished by the Mongol's knowledge. 'This is true,' he said.

'Then do not go into the wolf's lair with only Begter and Chankai – let us all go together. If it goes bad, we have a better chance of cutting ourselves free of the trap.'

'I have made my decision. If we all go, we will seem more of a threat to them. Begter and Chankai, you're with me, and Idar. The rest of you wait three days.'

‘As you command, *ezen*,’ said Arslan.

As Robert rode down the slope towards the gatehouse, he wondered if he had made another blunder. But he had made his choice; now it was all in God’s hands.

The dice were cast.

-

The heavy double doors of the gatehouse swung closed behind him with a thud and Robert and his three companions found themselves in a narrow street that led south towards the harbour. He could even glimpse a sliver of blue sea at the end of the street. He wondered how many souls were crammed into these close-packed houses – a thousand? Maybe two? And very few were Genoese, he judged, from the faces that stared out curiously at him from upper-storey windows.

They seemed to be raggedly, hungry folk, dark haired, hard-looking and steppe-weathered. Not too dissimilar to the hard men of his *arban*, if the truth be told. Kipchaks or Cumans, he thought, and maybe a few Khazars among them and a scatter of Greeks.

There had been no difficulty in gaining admittance; the mention of Barisone Adorno’s name had had the gates yawning wide. And the guards who formed up around him – a dozen crossbowmen in their yellow surcoats, with swords at their waists – had the sleek look of Italians, and they had responded to his speech in that tongue. Robert was glad he had taken the time that morning to change his clothes. He wore a hauberk of iron links that day that fell to his knees over a padded gambeson, and a Templar surcoat over the top, black linen with a bright white cross on the chest. His curved Mongol blade hung at his left side.

He wanted to look like a Templar knight, which he was, and to imply the whole might of the Order was behind him, which it certainly was not.

They were escorted down the street towards the harbour. He and his three men mounted, and the crossbow men, under a cheerful, curly-haired captain, on marching foot all around them. They turned right after a hundred yards and immediately came into a large stone-flagged courtyard, as big as a market square, with a large brick-built house on the far side of the almost empty space. On the south side of the yard, under a capacious and rather jolly, yellow-and-red striped awning, was a gathering of a few dozen folk, clustered round a huge throne – and seated in it, and, indeed, spilling out over the armrests, was the fattest individual Robert had ever seen.

The curly-haired captain led the four men towards the awning, then asked them to dismount. All four obediently did so. Robert passed Samson's reins to Begter.

The cheery captain pushed through the crowd around the enormous man in his throne, and when he found himself in space, he bowed and said, 'Your Excellency! Visitors. Strangers but good Christians, they say, who crave an audience with you.'

Robert who had followed the captain forward on foot stared in fascination at the grotesque figure filling the chair. He was three times the size of an ordinary man, vast around the belly and thighs, thinner towards his rosy-cheeked face – the whole man the shape of a gigantic pear. He was clad in an enormous red robe, with a black over-mantle fringed with many golden tassels, and his small, almost cherubic head was topped with a high, square hat, not unlike a bishop's mitre, but in gorgeous crimson velvet and with tiny golden tassels hanging from the four corners. His thick blubbery lips were stained deep purple with wine, and he held a massive golden goblet – a chalice – in his small, heavily be-ringed hand, which he drank from almost constantly.

'Strangers, eh?' said the huge man, in a high-pitched, whistling voice. 'But good Christians, you say. So, come on, come forward then, and present yourselves.'

Robert stepped forward and bowed. He was aware Idar was beside him, also making his bow, just off at his left shoulder and knew that the two Mongols were a few paces back holding the reins of their four mounts.

'Your Excellency, I am Robert of Hadlow, a Poor Fellow-Soldier of Christ and of the Temple of Solomon. I am also the partner of Niccolò Ziani of Tana.'

'Ah, yes, the Venetian viper,' piped the fat man, smiling hugely as if speaking in jest.

'This is Idar, Signor Ziani's servant and my guide.' Idar bowed again.

'I know of you, Templar,' the fat man said. 'I am Barisone Adorno, Podestà of Genoa. You have arrived just in time, signor. I am at present loading cargo into my ships and making ready to depart this God-forsaken flea-pit and return to civilisation for a short while. I presume you are come here at last to pay ransom for your brother.'

'I am here to *discuss* the ransom,' said Robert.

'Oh-ho! You will attempt to negotiate, very well. I'm sure I shall enjoy this.'

'Indeed. However, before we begin, Excellency, I should like to see my brother Gilbert and to speak with him. I must ascertain that he is in health and unharmed.'

'And if I refuse? What would you do then, Signor Templar?'

'I shall assume my brother is dead and there will be no need to pay ransom for his corpse. There would be no profit in it for you, Excellency.'

Adorno giggled squeakily to himself, looking at Robert, then Idar, and back to Robert again. He took another gulp of his wine. A servant came forward with a silver jug and refilled his huge chalice. 'You resemble him, you know, your younger brother – well, as I imagine he looked before his incarceration. Now, of course…'

Robert felt a flicker of anger. Was this gross sack of meat mocking him?

'I would be gratified if you would conduct me to my brother at your earliest convenience. I have many calls on my time and—'

'Gilbert of Hadlow has been my prisoner for many, many months, he can wait a moment longer to see his brother. I would speak with you, signor.'

Robert said nothing. He rolled his shoulders to ease the tension in his back.

'I believe you have recently returned from the East, signor,' said Barisone Adorno. 'From the presence of a mighty Asian monarch – the King of the Tartars.'

Robert did not bother to reply. He half-lifted the letter from Adorno to Ziani that was in his right hand, as if to reply, 'I know that you already know this.'

'What manner of ruler is he, this great and savage Tartar king?'

Robert was surprised by the question. He had spoken for many hours with Ziani back in Tana but he had never been asked anything like this.

'He is… a good ruler, I think,' he said. 'He is fierce to his enemies, of course – and there is very little mercy in him. But he is most benevolent to his people. And just in his punishments, tolerant of their small mistakes. He is much revered.'

'Do you revere him, signor?'

'I… I would say that I respect him. I would not care to cross him. Nor would I care to face his armies in battle.'

'Do you fear him?'

'He is powerful. More powerful than any Christian king. Or podestà.'

'And your own king – you are an Englishman, I understand. Do you respect the king of your own land? The young Henry of Winchester?'

'I do not know him. I have not been in England these many years. I am a Templar knight. My loyalty is to the Grand Master of the Order. But what is this interrogation? Why do you ask these questions? You will now kindly conduct me to my brother or I shall take my leave of you.'

'I am trying to get a sense of this Tartar potentate, signor, and of you.'

'My brother, Excellency,' said Robert, with more than a little iron in his voice.

Barisone Adorno took another mighty swallow of his wine, wiped his purple lips with the back of his small delicate hand and said, 'A final question, Templar, then I shall have you shown to your brother's apartments. Is this great king – this Genghis Khan – a man who can be trusted? Is he true to his word?'

Robert paused before answering. He had not named the Lord of the Steppe to Adorno and yet the fat man seemed to know his Mongol title.

He said, 'I believe he is. It is considered a matter of honour among his people to keep a promise, freely given, and sworn by the sky god Tenggri that these heathens worship. I also think that, were the circumstances to his advantage, or were he or his people to be threatened, he might break his sworn word out of expediency. Much like any great monarch on Earth.'

'Thank you, signor. Captain Carlo will conduct you to your brother.'

He waved his small plump left hand in dismissal.

Robert bowed again, he tucked the safe-conduct letter in the big leather purse on his belt and began to back away.

Just as he was doing this, the Podestà spoke again in his high, squeaky voice, 'You will dine with me later, signor, when you have satisfied yourself as to the health and well-being of your brother. We can discuss the ransom then. Your horses will be cared for and your men fed. Captain Carlo will bring you to my table in one hour.'

Chapter Five

Robert left Idar with the two Mongols in the stables, which were at the other side of the courtyard, and followed Captain Carlo, the same curly-headed soldier, across the flagstones and inside the large brick building, through a high-ceilinged hall, up a short flight of stairs and down a long white corridor. He found he was genuinely impressed with the luxury of this grand Genoese house in the wilds of the North.

Firstly, it was built from red brick and Robert knew that each individual kiln-fired brick must have been carried here by ship all the way from Italy. There were no brickworks on the northern steppe. Secondly, there were rich silk tapestries hung on the walls, and silver sconces for candles every few yards. Unlit now, of course, at near noon, but holding fat beeswax columns. All this must have been imported, too.

There was more than enough light streaming in from the flung-open windows on that hot day, and a cool breeze too. The floors were made of a golden polished cedar wood, and he could even smell the faint perfume of the wood as he walked. This brick-built palace was far grander than Niccolò Ziani's timber house in Tana, he thought – and it was certainly much bigger.

When he reached the end of the corridor, he found himself looking out a large window, with the shutters pinned back, down at the west part of the town.

There was a narrow alley twelve feet below the window, running parallel with the side of the house and, at the end of that, at a right-angle, was a wider street with many houses and workshops, with a dozen locals walking and chatting with their neighbours around a busy cook-shop selling some kind of fragrant meat-filled pastry.

The street ended at the palisade with a gate set into it, wide open and unguarded, so far as Robert could tell. Beyond the palisade was the enclosure where he could see hundreds of half-naked slaves, still moving about like a great shoal of dark fish inside the flimsy wooden barrier.

Captain Carlo was knocking at a plain, white-painted wooden door. He heard the sound of bolts being drawn and the door was opened by a man in another yellow surcoat, with a sword at his belt. Carlo conferred with the guard and the door was thrown open, and Robert went inside.

He had braced himself for some dank, stinking prison cell, a grim, dripping stone box, but once inside the airy, white-washed room, all he saw was a three-legged stool and a small table, which held the remains of a simple meal: broken bread, a curling cheese rind and a jug of wine; and on the far side of the room another white door, which was secured with iron bolts, both top and bottom. The guard, who had clearly been interrupted at his noon-day meal, called out, 'Coming in, signor,' in the Genoese dialect of Italian, and slid back both the well-greased bolts.

The guard pushed the door half-open, and made a courtly gesture with his hand, a sort of half-bow, inviting Robert to enter the room within.

Once Robert had squeezed through the doorway, the first thing he saw was a large plant, with wide dark-green fronds growing from a blue ceramic pot as large as a Bordeaux wine cask. Beyond that was a day-bed, an odd Turkish-looking item, made of a long, padded shelf and a high back at one end. There was a small table holding various bottles and cups and a full bowl of fruit, with a three-legged stool beside it, and another shoved underneath, and a high metal stand bearing a large water basin, an earthenware jug underneath on its own shelf below, and a damp towel hanging limply from the basin's white ceramic rim.

A light voice said in Italian, 'A moment, signor. I'll be with you momentarily.' Robert looked towards a dark doorway that seemed to lead into yet another chamber.

While he waited, he completed his inventory of the room: a pile of crumpled clothes by the wall, dirty, he assumed – puddled green hose and a wine-stained white linen chemise and a pair of grubby grey braies. A small, polished lute was propped up against the Turkish day-bed, an empty wine cup sat on the windowsill next to a browning apple core. And a window! Barred with strips of iron but allowing the good clean sunlight to flood into the room.

A moment later, Gilbert was framed in the doorway. He was dressed in a fresh white chemise and russet hose attached to a good leather belt with a silver buckle. He was very thin, his cheekbones horribly prominent, and Robert could see the sharp lines of his collarbones at the open top of his linen chemise. His fair hair was longer than the last time Robert had seen him, but also much more sparse and filled with fine strands of white. He looked frail and weak, and a little older, his face much more lined with care, but he was clean and in reasonable good health.

Gilbert's mouth fell open when he saw Robert and, with a wordless cry, he rushed straight towards his brother and embraced him, hugging him tight and crying, 'I knew you would come, brother. I always knew it in my heart.'

His words were muffled since his face was pressed into Robert's neck.

After a few moments, Robert took Gilly by his shoulders and pushed him back to arms' length, holding him there and looking into his face.

Gilly stared back at him, the tears falling freely and running down his cheeks.

'I knew you would come eventually to set me free,' he said.

'Let us not get too far ahead of ourselves,' said Robert. 'For I have not yet arranged for your freedom, brother… not quite yet.'

'But you will, Rob, I know it,' said Gilbert. 'And whatever the ransom, I'll pay you back. I swear by the Virgin, I will repay you every penny.'

'We'll see about that. First, tell me how you are? What do you lack?'

'Nothing but my freedom. They bring me fresh food daily, although I have a very small appetite these days. My needs are well cared for. But I wish to be out of these accursèd rooms and back at home with my Brethren. Tell me, Robert, what news of Acre, of the Order, of our Brethren and the war in Egypt…'

The words were tumbling like a waterfall out of Gilbert's mouth.

'They tell me nothing here,' said Gilly sadly, 'I see by your surcoat that you have been reinstated to the ranks of the Knights. I knew they would see reason – gambling is a sin, yes, but for a man such as you, winner of First Lance three times, surely a reprimand would suffice. Where have you been? What news of our—'

'We have only a little time,' said Robert. 'Tell me what you need. A doctor?'

'No, I am hale and whole… well, I am now. I was very, very sick in… in Jerusalem, and likely to die. In that filthy hole, I truly thought I would perish. I made my prayers and readied my soul but I was raised up by the Hand of God, delivered from that Hell by the Almighty, through the person of my good friend Lanfranco. You remember Lanfranco Adorno, Rob? He was in Acre with us – dark fellow, very strong. He was the brother-knight who commanded the west rampart of the citadel, and I his lieutenant. I stood duty with him many times. You must remember Lanfranco?'

'I remember him – it is his father, Barisone Adorno, who now holds you captive. But tell me what happened to you. You were captured at Damietta, is that right?'

'Let us sit, and I will tell you everything. And you must tell me your news, too.'

They sat down on stools at the small table, and Gilly offered his brother a drink.

'I am allowed a little wine, and other comforts, too. Would you care for a cup?'

'No, Gilly, but tell me your story. I beg you.'

'An apple, perhaps? No? So then… Damietta. That was bad. Very bad. When we arrived in Egypt in May we found the grand harbour was guarded by a great iron chain that kept our ships out, and so the Count of Saarbrücken, who had command at that time of all our forces, ordered that a tower that guarded one end of the chain be taken. He sent his own men three times, and three times they were bloodily repulsed. Hundreds killed. Then, of course, we Templars offered to take the tower for the count.

'And take it we did. But it grieves me to tell you, Rob, that William of Chartres, our Grand Master, was gravely wounded in the second assault on that accursèd tower. He was fearless, as ever, and in the vanguard fighting like a lion. Indeed, I was beside him at the base of the tower, when a spear hurled from above pierced through his mail at the neck and he fell. I carried him back to the ship with the help of three sergeants.

'We took the tower, eventually, with a battering ram at the gates, quick steel and our own God-given courage. Yet our victory came at a cost: a dozen brother-knights and two score of sergeants were lost; a fearful price, but we took that tower, Rob, we showed them, and Simon of Saarbrücken said he had never seen anything like it.'

The pride in Gilbert's voice was unmistakable.

Robert regarded his brother fondly. He'd had mixed feelings when Gilbert had joined the Order; he had worried that the brutal nature of a martial life was not right for his sensitive younger brother – little Gilly had seemed to be hurt so easily when he was growing up. And Robert had spent much of the past two years concerned for his life. But here he was, in health, having survived a terrible ordeal. He had proved himself as a man and a knight. Robert felt the swell of pride and affection in his heart.

'Now that the way was finally clear,' continued Gilbert, 'our ships came into the harbour and we disembarked the rest of the army and surrounded Damietta, and we pitched our camp in the marshy lands to the east of the city, preparing for a siege.

'The Sultan's men defied us, of course, and we made two unsuccessful assaults on their walls that summer. Alas, William of Chartres had never recovered from his wound. It was late August, and the siege was going nowhere. The Grand Master lingered in his sickbed for a month or more becoming ever more delirious and wild in his fever. The physicians gave him the milk of the poppy to soothe his spirit but he died, saying that, at last, he would see the face of God, and he was exceedingly glad.'

'I am sorry to hear of his passing, brother,' said Robert.

'Yes. We all felt the blow of his death, all the Templars in the camp. There was a great despondency among all the brother-knights. For some weeks many of us did nothing but grieve, and many felt God had turned His face from us and our cause.'

'I cannot believe that, Gilly,' said Robert.

'No, perhaps not. But what followed a little more than a month later seemed to us to be further proof of God's disfavour. The Saracen enemy made a sortie from the city – in force. Our attack on Damietta was no great secret and the Ayyubid Sultan had had many months to prepare for the siege. He had strengthened his city walls and filled Damietta with men-at-arms from across the Levant, thousands of them. They were ready for us. When they made their sortie and attacked the Templar camp in the dead of night, they came upon us in great numbers. I do not know if our sentries were negligent, or drunk, or what, but they were swiftly overrun and I awoke in my tent to the shouts of alarm, the crash of steel and the flames of a great conflagration…'

Gilbert paused then, seemingly embarrassed. 'Forgive me, Rob, but my memory of that night is clouded and of the days and weeks after, too. I came running from my tent in only my braies and chemise, my sword in hand, and saw Saracens everywhere and the camp in flames. Before I could strike a blow, I took a crack to the back of my head – feel right here, brother, there is still a hard knot in my skull from that unseen strike.' Robert leaned forward and obligingly felt the back of his brother's head.

'I know not from whence the blow came, nor who struck me. I fell to the ground and knew no more. I awoke in a large wooden cage on wheels, my hands and feet bound, and my head aching – indeed my whole body was in great torment. I was in and out of myself for several days, but I knew we were travelling east in that hellish wooden cage and that I was among other members of the Order, and that gave me some small comfort. The Saracens had captured three of us brother-knights, all taken alive: me and Lanfranco Adorno, and Guillaume de Toulouse – you remember him?'

Robert shook his head.

'And they took nine of our sergeants, too, including old Rufus le Blanc. You must recall *him*: he had such a fine singing voice. He would lead the choir in chapel.'

'I remember Rufus.'

'He died. He had taken a wound to the thigh and it began to rot in the wooden cage and he died. Poor Rufus never sang the *Te Deum* for us again.'

'Where did they take you in that foul cage on wheels?'

'Signor Templar,' said the guard. 'It is nearly time for you to dine with the Podestà. You must not be late.'

'Go on with your story, Gilly,' said Robert, ignoring the guard.

'They took us to Jerusalem – to the Holy City itself. I do not know why. I think the Sultan meant to use us as bargaining pieces with the Order, and they needed us to be nearer to Acre. But we travelled for three weeks to Jerusalem and once there they threw us in an underground gaol, not much more than a pit in the earth. All my life I have wanted to see the Holy City and all I saw of it then was a dank, slimy, rock-walled chamber deep in the earth's bowels. I stood ankle-deep in filth every day. One barred window, high above, and about threescore other wretches, our people and local miscreants, for company. The guards would simply hurl a bucket of food scraps into the cell, as if we were pigs, and, indeed, we would fight each other like animals for mouldy peelings. Our thirst became so great that we licked water from the dripping rock walls. May God forgive me for the things I did in there. Terrible things. I once killed an old man with my hands, like a ravening beast, for possession of a rotten melon.'

'I am so sorry I was not there for you, Gilly.'

'You are here now, Rob, that is what matters. And I had Lanfranco. He helped me; saved my life really. We made a partnership in that stinking prison, just the two of us, after Guillaume died of gaol fever. Lanfranco and I looked out for each other, shared our food, watched over each other while we slept. I would not be alive but for Lanfranco. And he got me out, in the end, too, at Christmastide. Or his rich father did. Barisone Adorno paid the price for both of us, and the surviving sergeants. And it cost him a pretty penny. You should have heard him grumbling in Genoa. A fortune he wasted, a king's ransom, and he seemed to blame me for the cost of our salvation.'

'They released you at Christmas?'

'We were taken to Genoa by ship. Just me and Lanfranco. I know not what happened to the sergeants. They were set loose in Jerusalem, penniless and starving.'

'It is time for your dinner, Templar,' said the guard. 'His Excellency does not like to be kept waiting.'

'One more moment,' said Robert. 'Go on, Gilly.'

'There is not much more to tell: Lanfranco asked his father to release me but Barisone refused. He needed to recoup his outlay, he said. He was going up to Soldaya, to arrange his affairs in the North, and took me with him, under heavy guard. But Lanfranco made his father promise to treat me well until the ransom was paid.'

'And has he treated you well?'

'As you see,' said Gilbert. 'Not badly. But after Lanfranco left to return to the Order, I waited and waited. I have been here ever since. Two years in these rooms.'

'I am so sorry, Gilbert. I was in the East all this time. I am rich now – not rich like Adorno but I can arrange your ransom. You will soon be free, Gilly.'

'Signor Templar?' said the guard sternly. 'It is past time to leave.'

'You are rich – how?'

'I cannot tell you everything now, Gilly. But you must trust me. I will have you out of here soon. Stay strong and I will return.'

'You would leave me here, Rob?' said Gilly. And his brother's plaintive tone twisted Robert's heart strings.

'Put your trust in God, brother. We shall meet again soon. I promise you.'

The impatient gaoler was now actually tugging at Robert's black surcoat.

'Farewell, Gilly,' Robert said, and he stood, turned and walked out the door.

Captain Carlo led Robert back along the corridors and down the stairs of the house, and out into the courtyard, where a long table covered with a shining white cloth had been set up under the brightly striped awning.

It was past noon and the sun was fierce. Carlo bade him farewell and disappeared into the stables on the far side of the courtyard leaving Robert alone.

After all the chivvying in Gilly's rooms, Robert was irritated to find that there was no sign of the Podestà. He tapped his foot on the paving stones, contemplating returning to his brother's prison to resume his conversation. Then, quite suddenly, a train of servants appeared, bringing out mountains of food on several silver platters.

They placed the food on the long table, a veritable cornucopia: a pair of roasted pheasants, basted to a glossy brown shine, then redressed with their own long brilliant green and brown tail feathers. A huge platter of grilled silvery fish on a bed of boiled green stuff. Half a dozen roasted capons, golden and shiny with grease. A whole suckling pig, slow-cooked with its belly packed with saffron-yellow rice, raisins and sultanas, the rich stuffing spilling out in a yellow wave from its sliced open belly. There were steam-wreathed pies of all kinds, and huge round cheeses, big bowls of pomegranates and apples and baskets of fragrant bread rolls. Silver flagons of wine.

It was a feast fit for a mighty king, or an emperor – or for this Genoese merchant prince of the House of Adorno, who was clearly as rich as any anointed monarch.

In spite of himself, Robert felt the juices flowing in his mouth. He had not eaten since before dawn. He poured himself a goblet of wine from a heavy silver jug, and took a sip. It was delicious – perhaps even better than the wine from Ziani's cellar.

A trumpet fanfare – and Robert turned to see the Podestà, borne on a huge gilded chair by four burly servants, in yellow silk tunics and scarlet hose, emerging from the house. They carried Adorno's bulk without any apparent effort, and Robert wondered when the enormous man had last taken a few steps on his own two feet. It might have been months. Several years even.

The servants carried Adorno to the head of the table, and while they fussed around him, arranging his crisp linen napkin, bringing a golden goblet and various silver platters within reach of his short arms, the Podestà flapped a podgy hand in Robert's direction and said, 'Come, sit beside me, Templar, so that we may more easily converse while we take our dinner.'

At Adorno's instruction, the servants filled Robert's large silver plate with choice cuts of suckling pig and roast pheasant, and refilled his wine goblet to the brim.

Robert allowed himself to eat and drink with a genuine enthusiasm. However, when he tried to broach the subject of his brother, initially to thank him for his good treatment during his captivity, Adorno hushed him and beckoned an attentive servant forward to give his guest another fat slice or two of some dripping, meaty delicacy.

So Robert ate and drank and held his peace.

Despite an invitation to talk, they completed their meal in near silence and Robert was not much surprised to see that his enormous host gorged like a starving ogre, stuffing juicy wedges of meat into his mouth, several at a time, with his fat little fingers and washing them down with huge draughts of red wine.

He made nasty, wet, crunching noises as he ate – like a herd of pigs in an autumn orchard. And, from time to time, a servant would come forward to refill his golden chalice and recharge his plate, sometimes accompanied by a little man who wiped the grease from Adorno's many chins with a napkin. Robert ate till he was sated, then sat back and watched, fascinated yet repelled, as the Podestà continued to ravage the dinner fare like an army sacking a captured city.

Eventually, Adorno's eating slowed, and finally stopped. The little servant came forward once more to mop at his grease-shined cheeks. Robert's host took one more mighty gulp of wine and then turned his tiny brown eyes on Robert.

'Let me tell you a few things, Templar,' he said, smacking his lips, 'about your *friend* Niccolò Ziani, the man called the Viper of Venice. If he is indeed your friend.'

Robert was taken aback by this sudden sally. He replied, 'Ziani is my partner and my benefactor. But, yes, I am also proud to call him my friend.'

'Then listen to my tale. And maybe you will understand a little more of him.'

Robert drank off the last dregs of wine in his goblet but he said nothing.

'Niccolò Ziani came from humble stock – Venetian for centuries, of course, but not one of the great trading families. A humble background, in truth. His people were shipwrights, who plied their trade on the Rialto, skilled artisans for generations, until Ziani's father began to invest his savings in the cargoes of his betters. He made a little money, and when he died he left Ziani a modest fortune and a single cargo ship, a cog, of his own. Young Niccolò possessed only one cog but he was a popular lad with many friends, who also had ships or who had the use of their fathers'. He was clever and charming. He persuaded his friends to come together in a company; they called themselves the Brotherhood of the Rialto, after their district. And they prospered.'

Robert nodded. He wondered what the point of this story was, but he was feeling sleepy with the food and wine and the heat of the afternoon, and was content to listen.

'So Ziani became rich,' Robert said. 'I know this already. He is a successful trader, now with many ships at his command.'

'You do not know *how* he became rich,' said Adorno. 'Possess yourself with patience and attend to my tale. You will learn a great deal from it.'

Robert shrugged and helped himself to another splash from the wine jug.

'The principal business of the Brotherhood of the Rialto was sugar. They sent their ships to Famagusta and purchased shiploads of sugar loaves from the Cypriot beet growers. They transported the sugar to Montpellier in the Gulf of Lions where they sold it to the merchants of the Languedoc to distribute to the European cities.

'As it happens, my family also traded in sugar and spices, and this is how I came to know this story. Now, Famagusta is not so far from Antioch in Syria, and their famed spice markets, and before long Ziani and his friends were also buying rare spices from the Arabian and Turkish traders and adding them to their cargoes of sugar before shipping them west to Montpellier.

'However, the European tables were already well served in all manner of spices supplied by our own Genoese ships and so, when the Brotherhood of the Rialto arrived at Montpellier, they found few takers for their wares and they were forced to sell off their sugar and spice at a loss just to recompense their ships' crews.

'This infuriated Ziani. So, the next year, your *friend* went to visit the pirates of Tunis, those fierce Saracen sea-wolves feared by all honest sailors in the Middle Sea, and he made an infernal arrangement, a secret evil pact, with these heathen corsairs.

'In exchange for gold from the Saracens, he furnished the pirates with the dates of the sailing of all the Genoese spice ships and their approximate time of arrival in the waters near Montpellier. The Saracen pirates kept their bargain with Ziani and they lay in wait for the Genoese ships, which they duly attacked and easily captured.

'They enslaved the Genoese crews, and sold the valuable cargo of spices back to Ziani. He then secretly transported these spices north from Venice – overland – to the German realms, via Augsburg and Frankfurt. He played this same dirty trick on the Genoese fleet three years in a row before they discovered his perfidy. And, know this, some of the ships that Ziani betrayed were owned by members of my own family. My cousin Marco was captured and sold into slavery and has never been heard of since.'

'I can see why you would hate him,' said Robert. 'But I already know that Ziani is ruthless. And few men of great wealth can boast of a spotless conscience.'

'Yet that is not how Niccolò Ziani grew so wealthy,' said Adorno.

Robert waited for him to continue.

'The increase in the frequency of the attacks on Christian shipping caused an important innovation in both Venice and Genoa. Shipowners were concerned that their vessels might be pirated by the corsairs or lost at sea in a bad storm, and they developed a system of mutual compensation. The shipowner, or more usually a consortium of shipowners, paid a fee to specialised groups of moneylenders to assure the value of their sea-borne goods. If the ship was lost *en route*, sunk or pirated, the moneylenders would pay the shipowner for a part of the value of the lost goods. Enormous sums, sometimes. But it lessened the risk of these dangerous ventures; do you follow me, Templar?'

Robert nodded. The Templars, too, were deeply involved in commerce.

'Ziani wanted his friends in the Brotherhood of Rialto to assure their cargoes,' continued Adorno. 'Who knew better than he the risk that a cargo might be lost at sea? But his colleagues of the Brotherhood refused to pay the fees to the assurers, preferring to save their money and put their trust in God and the skill of their captains.

'One year, they sent a convoy of five ships, their holds packed with spices and sugar, across the Mediterranean to Montpellier. All was well until they sighted the coast of Sardinia. Then, from behind a headland, a fleet hove into view, a hundred galleys, rowed by slaves, and filled with cruel Tunisian pirates, and they swiftly bore down on the defenceless Rialto convoy of fully laden spicers.

'After a brief battle, in which the Christians sold their lives dearly, the five ships were overwhelmed. However, this time, instead of enslaving the crew, all of them were immediately put to the sword, every last man. Hundreds of good Christians were butchered and the sea for a mile around was dyed red with their blood.

'The Brotherhood of the Rialto was broken by this catastrophe. One of their number took his own life, another younger man turned pirate himself and was killed in a great sea battle off Corfu a few years later. But Niccolò Ziani was made very wealthy by the loss of those five spice ships. He alone had paid the premium to the assurance people to ameliorate the risk of such a disaster, and so he alone was paid the vast sum his private agreement with them had stipulated.

'The moneylenders complained, of course. And many Venetians whispered that it had been Ziani himself who had given the vital information to the Tunisian corsairs about the movements of the spice fleet. Some even said that it was Ziani who had purchased the sugar and spice back from the Tunisian pirates, and who sold them on via his land routes into Germany. But nothing was ever proved. A young lawyer, a kinsman of one of the members of the Brotherhood, who tried to investigate the disaster was murdered in an alley and his house, where he kept his papers, was burned to the pilings. It was never proved who was responsible yet all knew who was guilty.'

Adorno's face was now slick with oily sweat. His beady little eyes glittered with malice and hatred. 'This is how your partner earned his title – the Viper of Venice.'

'You are telling me that Ziani consorts with Saracen pirates?' said Robert.

'I am telling you what your *friend* did to his old partners and colleagues – his Rialto brothers. He betrayed them all to the Barbary corsairs simply to enrich himself.'

'I do not believe you,' said Robert. 'To be frank, I have had enough of your old sea stories. I would prefer you to attend now to the matter of my brother's ransom.'

'All in good time, Templar. Only ask yourself this: why is Ziani, with all his wealth and power, sitting up there in Tana, in the arse-end of nowhere? Why is he living on the lip of the wilderness? Because he cannot go home to Venice. I can go back and forth to Genoa, as I please. But he cannot. He is self-exiled. There are still too many powerful Venetian families who would see him prosecuted for his crimes, or if that did not serve, then simply murdered one dark night.

'The families of the Brotherhood are still alive, some still trading, and he has made yet more enemies since those early days. I am warning you, Templar, as a kindness, that Niccolò Ziani will surely treat you as cruelly as he treated his former colleagues. I am saying plainly that you are a blind and blinkered fool to trust him.'

'Nevertheless, I do trust him. He has always dealt honestly with me.'

'I very much doubt that. If you have not yet discovered Ziani's lies, you will soon do so. Now, I have a proposal to put to you – a better arrangement for you and for me – and all I ask is that you give my proposal the full and proper consideration.'

Adorno fixed his little bird-like eyes on Robert.

'Tear up this treaty you have with Ziani and the great Tartar warlord. Destroy it. Burn it. You said yourself that this man Genghis Khan would break his word if it were to his advantage. Return to Asia and make another arrangement, make a better one – this time between you and the Tartar warlord and the House of Adorno. You shall have a two-thirds share in this new agreement, and I shall take the other third.

'We shall be true partners, you and I. Furthermore, I shall give you back your brother, hale and whole as you have seen him, and without asking for a single silver penny in ransom money. And, unlike Niccolò Ziani, I shall never lie to you or betray you. I will always deal with you truly and honestly. I swear on my immortal soul.'

Chapter Six

Robert stood up abruptly. 'Enough!' he said. 'Enough of your silken lies and serpentine promises. I have made a treaty with the Great Khan and the House of Karacha – my house, in which Niccolò Ziani has a share equal to mine. I trust Ziani. And I shall not forsake him for a… for you, signor.'

Robert found he was breathless with rage. He tried to calm himself. He sat back down and took a great, long breath, feeling the thudding of his heart.

'Since you mention my brother,' he said, after a moment, 'whom you hold as *your* captive – like a God-damned Saracen pirate yourself – I shall tell you this, signor. I have determined the amount that I can pay. The full amount that I shall pay, and it is this: I shall give you ten thousand marks of silver for Gilbert of Hadlow, and not a penny more. It is a more-than-fair price for a young Templar knight; indeed, ten thousand is an excessive sum. Nevertheless, I shall pay that sum. I *can* pay that sum. I cannot pay any more. And, if you will not accept it, I shall be forced to find another way to free my brother from your unchristian, nakedly avaricious grasp.'

Adorno stared at the Englishman. He did not move; he did not blink.

'This is your final word?' he said. 'You will not even consider my offer?'

'Ten thousand for my brother. That is all I have to say to you, signor.'

Adorno let out a breath. He flapped one small hand in the air, some sort of signal to his people, and suddenly there was movement all round the table. At first, Robert assumed that it was the army of servants come to clear away the empty platters and cups, then he realised the people surrounding him were soldiers, men-at-arms in yellow surcoats with drawn swords, spears and spanned crossbows with bolts already in the groove.

Captain Carlo was standing beside his bench, smiling genially down at him.

He saw that, on the far side of the courtyard, his three men, the two Mongol troopers and Idar, were being herded at crossbow-point towards the dinner table. Their hands were tied behind their backs and they had been stripped of their weapons.

'What is this?' said Robert. 'I came here at the invitation of your letter, sealed with your signet, under solemn promise of truce and safe conduct.'

He fumbled at the pouch, seeking the letter that Ziani had given him.

'If you have no more to say about my generous proposal,' said Adorno, 'or an appropriate ransom of your brother, than let us talk about the murder of Father Pietro.'

'What?' said Robert.

'Father Pietro – a man of God who was my servant and my friend. You brutally murdered him in the heathen wilds of Asia. Do not attempt to deny this.'

There was a man now standing at Adorno's shoulder, and with a sinking heart Robert recognised him. He was a large, lumpish blond man with a great hedge of beard. A Rus'. He had last seen this man on the battlefield outside the town of Ray, a few miles south of the shores of the Caspian Sea. He had been a bodyguard or servant of Father Pietro. Robert had indeed killed Father Pietro – but it had not been murder.

'I am here under promise of safe conduct,' said Robert. 'You swore to deal truly and honestly with me. Is this your honesty? Is this fair dealing?'

'You do not deny you killed my servant, Father Pietro?' said Adorno.

'That man,' said Robert, pointing at the Rus', 'knows that I killed Pietro fairly in the heat of battle. And your priest had attempted to murder *me* several times.'

The Genoese soldiers were all round Robert. A dozen men. Captain Carlo put a firm hand on Robert's shoulder pinning him to the bench.

'An eye for an eye, says the Bible,' Adorno was grinning, his own little eyes shining with glee. Despite all the rich food, Robert's stomach suddenly felt hollow.

'You murdered one of my best men in the heathen dust of Asia, and so...' The Podestà lifted his fat hand in the air and made another odd gesture.

Robert whipped his head round and saw one of the Genoese guards in the very act of drawing a dagger blade across Chankai's throat. The Mongol warrior gasped, spluttered out bloody froth, and slowly crumpled to his knees.

Begter and Idar were now madly struggling in their captors' grips.

Robert surged to his feet.

He felt Carlo's hand trying to hold him in place but he was still rising, driven by all the power in his muscular thighs. At the same time, he stretched out his arm and grasped the handle of the silver jug on the table before him, turned lightning fast, his right arm swinging, and he smashed the heavy metal vessel full into the captain's face, knocking him back a step or two in a great splash of blood-like red wine.

Robert jumped straight up on to the table itself, his boots shivering the wood and making all the remaining silver platters, knives and spoons dance. He transferred the heavy jug to his left hand and drew the Mongol blade with his right, and slashed at the outstretched arms of the Genoese guards who were reaching for him.

The steel flashed, severing half a dozen fingers, the digits falling like broken twigs. Robert bounded off the table on the far side, landing lightly on the courtyard flagstones.

He paid no heed to the shouts of anger and cries of pain behind him but simply sprinted towards the knot of people around Idar and Begter. There was no one between him and his men and, a short moment later, he had cut down the man who was holding Begter and was exchanging sword cuts with a second Genoese, using the silver jug as a kind of shield.

Someone loosed a crossbow bolt at him, and he felt the wind as it passed by his cheek. His opponent was staggering away bloody, sliced laterally across the face by Robert's razor-keen blade. Begter was free of his captor, had stolen a dagger from one of them, and was stabbing one of the guards in the chest and belly. Idar had also freed himself and was reaching for a sword, sheathed at the waist of a dead Genoese.

Robert heard Adorno shouting, 'Stop this nonsense! Stop this right now!'

He fended off one attacker with a swipe of the wine jug and ran his blade through the belly of another man – a Genoese crossbowman who was hurrying to reload his weapon. Idar was battling someone with the stolen sword, now killing him. Begter had found himself a hand axe, and buried it in the head of a snarling Genoese.

The one living Genoese was backing away, waving his sword in a loose and terrified manner. But there were boots slapping on the stones in the yard, Captain Carlo, face bloody, was running forward with a dozen yellow-surcoated men at his back.

Adorno was shouting. 'Kill them all! Kill them!' The big Rus' was still beside him, a long knife in each hand, and two Genoese with drawn swords stood on either side of his chair.

Robert felt the burn of anger deep inside. He had come here in good faith to discuss a ransom like a civilised man with this turd-mountain. He had been tricked and his man had been murdered. His brother was imprisoned by this monster. He glanced quickly over at the stables, where he could just see the nose of Idar's creamy thoroughbred and thought – *no, it's impossible.*

Time seemed to slow. 'On me,' he said in Mongol. Then, seeing Idar, he said, 'Stay close,' in Italian. He ran straight towards Carlo and his dozen charging men.

Robert of Hadlow began his training as a knight at the age of seven. Since them almost every day of his thirty-two years he had practised and honed the craft of war.

He had been schooled by the finest masters in the halls of the Templars, men who were themselves accounted the most skilled warriors in Christendom, for a full decade. And he had surpassed them. He could even kill a man with one empty hand, should he choose to do so.

He chose to.

As he ran towards the Genoese captain, he hurled the wine jug hard overhand and was pleased to see it thud, once again into Carlo's handsome, curl-fringed face. The captain dropped like a poleaxed heifer to the courtyard flags, clutching his face, then Robert was in amongst his enemies, his blade flickering out like a shaft of lighting.

He sliced through the belly muscles of one man, and punched stiffened fingers into the soft side of the throat of another, completely crushing his windpipe and dislodging the cartilage box entirely from its fleshly moorings. He left the Genoese man-at-arms choking, scrabbling madly at his own neck, and dying for lack of air.

Robert ripped through the pack of Genoese men-at-arms like a fox in a hen house, his Mongol blade stabbing, slicing, hacking, killing and, at his shoulder, he was aware that Idar was doing similar terrible damage with the stolen arming sword.

He took a few hard cuts from the flying Genoese swords but, by the Grace of God, his mail coat kept the enemy steel from his flesh. A crossbow bolt ripped through the loose material of his surcoat but missed his waist by a good two inches.

Begter, a horse-borne archer, was wielding the unfamiliar dagger and axe beside him with a surprising precision, stabbing and slicing at the men that Idar and Robert wounded, finishing them off. Then, in less than a dozen heartbeats, all three men had burst through the blood-spattered pack of Genoese, leaving five lying in bloody puddles on the courtyard and half a dozen whimpering and cringing behind them.

'This way,' said Robert, pointing with his bloody sword at the doorway to the large, brick building on the far side of the dinner table. It had been in his mind to kill Adorno, but there was now a large bristling knot of armed men around the enormous merchant.

'This way,' he said again, and led his two surviving men at a dead run straight into the dark entrance. He could hear the sound of angry shouting and pounding feet behind him, but he did not pause even for an instant to look back. The three men found themselves in a high-ceilinged hall and Robert led them at the run up a flight of stairs and down a long corridor with sweet-smelling cedar floors. They could hear the pursuers behind them, the clatter of boots, the hard shouts of frightened and furious men.

Robert stopped, panting a little, outside the white-painted door at the end of the long corridor. He calmed his breathing, knocked, and said in his best Genoese dialect, 'Open the door, comrade, if you please. The Podestà wishes to see the prisoner.'

Robert waited to hear the bolts being drawn, his body tense. Idar and Begter were beside him, Idar looking away down the long corridor. The noises of the pursuers were getting louder.

An officer bellowed, 'Get up there, you sons of whores. Go and get at them!'

'Open the door, comrade, if you please,' said Robert again, he was trying to keep the rising panic out of his voice.

'On whose authority… *comrade*?' came a muffled voice from within.

Robert hurled himself at the door, his full weight slamming against the painted wood. But the door was reinforced in some manner and he simply bounced off.

There were men in the corridor. A score of them. And advancing slowly.

'*Ezen*,' said Begter, 'they are coming, *ezen*.'

Robert threw himself at the door again, once more there was no result. Then Idar hurled his full weight at the white-painted wood; and he rebounded too. Robert hacked at the wood with his sword, with no more effect than a few slivers carved off.

The Circassian wrapped one hand in his shirt and seized the arming sword by the hilt and blade and dug the point into the painted wood around the door handle; once, twice, he slammed home the steel, but only a few chips of wood were worked loose.

A crossbow bolt hissed between them, hit the door jamb and clattered away.

'It cannot be done,' said Idar.

'*Ezen!*' said Begter.

Robert glanced left. The Genoese were advancing, in some kind of shield-wall, behind three large red-and-gold kite-shaped protectors, rims overlapping; a moving wall that spanned the corridor, with half a dozen heads behind them, spears extended.

The crossbow loosed again, from behind the shields, the bolt scraping along the brick wall. The creeping block of Genoese men-at-arms was a dozen paces away.

'I swear I will return, Gilly,' shouted Robert. 'I will be back for you soon.'

They ran.

They sprinted to the end of the corridor, where the window shutters were flung wide. Idar went first, vaulting out and over the sill, hanging briefly by his hands and then dropping to the muddy alley below. Begter went next, pausing for a moment at the sill to look down at the twelve-foot drop beneath, and Idar below him, beckoning.

Robert stood erect, sword in hand, and faced the Genoese, who all peered at him over their shield rims, still coming on. A crossbow cracked, the bolt buzzed by him.

'You hurt one hair on my brother's head and I will slaughter you all,' he said. 'By God, I swear I shall kill every single one of you motherless dogs, if my brother is harmed.'

Then he sheathed his sword, turned and ducked out of the window. As he hung from his fingertips, he heard the roar of triumph from inside the corridor, and the stamping of feet, then he dropped and rolled in the soft, wet filth of the narrow alley.

Idar helped him up and they ran, limping a little, down the muddy passage, heading south towards the sea and a wider street. Robert glanced behind him, just once, and saw two black heads poking out the window, a spear shaft and the T-shape of a crossbow. But there were several knots of townspeople in the street ahead, some gawping and pointing at the three running men emerging from the alley, and asking each other idiotic questions; Robert and his men were forced to dodge between them.

Robert looked up at the brick wall of the building as he quit the alley and saw a high barred window and a glimpse of a pale face with blond hair staring down at him.

He turned right at the wide street and sprinted towards a portal in the town's wooden palisade, where a trio of Genoese were just beginning to close the gate.

The three fugitives said nothing and simply charged straight at the closing gate. Idar's long legs carried him there first. He said not a word, but simply hacked down one of the Genoese guards with his stolen sword and the other two fled before him.

A moment later all three were outside and running up the muddy track that ran between the town palisade and the fence of the slave stockade.

'This way,' shouted Robert. And his comrades ran behind him as he followed the fence around a gentle curve towards the entrance to the slave pens. Behind them a swarm of Genoese erupted from the gates, scores of them, spearmen, crossbowmen, even some mailed men-at-arms on horseback. They were shouting in their war fury.

Robert could clearly hear the drumming of their hoofbeats.

They charged into a small squad of guards outside the slave pen gates.

Robert whipped out his sword, and slashed across a man's throat, near severing head from neck. Idar struck down another, in one, two lightning blows.

Begter said, '*Ezen!*' and Robert saw he was pointing north.

There was a small knot of horsemen galloping recklessly towards them. Short stocky men, on small ugly ponies, riding like centaurs, bows in hand, arrows nocked.

Robert ran towards the entrance to the slave pen, cutting at a Genoese man-at-arms who stumbled away blindly, his face torn and bleeding. The gates were two paces wide and made of wickerwork, secured to the fence by mere leather thongs.

Robert made short work of the thongs and tore the pen gate open – he stared inside at the milling humanity. Skinny wretches in dark rags, a multitude staring back at him from despairing hollowed-out faces, pale and weak beings like walking ghosts.

'Run,' shouted Robert, 'run now, if you desire your freedom!' He was yelling at them in Italian, the Venetian dialect, and the dead-eyed slaves stared back at him in bemusement. He repeated his message in bad Cuman, then for some reason again in Mongol. Then turned and ran back to his friends, who were surrounded by a knot of half a dozen stamping, snorting horsemen.

Mongol horsemen.

Robert locked eyes with Arslan, who frowned disapprovingly, but extended his hand. The Englishman took it and swung up behind his lieutenant, gripping him round the waist. Some of the *arban* were already busy loosing arrows at the Genoese, a deterring shower of death that had quickly slowed, then halted the enemy advance. Idar and Begter were mounting up, too, behind two of their comrades.

'Go!' said Robert. And, as Arslan dug his heels into the double-laden pony, the Englishman looked back at the slave pen and saw to his relief that hundreds of the wretched captives were pouring out of the open gate and fleeing for the high ground.

The space between the town and the slave pen was filled with scores of raggedy running folk. And on the far side of the mass of freed slaves, he saw the knot of Genoese men-at-arms standing completely still, hefting weapons and merely glaring at them.

The Mongols threaded their way through the crush of running humanity, touched their spurs to their horses' sides, and galloped away towards the distant green hills.

Chapter Seven

'Chankai is dead?' said Arslan, as he dismounted lithely from the tired steppe pony.

Robert, who was already on the ground, could not look him in the eye.

'I saw them cut his throat,' he said. 'I realised then they meant to kill us.'

'Huh,' said Arslan. 'Then?' There was a cold silence. 'So you fled the town and left four good horses and your imprisoned kinsman behind?'

Robert stared at him. It was undeniably true. He had allowed Chankai to be killed and had lost Samson, Idar's cream-coloured thoroughbred, and two other good steppe ponies. He wished more than anything in that moment that Altan were with him. Not this cold-eyed contemptuous brute of a lieutenant.

'Do you mean to return to Soldaya and bring out your brother?' asked Arslan.

'The steppe is wide,' snapped Robert, and he turned and walked away.

Robert, Idar and the eight surviving members of his *arban* were on the edge of a small lake, little bigger than a castle fishpond, shallow, soupy and green with algae. The lake was a good ten miles from the town of Soldaya, and they had stopped there to water the horses. And rest the poor beasts, too. There had been no pursuit, at least none that Robert had been able to discern from the jolting back of Arslan's overladen pony. Dusk was now falling and Robert was feeling more exhausted than ever before.

They made a small fire, but only to boil water and make *shulen*, then they extinguished the flames and stamped out the embers, and Robert set two sentries to watch in the darkness. He wrapped himself in his cloak and tried to sleep. However, the image of Gilly's pale face at the bars in the brick wall above him kept him awake. He was consumed with fear at what the Genoese might do to his brother in revenge. He had to face the truth: his mission to Soldaya had been an abject failure and he had thrown away the life of another one of his men. Arslan was right to be contemptuous.

Eventually, knowing he would not sleep, he got up and went to relieve Saka, who was on sentry duty.

'Any sign of the enemy?' said Robert, as he stood beside the Mongol in the darkness, looking south towards the coast in the direction of Soldaya.

'Nothing. Not even the hoot of an owl,' said Saka.

'Then you can go to your blankets,' said Robert. 'I will take this watch.'

He could see the gleam of Saka's teeth in the darkness as the man smiled with pleasure. As Saka turned to go, Robert put a hand on his arm to stop him.

'Tell me,' he said, 'how did Arslan know to come down from the hills at that exact moment and save us from the Genoese?'

'Do not be angry with us, *ezen*,' said Saka. 'We watched you go inside the town but instead of obeying your command and retreating to that hill, Arslan made us stay – hidden, of course, but on that same ridge you rode out from.

'He said that he'd had a dream the night before of you, Chankai and Begter drowning in a great black sea, struggling to swim to the surface. He believes in dreams, Arslan. I think they are yak shit, but Arslan swears it is how gods speak to us. So we stayed on the ridge, no more than half a mile from the walls, and watched the town. When we saw you fleeing out of the gate, pursued by soldiers, we mounted up and came down to get you. You are not angry that we disobeyed you, *ezen*?'

'How could I be angry? I owe Arslan – all of you – my existence.'

'I'm sad about Chankai,' said Saka. 'He was a good wrestler, a strong man.'

Robert could think of nothing to say except, 'God in his mercy will surely forgive his sins and welcome him into Heaven… Now, go to your blankets, Saka.'

When the half-moon rose, Robert looked up at its silvery beauty and realised with a violent pang that there was one person he missed even more than old Altan.

He slept three hours in the deepest part of the night and woke thick-headed at dawn, with the knowledge that mosquitoes were feasting joyously on his neck. He slapped them away and roused the *arban*. An hour later they were on the road.

Six days after that, they rode through the gates of Tana, a bedraggled, dusty crew, drooping with both fatigue and failure.

–

After washing and changing his linen at the inn where the *arban* was lodged, and dispatching Idar to report to Ziani, Robert went to pray in the church of St Mary's in the town square.

The interior was cool, dark, lit only by a handful of candles on the altar, and completely empty, save for an elderly priest called Father Michel, a Frenchman from the city of Orléans, who had been a missionary among the Kipchaks, attempting to preach God's Word to the heathen in the wilderness north of the Don. After a single year, he was attacked by his flock, who broke his leg and robbed him of all he owned.

Father Michel hobbled around at the back of the church, sweeping with a broom, and after a polite nod of greeting when he had entered, Robert ignored him. He needed to pray. He needed to ask the Almighty a question and hear the answer in his heart in the quiet stillness of His House. He knelt before the wooden altar, looking up at the huge wooden crucifix affixed on the whitewashed wall above. The image of Christ in his Passion seemed to him to resemble his poor brother Gilly, emaciated, with long flowing hair and such a gentle and sad expression.

He prayed to St Christopher, his favoured saint, the guardian of travellers, and believed that he had the answer to his question. Then he went to the side of the church and sat on one of the benches. He breathed in the familiar church scent of beeswax candles and incense, and the hum of ancient sweat ingrained in the wood of the benches. And was comforted by it. It was, for him, the scent of Godliness.

He closed his eyes. After a while, he heard the door of the church creak open, but since he did not wish to speak to anyone, he kept his eyes tightly shut.

He could not ignore, however, the sound of someone sitting down on the bench right next to him, barely a foot away. His eyes flared open, indignant that he should be disturbed in this sanctuary. He glared at the man beside him, a tall, lean, middle-aged fellow, with sparse dark hair, who was dressed in the plain garb of a monk or friar, a wooden cross hanging at his chest. He blinked, utterly astonished.

No, it could not be true.

It was Jean de Malemort, Seneschal of the Templar Order – the last person Robert expected to see in this remote outpost. He let out a muffled sob of gratitude – God had answered his prayers – here in the flesh was the man he revered most on Earth. The only man to whom he could speak freely about his troubles.

'God be with you, Brother Robert,' said Jean de Malemort. 'You seem at first glance to be in rude health despite all your travels and travails.'

Robert found he had seized Malemort's right forearm, perhaps to reassure himself this was a living man, not some spectre of his imaginings.

'You came here, my lord,' he said stupidly. 'You came to Tana – for me.'

'For you, for Christ, for our mutual venture – for the salvation of Outremer.'

'My lord, I have so much to tell you…'

'Aaron of Sana'a has already made a full report to me, Robert, and the Venetian merchant, Niccolò Ziani, too, writes to me from time to time with his tidings, as I'm sure you know. It seems that you have brought a mighty Eastern army to the very edge of our Christian world, and I congratulate you heartily on that extraordinary triumph.'

Jean de Malemort was smiling at the Englishman.

'I knew you could do it, Robert. I knew I was right to choose you among all the others, knowing that you alone had the strength and determination – and the guile, let us not forget that – to see this matter through. Now we must bring our new Eastern allies over the final hurdle and launch them swiftly against the Saracens. But first, tell me, Robert, are you well? Are you in good spirits? Ziani says you have made a great treaty with the fearsome Tartar king that will make you both quite sinfully rich. And where have you been? I have been waiting all this past week here in Tana for you.'

It felt like a confession, with all that sweet relief at the unburdening of his tormented soul. Robert spoke for an hour to his master, the Seneschal of his Order.

Jean de Malemort took him right back to the beginning, to his first exploits in Asia, the desert crossings, the battles on behalf of the Mongol monarch, the victories, the hardships. He even admitted to the Seneschal that he had broken his Templar vows of chastity and found true love with Sarantuya, the adulterous wife of another man, and yet Malemort did not chastise nor even criticise him, only saying, 'We are all of us sinners, Brother Robert, even I, but God's love is forgiveness for all of us.'

He told Malemort then about Soldaya, and his failure to free his brother, and the death of Chankai, and even of Arslan's cold contempt. When he had finished, he felt spent, but also strangely light, as if he had been thoroughly cleansed both inside and out.

'You have ridden a hard road, Robert,' said Malemort, his eyes soft with kindness. 'I am sorry I have not been able to help you. But may we now speak of the great Mongol army in Georgia? What are their plans? Can they be persuaded to come to the aid of Christendom?'

'I fear not,' said Robert sadly, 'at least, not for some time. Their supreme commander General Subutai has been ordered to come north of the Caucasus to deal with a rebellion of Cumans under their leader, a man called Khan Köten. I have given Subutai my word to lead their army north through the high mountain passes.'

'Leading their army in the wrong direction, from our point of view,' said Malemort. 'Can this Mongol's mind be changed? Can he be persuaded to go south?'

'I promised,' said Robert. 'I am loath to break my word. Also, I wish to ask a great boon of General Subutai in due course while he is in these northern lands.'

'Hmm,' said Malemort.

'However, Subutai has sworn to me that if I do this arduous task for him – guide him through the high passes – he will come south after the rebellion is defeated and perhaps then he may be persuaded to capture Baghdad, and after that…'

'Our poor Brethren are dying every day in the Holy Land,' said Malemort. For the first time, the Englishman sensed a tone of rebuke in his voice.

Robert dropped his eyes. Yet he knew he still had to bring the Mongol army north, or his secret plan to save Gilbert had little chance of success.

'How goes the war?' Robert asked the Seneschal, just to change the air.

Malemort let out a sigh.

'The day I left Trebizond to take ship to Tana,' he said, 'I heard we had been expelled from our last foothold in Egypt.

I am sorry to tell you, Robert, that the Army of God has broken against the Sultan's walls. The men were exhausted, many wounded. Many more dead. Our camps, too, were full of plague and sickness – some cried aloud that God had forsaken us.'

Robert paused to reflect on this news. 'And the Latin kingdoms?'

'They, too, are beleaguered. Too many knights were destroyed in the fighting in Egypt. The Saracens smell our weakness. Last month, the castle of Belmont in Syria was razed by the Saracens after a ten-day siege, the captured walls were pulled down and a hundred Christian knights were put to the sword by this implacable foe. Worse, the reinforcements coming from Europe have slowed to a trickle. The kings of Christendom believe our cause is lost. Their noble lords choose not to demonstrate their prowess in Outremer. They believe their efforts there will be in vain. Yet our cause is *not* lost, Robert. Our knights have not died in vain. For, as you know, this is the cause of Christ. The cause of Christendom itself. It is God's will. *Deus vult.*'

'I can try again to persuade the Mongol general, my lord, but I fear...'

'Tell me this, Robert,' said Malemort, fixing him with his intense eyes. 'This Mongol king – this Genghis Khan – he is not a Christian, is that correct? He is not King John the Presbyter – or Prester John – the puissant Christian lord of Asia whom we once hoped you might discover?'

'No, my lord. I no longer believe Prester John exists. He is a mere fable. Even if he does exist, Genghis Khan is not him. The Great Khan is no Christian, though there are some among his family who are of the Nestorian faith. More than a few, I'd say.'

'If this Genghis Khan were to perish, who then would succeed him? One of his Christian children, perhaps? One who might look more favourably on our plight?'

'The Great Khan is in health, my lord. And not yet old. I have met his favoured son, a brute called Ogedei, who sits at the khan's right hand in council. He is a sad drunkard, and no kind of Christian: he laughed at a holy relic I gave his father…'

'A pity. Then we must persuade General Subutai to come to our aid. You have already moved mountains to bring him west. How might this best be achieved?'

'As I said, my lord. I plan to oblige him greatly by guiding his Mongol army over the Caucasus, and we can only hope and pray that he will honour that obligation to me – and fulfil his promise to turn south to attack and capture Baghdad.'

'So all our hopes rest on the gratitude of a heathen warlord? That does not fill me with confidence. I wish Aaron were here. But he is down in Sana'a, having completed his southward journey. I believe we must seek counsel with our good friend Niccolò Ziani. Mayhap he can help us to shift this Mongol general's mind.'

–

They found Ziani in the rose garden behind his great house. The garden was a sad, botched affair, the few surviving blooms small, mean, brownish things, much eaten by insects and rot, and, when they were brought into his presence, Ziani, dressed in a leather apron, was wielding a pair of iron shears with a vigorous ruthlessness.

The Venetian merchant set down his shears and ushered Robert and Malemort to a stone table in a shady part of the garden and gave instructions to his servants that wine and biscuits be brought for his guests. Robert gave Ziani a brief account of his disastrous mission to Soldaya and, when he had received his sympathetic response, the talk turned to the matter that Malemort considered far more urgent. Robert was slightly surprised to see that Ziani showed no astonishment that Malemort should be in Tana, until he realised the Seneschal must have been residing with Ziani for this past week. There was no Preceptory within a thousand miles, so where else was the Templar knight to stay?

'From what Robert has told me,' Ziani said, 'this General Subutai is loyal to the Great Khan, and will not go against his master's will. Is that not so?'

'He has a surprising amount of latitude,' said Robert. 'Genghis Khan trusts him completely – and rightly so, since Subutai is his loyal dog – but the general may go wherever he chooses, and take whatever city he likes, unless he has direct orders to the contrary. I have seen this with my own eyes in Khwarazmia. If Subutai chose to capture Baghdad, for example, Genghis Khan would not be angered. I even discussed that notion with the Great Khan in Samarkand. And the capture of Baghdad might be enough *in itself* to help us.'

'How so?' said Malemort.

'With a powerful Mongol army inside Baghdad, on the eastern flank of the Sultan of Egypt's territory, the Saracens would be obliged to divert a large number of troops away from the Latin kingdoms to defend themselves from the Mongol threat, would they not? Word must have reached the Sultan of the demise of the Shah of Khwarazmia and the swift overrunning of his empire. I believe the Sultan would be most discomforted to find twenty thousand Mongols at his back door. He would be forced to take swift action; to send an army to cover his eastern borders at the least.'

'This is true,' said Ziani. 'However, there is something I must tell you. Something I heard only today from my informants. The Mongol army may no longer number as many as twenty thousand. They fought a great battle earlier this spring against the Georgians. King George the Brilliant led fifty thousand men-at-arms against them. There was a great slaughter in the Kura Plain and the Georgians were badly defeated. The Mongols, too, suffered great losses and were forced to retreat…'

'To retreat?' said Robert. 'Where did they retreat to? Not to Persia?'

'Not so far,' said Ziani. 'They retreated to the shores of the Caspian. They are encamped now around Derbent, licking their wounds. But I fear there may be another battle brewing. The Georgians, I hear, are determined to expel them from their lands.'

The servants came out into the garden, bringing vessels full of the sweet red wine of Trebizond and delicate honey biscuits made from crushed almonds and—

–

'Cease your idle rambling, prisoner,' said Wilhelm von Eslarn. 'Do not squander the court's time with talk of honey biscuits and rose gardens.'

Robert, thin, meek and drab in his penitent's chemise, looked up at the Provost of Vienna, who was strutting up and down, directly in front of the duke's throne.

'I merely wish to describe fully the—'

'We have heard enough talk of your sweet wines and rich meats,' snapped Wilhelm. 'The important question before this court is whether you consorted with the Tartars in their crimes against Christians. And I have a query for you pertaining to this matter.'

'Someone should give that poor skinny wretch a couple of biscuits and a cup of wine,' said a voice from the audience. 'He looks sorely in need of it.'

'Silence!' shouted Wilhelm. 'I will have silence in His Grace's court. The question I have for you, prisoner, is this: you have mentioned a battle fought between the King of Georgia and the Tartar horde in the Kura Valley. Did you know that this battle – and another one between the same antagonists a few months later – in effect ended the participation of the Christian Georgians in the holy struggle in Outremer?'

'I did *not* know that,' said Robert. 'I know very little of Georgian affairs.'

'It was His Holiness Pope Innocent, may he rest eternally in God's bosom,' said Wilhelm, 'who persuaded George the Brilliant to raise a mighty army of knights to come to the aid of the Holy Land, and that noble Christian king was in the very act of raising such a force, for exactly that purpose, when he was obliged to defend his own territory against an attack by your savage Tartar horde. These fiends destroyed his army, tens of thousands of knights. So my question to you is this: did you participate in the battle at the Kura Valley that destroyed so many of Georgia's valiant knights?'

'I did not,' said Robert. 'As I have said, I was in Tana—'

'Eating biscuits!' said the voice from the audience. Laughter erupted.

'Silence!' shouted Wilhelm. 'No more outbursts or else I will clear the hall.'

The provost waited a moment for the mirth to subside, then he continued, 'Did you then, Robert of Hadlow, participate in the *second* battle between the Christian Georgians and heathen Tartars in which poor King George was mortally wounded?'

'I did not,' said Robert.

'Why not? You claim you were eager to rejoin the general of the Tartar army to attempt to persuade him to turn south and attack Baghdad. You were only a week or two's ride away from him. Why did you not rejoin this hellish legion of Tartarus and revel in the ruin of the Christians of Georgia?'

'I would not do that. I could not,' said Robert. 'I… I fell dangerously ill.'

'He had eaten too many honey biscuits,' said the voice.

The court erupted in mirth once again. And as Wilhelm shouted his threats, and bellowed for immediate quiet, Robert scanned the faces of the people on the benches. He could recognise none of them, yet he had the strongest sense that at least one man among their number was on his side – which was a heartening thought.

When order was finally restored, Wilhelm turned his angry gaze once again on Robert.

‘So then, prisoner, you deny taking part in the destruction of the chivalry of Georgia?’

‘He has already denied it, Provost,’ said a mild voice from the dais. And Robert saw that little Geoffrey of Beaulieu was now speaking.

‘Unless you have any evidence to the contrary,’ said the Dominican, ‘I suggest we move on with the prisoner’s story. Perhaps Robert of Hadlow would care to resume his narrative. You fell ill, you claim, which prevented you from rejoining the Mongol army, which was at that time to the south of the Caucasus Mountains…’

Robert saw Wilhelm swiftly deflate like a pig’s bladder pricked by a thorn and meekly resume his original place, standing quietly by his master, the duke.

Chapter Eight

The sickness took Robert a week after the meeting in Ziani's rose garden, while he was preparing to return to General Subutai's side with the remaining men of his *arban*. It fell on him like an avalanche. He did not know the cause of the disease – foul night airs, perhaps – but grief and horror must surely also have played their part.

That same morning, Ziani had summoned him again and showed him a small wooden box that had been delivered by an unknown man to his house, just before the dawn. The porter had received the package from a horseman, someone who looked like a Kipchak, but he had not thought to detain him. He had taken the well-wrapped parcel from him and watched the stranger gallop away down the main street of Tana.

Robert opened the wooden box, which was no bigger than his own fist, and immediately gasped in revulsion at its contents. For inside the box was a small, round gelatinous object with a long bloody thread of a tail.

It was a human eye. Blue. And underneath it lay a canine tooth, still bloody at the root. With these items came a note, written in good, clear Latin, which read: '*The price for your brother is now two hundred thousand marks. These items are for the hurts done to Captain Carlo. Adorno.*' There was a Bible reference: Exodus 21:23–27.

'What does this mean?' said Ziani.

'It means the Podestà threatens to dismember my brother Gilbert if I do not pay him that new sum. Exodus 21:23–27 reads: "Whenever hurt is done, you shall give life for life, eye for eye, tooth for tooth, hand for hand, foot for foot…"'

Even as he said these words, Robert felt the world swimming around him, his vision blurring. His legs felt weak and he had the overwhelming urge to sit down.

'My friend, I am so sorry but I cannot afford…' said Ziani. 'Even for me, it is too much – two hundred thousand marks? It is not within my power to—'

Robert collapsed in a dead faint.

The sickness was a savage tempest that tossed the Englishman's body and his mind hither and yon at its whim, like a cruel house cat toying with a half-dead mouse.

He was racked with fever for days, now freezing cold, cowering under a dozen heavy blankets, now burning hot, the sweat coming off him in stinking rivers, all the blankets drenched. Niccolò Ziani housed him in his own chamber and teams of his servants tended to Robert's needs day and night. They tried to feed him egg possets and much-watered wine but he fouled himself and vomited copiously. And his frame was convulsed in such agonies between these fever bouts as he had never experienced before. But his dreams, his hateful dreams, were so much worse.

He saw in his fevered nightmares Gilbert being sawed into pieces by a team of grinning slaughter-men, taking iron tools to his pale limbs, cackling with unholy glee. His brother cried out to him, 'Why did you leave me? Why did you forsake me?'

Adorno, that great wobbling turd-mountain, visited his sickbed, chuckling and plucking at his sleeve and saying, 'Trust me, Templar, if you would but trust me…'

The fever broke after four days of terrible suffering, but it left Robert too weak to raise his own head from the pillow, let alone get out of the bed.

He slept long and deep, many hours of every day, and still he could find no strength to rise. Saka and Taka came to see him asking for orders for the *arban*, which was ready to depart, but he had none to give them, save not to drink too much while they waited for him to either live or die. A Greek physician came after a week in this feeble condition and bled him, plunging a lancet deep into his left forearm and draining out a pint of his dark blood. Yet this seemed only to make him even weaker.

Eventually, slowly, his strength began to return and, pale and wraith-like, he rose from his bed after three weeks and managed to drink a little mutton broth with Ziani.

The merchant told him Jean de Malemort had visited and prayed over him in his sleep, several times, but the Seneschal had been called back to Acre – the crisis of the Latin kingdoms was at hand, he said, and he must stand beside his Brethren. Robert had no memory of this at all but was he grateful for his master's prayers nonetheless.

'Malemort left a message for me to give to you, if… if you should recover from your illness,' said Ziani, holding out a small folded piece of paper.

Robert looked stupidly at Ziani, struggling to keep his eyelids open. 'Message?'

'Shall I read it to you?' Ziani asked. Robert managed a nod.

Ziani cleared his throat.

> 'I pray daily that Almighty God will return you to your full health and strength, Brother Robert. I am certain He will do so – and soon. And when you are fully recovered, I do earnestly urge you to return to your Mongol general with all haste and say and do whatever you must do to persuade him to our cause. The cause of Christ that we serve is paramount – nothing else matters, not our own lives, nor even the lives of our comrades. Remember this: Deus vult. God wills it. I trust we shall meet again soon, in this earthly life or in the glorious Hereafter.
>
> 'Yours in eternal Brotherhood, Jean de Malemort.'

'Just that?' said Robert. 'No verbal message?'

'He told me to impress on you that returning to your Mongol general's side was your most pressing duty – and must come before anything else.'

'He was referring… to my brother Gilbert, I think.'

'Yes.'

'Has there been any word?'

'My informants tell me Gilbert of Hadlow is still confined in Soldaya but his accommodation has changed for the worse – they have locked him in an iron cage.'

–

A week later, in the dying days of summer, still as weak as a kitten, Robert rode out of Tana, heading south towards the passes of the high Caucasus. With him rode the *arban*, all eight of them either badly hungover or still drunk from the carousing of their last night. The only man who was truly fit to fight that morning was Idar, who had been loaned out to Robert by Ziani once again as his guide.

'Idar knows the Caucasus. His family are hillmen from way back,' Ziani said. 'He knows every pass and defile, and how to read the swift-changing weather. He says that if you do not depart within ten days you will be in Tana till the spring.'

Ziani leaned in closer and said, 'He is very accomplished in all the arts of war and I have told him to ward your life as if it were his own. I cannot have my partner in the House of Karacha murdered by some Cuman bandit on the road. He can also convey messages back to me, should the need arise. Take Idar with my blessing.'

Robert was glad to have him. The Circassian was unobtrusive, and when he spoke it was always with good sense. Furthermore, Robert was glad to have someone to counteract Arslan's obvious contempt for his many failings as a leader of men.

The *arban* leader regarded Robert's second attempt to mount his horse on their first day out of Tana with an icy eye. He said nothing but Robert could feel his gaze, and was furious he could not thump into his own saddle without an old man's grunt.

By mid-afternoon, Arslan suggested that they stop and make their camp. 'You are weak,' he said to Robert. 'You should rest here before you fall off your horse.'

'We will ride on another five miles,' said Robert, although every muscle, sinew and fibre in his body was shrieking with the strain.

'There is a wood, a mile yonder, over the rise, with a little stream,' said Idar. 'It would make an excellent campsite. The best for twenty miles.'

'I will take a look at this place, Idar, and make my decision then,' said Robert.

The Englishman grew stronger, day by day, and his body hardened once again to the road and his leather-covered wooden Mongol saddle. He tried not to think about poor Gilly languishing in his iron cage, eyeless and bloody-mouthed. There was, in truth, nothing he could do now for his brother anyway. He did not have two hundred thousand marks to pay the ransom and Ziani claimed he did not have the coin either.

Even if the Venetian could raise that enormous sum from his fellow Tana merchants, how could Robert ever hope to repay it? He would be beggared for decades. Besides, he *did* have a plan for rescuing Gilly. He just needed a little time.

The *arban* arrived at the foothills of the Caucasus in a black rainstorm, a driving torment of water and wind, and took shelter in a tiny village, where Robert asked for food, wine and news from the locals, in exchange for a shiny silver penny.

Idar could understand their local dialect and relayed back what he had learned to Robert.

'There has been a second great battle,' he said, 'on the far side of these mountains. The Georgians fought the Mongols again – and were defeated again.'

The crossing took a full week and it was hard going for every man in the company, not just for Robert in his weakened state. The steppe ponies had to be led by the men on foot in some of the narrower pathways, and some tracks were only a foot or two wide, with sheer drops of several hundred feet on one side and a bare cliff-face on the other. The nights were already freezing, even though they remained below the snow-line. Robert deliberated long and hard and finally allowed a tiny fire to be built on the coldest night. He feared his frozen men would perish otherwise.

They finally came down into the soft green hills north of Tiflis, but immediately turned off the main road south to the Georgian capital, guided east by Idar along faint goat tracks at the southern base of the great mountainous barrier.

They were, if anything, in far more danger here than in the high places or even in the Kipchak badlands beyond. After the shattering defeat of the Georgian army, if they were taken as prisoners by King George's men, they would likely be immediately put to the sword. So when there was sufficient moon and only a little cloud, they travelled by night; and when they were blessed by a few warm days, the last remnants of summer, Robert had the *arban* take off their distinctive *deel* robes and fur-lined hats and ride bareheaded in just their light silk undershirts, baggy trousers and boots.

Idar moved his horse up close to Robert's at dusk on their third day in Georgia.

'There is a little-known pass through the mountains, lord, at this eastern end of the Caucasus. It is narrow, and used mostly by smugglers and bandits, and it emerges into the plain of the Terek River. It is not so high as the road north from Tiflis, which we have just travelled, and this route is passable in late autumn, even in early winter, by those who know it. I tell you this because I know you are eager to lead the Mongol army back into the Kipchak lands as quickly as possible.'

'I am. But I was thinking that the coastal road north from Derbent might be the simplest. Do you know it?'

'I know it, lord. That route is too hazardous, in my view. On the left side, as you ride, are sheer cliffs and rocky spurs where the bandits roost. They shoot arrows down upon travellers from the commanding heights, their spears fall, too, and only skilled mountaineers can climb up to attack them in return – by which time they have fled. And the sandy road washes away often after any heavy rainfall, which can leave a column of men pinned helplessly between the rock face and the deep blue sea. That Derbent road can be easily traversed in high summer, in the warmth of the sun, but, at any other season...' Idar dolefully shook his dark-maned head.

'This other pass, the little-known one you mentioned, which comes out into the Terek Valley,' asked Robert, 'you are quite certain that it can be safely traversed in the autumn?'

'It will be hard, lord. But, yes, it can be done. I have passed by that way.'

The faint road took them up into the hills as they pushed on east towards Derbent. They encountered a few local fruit farmers and several herdsmen with their flocks, who for the most part either ignored them, or ran away as soon as the riders appeared. But they managed to purchase fresh milk and meat at a surprisingly busy market on the banks of the Samur River on a sunny, chilly day and there they garnered some more useful tidings.

The Mongol army was still encamped at Derbent and was recruiting thousands of fighters from non-Georgian populations – wild Kurdish horsemen, for the most part.

Two days later, descending from the bare hills and with the shining blue expanse of the Caspian stretching out before their eyes, they were stopped by a trio of Mongol sentries, with arrows nocked to their bows, who demanded to know their intent and destination.

Two hours after that, Robert was standing in the centre of General Subutai's huge *ger* outside the coastal town of Derbent, being welcomed by the great man himself.

Chapter Nine

Robert and Idar galloped along the side of the column, travelling in the opposite direction to the thick stream of thousands of Mongol horsemen hunched in their saddles against the relentless icy drizzle. The two men reined in, breathing hard from the run, beside the party of General Subutai and his half-dozen mounted lieutenants.

The Mongol general, the kind of high commander known as an *orlok*, was a bald, barrel-chested veteran, with intelligent but oddly yellow eyes. Subutai grunted an acknowledgement of their clattering, panting presence, but said no words to them. He was looking intently at something high above him on the rocky hillside. A few moments later, he extended a gnarled index finger, and jabbed it upwards.

'Tell me, who are they, *Elchin Baghatur*?' he asked.

Robert had been granted the title *Elchin Baghatur* – meaning Hero Envoy – by Genghis Khan, and it gladdened his heart to hear Subutai employ it. The *orlok* was pointing at two half-visible figures a thousand feet above them, crouching on a mist-obscured rocky outcrop above the left side of the road, their shapes framed by the leaden sky beyond. They were poor, raggedy creatures, Robert saw, in conical blue felt hats with extended ear flaps on the sides, the outline of their bows and spears visible.

Robert conferred with Idar.

'Alans,' he said in Mongol. 'Alan scouts. Mountain folk and bandits. Likely they are allies of the Cuman rebels. They are our enemies, *Orlok*.'

Subutai grunted. He was still watching the pair on the rock high above them.

'There is a steep, narrow path about half a mile back that leads up the crags in that direction,' said Robert, 'I could take my *jagghun* up there and try to locate them, then either kill them and drive them off. Or perhaps capture one alive for questioning. Shall I do that, General?'

'You would not catch them,' said Subutai. 'This is their land. They know it like they know their wives' soft thighs. Don't break your horses' legs on their rocks, *Baghatur*. Let them watch us. Let them count our numbers – and tremble in fear at our coming.'

'As you command,' said Robert, with relief. It would have been a horribly perilous task to take his hundred horsemen up into that rocky wilderness. And he was still not entirely back to his former strength after the shattering bout of fever in Tana.

The entire Mongol army was advancing that day in column up a narrow defile, with two bare mountainsides on either side of the road. The grey rock faces on both left and right seemed about to close together like a giant pincer and crush them to death – all twenty-three thousand of them, including the new Kurdish recruits, the Mongol women, all their children, and many thousands of horses, goats, sheep and camels.

And, if that were not enough of a multitude to move through high mountains in late autumn, there were six four-wheeled wagons in the centre of the long column pulled by six teams of eight oxen, the wagons containing huge baulks of timber and coils of ropes, stone missiles and hundreds of boxes of iron tools. This was the Mongol artillery train, a part of Subutai's army run by two hundred expert Chinese craftsmen, informally called the marmot-men for their skill in digging. The wagons also carried spare food, wine and several iron-bound treasure chests filled with something very heavy.

The marmot-men were an elite, specialised arm of Subutai's army, who could construct from scratch, in just two days, a battery of five trebuchets and site it on perfectly levelled ground. On the third day, these huge machines could be hurling boulders the size of a piglet against the enemy's walls to bring them tumbling down.

Robert had been riding with his own *jagghun*, the company granted him by Genghis Khan, near the vanguard of the ponderous column, when General Subutaï sent word to summon him. He had been walking his horse alongside the *jagghun*'s temporary captain, Taghachat, a veteran warrior and good friend.

Robert had spent the past two weeks in Taghachat's *ger* outside the small town of Derbent, getting his men ready to cross the great barrier, and fretting daily at the delay to their crossing. Winter had been fast approaching; in fact, the weather had already turned foul and their round felt tents pitched outside the sprawling town had been lashed with rain and wind on most days.

Despite the bad weather, three days ago they had finally departed from Derbent, taking the route north and west that Idar had suggested to Robert. And now it seemed that their tortuous advance through the high hills had already been observed by the enemy.

'How many times have you crossed these mountains, *Elchin Baghatur*?' Subutai asked Robert, surprising him with the question after such a long silence.

'This will be my fourth time,' he said. 'But I've never taken *this* road before.' He muttered something then to Idar. 'My servant has traversed the Caucasus range more than twenty times, he says. He swears this road is good. And says it is our only viable choice at this time of year.'

'Let us hope he is right,' said Subutai. 'But knowing is better than hoping. So take your *jagghun* forward, *Elchin Baghatur*, and scout the road for at least ten miles ahead. I do not wish to receive any unpleasant surprises on the march. Go!'

Robert did as he was ordered. He sensed that his relationship with Subutai had altered subtly while he had been away from the army. He felt, somehow, that Subutai no longer completely trusted him. And it was true, he reflected, that he had been away from the general's side for much longer than promised – more than six months had passed since he had ridden away to deliver the treaty to Tana. But he had not promised the Mongol general that he would return to him by any particular date.

The lack of trust was perplexing but he tried not to let it concern him.

That same evening, after he had made his report to the *orlok* that the road was clear of enemies for the next dozen miles, he lingered in the general's camp, half-expecting to be invited to dine with the lieutenants, as he'd done many times before.

'We should be through the highest passes and down into the Terek Valley beyond in four or five days, if the weather does not get any worse,' said Robert at the door of the *ger*. Subutai nodded and waved him away, returning to his conversation with his stern-faced senior lieutenant, a Mongol called Chormaqan, and his fellow general, an older man called Jebe, a famously dashing cavalry commander.

Robert shrugged at his curt dismissal and went out into the freezing night.

The next day it began to snow heavily.

The progress of the column, which had already been horribly slow, was now further impeded by the thick, white drifts that had filled the narrow pass to chest height overnight. Mongol troopers were forced to dismount and dig through the snow to clear a path for their horses, using their swords, spears, even bare hands – along with what few spades and picks they could beg or borrow from the marmot-men.

On that first snowy day, the column made only three miles. Worse, they were still climbing and it was likely to become far colder the higher they rose. On the second day of travel in the blinding white landscape, they achieved only two miles of progress. One of the ox-drawn wagons, carrying its heavy cargo stored in iron-bound chests, had snapped its wooden axle, fallen into a deep rut and spilled its contents in the road.

Robert who, with his whole *jagghun*, had helped lift the massive wagon free of the snow, then repair the broken axle and repack the cargo on the wagon bed, had been astonished to discover that the boxes it carried were filled with dozens of small, gold bars. The value of that treasure was enormous – and Robert eyed the bullion with interest. It was, he reckoned, enough gold to free Gilly from Adorno's iron cage.

The snow continued to fall and more than a score of Mongol troopers froze to death during the next frigid night. But the ice-gripped ground was too hard to dig graves, and they did not have enough spare fuel to burn them. So the stiff bodies were simply stacked up like logs at the side of the road for every living Mongol to observe through the whirling flakes as he laboured past them leading his shivering pony.

Robert, making his daily report to Subutai the next evening, overheard General Jebe saying, 'This is much worse than when we crossed the Tien Shan to attack the Ferghana Valley, *Baghatur*. And we lost one fifth of our horses in that little escapade.'

Subutai, throwing a hard look at Robert, said to the Englishman, 'Did your tame Circassian, who claims to have ridden this road in winter, have two *tumet* with him?'

Robert had to admit that Idar had not.

On the fourth snowy day, less than a mile from their camp, they were attacked by bandits; and the struggling ox-wagons of the marmot-men were the chosen target.

The first sign was a small avalanche of rolling rocks, thundering down from the white mountainside above the narrow road. The grey boulders bounced recklessly down from the heights, dislodging great scads of ice and snow, before smashing into the wooden wagons, breaking them apart and crushing some of their hapless Chinese drivers.

This stunning boulder assault was immediately followed by a lethal rain of hurled javelins and arrows, and then a force of four or five hundred Kipchaks and Alans descended on to the centre of the column, swarming over the shattered artillery wagons, slaughtering the draught oxen and killing some of the marmot-men, who were ill-equipped, anyway, to fight off the screaming enemy. Before the Mongol flank guards could come up, the Kipchaks began looting the ox-wagons, making off with many of the vital iron tools, as well as baskets of food and skins of good wine, and several other choice Derbent luxuries. When the Mongol horsemen came galloping up, the bandits scampered away back up the sheer cliff faces like excited chattering monkeys, with their arms full of Mongol goods and their packs laden with booty.

The Mongol cavalry, riders from one of Chormaqan's *mingghat*, hampered by the dragging, deep snow, had been too slow in coming to the rescue of the ox-wagons, but once they arrived at the scene, they threw themselves fearlessly at the remaining bandits and managed to slaughter a dozen of these wretches before they could flee.

Subutai convened a council of war that night in his *ger* – attended by a dozen officers, including Robert. Wine was served and bowls of hot *shulen*.

Robert listened, slurping his scalding mutton stew, as the general outlined the new order of march. The Englishman had entirely missed the assault by the bandits, being ordered to the vanguard of the column that day, but he had seen the aftermath, the shattered wagons, the broken goods strewn across the road, and the patches of scarlet blood staining the white snow.

Subutai's orders were thus: the remaining baggage and artillery wagons and the surviving marmot-men were to be left behind. So, too, would be the Mongol injured, the women, children, most of the army's spare horses, and almost all the herd animals. Subutai detailed off two *mingghat* of his troops to guard them. Two thousand men should be enough, Subutai told his officers, to keep the bandits at bay, if they remained alert. Anyway, he could not spare more.

This rump of the Mongol column – some four thousand women and children and two *mingghat* of fighting men – would attempt to continue the journey over the high passes but, if they found the task impossible, they were ordered to return to Derbent, as best they could, and attempt to make the Caucasus crossing again in the spring.

The rest of the army – about seventeen thousand Mongol riders, with only two spare ponies each – would struggle on through the deep snow, aiming to get over and down the other side of the mountain range as swiftly as possible.

They set off the next morning at dawn. It was a warmer day, and the pallid sun made the individual snow crystals glitter like a carpet of tiny diamonds on the endless white hillsides, and the peaks to the west poked sharply into the blue sky like a giant's icy fingers.

Robert, riding between Idar and Taghachat, looked back along the column from time to time and could see the forlorn rump, with its few outriders and the perpetually stirring mass of horses and beasts, falling further and further behind them as the hours passed. He'd left Arslan and his *arban* with his herds, but took the rest of his *jagghun* with him. In a gloomy moment, he wondered if he would ever see the *arban* again.

Yet they made better progress that day, without the encumbrance of the beasts and the baggage – although Robert noticed that they retained a pair of donkey carts carrying Subutai's heavy iron-bound chests – and, late in the afternoon, seven miles further along the road and near the saddle of the pass, dark clouds closed swiftly in from the west, like the drawing of a black curtain and the white world began to hiss with rain.

A hard, drenching rain, to be sure, but wet – that was the crucial point. As it fell, the thick drifts of snow began to shrink and melt and slowly drain away.

Chapter Ten

They were waiting for them on the Terek Plain, fifty thousand fighting men of the rebel army, standing there in full battle array. Cumans, Kipchaks, Alans, Bulgars and Khazars and an assortment of peoples from the other warlike tribes of the Caucasus region – a multitude of foes gathered, united by a hatred of the invader.

Subutai had summoned Robert and, once again, when the Englishman arrived, the *orlok* said nothing to him but simply gestured with his hand to indicate the host spread out on the plain below. It was an hour after dawn and Subutai and Jebe and a dozen of his mounted officers were gathered on a spur of hillside. The general seemed to be implying by his hand gesture that Robert was to blame for this situation.

'Your Circassian servant led us into a trap,' he said, in a mild, almost casual tone. 'I should take his head. And maybe I should take yours, too, *Elchin Baghatur.*'

Robert looked across at Subutai. But he saw with some relief that the *orlok* was grinning at him. He was joking, apparently. Subutai's sense of humour had always been rather odd. But he *had* beheaded a local guide in Georgia, Robert had heard from Taghachat, for leading him astray.

Robert stared at the great mass of enemies below and his heart sank. Away to his left, the road down from the mountains followed the path of an icy river that tumbled over small rocks and large boulders and spread out on to the broad expanse of the Terek Plain, which was very nearly featureless in all directions except for a few wind-stunted trees and bushes.

The Mongol column was even now making its way down this rocky road, moving faster than it had done in many days, but still at a very slow pace. Many of the tired troopers were oblivious to the threat that lay in wait for them on the plain.

Robert examined the assembled foe closely. On their right wing, over to the west, sat row upon row, rank upon rank, of Cumans and Kipchaks, grim as death on their shaggy ponies. Ten thousand riders, Robert estimated, and well-armed with swords, axes, bows and javelins. They sat there like pagan statues under their tribal totems, wooden poles topped with ferocious painted animal skulls, and made garish by long strips of coloured silk, scraps of animal fur and the scalps of slaughtered men.

The centre of the combined army was composed of ten blocks of Khazar foot soldiers, all neat and orderly; a thousand disciplined spearmen in each massive block, with ten-foot pole arms and short swords hanging at their waists, and polished iron shields fitted with spikes, which flashed as the metal reflected the low winter sun.

On their left wing, nearest to the spur on which Robert and the Mongol generals observed them, were two full Bulgar legions containing five thousand knights in each, proud men seated on huge destriers, faceless in steel helms that had iron masks attached, with mail aventails draped over their necks and shoulders. Their colourful kite-shaped shields were decorated with wolves, eagles, dragons and weird geometric shapes; and they sported ivory-hilted swords, and sat on beautiful, gold-inlaid red leather saddles to demonstrate their superiority over the common man.

On both flanks, and behind the main battle lines, stood loose packs of hundreds of archers from the various Alan tribes, wearing bodices stitched with iron lamellar strips. And beside them were many companies of Durdzuk axemen in conical helms, leaning on the long shafts of their weapons like woodsmen at rest, as well as swarms of javelin men and slingers, message-runners and servants, and scores of mongrel dogs barking excitedly around the boots of their masters.

'Idar did *not* lead us into a trap, *Baghatur*,' said Robert. 'Our coming was no secret. But I am much surprised that they managed to assemble such a varied army under one leader. Cumans hate Bulgars, and Durdzuk are famously at feud with the Khazars.'

'They all fear us,' said Subutai, 'that is what has united these motley swine.'

The general continued, 'They are led by a rebel from the North – a Cuman called Khan Köten who has long held a grudge against us. And whether your Circassian betrayed us or not, we are still stuck tight in the jaws of a trap. We cannot go back into the mountains. We are too weak and would starve this winter. Few would make it back to Derbent alive. And if we engage them down here... well, as you can see, *Baghatur*, we are outnumbered three to one.'

'I say we attack them,' said Jebe. 'Full frontal attack, nothing clever, nothing fancy. Sweep them away with one massive charge, while we still have the strength to achieve it.'

Robert heard Chormaqan, Subutai's lieutenant, sucking his teeth in disapproval but the man said nothing aloud. The Englishman could see Jebe's point. The army was tired and hungry. And they would only become more hungry. Many of their horses were lame after the hard crossing. And there was no room for manoeuvre. Even the fittest horsemen could not make play in the rocky scree at the base of the mountains, which was so lethal to horses' hooves.

They could not employ all the usual Mongol tricks, so successful in the past, such as feigned retreat or a flanking attack. They were well and truly trapped.

'I have the beginnings of an idea, *Baghatur*,' said Robert. 'If you will pay heed to it. Though, I must warn you, the price may be much higher than you can stomach.'

–

Robert picked his way on foot across the rocky plain, heading towards the fires of the enemy camp. At his shoulder stalked Idar, silent as a cat, and beyond him was the dark form of Taghachat, stumbling noisily, it seemed, over every single tussock and pebble. Robert wondered if he had been wise to bring his *jagghun* lieutenant on this mission, but there had to be a Mongol among them for their message to be credible. He trusted Taghachat with his life, and he was a superb rider and one of the bravest men he knew, a veritable wizard at scaling the outside walls of enemy fortresses – but he wished his friend was a little less heavy on his own two feet.

It was three days since the Mongol army had come down from the mountains and arrayed itself at their base with the steep slope behind them. General Jebe had had his way. Subutai had, with some reluctance, allowed the dashing cavalry commander to make a headlong attack – of a kind – on the enemy formation on the first day.

So Jebe and three *mingghat* of his cavalry, three thousand Mongol horsemen, had charged the Khazar foot soldiers in the centre of the enemy line. They had come almost within touching distance of the foe, loosing arrows directly into their stationary ranks before peeling away, and returning swiftly to the uneven ground where the rest of Subutai's dismounted force had made its stand behind concealing rocks.

It was, in truth, not a serious, committed assault, but instead an attempt to lure the Khazars out of their formation, and perhaps provoke the rest of the enemy as well.

Subutai's twelve thousand men were waiting for the enemy to attack. The wily Mongol general hoped that a full-scale enemy assault would be triggered by General Jebe's provocative charges. If they could entice the rebels into making a headlong attack on the Mongol positions, their tight formations would be destroyed by the rocky terrain and they could be cut down by the Mongol archers.

Sadly, the enemy had failed to oblige him. Despite repeated charges by Jebe's men, and their equally swift retreats, the huge force of combined Kipchak, Cuman, Alan, Bulgar, Khazar and Durdzuk warriors declined to follow the whooping riders into Subutai's well-laid trap.

Instead, they all waited in position, patiently, stoically for the Mongols to attack them.

Which was why, after two more days of stalemate, two days in which the two armies eyed each other warily at a distance of five hundred paces, Robert had been allowed to attempt his own hare-brained scheme. And earlier this evening, after sunset, so as to be cloaked by the night, Robert and his two companions had set out on their perilous mission.

Taghachat kicked a clattering stone, and a voice up ahead in the fire-lit darkness called out, 'Who is there? Name yourself, if you be a friend!'

The language he spoke was Cuman. And Robert replied in the same tongue, 'We are friends with a message for Khan Köten. Let us approach you without fear.'

The sentry was a young man in an embroidered padded coat, leather leggings to his knees, a steel helm with a spike on the crown, a mace tucked in his belt next to his quiver of arrows. Behind him was a watch fire where three of his comrades were rolled snug in their blankets.

Behind these pickets, Robert could make out the dark shapes of half a dozen low, round tents and horse lines where dozens of sleepy beasts were tethered.

'Who are you?' said the sentry. He seemed a little bemused by the appearance of strangers but not particularly frightened. His right hand held his strung bow; his left was on the flights of an arrow in his belt-quiver.

Robert stopped three paces from him, his eyes were dazzled by the dancing red firelight, and he squinted at the dark silhouette of the young man.

'I am a Georgian knight from Tiflis,' Robert said, touching the red cross on the chest of his white Templar surcoat, which was close enough to approximate the flag of the Georgians. He knew that he looked every inch a Christian knight in his surcoat and mail. Only the curved Mongol sword at his hip gave the lie to his subterfuge. Mercifully, the sentry did not notice it.

'This is my servant-companion Idar, a Circassian warrior, and my faithful guide Taghachat, of the Reindeer People of the eastern steppe.'

'Always stick as closely to the truth as you can,' Jean de Malemort had once told him. 'Nothing gilds a lie better than a large measure of good, honest truth.'

'We have a message for Khan Köten – can you take us to him?' said Robert. 'It is of vital importance that we see your khan as soon as possible.'

'I will wake my officer and ask,' said the sentry. 'Stay here. Do not move.'

–

It was as simple as that. A half-hour later they were in a round felt tent – very similar to a Mongol *ger* – and a middle-aged man was rubbing his sleep-crusted eyes and staring at them in mild disbelief. A pretty young woman, clearly his wife or concubine, was offering the three visitors cups of fermented mare's milk to drink.

There was a huge, thick-chested bodyguard with a long-handled axe standing on the far side of the space, glowering over at Robert, and two more armed men outside the wooden door of the tent. Despite them, the Englishman knew that he could easily murder this Cuman khan, if he chose to. But Robert had no plans that night to play the assassin.

'They said you had a message for me?' said Khan Köten.

'I come as an emissary of Subutai Baghatur,' said Robert. 'With a personal offer from him to you – and only for your ears.'

Khan Köten straightened up quickly and peered again at Robert. He was a plain-featured man of medium build with a large, bulbous nose; beardless but with a long drooping moustache like a pair of fangs draped over his upper lip. He was balding on top but hirsute on the sides and back, with his thin, stringy black hair falling down to his shoulders. He was about forty years of age, Robert guessed, but he moved with the agility of a younger man. His eyes were light brown and very intelligent.

And this night they sparkled with suspicion.

'So the enemy is here in my tent,' he said, his hand resting on his sword hilt.

'An envoy of your enemy, who seeks to talk peace with you,' said Robert. 'And perhaps even to cease from being your enemy.'

'Talk then,' said Köten.

'This is for your ears alone, Great Khan,' said Robert, glancing at the bodyguard.

'Talk or leave my camp,' said Köten.

'May we sit together?' said Robert.

'No. Say what you would say then go. Be quick about it.'

'General Subutai says that there is no need for us to be enemies, Cuman and Mongol, we are one people, brothers of the steppe. There's no need for us to quarrel.'

'Tell that to my Kipchak brothers in the east who have been slaughtered in their thousands by the Great Khan's *tumet* for a generation and more. Tell that to their rotting corpses. Tell that to their widows, raped by the Great Khan's brutal men. The Mongol wolves have pressed on our lands since the rise of your Genghis Khan in Mongolia. To this day, many Cuman and Kipchak families weep at the mere mention of his name.'

'There has been war between the Great Khan's people and yours for many years – this is true. But now it is time to end the bloodshed. It is time for us to agree that you have your lands, and we have ours. General Subutai, who speaks with the Great Khan's voice, suggests that all the lands north and east of the River Don shall be yours. All the land from the River Don, north of the Sea of Ravens, until the Aral Sea, shall be Cuman land. The Great Khan makes no further claim on it. This shall be inscribed into Mongol law. That part of the great steppe is yours till the ending of the world.'

'That land is already ours. You offer us only what is ours by right.'

'And you shall be free to enjoy it, without Mongol interference, for the rest of your lives, and your children's lives. All that General Subutai asks is that you withdraw from this field of battle and return to your lands north of the Don. And, to compensate you and your brave men for the loss of plunder, Subutai would offer you gold – a shining mountain of treasure. More precisely, he offers you the weight of two full grown men in pure gold ingots.'

And there it was. The reaction in Khan Köten's eyes that could not be hidden.

The Cuman opened his mouth. But no sound emerged. A moment later, he closed it again. He seemed to be struck dumb by Robert's offer of such a vast amount of wealth.

'Who are you?' said Köten. 'I mean who are *you* to make such an offer?'

Robert reached into the pouch at his belt and pulled out an object wrapped in linen cloth. He unwrapped it and handed a small, shining gold bar to Khan Köten.

'I am the man who gives you this ingot, as a personal gift. A man who promises you that you shall receive a thousand more, exactly like this one, when the sun rises on the morrow, if you should choose to accept Subutai Baghatur's most generous offer.

'But… who are you – how do you know our Cuman tongue?'

'I rode with Altan, son of Altrak. He schooled me well in your tongue and your customs. We rode and fought together as brothers against the Muslim horsemen.'

'I have heard of Altan, son of Altrak. I heard that he died in Khwarazmia.'

'He died in my arms. Courageous to the end. I ask for this peace in his name.'

'What do you want of me, friend of Altan and envoy of my enemy?'

'Take Subutai's gold. Withdraw north of the Don. Let there be peace at last.'

'But the alliance, all our allies, the Bulgars, the Alans and Khazars…'

'Do not trouble yourself with their fate. Think only what will happen to your people if you Cumans and your Kipchak cousins do *not* choose to accept Subutai's bargain. We have many more troops coming over the mountain pass. Another twenty thousand. They may even be here in the morning. Once we are reinforced, we shall destroy you. You have shown yourselves unwilling to attack our lines in the present situation. You fear us. When our reserves come down from the pass – the same number again as we now possess – we will swiftly annihilate you all.'

Khan Köten was staring at him, eyes wide. But was it fear or fury in them?

'We shall attack you in the morning with our far superior strength,' continued Robert, 'and we will slaughter every man, woman and child who stands against us in the traditional Mongol way. Have you ever heard tell of the Great Khan's Choice?'

Robert could see by the Cuman's eyes that he had.

'This is your Choice, Khan Köten. Take our gold – more gold than exists in all of Cumania – and depart. Go and live life in peace with the Mongols. Or, refuse me and face annihilation in the days to come. It is time for *you*, Great Khan, to choose!'

–

The enemy line was breaking apart. The entire right wing was dissolving in a vast cloud of dust and slowly moving backwards, the cavalry leading the way and the infantry, tents and hastily packed baggage, retreating more slowly after them.

And Robert knew exactly what had turned the tide in the Mongols' favour.

It was not only the two donkey carts full of gold bars, pulled by those stoic beasts of burden, that had trundled over the gap between the lines just as the first pink streaks of dawn were lighting the east. Not only that. Robert had feared that the Cuman khan would simply take Subutai's gold and remain in his battle position. But what had turned the tide, in Robert's view, had been the dust cloud on the mountain road above the plain, the sign that large numbers of folk were approaching from the high passes.

It was, in truth, the massive herds of the Mongol army, as well as their spare horses, wives, children and two thousand Mongol guards. The rump of the column.

But the Cuman khan did not know that. Robert had thrown the dice – and won.

'You have done very well, *Elchin Baghatur*,' said Subutai. He was sitting on his horse beside Robert, with Idar also mounted a few paces behind them both.

'In truth, I did not believe your trick would work, but it did and you have rendered great service to the whole Mongol nation.'

'I am glad you feel that way, General,' said Robert, 'because there is one thing I would like to ask of you – a small boon, or a simple favour, you might call it.'

Jebe came galloping up to them on a lathered horse, a dozen riders round him.

'The time is ripe, Subutai,' he shouted. 'You cannot deny this to me!'

'No, indeed,' said Subutai, grinning at his fellow general. 'It is ripe as a soft peach. Your *tumen* will break them, Jebe; then I will follow after you to crush any enemy who survive.'

'General,' said Robert, 'if I could just speak to you about—'

'Not now, Robyert; not now, my clever friend. We will speak of favours and boons later, when we are at leisure. Today we have a battle to fight. Bring your full *jagghun* up to attend me personally, *Baghatur*. I shall have need of your horsemen!'

Jebe had arrayed his *tumen* – ten thousand Mongol warriors on their fittest horses – at the very front of their position in the shadow of the mountains. And, as Robert looked on, further back and surrounded by all his own hundred men, since his scouting *arban* had now rejoined him, he could see the enemy desperately scrambling to extend their lines westward and fill the gaping hole left by the departure of the whole Cuman and Kipchak force.

Half the enemy strength had evaporated in a few hours, and the dismay in the ranks of the remaining Bulgar, Alan and Khazar foemen was plain for all to see.

At the edges of the enemy line, and the rear, more of the opposing horsemen were turning and galloping away. Their comrades called out that they were cowards and old women, but these cravens were the wise ones. They fled to preserve their lives.

On the left, Robert could see a company of Durdzuk javelin men – two hundred strong – turn and begin jogging north, away from the battlefield.

General Jebe gave the agreed signal, the red flags were raised at both ends of the Mongol front line and, as one man, his *tumen* surged forward – ten *mingghat* of superb horse-warriors – and began trotting towards the distant enemy line.

They rose to the canter, then the gallop and began loosing their shafts at two hundred yards out. By the time they had crashed into the enemy line at full gallop, they had shot three arrows apiece at the rippling mass of their enemies, the dense formation already shivering like a great beast in mortal terror.

A Bulgar warlord on a huge charger with a silver dragon on his helm was out in front of their battle lines, waving his shining sword in the air and shouting to his men to 'Have courage, hold fast! Make your mothers proud this day!' Then ten thousand charging Mongols smashed like a living battering ram into their thinned, disheartened and wavering ranks.

The carnage was horrible to watch. The Mongol force of heavy cavalry sliced into the disorganised ranks of the allied army, the couched Mongol spears punching through armour and into soft flesh beneath; then the keen, curved Mongol blades rose glittering, swooped down and came up bloody. The Mongol attack punched straight through the thin lines in three or four separate places, and most of the rebel horsemen were now openly fleeing the Mongol wrath – or dying under their silver blades.

Some of Jebe's men were fighting individual duels, with the Bulgar knights resisting them magnificently, their swords clashing, sparks flying, men screaming in rage and fear; other Mongols were simply chasing after the fleeing infantry. Only a few moments after the attack struck home, the enemy line began to disintegrate into dozens of knots of struggling men, falling men, dying men, the wounded moaning on the torn and trampled ground beneath, men yelling battle cries, horses biting, kicking, the stink of shit and blood clogging the back of every throat.

Then Subutai gave the order for his own light horsemen to move forward, and a few moments later the second Mongol wave of the attack crashed into their shattered lines.

Robert exchanged cuts with a mounted knight, a roaring man in mail and helm who battered at him, then disappeared into the swirling dust. He narrowly avoided being speared by a pair of Alans on foot, then he cut down a trio of mounted Khazars in quick succession – slice, cut, slice, lunge – and three enemy saddles were swiftly emptied.

His white surcoat was splashed with blood and, quite suddenly, he felt a great wave of disgust engulf him. He killed a stumbling man who came within reach of his sword and paused to see Idar dispatch two Alans, one on either side of his horse, in two savage, hacking blows.

The battle was won, and the enemy was defeated. Yet the slaughter continued long into the afternoon. Subutai had given the order that no quarter be given, no prisoners taken, and rather than participate in the slaughter, Robert quit the field, with Idar, leaving Taghachat, overexcited and gore-soaked, to direct the men of his *jagghun* in the important activity of loot-gathering.

The enemy was utterly destroyed and by nightfall the field was a reeking charnel house, with flocks of feasting crows and a few Mongol women still picking over the bodies of the dead. Robert washed his face and hands in a basin of water, changed his filthy surcoat, and waited with his own exhausted *jagghun*, sipping *airaq*, the mildly alcoholic fermented mare's milk beloved of all Mongol troopers, and chatting idly to Saka and Taka.

They lost only one man of their company that day, with only three wounded – and Robert took a moment to thank God for his mercy and pray for his trooper's soul.

Arslan was drunk and parading around the camp with two severed heads of enemies he had killed that day. And while this barbarism offended Robert's notions of chivalric behaviour, he decided to let it pass. These brave men had risked their lives at his command. Let them have their fun. He waited, taking his ease with the baggage train, until it was full dark and the noise of wild carousing echoed throughout the whole camp. The remainder of the Mongol women and children, and all the herds, had now rejoined the army and the camp was in a mad, joyous mood. The sounds of sweet victory filled the air.

Robert wanted to make sure Subutai had also drunk a good deal of alcohol – indeed there was scarcely a sober Mongol in the camp – before he went to visit him.

It was time to ask the general for a favour.

Chapter Eleven

'Yes, Robyert, it is indeed a time for rewards,' said Subutai, with a heavy sigh. 'But I can save you a good deal of breath if you are going to ask me to turn about and go back over the Caucasus to ride on Baghdad. The answer to that is still no. At least, not for now. We have won one battle but the Cuman rebellion is not yet snuffed out.'

Subutai was feasting with his senior officers in his command *ger*, and the fare was lavish – roasted kid, boiled mutton and a huge piece of half-raw beef from one of the train oxen, which had died of exhaustion after the difficult trek over the mountains. There was wine by the jugful, and *airaq*, too, and many Mongol officers were extremely merry, some already at the red-faced, singing stage. But Subutai was no more than moderately drunk.

'I was not going to ask you to take Baghdad,' said Robert, smiling hard. 'Not yet. But I shall hold you to our previous agreement. I understand that you must finish this Cuman business before we can contemplate turning south.'

'We snapped the spine of the rebellion today,' slurred Jebe. 'They were only truly dangerous when united. Now we shall wipe out that dog Köten and all his Cuman scum.'

'And recover all my gold from their greedy hands,' added Subutai.

'That too. But, to be fair, the *Elchin Baghatur* more than deserves his reward, Subutai,' said Jebe, squinting at Robert. 'You cannot deny him a boon on this glorious day of victory.'

Robert nodded his thanks to Jebe. Victory was all very fine yet he felt it was tainted by the way it had been accomplished. He had tricked Khan Köten, he knew that. He had bribed a weak, greedy man into behaving disgracefully. All his talk of peace between Mongols and Cumans had been a black lie. He knew Subutai and Jebe would hunt the man down – remorselessly. Not least to reclaim the fortune in gold from him. Khan Köten's days were now numbered, thanks to Robert's plausible falsehoods. And although he had lied in the cause of Christ – and for a far more urgent reason – the knowledge of his gross deception didn't sit comfortably with him.

'Ask me then, Robyert, what is this great favour you would demand of me?'

'I want a *mingghan*,' said Robert.

'What!' shouted Subutai in mock outrage. 'You want to be a *noyan*? You want to command a thousand Mongol troopers; you, a foreigner from who-knows-where, you who have *already* been so lavishly rewarded by the Great Khan. You want more than the titles, the honours and riches our master has already generously bestowed?'

Jebe was laughing like a donkey at Subutai's rage. A drunken donkey.

Robert knew he was being teased and he grinned as if he did not care.

'Let me explain my plight, *Orlok*,' he said, smiling with his teeth clenched.

Robert then told Subutai about his brother, who was languishing in an iron cage in Soldaya, and all about Barisone Adorno, the Podestà of Genoa, who was holding Gilbert captive. He spoke about the eye and tooth that had been sent to him in a little wooden box, and his fear that more parts of his poor brother would soon be delivered.

'I have tried to negotiate in good faith with Adorno – offering him a fair sum for my brother's freedom – and he refused and murdered one of my Mongol troopers in front of my eyes. I had to cut myself free of his guards to escape his grip. So I am done with negotiation. I am done with offering him money. I would go to Soldaya – it is only a few weeks' ride from here – and take back my brother by main force.'

'This merchant from, uh, Genoa murdered a Mongol trooper?' said Subutai, his expression now deadly serious. Even Jebe had stopped making his stupid drunken noises.

'He cut the throat of Chankai of my *arban*. Chankai was a very good man.'

Subutai waved this last extraneous comment away. 'Then this wretch must pay with his life,' the general growled. He suddenly sounded completely sober.

'I will give you a *mingghan*, Robyert – the Black Falcons are yours. Their *noyan* – you know Noyan Shulet? – was wounded today and will be laid up for weeks. His *mingghan* lost a hundred troopers, too, in the battle. So you will add your *jagghun* to the Black Falcons to make up their strength. Go north, my friend, and punish this Mongol-murderer: slaughter his men, possess his herds, burn his town to the ground and savour the lamentation of his women. Then you must swiftly return to me.'

Subutai paused, and Robert opened his mouth to thank him.

'Wait,' said Subutai. 'I am not finished. Understand, Robyert, that I give you this command only with the following conditions. First, it is only a temporary command. When Shulet recovers his strength, he will resume his role. You shall be *noyan* no more. Understand? Second, you must not stray or wander off on your own ventures; I do not want to hear of any more brothers in peril or vital treaties that must be delivered. Destroy this Genoese murderer, rescue your imprisoned brother and return swiftly to me. I will soon need your *mingghan* to destroy the Cumans. Am I clear?'

'As a mountain stream,' said Robert. 'I want to thank you—'

'I am still not finished. You have good friends in this place called Tana – the same men of the city of Venice, I believe, who made the treaty with our Great Khan for trade in goods on the Mongol dominions. Yes? Tell them we are coming north, and that any help that they may offer us, in terms of shelter, information, food and fodder for our horses, will be richly rewarded. We Mongols are bound to them in friendship by your famous treaty, *Baghatur*. That is all. Take your *mingghan* and go and punish your enemies. And now that I have granted you this favour, I never want to hear you grumble that I have not been fair to you, that I have not rewarded your service to the Mongol nation. You cannot ever say again, Robyert, that I have not been generous to you.'

Subutai grinned. And Robert was fairly sure he was teasing him again.

He did not care. He had his *mingghan*. He had a thousand iron-hard Mongols, enough to take Soldaya, destroy Barisone Adorno and free his brother from his cage.

'I will tell my friends at Tana, *Orlok*, that you will require quantities of fodder and provisions. And intelligence of the Cuman forces. I shall tell them to receive you with courtesy.'

–

Two weeks later, Robert cantered up to the summit of the rise and looked down at the town of Soldaya half a mile below him. It was near midnight and a freezing full moon watched over his fine new *mingghan*, which was spread out all around him.

This was the exact same spot from which he had looked at the town in the summer – a lifetime ago, it seemed – and yet the town walls, the thick-built gatehouse and snow-covered roofs of Soldaya appeared very different to him that night.

He saw them now through eyes of unquenchable hatred.

During a brief halt in Tana with the Black Falcons, two days to re-provision and alert Niccolò Ziani to the imminent arrival of the Mongol army, he had found out that Adorno, or his brutal executioners, had wreaked yet further damage on his brother Gilbert.

A putrefying left hand, looking like an enormous spider, pale as death in its coffin-like wooden box, had been awaiting his arrival in Tana.

Ziani had passed it to him with an apologetic wince, and watched as Robert clenched his teeth in fury as he opened the lid and released the stench. There had been no accompanying note. None was necessary – the first message from Adorno citing Exodus had been perfectly clear. Robert, shedding bitter tears, had taken the rotting hand to the graveyard at St Mary's in Tana, and had buried it there amid the prayers and chants of old Father Michel, the crippled priest. Robert had ridden away west into the snowy wilderness with his Black Falcons the next dawn.

This freezing winter night, six days after their departure from Tana, as he looked down on Soldaya, Robert felt like God's avenging angel poised to exact His just retribution.

Somewhere inside the snow-capped town was his brother, what was left of him, if he yet lived. Inside those walls were his cruel tormentors, too. He turned to his new lieutenant, a bear of a fellow called Borchu who had previously served the injured Noyan Shulet.

'Give the signal,' Robert said.

Borchu bowed his head, spun his pony and galloped down the slope, shouting out to the *mingghan* messengers. Robert wished the big man did not have to shout quite so much, it jarred the stillness of the moonlit night. But he supposed that it made no difference, and shouting was Borchu's way of showing that he was obeying with alacrity.

Robert stayed where he was and watched as two large groups of his riders – a *jagghun*, a hundred men, in each – emerged from concealment in the countryside on both the left and right sides of the town and raced towards the gatehouse. Taghachat had begged for the honour of leading the left-wing attack with Robert's old *jagghun*, and a Black Falcon *jagghun* leader called Shigi had volunteered to lead the right-wing assault.

Robert checked his own thought – they were all Black Falcons now. He watched silently as the two dark masses of men, indistinguishable in the icy night-time, thundered towards the walls. He felt nothing but hatred – no apprehension, no fear, just a raw, grinding anger.

He watched the first *jagghun* reach the walls over on the left and saw, in the moonlight, the gleam of grappling hooks hurled upwards at the ramparts, and the line of the trailing knotted ropes, then the dark bodies hauling themselves, hand over hand, towards the battlements. There was no sign the enemy were even aware of the attack. He had seen the black outline of two sentries walking on the walls half an hour before and, more recently, the red glow of a brazier inside the tower at the western end of the wall as a door was briefly opened, and he reckoned the sentries were avoiding their duty and keeping warm that cold night inside the cosy watch-house.

Beyond the town walls, he saw that the slave pens were standing empty. He wondered what had happened to all the wretched folk he had released from the pen during his escape last summer. He hoped that some had made their way back to their homes. But he also knew that the empty enclosure did not mean the vile trade was ended. Adorno's slave-takers could easily have refilled the foul pens many times over.

Such was life in this cruel northern land.

His eyes snapped back to the town walls, and he saw a flicker of red as the door to the watch-house opened and, at last, there were wild shouts of alarm from the battlements and figures hurrying along the ramparts with torches. The Mongol assault was discovered at last.

On both the left and the right of the gatehouse, he could see black shapes still climbing the knotted ropes to reach the battlements, but he knew that some of his men had already reached the top. He could hear the sharp crack of steel on steel, the thud of hard blows on flesh, the shouts of frightened men and cries of the wounded.

He turned to Idar, who was sitting on his horse three yards away.

'Be ready to ride,' he said. 'They will have the gates open very soon.'

That was Robert's plan: a double assault on the walls on either side of the gatehouse by the two *jagghut*, who would kill the defenders and secure the main gate, and open it for the rest of his *mingghan* to ride through.

He had no doubt in his mind that he would succeed in taking this town. He had counted no more than a dozen sentries on the walls earlier and he had given no warning of his assault. Who, after all, would expect a thousand Mongols to gallop out of the steppe and fall on this town in the middle of nowhere? And in the winter, too – sometime around St Nicholas's day, he believed. Barisone Adorno would not be expecting an attack in mid-winter. Robert reckoned the Genoese had, at most, three hundred troops in the town. No match for a war-seasoned Mongol *mingghan*.

No match for two Mongol *jagghut*, in all truth.

Now the gates were swinging open and there was Taghachat, standing tall in the moonlight in the centre of the opening gate, the blood gleaming black on the steel of his sword.

Robert rode slowly through the narrow streets of the burning town, the smoke drifting in fire-lit skeins in front of his horse's twitching nose. The Englishman had not even drawn his own sword, let alone struck a blow. Yet all around him were the horrible, crunching sounds of sack and slaughter. The garrison of the town had been overrun very swiftly – there had, indeed, been no more than a hundred or so Genoese men-at-arms, fewer than Robert had been expecting. However, it had been reported that a squad of desperate, cornered, crossbowmen had accounted for three of his troopers before they were sliced into meat by a swarming rush of his men.

When there appeared to be no more resistance in the streets of the town or on the walls, Robert released his *mingghan* to plunder the houses of Soldaya as they wished.

He was making for the courtyard in the centre of the town, where he had dined so lavishly with Adorno, and the palatial brick house where Gilly had been imprisoned.

Idar rode just behind him, the Circassian had drawn his arming sword, and he also had a pair of javelins in a leather boot by the horse's withers. His dark head turned left and right looking for the danger that Robert in his cold and furious hatred did not deign to notice. Behind Idar came a single *arban* of guards and messengers, led by a sullen Borchu, whom Robert suspected would rather have been kicking down doors, and searching for loot with the rest of the victorious *mingghan*.

The whole town was now lit by the burning houses, creating a weird orange glow that came and went, flaring now and dying back to leave shadows darker than before. They passed through patches of smoke and back into clean air. At a side street, Robert glanced left and saw a knot of joyful Mongols gathered round a pathetic, huddled group of Soldaya citizens, men, women and children crying with terror, holding out their hands in piteous supplication, the troopers gleefully hacking them apart. He rode on without a qualm. The only victim in his mind that deadly hour was Gilly. The only other man existing inside his head was Barisone Adorno.

Where was he? The Podestà could not have run – he could not run.

They came into the wide courtyard, and a few black scurrying shapes, like human rats fleeing the light, disappeared into various doors and corners the moment their horses' hooves sounded on the flagstones. In the centre of the space was a large black object, a huge cube, covered with a dark, waxed-linen tarpaulin.

Robert stepped down from his horse and threw his reins to Idar. He walked over to the square shape and tugged the tarpaulin free. By the intermittent orange light of the burning town, Robert could see that the cube was a cage of iron bars nine feet high and in the far corner was a small, huddled shape. Then the shape moved.

'Gilly?' said Robert. 'Gilbert is that you?'

The only response was a pain-filled groan. His brother was alive, at least.

Robert found a door to the cage, an iron padlock securing it.

'Idar,' he said. And the Circassian tossed him one of the javelins, which Robert caught with his left hand. He jammed the steel point in the hoop of the padlock and, with a hard wrench, he snapped the lock.

A moment later he was inside the cage and kneeling on the ground with Gilbert's bony, naked form cradled in his arms.

'Gilly, Gilly…' Robert found that he was weeping.

His brother stirred in his arms, and a flare of firelight illuminated his gaunt face, the ruin of one eye, crusted over with a huge, half-healed scab. His brother smiled horribly at him, showing the awful wreckage of his black mouth, and Robert noticed that more than one tooth was missing. Gilbert mumbled something incomprehensible, then coughed weakly.

'I am here Gilly,' said Robert kissing his pale, papery forehead.

'I knew…' said Gilbert. 'I knew you… would come… I waited.'

'I'm here, brother,' said Robert, choking on his own free-flowing tears. 'All will be well. We will get you away from here, take you to a safe place. Where is Adorno? Where is that God-cursed Genoese monster who did this to you?'

Gilbert stared up into his brother's face. 'Go… gone,' he said. 'He went more than a month… ago. After he watched his men-at-arms do… this…'

He pulled his bare left arm out and thrust it towards Robert. In the dancing orange light, Robert could see the bloody stump, untreated, scabbed with thick black matter and leaking a trickle of yellow-green pus. He took the arm, as gently as he could – and felt Gilbert flinch even at his tender touch – and examined what was left of the emaciated limb. It was a greenish-grey colour, so far as he could tell in the firelight, all the way up to his bony shoulder. It reeked of rotting meat, too.

'We will get a good physician to see to this,' he said, trying to sound confident. 'A doctor will fix this up in no time at all, you will see, Gilly.'

Gilbert grinned mirthlessly at him. His face was a flesh-stripped skull, at the same time both ancient and horribly young. 'I've seen… bad wounds… like this, brother… this same hue,' he said. 'In… gaol in Jerusalem. I know… what it… means.'

'Where did Adorno go? Tell me, I beg you. I will hunt that fat bastard down.'

'Back… to his… city. He said he would… return in the spring… and take my right foot. Pray with… me, Rob. Pray… for me.'

Huddled together, the two Templars began to say the familiar Latin litany of the *Pater Noster*, Gilly's words so faint they could scarcely be heard. And when they had finished, Gilbert let out a long sigh. 'You came back… Rob. You came back for me… I knew you would… be with me… in the end.'

Then, with a loud rattle of breath, his immortal soul left his poor ruined body.

Chapter Twelve

Robert buried his brother in the churchyard of St Mary, in Tana, beside his severed left hand, his eye and tooth, so that on the Day of Resurrection, Gilbert would be made whole once more. Robert wept over the grave and gave Father Michel a pouch of silver coins to say Masses for his brother's soul every week for a full year.

In his heart, Robert swore he would be revenged on Barisone Adorno. He had left Soldaya a smouldering ruin, carpeted with the bodies of its slaughtered citizens, and with scarcely a dog still alive, but it was still not enough – it was not nearly enough. He vowed he would carve that obese Genoese monster into a hundred pieces, and leave him weeping, handless, blinded and begging for the sweet mercy of death.

However, if Robert's humour that Christmastide was one of grief and sorrow, rage and revenge, Subutai's army, now encamped in the town of Tana and in the snowy woods and fields all around, was celebrating another great Mongol victory.

General Jebe had followed the Cuman and Kipchak army north to the River Don, and when his scouts reported that their army had divided in two to return to their own lands for the winter season – some going west, some east – Jebe fell on Khan Köten's much reduced force of Cuman warriors heading west and routed them in one terrible morning of charging horses, screaming men, spraying blood and lethal swinging steel.

Köten himself managed to flee the battlefield but Jebe captured the Cuman baggage train. He had ridden triumphantly into Tana, a few days later, with his victorious *tumen* and two little donkey carts bearing two grown men's weight in gold ingots.

They celebrated their success in true Mongol style, with vast quantities of wine and *airaq* and roasted meats of all kinds – all provided by Niccolò Ziani and his merchant friends – in a grand feast worthy of an Emperor of Cathay, which lasted for several days.

On Christmas Day, after Mass at St Mary's, Robert joined Subutai and Jebe, Ziani and the more prominent men of Tana, for their own feast at Ziani's house. The Venetian was pleased with Robert for, by destroying Soldaya, he had, in effect, removed Venice's greatest rival in this part of the world. Ziani made a gift to Robert of a beautiful bay stallion, a big, sleek creature of mingled Persian and Arab blood, swift of limb but also strong, which had also been trained for years as a warhorse.

Robert was entranced by the animal and named him Bayard.

The Englishman had little time to dwell on thoughts of his brother's death at the Venetian's festive board, because he was in constant demand as an interpreter, translating jovial sallies from Subutai and enquiries about the Mongol world from Ziani. These two men – so different to each other – had formed an unlikely friendship, albeit one that depended on Robert for any dialogue.

However, the centre of attention during that lavish celebration was a Venetian merchant called Morosini, a very successful fur trader. Morosini had much commerce with the Rus' amber and fur traders from the North, and he had just returned from a visit to Kiev, a great city in the Rus' lands, where he had prayed at their beautiful St Sophia Cathedral.

So much of the talk round the long table that Christmas Day was of the doings of these Kievan Rus'. After his crushing defeat at the hands of Jebe, Khan Köten and his few remaining followers had fled into the lands of these boisterous Rus' princes – who now laid claim to a vast area of land to the west and north of the River Dnieper.

For generations, the Cumans, a horse-borne steppe people, had plundered the grain farmers of the Kievan Rus'. Yet Khan Köten had been warmly received by one of the Russian princes, a man named Mstislav the Bold, who was the lord of a region called Galicia in the west of their land, near the Kingdom of Hungary. This was less surprising than it might seem, Morosini told them at the Christmas table, since Prince Mstislav was married to Khan Köten's daughter.

Mstislav was a very common name among noblemen of the Rus', Morosini informed them. The Grand Prince of Kiev – the leader of these Orthodox Christians – was also called Mstislav, as was the prince of a town and region called Chernigov. While the mass of the Rus' were simple farmers or hunters, just stupid lumpen peasants, Morosini claimed, a few Rus' princes, dukes and great lords of lands thought very highly of their lineages, and were precious of their honour.

Morosini had something interesting to say about the fugitive Khan Köten and his friendly reception by the Rus' nobles in Kiev, and as the Venetian merchant told his long story, Robert translated the tale for the benefit of Ziani's Mongol guests.

'Khan Köten appeared before the Grand Prince of Kiev still in his filthy, battle-torn rags,' said Morosini, 'and when that noble prince asked him why he should grant him sanctuary, since he was a heathen and a notorious plunderer of the Rus' farmlands, Khan Köten replied to the Grand Prince thus, "Today we have been defeated by the Mongols, but tomorrow it will be you who tastes bitter defeat; today they have taken our lands from us, but tomorrow it will be your villages that are in flames. Only if we stand together, united as brothers, can we defeat this great evil from the East."'

'Did these Rus' princes heed Khan Köten's pleas and welcome him to their lands?' asked Subutai. Robert translated this and Morosini admitted that they had.

'Indeed, signor. I have heard they are busy preparing for war in the spring.'

Subutai did not reply to that. He grunted, turned and made a jovial toast to their generous host Ziani, who had provided for them so lavishly at his Christmas feast.

–

During the long days of winter in Tana, Robert brooded for much of the time over Gilly's death. He reviewed his own actions and concluded miserably that it had been at least partly his fault that Gilbert had died of his mutilations. If he had not gone to Soldaya to negotiate with Adorno, Gilbert would still be alive in his comfortable accommodation, hale and whole, with wine and fruits and sunlight. Or if he had somehow found the hundred thousand marks in silver to pay the ransom – then Gilly would be free and with him now in Tana. If Robert had immediately set his mind to getting Gilbert out and had not travelled to Asia in search of riches and to fulfil his mission for Jean de Malemort, then his brother might be alive now.

Even when he applied the stern logic that his Templar instructors had taught him, he felt no better. He simply had not had a hundred thousand marks to pay the Genoese's extortionate ransom, and to borrow it would have crippled him financially for decades. And Adorno had, in truth, cleverly used Gilly as bait in a trap to punish Robert for killing his man Father Pietro. Furthermore, Robert's mission to the Mongols had been in the service of Jesus Christ, not merely in the service of Mammon – and surely that cause must supersede rescuing one knight from a fairly comfortable captivity.

All these were reasonable rebuttals to his profound feelings of guilt at his brother's awful demise, yet his conscience still tormented him every hour of every day.

Feeling useless and ashamed, Robert was seized by a melancholy humour. He drank too much each day and slept for twelve hours a night in the inn. Noyan Shulet had now recovered from his wounds and had resumed his command of the Black Falcons, including Robert's own *jagghun*, and so he had few duties that might have distracted him from his grief and guilt.

Some weeks after Christmas, following a long period of inactivity, he managed to rouse himself from his melancholic torpor and begin to take an interest in the world.

There were various commercial messages, he understood, that Ziani wished to dispatch to Karacha in Samarkand: instructions about which goods he should buy, advice on prices of items in Europe and questions about silk-trade related matters.

Robert recognised that he had neglected his affairs too long. So, a little after dawn, Robert saddled up Bayard and rode out on a cold, crisp February day, with the blue arc of heaven above, and rode the two miles to the Mongol camp and Subutai's huge *ger* in the centre of the bustling mass of tents, carts, goats and tethered horses.

The general was in an exuberant mood when Robert was admitted by his guards. '*Elchin Baghatur*, welcome! You are the very man I wished to see this morning. Have some *airaq*? Or wine? But first tell me what brings you so handily to my door?'

'Nothing to drink, thank you, General,' said Robert. 'I come here as an envoy from Ziani, who seeks to employ the magnificent Arrow Riders to communicate with our partner in Samarkand. I come also on my own behalf. But tell me first how I may serve you, *Baghatur*? Tell me why you particularly wished to see me today?'

'Yes. Indeed. You have ridden across the lands to the west of here, is that not so? Beyond the Kalka River and to the great peninsula that they call the Taurus?'

'I took the Black Falcons there two months ago in an attempt to rescue my brother. As I believe I mentioned, the attempt was a sad failure. My brother died.'

'Yes, yes, very sad,' said Subutai. 'So you *are* familiar with the lands to the west of here, along the northern shore of the Sea of Azov. Have you perhaps also ventured even further west – as far as the great river they call the Dnieper?'

'I have not. I know only that it marks the traditional border with the Rus' lands.'

'Just so. I regret to tell you I have had grave news from that direction. You will doubtless know that I dispatched ten envoys to the Grand Prince of Kiev. I sent him lavish gifts and a friendly message saying that I had no quarrel with the Rus'. My fight was only with the Cumans and Kipchaks who rebelled against the Great Khan's authority, and I politely requested that the Cuman Khan Köten be delivered up to me for punishment. Did you hear what happened next?'

Robert felt his heart begin to sink. 'I have not heard, General,' he said.

'They murdered my envoys! All ten of them. Impaled them alive on stakes.'

Robert suddenly felt very cold. He knew exactly what the murder of a Mongol envoy meant. The Mongols deemed all ambassadors sacred. To injure an envoy was to injure the Mongol lord who dispatched him. Genghis Khan had descended on the Empire of Khwarazmia full of wrath and determined to seek vengeance because a party of his sacred trade envoys had either been either killed or utterly humiliated.

'You will now make war on the Rus',' said Robert. It was not a question.

'Naturally, and I desire you to go with the Black Falcons to the Dnieper River, and scout the way for my *tumet*. Will you do that for me? Noyan Shulet is a very fine leader, no doubt about it, but he does not know these western lands as well as you.'

'General, with respect, you gave me your word we would turn south to Baghdad when the Cuman rebels had been beaten. And they *have* been destroyed. When spring comes, and the passes open, I hoped you would lead the Mongol army south. Besides, I'm far too busy to guide your *tumet* west. Ziani wants me to arrange for messages to be sent to Samarkand. I need to organise packhorses to carry our goods east from the

Sultanate of Rum. I must set up the links that connect with my partner Karacha—'

'You misunderstood me,' said Subutai, interrupting him. 'I actually said that, if you helped to guide me across the high mountains, I would seek the Great Khan's *permission* to take an expedition down to the city of Baghdad. I shall indeed do that once the rebel Cumans and their Rus' allies have been properly punished.'

Robert glared at him. The air of jollity in the tent had suddenly soured.

'I swear this to you. I swear by Tenggri, by the Eternal Blue Sky,' said Subutai. 'I will seek the Great Khan's permission to go south after we have accomplished what we need to do here. Surely you, Robyert, who have enjoyed the privileges of an envoy among our people, surely you would not allow the brutal murder of ten of our ambassadors to go unpunished? Help me find and defeat these Cuman pigs and their foolish Rus' allies and I shall send a swift message to Genghis Khan begging his permission to ride immediately on the city of Baghdad. Furthermore, I shall also allow the Arrow Riders to deliver your own private messages to Samarkand without demanding a single penny as my fee. Is that agreeable to you, *Elchin Baghatur*?'

Robert knew he was trapped. If he refused Subutai, he had no chance of bringing the Mongols into the desperate fight in the Holy Land. All his hard-won influence over Subutai would be lost. He would also be refused permission to use the Arrow Riders to communicate with Samarkand. 'So, Shulet is to command the Black Falcons?' he said, for something to say.

'You shall be his senior lieutenant, his second-in-command. And the No.4 *jagghun* will be yours again, under Noyan Shulet's command, of course. Then, when we have crushed the foe, if great Tenggri permits, we shall all ride south to Baghdad.'

–

Robert sat on the back of Bayard, his Arab-Persian destrier, and looked out at the dusty plain ahead of him. He was very tired, in bone and blood, worn down by months of hard riding back and forth on the rolling steppe north of the Sea of Azov, yet somehow his mind was sparkling bright, aglow with a keen, almost feverish excitement.

For it was the day of battle.

On his left sat Taghachat, the lieutenant of his *jagghun*; on his right sat Idar, his fearsome Circassian bodyguard. Behind him was the No.4 *jagghun* itself: ninety-three battle-hardened dauntless Mongols sitting on their ugly little steppe ponies; near a hundred hard men who called him *akhmad*, or captain, and some of them who even called him friend.

On either side of Bayard's flanks, stretching for half a mile each way, was Subutai's entire Mongol army of eighteen thousand horse-warriors, grouped into five blocks of mounted men, both light and heavy cavalry, with their backs towards the fast-foaming Kalka River, and their faces east towards the enemy. There was nowhere to run to. They must confront the enemy here.

And the enemy was surely coming. The heavily armoured knights of Prince Mstislav the Bold were a low smudge of brown in the distance but fast approaching. After an exhausting nine-day chase, the combined enemy force of Rus' and Cuman cavalry had finally caught up with the Mongols on the long western bank of the Kalka.

Robert had done as he was ordered and taken the Black Falcon *mingghan* west along the coast of the Sea of Azov. The Black Falcons had been the tip of the Mongol spear. Behind them came Subutai's entire force, nearly twenty thousand Mongol horse-warriors with wives, children, herds of sheep and goats, and thousands of spare ponies – the herd animals far outnumbering the fighting men – the baggage wagons, tents and everything else. It was the equivalent of a town on the move across the grassy, herd-feeding steppe, and moving surprisingly swiftly.

They had reconnoitred beyond the Dnieper River, even as far as the distant Dniester, and plundered scores of drab Rus' peasant villages, living off the steppe and their captured booty, and gaining more intelligence with every mile they rode and every Rus' steading they burned.

However, the intelligence they gathered was daunting: Grand Prince Mstislav of Kiev and Prince Mstislav the Bold, along with their ally Mstislav of Chernigov, and several other Rus' noblemen – Robert thought of them all as being called Mstislav, although he knew that some of them must have had other names – had raised a vast army between them, some eighty thousand men, outnumbering the Mongol force by more than four to one. True, much of the Rus' army was composed of peasant levies, thousands of poorly equipped men on foot, armed with only spears, knives or crude farm implements; and the various Rus' contingents were all commanded by their own independent Mstislavs – there being, as far as Subutai and his scouts could divine, no overall Rus' commander – but it was a formidable force to reckon with, nonetheless.

Robert wondered if Subutai understood what he had provoked, when he ordered his Mongols, burning and pillaging, to venture so deeply into the rich Rus' farmlands.

To Subutai's credit, when the Mongol general finally comprehended the true size of the enormous enemy force pitted against him, he did immediately begin to retreat.

He left a single rearguard *mingghan* of heavy cavalry under a dashing young *noyan* called Hamabek on the east bank of the Dnieper and fled back towards Tana. Hamabek's *mingghan* savaged the Rus' army's flanks as they tried to cross the river, his horse-archers cutting down Rus' cavalry in their hundreds. But they were only a thousand men, and were soon trapped and slaughtered, swamped by overwhelming numbers of their enemies and completely wiped out.

Hamabek did, however, buy Subutai just enough time to evade disaster.

The Mongol army fled before the victorious Rus' and their gleeful Cuman allies – Khan Köten and his Cuman riders up in the vanguard with Prince Mstislav the Bold. And this lord of the Rus' lived up to his fearless name, galloping boldly ahead of the main army with his ten thousand horsemen, while the rest of the Rus' army was left to straggle over a fifty-mile stretch of steppe between the Dnieper and the Kalka. Which was exactly what Subutai had hoped for.

The Mongol general halted his army on the western bank of the Kalka River, and turned it around to face the foe. Subutai, accompanied by Chormaqan and a dozen senior staff, now rode along the lines of his tired Mongol troopers, calling out encouragement to favoured individuals and repeating his orders for the day in his brass-lunged battle-voice.

The massed Mongol horsemen sat there, stock still, their flat, weather-battered faces, pale, dust-grimed and impassive under their steel helmets or fur-lined felt hats, not a man among them displaying his fear. They trusted Subutai. They trusted, too, in their own prowess. It was time to show the enemy they were Mongols, not fleeing vagabonds. Above their heads the spirit-banners, the *sulde* – tall spears that had a crossbar adorned with horse-tails – fluttered in the breeze, one for each *noyan*. They were the soul of the *noyan*, the rallying point and sacred symbol of a *mingghan*.

Subutai spotted Robert sitting on Bayard with his *jagghun*, and raised his riding whip in salute to the Englishman. Robert thought he might stop and address him personally – instead General Subutai, in his carrying battle-voice, called simply out, 'Remember, my brothers: the yellow flag is for you light cavalry, the red flag is for the heavies. Make all your mothers proud this day. Make me proud, too, my boys!'

The Black Falcons were light cavalry scouts and Robert, a trained Christian knight, used to fighting in full mail and great helm, with lance and shield, felt ill-protected that morning, dressed in his woollen *deel* and fur-lined hat. He was no bowman but he had six throwing javelins in a bucket-holster at Bayard's withers, a flanged mace tucked in his belt, and his Mongol sword at his left side.

He had donned his mail hauberk beneath his *deel* and under his fur hat was a basic steel cap with a nasal guard. Yet he still felt horribly vulnerable to the Rus' heavy knights.

Today, he told himself, he would fight as light cavalry. His task was to wield the No.4 *jagghun* as a weapon; and make sure they followed all Noyan Shulet's orders to the letter.

Robert had no particular desire to impress his *noyan*. He was a red-faced, rather stupid man, much given to shouting at subordinates. Shulet treated Robert with a wary civility, since he knew Robert was a *baghatur* and confidant of Subutai. But Robert suspected that Shulet resented the fact that he had taken the Black Falcon *mingghan* off to plunder the wealth of Soldaya, when the *noyan* himself had been left behind recuperating from his wound.

As Subutai spurred away along the battle line, loudly repeating his orders, Robert realised it was not true. He was no longer a confidant of Subutai. In previous engagements, he had ridden beside the general as his aide or lieutenant, now he was reduced to a captain of a *jagghun*, part of another man's *mingghan*.

He wondered, not for the first time, why Subutai was acting so coldly towards him.

The smudge of brown had come closer, and resolved into a mass of cavalry. Two distinct formations, as far as Robert, squinting hard, could make out. On the right, from his perspective, were the Rus' – Western-style knights and mounted men-at-arms, glinting in polished mail with long lances upright, perhaps ten thousand of them. He saw high helms and painted shields – Mstislav the Bold's heavy cavalry.

Over on the left, was a looser formation of shaggy men on little steppe ponies, some mail visible, but a raggedy, fur-clad mass of irregular troopers – Khan Köten's Cumans, he had no doubt, and massed in similar numbers to the Rus' knightly vanguard over on the right.

Both formations were coming up swiftly on the Mongol line, not seeming to slacken their pace in the slightest. Robert expected them all to rein in soon, order their ranks, take a pause for breath, before attacking in the usual, well-measured manner.

But on they came, at the trot. Unceasing. Relentless. He could now make out individual riders in the first rank of Mstislav's force. Five hundred paces away. It was puzzling. They made no pause to reset themselves. It seemed they meant to charge the Mongols without delay.

Chapter Thirteen

Noyan Shulet rode out in front of the battle line. He turned his pony briskly to face his *mingghan* and bellowed, 'Black Falcons – it is time to do your duty! Follow me!'

All the way up and down the Mongol lines, Robert could see big yellow flags being waved by the designated signallers. And the first of the whistling arrows, shafts with small tubes attached to create an eerie fluting sound, was soaring up across the face of the army, to reinforce the Mongol general's flag message.

It was time to face the enemy. Time to fight. Time to deploy the fire-pots.

His *mingghan* began to move forward at a walk. All along the Mongol line the light *mingghat* – eight thousand riders – were doing the same. Heading towards the oncoming Rus' cavalry.

Robert turned in the saddle to look at his designated fire-pot men, a picked group of a dozen riders commanded by Arslan, many of them from his *arban*, who were bunched together behind him. Robert nodded at the trooper, and Arslan gave him a curt nod in response. Then the Mongol let out a whoop, and he and his comrades, galloped forward and hurled themselves at Mstislav the Bold's advancing cavalry.

The fire-pot men seemed to cover the ground between the two forces in a matter of moments. Each man in Arslan's command carried a small clay pot in a basket of rope, the pot containing live coals, tar-soaked straw and wet leaves or grass. As they rode at the enemy, they whirled the fire-pots around in a wide circle on the right side of the horse, and the clay pots burst into flame, emitting a thick black stinking smoke.

When they came within fifty paces of the enemy, the fire-pot men hurled their clay missiles in the manner of slingshots towards the enemy horse, and they landed, spilling showers of red sparks, right in front of their pounding hooves. All along the front, small groups of Mongols from each of the eight light *mingghat* were doing the exact same thing, and in no time at all, a thick wall of black smoke was rising through the air, obscuring the sight of the Rus' attackers and terrifying their charging horses. And into this dense barrier of smoke, hurtled eight thousand Mongol light horsemen.

Yet the galloping Mongols did not confront the enemy head on, they did not smash directly into their ranks, instead they came galloping in, whooping and screaming like fiends, at an oblique angle to the oncoming Rus'. The Mongol riders emerged suddenly out of the wall of smoke and skated across the face of their regiments, loosing arrows from their bows at close range, before turning and galloping away.

Robert, with his howling *jagghun* around him, spurred Bayard along the front line of a smoke-wreathed Rus' cavalry regiment. He grabbed a javelin from the bucket-holster, hefted it and hurled the light spear to his left into the body of an astonished Rus' knight, perhaps even a Mstislav, given his elaborate silver helm. The javelin sank a good foot into the man's chest, and the man let out a horrible bubbling cry and slumped back in his saddle.

Robert heard an arrow hiss past his ear and reached for another javelin.

Behind him Taghachat was shooting his short, horn-and-sinew bow like the master horse-archer he was. The Mongol warrior plucked a shaft from his quiver, nocked and loosed it into the mass of enemy horse; then, almost faster than thought, he plucked another, nocked and loosed again. Arslan was now at Robert's other side, shooting his own short bow like a centaur. The Englishman pulled back his right arm and hurled his second missile deep into the enemy ranks, and found himself at the far end of the Rus' regiment, with Idar now at his side.

The Circassian was also shooting a bow but at a slightly slower pace than the Mongol troopers, taking time to aim his shots. Then they both turned their horses at the same time and galloped away, the angry taunts of the Rus' echoing in their ears.

The wall of smoke and the close-range arrow storm slowed, then halted the Rus' advance. There was now confusion in their ranks. There were horses screaming on the ground, riddled with arrows, and dead and wounded trampled underfoot. Some Rus' horses refused to go through the smoke, which drifted in thick, stinking skeins across the field.

But not all.

Formed bodies of Rus' horsemen appeared like armies of wraiths out of the dense clouds. Robert turned Bayard around, calling his *jagghun* to him and, after a moment in which they reformed the ranks, they charged again at a Rus' squadron, a mass of a hundred horsemen, their faces covered to the eyes in mail aventails under plumed helmets; frightened men who seemed to have lost all direction in the chaos.

Their leaders were shouting in an alien tongue, and pointing in three different directions, as Robert's *jagghun* swept out of the smoke and across their front once more. The Englishman and his men showed the Rus' no mercy. They rode in fast and lacerated their ranks with a blizzard of lethal shafts, loosed at a range of no more than twenty paces. Three, four, five times, the steel-tipped Mongol arrows, propelled by their powerful bows, slashed deep into the roiling enemy ranks, the shafts easily penetrating the Rus' iron-link mail at that catastrophically close range.

Robert hurled two of his javelins in quick succession, knocking one mail-masked knight clean out of the saddle with the first; the second disappearing into the tight-packed, shifting mass of Rus'. The enemy howled in rage and spurred after them, but Robert's nimble men whipped their ponies round and cantered away.

Robert led his *jagghun* back out of the smoke, to a clearer patch of the field. A whistling arrow tootled over his head – continue the attack – he knew that signal meant. He could see two other *jagghut* of Black Falcons regrouping to his right, and there was Noyan Shulet, under the Spirit Banner, pointing his sword at the mass of enemy. Ordering another assault on the disordered ranks of Mstislav the Bold's men.

Robert turned to Taghachat. 'We're going again. *Jagghun*, all of you, on me!'

As they galloped again towards the nearest Rus' formation, with Noyan Shulet and two other *jagghut* riding immediately on their right, Robert had just enough time before they hit the enemy to glance left, then behind him, at the rest of the field.

The army of Khan Köten had been pushed further to the south, beset on all sides by buzzing swarms of Mongol light horse. There was a widening gap of several hundred yards between the beleaguered Cumans and Mstislav the Bold's chaotic regiments. Behind him he could see the heavy cavalry *mingghat* ordering their ranks.

He looked ahead, beyond the mass of Mstislav's troops, which seemed to be hemmed all around now by Mongol light cavalry. And what he saw chilled his soul.

There were two more huge blocks of Rus' heavy cavalry – tens of thousands of horsemen in total – coming forward. They were still half a mile's distant, but they were hastening towards the fight, and beyond them, three or four miles away, were yet more enemy regiments – infantry formations this time, he thought – thousands of peasants tramping stolidly towards the whirling dust and smoke-obscured battle.

Robert had no time for fear. He was galloping with a score of Black Falcons at the shaky lines of enemy cavalry. Once more they rode in obliquely, Robert hurled his second-to-last javelin, missed the man he was aiming for and saw his spear sink into the haunch of a dun mare. The horse went wild, kicking and bucking off his rider.

The Rus' formations were coming apart now, the enemy riders surging forward in ones and twos out of their ranks, shouting out their hatred for the gadfly Mongols, and Robert found himself ducking under the strike of a long lance, which passed over his right shoulder. Bayard snapped his great yellow teeth at the oncoming horse's neck and caused the animal to rear up in panic, nearly throwing its rider. Which gave Robert time to draw his blade and hack at the Rus' rider's right arm as he passed.

He felt the contact of the blow, the crunch of steel against mail and bone. There were horses and enemy knights all round him. His opponent had disappeared in the swirling melee. He exchanged ringing sword cuts with a giant, red-bearded man, then sliced his blade across the fellow's big shouting face, opening his nose with a spray of hot blood, before spurring Bayard quickly out of the crush and into a patch of space.

The din was appalling. His view of the field came and went in wind-shifted patches of smoke. Yet, over the screams of the wounded and the war cries of Rus', the clash of steel, the crack of wood and bone, the neighing of frightened horses, the Englishman could hear the drumming of thousands of iron hooves on the dry earth.

He turned his head eastwards and saw that Subutai had chosen that exact moment to launch his superb heavy cavalry into the fray.

Ten *mingghat* – ten thousand Mongol warriors clad in iron mail and steel plate, on massively strong armoured horses – threw themselves into the fight.

Ten thousand steppe-hardened riders wielding long lances, swords and maces, surged forward from the Mongol battle lines. They smashed straight into the mass of frightened, milling, arrow-thinned cavalry of Khan Köten.

They plunged deep into the Cuman ranks like a sharp knife sinking into a block of wet curd. As the *sulde* poles danced above the heaving, dust-cloaked, deafening scrum, the horse-tails whipping in the steppe wind, the Mongol cavalry crushed the Cumans; they cut them down in bloody sheaves, culling them like pigs in a slaughterhouse.

Their long Mongol spears, driven by the full weight of mailed rider and charging horse, tore into the lightly covered bodies of Khan Köten's men, sinking into their flesh up to the hook behind the blade. When the lances were embedded in bodies, snapped or discarded, the Mongols drew swords and began to hack and slash the foe into bloody ruin.

They fled. The whole Cuman force ran, turning their nimble steppe ponies, and galloping back the same way they had come. Thousands began to flee the field, like a flock of sheep before a wolf pack, throwing all caution and courage to the winds in their haste to escape the chopping fury of the Mongols' and their glistening red blades.

The fleeing Cumans were pursued by the Mongol cavalry, who screamed and yelled in joy as they spurred after their terrified enemies. The Cumans tried, at first, to find safe refuge in the advancing ranks of Mstislav of Chernigov's men, galloping full pelt into their oncoming mass, soon becoming hopelessly entangled with the Rus' horsemen.

Into this panicked maelstrom of horses and men, surged the heavy Mongol cavalry, driving into the gaps between the Rus' files created by the Cumans.

The slaughter was appalling: battle-hardened Mongol warriors slaying nervous, raw Rus' recruits on both the left and the right, slicing at them, lacerating them with dripping swords. Soon the Chernigov army was infected with the Cuman panic, and when Khan Köten's broken men continued their flight through the ranks and beyond, they broke apart the Rus' formation. Now tens of thousands of fear-crazed horsemen – both Rus' and Cuman – were galloping west as fast as their horses could be driven.

The Grand Prince of Kiev, another fellow called Mstislav, who was coming up on the right, saw his Chernigov allies running from the field, pursued by a mass of Mongol cavalry and promptly turned his own horse around and ordered his men to retreat, and all of them were soon cantering swiftly back towards the River Dnieper.

Robert could scarcely believe his eyes. All that was left of the enemy host, many times their number, which had come against them that morning, was a few thousand battered men belonging to Mstislav the Bold, the first Rus' contingent to engage them. And these mangled regiments were entirely surrounded by the darting light Mongol *mingghat*.

A wholesale slaughter began. Robert rallied his *jagghun*, and joined the jostling, jubilant ranks of Mongols around the huge, bristling ring of Rus' riders. He tossed his final javelin into the boiling cauldron of stricken men and horses, his ears deaf to the pitiful cries of the wounded. The Mongol arrows dropped like black rain on the heads of Mstislav's men, each lethal volley slaying or wounding several dozen riders.

Then, quite suddenly, he was once again overwhelmed by a feeling of disgust at this needless slaughter. Robert turned Bayard's head and shouldered his way out of the crush around the doomed, encircled Rus'. He'd had enough. Robert looked around him and saw Taghachat, and about a dozen men of his own *jagghun*, not more than twenty yards from him, and Idar with them, blood-splashed but grinning, and kicked his poor, exhausted Bayard towards them.

Mstislav the Bold, too, had had enough. There was a sudden convulsion inside the great ring of beleaguered Rus', a shrill trumpet blast and loud cries of defiance.

The bold prince and a few hundred of his best-armoured knights surged west *en masse*, and a few blood-spattered riders broke free of the ring of their enemies.

In one great flood, like a pig's bladder full of water being pricked, the horsemen erupted from the ring of Mongol cavalry, spurting out of a gap in the Mongol lines, and thundering away, followed by a final shower of shafts, and the jeers and laughter of their foes.

Terror gave them wings and, within a few moments, they were a good half a mile distant, obscured by a dust cloud from their horses' pounding hooves.

The unfortunate Rus' men who remained in their defensive ring were given no quarter. It took an hour of bloody butchery, in which Robert and his surviving *jagghun* riders took no part, but by noon not a man among the encircled enemy still lived.

–

Three days later, Robert presented himself at Subutai's *ger* and asked for admission. The general was seated on a mat on the floor of the tent with half a dozen Mongol officers around him, there was a mound of letters at his right hand, crisp squares of folded paper sealed with wax, and several rolls of parchment tied with bright red ribbons. Robert knew immediately what it meant. The Arrow Riders had found the Mongol army on the Kalka and delivered a cache of messages from Genghis Khan.

Subutai made him wait, refusing to look up at Robert. The Englishman stood there awkwardly, outside the ring of Mongol officers, in his last clean linen shirt and a new woollen *deel*, secured by the gold-appointed leather sword belt given to him by Genghis Khan himself, his body freshly washed clean in the freezing Kalka River.

While he waited to be acknowledged, Robert allowed his mind to wander. He was thinking about his poor brother Gilly and how he had foolishly chosen these cruel, alien people, these savage, murdering Mongols, over his own flesh and blood.

He thought then about Sarantuya, too, and the love he had left in Samarkand. If he had not undertaken his mission to the Mongols, he would never have met her. Would that have been a good thing? Or a bad one. He would not have broken his Templar oath. But he would never have known her. Did Saran ever think of him? Or had their love been a passing fantasy, a dream that fades away to nothing in the harsh light of dawn?

'*Elchin Baghatur*, I believe you wanted something?' said a voice. And Robert was wrenched back to the here and now. Subutai was finally addressing him.

'The passes are open,' Robert said.

'What is that you say?' asked Subutai.

'The passes in the Caucasus are clear of snow. They have been open for some weeks. The Cumans are defeated. It is time to take the army to Baghdad.'

Robert knew that the Mongol cavalry had pursued the beaten Rus' and Cuman army after the battle, chasing the beaten foe the nine miles to the Dnieper, cutting down the stragglers, and harassing the fleeing columns. There was no question that the assorted Mstislavs and the rebel Köten had been beaten at Kalka, their armies destroyed, their regiments broken, although the wily Cuman khan had escaped, once again.

Subutai sighed. 'Leave us,' he said to the gaggle of Mongol officers around him. When they had all collected their letters and departed, and Subutai was alone with Robert, he said, 'Sit down, *Elchin Baghatur*, I have something I must tell you.'

Robert sat with his legs crossed on the mat and looked across at Subutai, who seemed, if anything, to be embarrassed; his sun-browned face was a little flushed. Robert was puzzled. He had never seen the great *orlok* look anything like this before.

'Do you require a drink? We have wine, I think. A bowl of *shulen*?'

Robert shook his head. 'Tell me,' he said.

'I am sorry to say I have not been entirely candid with you about Baghdad,' said Subutai, fixing Robert with his oddly leonine eyes. 'I have been in communication with the Great Khan for some months now about the direction that General Jebe and I should take once the Cuman rebels were destroyed. We discussed capturing Baghdad – it was even mooted as a plan when we were in Georgia. And I advocated that plan to the Great Khan. I swear I did, Robyert. But, in the end, the Lord of the Steppe decided we should not go south. It distresses me to tell you this.'

'This is why you have been so cold to me,' said Robert. Inside, he was a ball of white-hot rage. *All my effort; all the blood and sacrifice – Gilbert abandoned. And for what? For the Great Khan to casually decide not to send his* tumet *to Baghdad?*

He managed to keep his face impassive and listened to Subutai's words.

'...so, you see, the Bulgars on the Volga River deserve punishment. They stood against us when we came down from the mountains, you must remember that, then there are some rebellious Kipchaks, too, who are sheltering with the Bulgars...'

'You would go east to fight against the Bulgars?' Robert somehow managed to say these words quietly, almost calmly – even while his entire world was spinning with fury.

'The Great Khan would have us complete a circuit of the Sea of Ravens, a reconnaissance of all the lands up here. Then return to him in Khwarazmia via the northern route. I know you have travelled these roads, when you were making your way east, and it occurred to me that you might agree to guide us to the Aral Sea...'

Robert stared hard at him, a hundred acid retorts scalding his tongue. But what was the point? He had tried and failed to bend Subutai to do his will, he had tried to save his beleaguered Brethren in the Holy Land but he understood now that it was no use.

'I thank you for your offer, General,' said Robert stiffly, 'yet I must most respectfully decline. Furthermore, I feel the need to resign my command of the No.4 *jagghun* from this moment henceforth. I will return immediately to my own folk, to the Brethren of my Order. My sword is sorely needed in the fight for Christendom.'

'Do not be hasty, Robyert,' said Subutai. 'I see you are angry. But know that you are truly valued by us – we need you, *Elchin Baghatur*, we Mongols need your knowledge. Take a day or two to reconsider. We shall not leave here for a full week.'

'I thank you again, General, but I have made up my mind…'

'Oh,' said Subutai, 'and there is this, too. A letter came for you by Arrow Rider from Samarkand. I trust it contains good news of your commercial ventures.'

Robert walked away from Subutai, blinking back his frustration, and clutching the square of white paper sealed with a red wax. He returned to his own *ger* near the east bank of the river. The woman who cooked his daily *shulen* and who, along with Taghachat, tended to his household, his horses and herds, a bustling matron called Jargal, a relic of his friend Altan, saw the expression on his face when he came in and went at once to pour him a bowl of *airaq*, and set a big pot of water on the *ger* stove.

Robert stared into space for a long while, even forgetting to taste his fermented mare's milk, and eventually he put down the bowl undrunk and reached for the letter. He was expecting something from Karacha, news of a trading coup in Samarkand or a statement of startling profits, although it was strange that he was communicating with Robert here in the wilderness, rather than with Ziani back in the town of Tana.

He cracked open the letter, and the first thing that fell out into his hand was a small metal pendant on an old leather thong. It was a medal, a cheap, stamped piece of low-quality silver depicting a blurred image of St Christopher.

It had once been Robert's most prized possession.

There was a note, accompanying the St Christopher medal, a few lines of neat Persian, written in a hand he recognised as Karacha's.

But the message it conveyed was not from his partner.

It was from Sarantuya and it read simply:

We have a child; a son born in the autumn last year. I named him Jalair and he resembles you more every day. Khuyag guesses he is not the father and I fear for my life. Come to me, my love. Saran.

On the creased white paper was a tiny, smudged handprint in black ink, a mark made by a baby not yet six months of age.

Chapter Fourteen

Robert stopped speaking. There was a young child crying somewhere out in the courtyard of Vienna Castle, a heart-broken girl. The hall had been deathly silent, all present rapt by his words. Robert heard a woman calling out in German to the crying girl, trying to comfort her with a few soothing words.

'Let me be sure I understand this,' said Wilhelm von Eslarn, Provost of Vienna, 'you, Robert of Hadlow, brought this destructive Tartar swarm thousands of miles westward from Persia in the hope that it would ride to the aid of the Latin kingdoms of the Holy Land, and save them from the Sultan of Egypt's wrath, is that correct?'

'The prisoner has admitted this,' said Ivo of Narbonne, jumping up from his stool. Robert said nothing. He stared at the provost with his unblinking blue eyes.

'And let me remind the court that my good friend Robert did all this at the behest of Jean de Malemort, the Seneschal of the Templar Order,' Ivo continued.

'Yes, indeed, the court has already taken note of that,' said Wilhelm. 'But my point is that this reckless Englishman brought an army of inhuman savages to the edge of Europe but then, instead of joining the good fight with our desperate Christian brothers in the Holy Land, these Tartars – or Mongols, as he calls them – destroyed the flower of Georgian chivalry – in two great battles six months apart, thus preventing good King George from sending his knights to join the struggle against the Saracens and harming the holy cause he loudly claims to support…'

Wilhelm paused dramatically. '…*then* he led these Tartars north into the Rus' lands, where they wreaked havoc on the Orthodox Christian princes of that region. It sounds as if these Tartars had shown themselves to be enemies of Christendom even then… long before their current catastrophic incursion to our peaceful God-fearing lands.'

There was a long silence.

'Will the prisoner not answer me?' said Wilhelm.

'I did not hear a question,' said Robert.

'Did you not recognise that these Tartars were the enemies of Christ by their warlike actions against these various Christian peoples?'

'The Mongol nation – and particularly its Great Khan – has no enmity towards Christianity, they neither revere nor revile it. Some Mongols are, in truth, Christians, of the Church of the East or the Nestorian variety.'

'Yet they did *not* come to the aid of Christendom in its hour of need.'

'I did not control the army of Subutai,' said Robert. 'All I could ever do was persuade, cajole and bargain with the Mongol general. All my persuasions failed.'

'Who is this Sarantuya?' asked Frederick, Duke of Austria. Robert was a little surprised by the question. He had thought the duke half-asleep in his chair. Wilhelm retreated, loyally yielding the questioning to his liege lord.

'She is… she was my love. The woman who lives forever in my heart.'

'Pretty little thing, was she?' asked the duke.

Robert declined to answer.

'A young Mongol woman with whom you had a child, yes?' asked Geoffrey of Beaulieu. Again Robert remained silent.

'Did your master Jean de Malemort know that you broke your sacred Templar vow of chastity?' the little Dominican persisted.

Robert dropped his eyes. His shame was almost a visible shadow on his face.

'I made my confession to the Seneschal,' he said, 'and was shriven.'

Wilhelm was back on the floor. 'You broke your sacred oath,' he said excitedly, 'therefore you are clearly a liar. You have admitted this. You lied to the Order about keeping your chastity. How can we believe a word that comes out of your mouth?'

Robert looked coldly at him. 'I have sinned,' he said. 'I am a sinner. We are all of us sinners, are we not? Every man and woman in this hall. Let he who is without sin cast the first stone, taught Our Lord and Saviour. Are *you* without sin, Provost?'

Wilhelm opened and closed his mouth. 'I am not on trial here,' he said. 'I am not accused of betraying the true faith of Jesus Christ.'

The Dominican said in a kindly voice, 'Well, then, you had tried to persuade the Mongol army to come south – and you had sadly failed in that attempt. What next? Did you abandon your secret plan – or rather Jean de Malemort's secret plan – to bring the Mongols' strength to the aid of the beleaguered Latin kingdoms?'

'I did not,' said Robert, in a firm voice.

'What then did you do?' asked Geoffrey de Beaulieu.

'I decided to address myself to a higher power than General Subutai.'

Geoffrey frowned at him. 'You mean God Almighty?'

'Not quite,' said Robert, with what might have been a glimmer of a smile. 'I was determined to personally petition Genghis Khan himself.'

'This Genghis Khan – I have heard of this man,' said the Dominican. 'They say he has slaughtered thousands upon thousands of innocent men, women and children; they say that he is sheer, unadulterated evil. Some even whisper that he is in truth the *Antichrist*. This monster was the higher power from whom you decided to seek aid?'

'He was but a man, but one I believed could save Christendom. So, yes, I decided to seek the help of Genghis Khan. I left the Mongol army and rode east.'

–

The words of Sarantuya's letter echoed round Robert's head, following the thudding rhythm of Bayard's hooves on the endless grasslands of the steppe.

> *We have a child; a son born in the autumn last year. I named him Jalair and he resembles you more every day. Khuyag guesses that he is not the father and I fear for my life. Come to me, my love. Saran.*

It was clear that the letter had been written by Karacha – which offered a small raft of reassurance in a stormy ocean of fear. This meant that his Persian partner knew of her plight and would do all in his power to protect her and their baby son, which, given the swift-growing wealth of the House of Karacha, was considerable.

However, Robert also understood that, if Noyan Khuyag wished to punish his unfaithful wife, or even to murder her, the *noyan* certainly had the ability to do so. Khuyag had command of the Golden Eagles *mingghan* – a thousand battle-hardened Mongol troopers – and if he ordered them to storm Karacha's mansion in Samarkand and snatch Saran and Jalair away from the merchant's protection, this might well be achieved within a single hour.

For all Robert knew, Sarantuya might already be dead, executed in some hideous Mongol manner about which he could only speculate.

She had told him once that when executing nobles – and Sarantuya was one of the Golden Kin, the daughter of Genghis Khan's sister – Mongols believed no blood should be spilled. Instead of ordinary beheading, the offending noble would be rolled up in a carpet and a whole *mingghan* of heavy cavalry would ride over it, so that the victim was trampled to bloodless death by the hooves of a thousand galloping horses.

Visions of Sarantuya, squashed and lifeless, tormented Robert as he rode east. Then there was his son – the boy called Jalair. He had never in his wildest imaginings thought that one day he might have a son. And that knowledge filled him with both loving pride and a bleak, formless terror. What if the little boy were killed before he even had the chance to set eyes on him?

Robert made haste.

He did not travel alone. He had ridden first to Tana, with only the Circassian Idar accompanying him. After a hasty conference with Niccolò Ziani about their future trading with Karacha in Samarkand, he equipped himself with food, bedding, spare clothes, weapons, a few trade goods and some money, loaded it all up on to a pair of packhorses, and set out on Bayard the next day with two spare steppe ponies and Idar accompanying him, with his own two spare riding horses.

On the third day out of Tana, Robert saw a dust cloud behind him, coming up fast and Idar and he, deciding they could not outrun their pursuers, took their horses off the rough track that passed for a road and into a brown forest of thick bullrushes on the swampy north bank of the River Don, hoping to hide until the danger had passed. Peering out through the thick reeds, with his reindeer-skin riding boots sunk in six inches of black mud, and his sword in his hand, Robert was amazed to see Saka and Taka galloping past his hiding place with half a dozen other Mongol riders.

He came stumbling out from the reeds, with Idar just behind him pulling the string of horses, shouting out to attract their attention.

The Mongols turned nimbly and came thundering back towards him and, for a moment, when he saw Arslan's scowling face, he wondered if they had been sent by Noyan Shulet, or even Subutai, to either murder him or bring him back to the Mongol army by force.

It had indeed been General Subutai who dispatched the *arban* to find him. But not to bring him back in chains. It was Khuchar, grinning at Robert from under the long white scar across his brows, who verbally relayed Subutai's message to him.

'Our friend Niccolò Ziani has informed me of the grave danger to your woman and child. And I would not have you think me ungrateful after the service you have rendered. So here is my gift: one *arban* of your former No.4 *jagghun*, to protect you on the long and dangerous journey. These eight men all volunteered to accompany you and are yours to command. When you have no further need of them, send them back to the Great Khan's army, wherever it may be. I also present to you this silver *gerege* to smooth your passage. Yours in friendship, Subutai Baghatur.'

Khuchar handed Robert an oblong leather wallet, heavy and bound with a thong. Inside was the *gerege*, a rounded slab of silver, about a foot long and three inches wide, with a hole punched in one end so that it could be carried on a rope or belt – the Mongol equivalent of a king's passport. There were words stamped into the metal in the Uighur tongue, which Robert could not read, but which he certainly recognised.

He had seen *gerege* before, in iron, silver and gold, and knew the great honour they conferred on the bearer. The Uighur words said, *By the power of Tenggri, the Eternal Blue Sky of the steppe, this metal object is a command from the Great Khan. Whoever does not respect the bearer and obey all his orders is guilty of an offence.*

He stared at the *gerege*, feeling an almost overwhelming wave of emotion. Subutai's gift was invaluable. It gave him enormous standing in any lands controlled by the Mongols. But Khuchar was not finished with his verbal messages from the army. 'Taghachat also sends his greetings and says he will care for the good woman Jargal, and faithfully tend your herds and horses until you and he shall meet again.'

There was an outburst of sniggering from the troopers of the *arban*. Robert looked round the sun-browned faces that he knew so well. Even Arslan was grinning slyly.

'So Taghachat and Jargal are now, ah…' Robert began.

There was general laughter. 'Oh, yes, *ezen*,' said Khuchar, 'they are like a pair of mating marmots snug in their winter burrow.'

'She is the best cook in the *jagghun*,' said Hasar. 'That lucky dog.'

As they were all mounting up again, Robert found himself next to Arslan.

'You volunteered to come with me,' he said quietly to the *arban* leader. 'Why?'

Arslan stared at him with his cold, black eyes. 'I had a dream, *ezen*,' he said, 'that you were a khan, leading a *tumen* into battle. And I was riding beside you.'

'What of Tuyuk? And Chankai? All my mistakes? Why do you all follow me?'

'Why? Because we are your men,' Arslan said. 'You belong to us.' Then he shrugged, 'And, as your dead Cuman might say, the steppe is long.'

'You mean the steppe is wide,' said Robert.

'I mean it is a long road to Samarkand,' said Arslan, turning away. And Robert was not sure but he thought he detected the twitch of a smile on the man's face.

They rode east, hard and fast, changing horses every ten miles or so to allow the animals respite from bearing their weight. The *arban* had brought their own strings, some men owning as many as nine ponies, and they rode in a cloud of their own dust.

Robert was not much concerned about meeting enemies, even though they were riding through Cuman and Kipchak badlands, and the powerful Bulgar army was somewhere to the north of them on the River Volga. He had travelled this part of the road before, and reckoned he could either outrun or outfight any enemy force he met.

At the bank of the Volga River, a sheet of water more than a mile wide, he found a Mongol outpost, commanded by a young *akhmad* of one of Jebe's *mingghat*. He was guarding the usual crossing point near a wooded island in the centre of the wide river.

The *akhmad* was impressed by the silver *gerege* Robert showed him and bowed to the Englishman as if he were the khan of Arslan's dream. They were fed lavishly and supplied with provisions, and their horses were given crushed oats and a rub-down, their hooves trimmed and oiled. Then they were rowed across the shining width of the Volga on the flat ferry by a gang of muscular Mongol troopers stripped to the waist.

On the far bank, the *arban* plunged again into the endless sun-baked steppe.

It was the very worst time of year to travel these parched wastelands: the sun was a bronze hammer in an endless blue sky, and the fine sand clouds stirred up on the road by their hooves sucked moisture from their skins and choked in their throats.

They found little water, and had to carefully husband all they did find, drinking mere mouthfuls each day – and, after a week, one of the older steppe ponies died of thirst. They encountered few people, and those they did – goat and sheep herders for the most part – fled before the sound of their hooves. They travelled by night in the mid-section of their passage, the hottest days, finding shelter at dawn and panting in the shade of rocks – there were no trees – as the sun crawled across the white sky and the hellish oven-hours passed. They mounted up again at dusk to ride onwards into the indigo-shaded night.

Robert and Idar prayed together every dawn and dusk, and Robert grew to enjoy the Circassian's company at their twice daily devotions.

Not once did this pale native of the Caucasian highlands complain about the heat or the dust or his constant thirst. One night, as the two Christians were sitting by the campfire,

Robert noticed the Circassian sharpening the long, slim dagger he carried.

It was an unusual weapon, with an eight-inch-long steel blade, only an inch wide, and with no cross-guard, but the tang of the blade held by a four-inch-long ivory handle, beautifully carved with an image of a man. Robert asked if he could see the weapon, and Idar handed the dagger over to him. Robert looked closely at the carved ivory: in the firelight he could see that the handle bore an image of what looked like a saint – indeed, St Christopher, his own guardian, with a little child on his shoulder – and this holy figure was also carrying a long traveller's staff.

'It is indeed the Christ-bearer,' said Idar. 'My father gave me this to ward me on my travels.'

'Do all Circassians carry St Christopher on their hilts?' Robert asked.

'No,' said Idar, 'some have the Blessed Virgin, some an image of Our Lord himself. Each dagger is different. We each carry two blades by custom: the dagger you hold in your hands, for close-up killing, and a longer sword for proper battle. There is a story told in my land that, a few years ago, the Circassians were briefly in the employ of the Old Man of the Mountains – have you heard of this fellow?'

Robert had: the Templars often spoke of the Old Man who lived in the highlands of Syria who led a clan of skilled assassins, and who killed rulers and great nobles for large sums of money. He did not know if this murderous clan truly existed or not.

'Tell me the story,' he said, handing the dagger back to Idar. So the Circassian tucked his long dagger away and settled himself to speak.

'It seems that the Old Man had made an agreement to murder a Turkish prince in the Sultanate of Rum,' he began. 'It was not the Sultan himself but one of his sons, who had offended a potentate of the Ayyubids. However, the foolish prince got word that he was to be murdered by the Old Man's clan, who all belonged to a Shia sect of the Prophet's followers. So the prince who, like most Turks was a Sunni, gave orders that no Shia strangers were to be allowed to set foot in his palace.

'The Old Man's most skilled warriors tried their best but they could not get close enough to the prince to slay him, so the Old Man turned for help to the Circassians, who were Christians and had a reputation for fierceness and discretion.

'The Old Man sent his secret emissaries to the old headman of one particular Circassian family and he promised him a large quantity of silver if he would murder the Rum prince on his behalf. This headman, who was very poor, agreed to the task.'

'Did it not offend his faith?' asked Robert. 'I mean: "Thou shalt not kill."'

'Huh, no, that was not a consideration,' said Idar. 'The Turkish prince who was marked for death was only a follower of the Prophet – a Saracen, you would call him – and at that time the headman's people were facing starvation.'

Robert nodded to show that he understood this calculus.

'So the headman of the Circassian family agreed to send his eldest son south into Rum to kill this unfortunate prince. But before he went off to do his duty, the son asked for guidance from the Assassin envoy as to how best to make the kill in silence and get away before the murder was discovered.

'The Assassin showed him a technique for killing, known only to his Syrian clan, which would dispatch a man instantly with a dagger without shedding any of his blood. The dead man would appear to have simply died for no reason at all. And his murderer could then make good his escape.'

'How is that possible?' asked Robert.

Idar whipped the dagger from its sheath, and brandished it high in the air, the reflecting firelight as red as fresh blood on the slim blade.

'With a dagger such as this,' Idar said.

Robert felt a chill of fear pass down his spine. His right hand began to creep, instinctively, towards his sword hilt. Arslan was on the far side of the fire and was watching, without comprehension, as the two men spoke to each other in Italian. But Robert saw that the *arban* leader, too, had his hand on his sword hilt.

Idar held the dagger up in his left hand and turned it over so that the blade was pointing directly downwards.

'The blade must be inserted vertically exactly here,' he said, putting his right index finger in the small hollow beside his own neck on the left side, in front of the lump of shoulder muscle and behind the clavicle bone.

'You will note that the blade is long and thin. If it is pushed down in here, it will reach the heart and lacerate that great, pumping muscle. The ruptured heart stops almost immediately and the victim dies. But all his blood remains *inside* the body. On withdrawing the blade, a cloth is used, wrapped round the steel, so any blood that comes out can be wiped away.'

'Ingenious,' said Robert. 'Have you ever used this technique?'

'Once or twice,' said Idar.

Robert waited but it seemed the Circassian was unwilling to elaborate.

'Were the kills successful?' he asked. 'By which I mean undetected.'

'They were,' said Idar, 'and I added a refinement to the technique, which I think makes it almost perfect. I took a plug of resin, from a pine tree, and placed it in the entry wound, like a stopper on a bottle. It ensures no leakage even after the body is moved. It allows more time to escape.'

'You were the oldest son who was sent to kill the prince, were you not?'

But Idar did not reply, he simply offered Robert a sly little grin.

They spoke no more of such gruesome matters that night, but Robert's dreams were torrid, and he woke the next day sweaty, with an undefined sense of dread.

After a gruelling three weeks, the company spied the glittering waters of the Aral Sea and, two days after that, Robert was flourishing his *gerege* at the bemused Mongol governor of the town of Yanikant on the Syr Daria.

'The whole Khorasan has risen in rebellion,' said the governor gloomily, a grey-bearded veteran of forty years of steppe warfare. He was referring to the eastern part of Persia, and the western part of Afghanistan, the lands beyond the Amu Daria, the parallel-running sister river to the Syr Daria.

Robert knew the region. He had fought several battles there with Subutai.

'They slaughtered the Mongol garrisons of Merv, Nishapur and Herat,' said his host. 'Three governors appointed by the Great Khan and three *mingghat* of our people were massacred by these filthy dogs. They want Shah Muhammad's son Jalal to rule over them. Not us. The fools. Do they not know what will happen to them now?'

Robert thought he knew exactly what would happen to them.

The governor and his guest were sharing a delicious goat stew, spiced with coriander, pepper and ginger, sweetened with apricots, in the governor's apartments above Yanikant's market. The meal was washed down with copious amounts of *airaq*. It was the finest meal Robert had enjoyed for weeks.

'Where is Genghis Khan now?' Robert asked. 'Surely he will not allow these massacres to go unpunished?'

'The Lord of the Steppe is returning to his steppe,' said the governor. 'He left Tashkent nearly a month ago and is taking all his herds, his horses and most of his *tumet* north, back to the heartlands. They say the khan now has his eye fixed firmly eastward on Cathay – the Hexi ruler in the lands below the Gobi has displeased him. He means to turn his attention on him and all those Tangut-controlled regions.'

'But what about the Khorasan?'

'His son Tolui has three *tumet*. He's been tasked with punishing the rebels and restoring order. He'll do it, too. The boy is a true son of the Great Khan.'

The 'boy' was in truth a full-grown man, and only two or three years younger than Robert. But Lord Tolui was already a successful Mongol general, with a reputation for ferocity and ruthlessness that almost equalled his father's. However, Robert did not know much more than that about Tolui except that his wife, a lady named Sorkoktani, was rumoured to be a devout Nestorian Christian.

'Where is Lord Tolui now?' Robert asked.

'Last I heard, he was at Balkh, heading south-west for Herat. These rebels will soon discover what it means to lay violent hands on a Mongol governor.'

Robert thought he heard a trace of concern, even a little fear in the governor's voice. 'And Yanikant?' he said. 'There is no rebellion around here, I take it.'

'No, I hanged one of their mad holy men just last week for sedition. Hung him in the market square yonder to teach them some proper respect. He was preaching that men must obey no law but God's holy law. I set him straight. He's still dangling there in the heat, if you want to take a look, but he is getting pretty ripe now.'

'If I wanted something fermented, I'd rather have another bowl of this delicious *airaq*,' said Robert, and they laughed heartily together.

'Tell me,' said the governor, 'indulge my curiosity, *Baghatur* – where are your people originally from? I mean from which tribe – before the Great Khan made us all one people under his glorious horse-tail banners. Your accent is touched with some Cuman, but you have the colouring of one of those Forest People from the far north.'

Robert was taken aback by the question. While he stumbled out an explanation of where England was in relation to this dusty little town on the edge of the steppe, he reflected privately on how he must have looked to this grizzled Mongol warrior.

He was wearing a well-worn *deel*, secured at the waist by a Mongol sword belt, with a curved Mongol blade at his side, and badly scuffed reindeer-skin riding boots on his feet. His face and hands were burned a reddish-brown by the harsh steppe sun, and he spoke the Mongol tongue now with an almost perfect fluency. The only thing to distinguish him from the next Mongol was his dusty blond hair, half-hidden by his fur-lined hat and his bright blue eyes. Yet he had seen more than a few men with not dissimilar colouring in the ranks of the Mongol army.

When he had first come east, he had been disparaged as a *gadaad khun*, an 'outside person'. Now, with his *gerege*, his title *baghatur*, and his own *arban* of Mongols, he was as much one of Genghis Khan's men as any man alive.

In the morning, two days later, when he and his *arban* trotted out the gates of Yanikant, heading down to the main road that ran south-east down the lush, eastern bank of the mighty Syr Daria, he reconsidered his private revelation: there was in truth one crucial difference between him and the next Mongol rider.

His faith. His unshakeable Christian faith.

His conviction that Jesus Christ was the salvation of mankind, and that God had sent his only son to Earth to die as a sacrifice for the sins of the world. Thus fortified, in spirit, by the knowledge of his faith and, in body, by two full days of food and rest, he gave the order to gallop and led his *arban* south towards Samarkand.

Chapter Fifteen

It took ten days of hard riding to reach Samarkand. They skirted round the fire-blackened, rat-infested, uninhabitable ruins of Otrar, which had been the scene of a horrific massacre in which every living thing – men, women and children, livestock, even horses – had been destroyed by the Mongol army. Robert had played no small part in the capture of Otrar and the sealing of its terrible fate, and his conscience still smarted as he observed the shape of its dark, brooding hulk on the western skyline.

They diverted west, briefly, to Burkhara to obtain news and rest the horses for a day. The Great Khan was somewhere north of the Kirghiz Mountains and, after questioning of the *noyan* in command of the Burkhara garrison, Robert discovered that the *mingghan* given the task of scouting Genghis Khan's route back to Mongolia was the Golden Eagles, a unit commanded by Sarantuya's husband Noyan Khuyag.

Khuyag had been Robert's host, his comrade and perhaps even his friend. And Robert was filled with a mess of contradictory emotions by the knowledge that the man he had cuckolded was now hundreds of miles away – and riding in a divergent direction from him. For, as Robert rode south-east, Khuyag led the Great Khan and his huge army north-east. A part of Robert wanted to look the *noyan* in the eye and tell him he loved Sarantuya and claimed her as his own; but another part of him dreaded the guilt, not to mention the bloodshed, that would surely accompany such a confrontation. He did not wish to kill Khuyag; he merely wanted the man's wife.

Robert occasionally wondered if Sarantuya and Jalair were with Khuyag, even now, heading back to Mongolia; or whether they had both been left behind safely in Samarkand, perhaps with Karacha. It crossed his mind more than once to change direction, ride eastwards, and try to catch up with Khuyag and the Great Khan.

However, he realised he needed more information about Sarantuya and Jalair and their current situation before charging into Khuyag's *ger*. His Templar trainers frequently used to hammer home the adage: time is rarely wasted by reconnaissance. So, after a single day's rest in Burkhara, he took the main road east to Samarkand.

One incident, however, did stick in his mind from their brief time in Burkhara. Arslan had come to him in the evening on behalf of the *arban* and asked if he and his fellow troopers might visit a nearby house of ill repute. They wanted to drink wine and spend a little time in the company of some pretty Uzbek ladies.

Robert was no prude – he had taken a vow of celibacy but did not expect the same from his men – so he readily agreed and even gave Arslan a small purse of silver coins to ensure that the evening went well.

He had asked Idar if he wanted to go with the troopers to this bawdy house but Idar had demurred. He said he preferred to remain true to his marriage vows.

'You are married?' asked Robert, astonished that he did not know this. The men of his *arban* were all young and unmarried – Begter was not yet twenty.

'I have a wife in Goro, on the coast of the Black Sea,' said Idar. 'She is very beautiful and her name is Yula. I have two daughters – twins, just six years old.'

'Why are you not with them?' Robert was intrigued. He realised he had never enquired about Idar's family, even after the thousands of hours they had spent in company, and all the miles of dusty road they had ridden together.

'I am a poor man,' said Idar. 'Yula and her father make their living from the sea but I am a man of the green hills. What would I do on the shore in Goro? I have not the skills to catch fish, or mend nets, or sail little boats – I was trained from childhood as a warrior, with sword and dagger. However, Signor Ziani has promised that if I serve him well for five years, he will give me enough silver to take a piece of land in the hills, and perhaps Yula, my daughters and I will learn to tend flocks of sheep.'

'I will make quite sure Signor Ziani rewards you handsomely,' said Robert, 'and I shall add my own gift to his when our journeying together is done.'

'I know that you will,' said Idar. 'You are a true Christian knight.'

–

The House of Karacha had changed little in the time since Robert had last seen it. It was a grand, two-storey lime-washed, brick-built house near the China Gate of Samarkand, with many arched windows, a long shady verandah and stout front door strengthened with iron bars. Robert led the *arban* to the barred iron portal at the side, which led to the sizeable stables at the back of the house, and while they were busy with the grooms, unsaddling the tired beasts and arranging fodder and fresh water, Karacha himself came striding out of the back door of the house, smiling broadly, and looking every inch the wealthy Persian merchant prince.

He was dressed in a flowing iridescent green silk robe, with a gold-and-black chemise under it, fastened with many pearl buttons, and baggy black-and-gold silk pantaloons. This apparition ended in two bejewelled lime green slippers with an elegantly curled toe. Karacha's tanned, long-nosed, handsome face was graced with a small black pointed beard and a pair of neat waxed moustaches, and on his head he wore a huge turban of the same magnificent iridescence as his outer robe, adorned with a nodding aigret fashioned from a small spray of glittering diamonds.

'Welcome to Samarkand, my friend,' he cried. 'Welcome home! My heart is filled with delight to see my esteemed partner returned to me once more!'

He swept Robert away into the house on a wave of questions about the journey and the doings of Niccolò Ziani and Tana and other news about their business.

'We have had a truly marvellous quarter here, Robert – a truly marvellous year, indeed. I trust you have been receiving my quarterly reports – and money – in Tana?'

Robert had. Although he had not given them the attention they were due. He had been preoccupied with thoughts of poor Gilbert and the Mongol campaign against the Rus' and with the Cuman rebels. However, Ziani had informed him that business was excellent, and had shown him the strong room in his house where chests containing linen sacks of gold and silver coins, and other treasures – gold cups, silver vessels, porcelain statues, boxes of pearls, fat bolts of silk – were kept under lock and key.

In the hour that followed, Karacha treated Robert to a similar exhibition, as well as showing him the thick, leather-bound ledgers of closely written vellum pages that contained the records of the House of Karacha, the monies taken in, goods purchased and sold, and expenses and taxes disbursed. Robert tried to pay attention to Karacha's tumbling words and to the figures in the long black columns on the creamy pages, but one urgent question in his mind was claiming almost all of his attention.

Finally, he asked it aloud, 'Karacha – where is Sarantuya?'

'She is safe, my friend, quite safe, do not trouble yourself about the good lady. Now let me show you our new silk store, we have been buying in bulk—'

'Karacha, I cannot lend my mind to all this,' said Robert. 'I have ridden two thousand miles to see Sarantuya. You wrote out that letter to me from her. In God's name, tell me what has happened.'

The merchant pouted. He seemed to feel deprived of his moment of glory. So Robert promised him that he would take the time to examine the accounts and make his own tally, in due course, and he would visit all the silk stores in Samarkand, if only Karacha would tell him what had occurred between Sarantuya and Khuyag.

They repaired to one of the salons, and sitting on huge silk cushions as soft as clouds, and sipping hot spiced wine to combat the autumn chill, Karacha told him what Sarantuya had said when she had arrived at the house the previous winter – weeping, bloody and recently very badly battered by Khuyag's angry fists.

After Robert's departure from Samarkand, she had been reunited with the *noyan*, and had accompanied him on the campaign in the mountains of Afghanistan with the Great Khan and his *tumet*, hunting the defeated Shah of Khwarazmia's son Prince Jalal, and sharing Khuyag's *ger* like the dutiful, loving wife he expected her to be.

Then her mother had died, after a long illness, and her pregnancy had become much more cumbersome, and she returned to Samarkand in the autumn of the year before – almost exactly a year ago – to give birth to a fine healthy son, Jalair.

Khuyag, who was able to visit her only sporadically – every few months or so between the Great Khan's wide-ranging campaigns – was at first delighted by the boy child; indeed, he was ecstatic. The child's eyes were grey-blue at birth, but then so are many children's, Karacha said. But after a few months, when Jalair began to develop light brown hair and his eyes remained resolutely blue, even Khuyag, who was not known for deep thinking, had begun to suspect that the child was not of his seed.

Sarantuya fought a valiant rearguard action, claiming her maternal grandmother, one of the Forest People from the north of the Mongolian realm, had had pale eyes. But, since both Khuyag and Sarantuya had jet-black hair and tar-dark, midnight eyes, this was not something that Khuyag was able to make himself believe for very long.

He might have swallowed his pride and raised the child as his own – after all, who wants to proclaim that his wife has lain with another man? – but the jokes and rumours started to circulate. One *akhmad* of the Golden Eagles said the *noyan*'s child would likely grow up to have a nose as big as the *akhmad*'s cock and, when Khuyag heard this, he went berserk, attacked the captain and hacked the poor man to pieces.

That made the story spread faster and further. Khuyag thought he heard a trooper snigger to a comrade as he walked past and, turning like a leopard, Khuyag beat the man very badly with his fists, very nearly killing the unfortunate fellow.

Then he turned his rage on Sarantuya, and his wife endured beating after beating until, at last, she and Jalair ran from him and sought refuge in the House of Karacha.

Karacha looked across at his business partner as he told this sad tale. Robert's face was bone white, his teeth locked. He was clenching both fists in fury.

'Where is she now?' Robert asked, through his teeth.

'We sheltered her and the boy here for three days,' said Karacha, 'during which time I wrote that letter and dispatched it to you by Arrow Rider. I happened to be engaged in a lucrative piece of business with General Tolui, the spoils from the Afghan campaign had been stupendous and we were in the middle of negotiating—'

'Enough of commerce, Karacha, where is Saran…?'

'Listen to the story, my friend, possess yourself with patience, I beg you. Tolui was with me and he saw the state of Sarantuya and immediately offered to take her into his household. He said his wife Sorkoktani Beki would care for her until Khuyag had regained his reason. That is where she is now. In Lady Sorkoktani's *ger* a few miles to the south of Samarkand, guarded by a *mingghan* of her own guards.'

'She is safe?'

'Safer than she would have been here. I have only a handful of Uzbeks – not enough to deny her to Khuyag. Lord Tolui has gone west to put down a rebellion in the Khorasan, and Genghis Khan ordered the rest of his *tumet* north back to Mongolia – and he took Khuyag with him. There was nothing Sarantuya's husband could do but obey his khan. But do not think Khuyag's anger is assuaged. There is trouble ahead.'

Robert nodded. 'I must go to her,' he said. 'I must go to her right now.'

'Tomorrow,' said Karacha. 'I will give you a guide to show you the way. But tonight we shall feast and, after dinner, have a proper examination of the accounts.'

-

Robert stood outside the red lacquered door of the huge, gaudily decorated *ger*, two miles south of the walls of Samarkand, and waited. The felt-wrapped tent was about twice the size of any normal *ger* and was mounted on a wheeled platform to allow it to be moved without daily dismantling, as normal *gers* were while on the march.

He could see lush grass growing round the enormous wooden wheels, which meant it had not been moved for months. The *sulde* pole, carrying the identifying banner of the occupant, depicted four blue wolves with a gold-stitched border, and was shoved in almost casually between the spokes of one of the iron-rimmed wheels.

Robert had been stopped and searched by guards before he got within a hundred feet of the *ger*. His sword had been taken from him, and then he was made to wait outside for a time, while two Mongols glowered at him as if he was a mortal enemy.

Oddly, this reassured Robert. Even though Khuyag was, presumably, hundreds of miles to the north, Robert knew his lovely girl was well protected from his fury.

'What is that horrible noise?' Robert asked one of the glowering guards.

From inside the *ger*, Robert could hear a kind of screeching, scraping noise. It sounded like a female cat proclaiming her availability to the local toms in some dark alleyway. Then it sounded as if another cat had joined her and was competing for male attention. More screeches, scrapes and a wailing sound like someone in distress.

'It is the great Jin artist, the music teacher. The ladies are having a lesson,' said one of the guards. 'Is this sophisticated Jin music not to your taste, *gadaad khun*?'

Robert listened for a moment, searching desperately for any rhythm or melody.

'No,' he said. 'I'd rather have both ears filled with molten silver.'

The guard grinned at him; his first indication of any kind of humanity. The man gestured with a stubby forefinger towards his comrade's ears, and Robert saw they had both been stuffed with something that looked like thick tufts of sheep's wool.

'Daritai feels the same,' said the guard.

What seemed like a long while later, the noise stopped and a few moments after that the lacquered door was thrown open. A small man in a scarlet robe came out, throwing farewells over his shoulder, and carrying a pair of long-necked stringed instruments, each with a small cylindrical soundbox at the end, and two horse-hair bows under his arm. He gave Robert a nod as he passed, but the Englishman ignored him and was already craning his neck to catch a glimpse inside the *ger* of his love.

Robert came inside and made his bow before three elegant Mongol ladies, who were sitting on the right-hand side of the large space on mounds of cushions, and sipping from tiny cups of some hot steaming liquid.

Sarantuya saw Robert and went quite still. She gave no other reaction except for a tiny widening of her eyes. And Robert was equally impassive.

He bowed again. 'I greet you, Sorkoktani Beki, and beg you will forgive my intrusion,' he said. His hostess was a *beki*, which meant a royal lady, one of the Golden Kin. She was older than Sarantuya, about Robert's own age, but still beautiful in a crisply elegant, almost bird-like manner. Not one hair of her elaborate coiffure was out of place. Indeed, more than anything she resembled a well-bred hawk, with a narrow and slightly hooked nose, rather like a beak – most unusual for a Mongol.

'I wished to pay my respects to Lady Sarantuya, who was kind enough to give me shelter in her *ger* when I was last visiting the Great Khan's Ulus.'

'You are the famous *Elchin Baghatur*,' said Sorkoktani Beki, smiling, 'I have heard much about your heroism on behalf of the Great Khan and the Mongol nation. You are welcome in my *ger* as an honoured guest. Be seated and taste some of this *tsai* – it is a drink from the empire of the Hexi, and is health-giving and invigorating, I am told. Sit, I beg you. May I present the Lady Töregene, wife of General Ogedei.'

Servants brought Robert a cushion and soon he was sipping a hot, slightly bitter drink that looked like peat-brown water. It was not at all to his taste. He was aware that he was in the presence of Mongol royalty – two daughters-in-law of Genghis Khan, and his niece – however, he could hardly tear his eyes away from Sarantuya.

She looked thinner than the last time he had seen her but infinitely more beautiful. Her midnight blue-black hair was piled up in an elaborate design, showing off her long white neck, with one endearing tendril of hair falling loose over her cheek. Her slender body was clad in a shimmering blue silk gown, with a printed pattern of white bamboo leaves. He longed to enfold her in his arms and kiss her with all his pent-up passion, but the presence of the two other noblewomen forced him to master himself.

His hostess asked him some inane questions about his travels from the West and Robert answered her without any thought at all. Then Sorkoktani Beki asked if he meant to stay in Samarkand for a long period, and Robert said, looking directly at Sarantuya, 'I will stay here for as long as I am needed.'

Then Sorkoktani said, 'Samarkand is a wonderful place to spend the winter months, many high-born Mongol ladies choose to do so, wonderful amusements, so many marvellous parties…' But Robert had by now stopped listening to her prattle.

Sarantuya had an index finger held up to her lips, as if she were pondering some issue deeply, but Robert knew that it was a signal, telling him to be discreet. Not that he needed to be told: he knew that illicit love was dangerous among the Mongols, lethal even. An adulterous woman might be put to death by her husband, if he chose.

He tried not to let the overwhelming desire he felt for her show in his eyes.

Lady Sorkoktani was apparently still speaking to him. '…of course, it will be a terrible disappointment to poor General Ogedei, not having his loving wife beside him on the long journey north, but Lady Töregene has endured several difficult births in the past and we all felt, Lady Sarantuya and myself, that is, and indeed all the well-born ladies of Samarkand, that a few quiet months residing in just one place would be the best and safest course for a healthy birth. What do *you* think, *Elchin Baghatur*?'

Robert had no idea what she was talking about. Somebody was pregnant, that much he understood, and would stay in Samarkand. As for who, he did not care. He was wholly consumed by the vision of Sarantuya. He could not take his eyes off her.

'The *Elchin Baghatur* does not concern himself with babies and children,' said Saran. 'He is more interested in manly things, such as long desert journeys, important trade treaties and distant foreign wars.'

'I do not distain all children,' said Robert, smiling lovingly at her. 'Some, I'm sure, are delightful. I've heard that you have a baby son, Lady Sarantuya, is this so?'

'This is true. A sturdy boy-child. But my little Jalair is with the horse-masters today, learning to ride. Perhaps I shall introduce you to him one day...'

'Learning to ride? How old is this prodigy?'

'He was born a year ago,' said Sarantuya. 'But we Mongols like to put our children on the backs of ponies at that age, so they grow up with no fear of horses. The horse-masters will take good care of him. Have no concerns for him, *Elchin Baghatur*. I shall take Jalair out riding in the lake-park of Samarkand every morning at dawn until he is able to sit on a pony without my aid.'

'An admirable ambition,' said Sorkoktani. 'I am sure he will grow to be a fine brave horse-warrior... *just like his illustrious father Noyan Khuyag*.'

She gave the final words a special emphasis, looking meaningfully at Robert as she said them. And the Englishman immediately understood her message. Sorkoktani knew he was Jalair's true father, but the other lady, General Ogedei's wife Töregene, did not.

'Talking of sons, mine is kicking urgently inside me,' said Lady Töregene, putting a white hand on her big, round belly. 'I think I must take some food, Suki, to placate my growing baby, if you would be so kind as to summon a bite.'

She smiled very sweetly at Sorkoktani as she said this.

'Of course,' said her host, clapping her hands for the servants. 'My dear *Elchin Baghatur*, would you care to eat with us? A simple repast, some dumplings, a little soup, some cold mutton... You can tell us of your adventures in the Rus' lands. And I understand you are in Samarkand to trade on behalf of your rich Venetian friends?'

Robert was surprised by how well informed she was. She was clearly intelligent, and an ally of Sarantuya's. Even so, he politely declined her invitation to eat.

'I only came to pay my humble respects,' he said, 'and to invite you to attend a Venetian-style banquet at the House of

Karacha, which will take place in one week's time. I am inviting all the notable Mongols in Samarkand. There will be the finest Venetian foods, gifts and entertainments. I hope you will join us, Lady Töregene.'

The next morning, an hour before dawn, Robert saddled up Bayard and rode slowly around the lake-park of Samarkand. The last time he had been here this pleasure park had been a drab place of mud, noise and detritus, with *ger* planted everywhere on the hoof-torn grass, and sheep, pigs and ducks running between them.

Samarkand had just been sacked by Genghis Khan's victorious *tumet*, and bodies still lay in the streets and between the ruined, blackened buildings. The three inter-linked lakes that gave the park its name had been used then as watering holes for thousands of Mongol ponies, as well as washing places for Mongol womenfolk.

The transformation was extraordinary: the city was cleared of any signs of war and, instead of legions of starving, crippled beggars shivering among the burnt-out ruins, the denizens of Samarkand thronged the streets and marketplaces, buying and selling all manner of goods, as well as arguing, eating and drinking in the many cookshops and taverns. The various Mongol campaigns in the region, and the enormous loot they had accrued, had not only benefitted the House of Karacha.

Since Samarkand had been designated the capital of the Mongol Ulus east of the Amu Daria, with the administration and tax authorities based there, the city had come roaring back to life. Troopers returned from the wars with loot money to spend, and the shopkeepers and tavern-owners of Samarkand welcomed them with open hands.

The lake-park was renewed. The park grass, no longer trampled by herds and horses, had returned to a lush and brilliant green, and the lakes had been dragged with nets to clear them of general rubbish and rotting corpses, and they now shimmered like mirrors, touched with pink and gold in the rising sun.

Robert walked his horse once around the path on the perimeter of the park, then he saw her, by the gilded gates of the entrance. A tall, thin Mongol woman standing beside an infant on a small pony, with another woman, older, holding the reins of two horses, allowing them to eat from their nosebags. Robert leapt from Bayard's back and sprinted the distance between them.

A moment later, Sarantuya was in his arms.

Chapter Sixteen

He held her in his arms and kissed her like a parched man drinking at a desert oasis, and for a long while they were locked together, their bodies pressed full length against the shape of the other. They kissed for a long, long time, then Sarantuya gently broke his hold and pushed him away.

They stood gazing at each other in silence, smiling like a pair of imbeciles.

Sarantuya sighed. 'We must not be seen together like this again, Robyert,' she said. 'Khuyag has his spies in Samarkand. And they watch me constantly.'

Robert looked around. He could see nobody nearby, other than the other Mongol woman, who now held the reins of two horses in one hand and the bridle of the pony with the infant astride it, in the other.

She was looking down modestly at her feet. Robert scowled at her, anyway.

'No, my love, Anya is no spy. She is my maid. She has been with Suki – with Sorkoktani Beki – for many, many years. And I trust her completely. I trust her with my life. I think we are safe at this early hour but still we must be very careful.'

'I have missed you so,' Robert said. 'I cannot bear to be without you.'

'And I you,' said Saran. 'But if Khuyag has proof – if he can produce witnesses to our love – then he will accuse me publicly in the Great Khan's court and I will be condemned to death as a faithless wife. If my husband can show that I have lain with another, borne another man's child, then not even the Great

Khan could do anything to save me. You would not survive either. Khuyag would have your head, my love.'

'The khan is your uncle, surely he can—'

'Genghis Khan made a new code of laws for all Mongols – the Great Yasa, it is called – but he is also bound by it. And he has many nieces. He can afford to lose one in the name of justice. You may not kiss me, Robyert, or even touch me in public, nor treat me differently from any other Mongol lady.'

Robert stared at her, appalled.

'However, we shall find a way, my love,' she said. 'We will find a path to happiness, I swear it. I knew you would come for me. And I cannot tell you how happy I am that you are with me now.'

Robert was reminded of Gilly's words – 'I knew you would come for me' – and when she said them, the emotion was running so strongly in his heart that he nearly embraced her again. He took a step towards her but she held up a hand to stop him.

'Would you condemn us both to death for a single kiss?' she asked.

Robert looked at her lovely face, the huge eyes, the planes of her cheekbones and her soft mouth. For an instant, he thought he might give up his life for a kiss.

It seemed a fair exchange.

Then reason returned. He took a step backwards.

'We cannot speak for long,' she said, 'this must seem like a casual meeting, by chance, between two old friends. You were a guest in my *ger* – it is perfectly proper that I should greet and speak with you in a public place. Now smile at me, my love – do not scowl like a demon with a toothache – and come and admire your fine son.'

Jalair was a fine, plump bundle of boyish happiness in a tiny *deel* and fur hat sitting on the back of the pony, with the maid, Anya, holding him in place. He had a round face, dimpled cheeks, a big, happy mouth and large, blazingly blue, guileless eyes. He gave a little crow of joy when Robert came close to him and, as Robert put out a hand to touch his face, Jalair grabbed his index finger and gave it a surprisingly firm squeeze.

'He is so strong,' said Robert in amazement; he felt as if a large bubble of air was expanding in his chest.

'Agwawh-wah,' said Jalair. He waggled Robert's hand with his grip.

'What is he saying?'

Sarantuya laughed, a lovely sound. 'He does not yet speak, as such, my love. Nor can he walk. He is saying, in his own way, that he likes you.'

Robert could not speak either – such was the strange hollow weight in his chest. He gazed on the boy – his boy, his son! – in astonished wonder.

'That is enough,' said Sarantuya. 'We old friends have met in the park, passed a few pleasantries, now you must go. We will continue our morning ride without you.'

Robert seized her hand. He opened the curled fingers and pushed something into her palm.

'This is for you, and for our beautiful son,' he said, trying not to weep for the fullness of raw feeling inside him. 'A token of my everlasting love.'

Sarantuya looked down at her hand and saw it contained the old St Christopher medal on its leather thong. She closed her fingers tightly around it.

'When can we meet again?' asked Robert, more than a little plaintively.

'In six days,' said Sarantuya. 'You invited me to your Venetian feast, did you not? Now say goodbye to Jalair and let us continue with our riding lesson.'

–

The so-called Venetian feast would have endured many a dismissive sniff for its lack of authenticity had any of the fifty-two guests ever set foot in that wealthy Italian trading port.

However, since not one of them, including their English host, had ever done that, it did not matter a jot. Robert asked only that the Uzbek cooks of the House of Karacha follow a few simple rules: no mutton or lamb, and absolutely no fermented mare's milk. Nothing that a Mongol might eat in the usual course of things.

The cooks accepted his challenge with gusto. They roasted a whole ox on a spit all day out in the courtyard by the stables and served it thinly sliced on warm wheaten flatbreads, with fried onions and a spicy sauce made from black pepper, cumin and ginger. They also prepared hundreds of skewers of grilled chicken pieces, and huge rice dishes made fragrant with saffron and laced with apricots and sun-dried grapes.

The Uzbeks fried small dumplings filled with minced beef and leeks in hot oil to make them crispy. They also made a light soup made from river fish and watercress. And, as well as all that fare, there were various game-filled pies, honey cakes and sweetmeats, and crumbly white cheeses and wine – vast quantities of good Persian wine – along with sherbets chilled by snow brought down from the Tajik Mountains and various types of fruit juice.

Each guest, both male and female, received a gift at the feast, a heavy silver bracelet, set with a polished hemisphere of deep blue lapis lazuli, transported to Samarkand from the deep mines in Afghanistan. Musicians wandered through the many rooms of the House of Karacha playing their stringed instruments and flutes, and singing, and outside in the courtyard, where trestle tables had been set up for the food, a Tajik juggler hurled balls, then burning torches and knives into the air for the amusement of the guests.

There was also an unexpected guest of honour. General Tolui had returned triumphantly from his campaign in the Khorasan and graciously accepted Robert's hasty invitation to attend the Venetian event. The word was that Tolui had ruthlessly destroyed the three cities of Merv, Herat and Nishapur, all of which had foolishly risen against their Mongol garrisons and murdered their Mongol governors. Tolui, they said, had exterminated all living things within the walls of these three ancient cities in just a few short months. People whispered that he had ordered his men to pile all the severed heads of the victims in great pyramids to serve as a grim warning to any other cities or lands that might contemplate any similar rebellion.

To his surprise, Robert liked Tolui. He was a short, cheerful, round-faced man, of about thirty, friendly, humorous and full of boyish enthusiasm. He looked about as far from his gruesome reputation as a man could get. But he was the youngest son of Genghis Khan and, as such, he must have known war from a young age. It did not seem, however, to have soured his almost perpetually sunny outlook in the slightest.

'*Elchin Baghatur*,' said Tolui, 'you honour me by this invitation to your home. And what a truly splendid home it is!'

They were standing in one of the large chambers in the House of Karacha, and Uzbek servants were hovering nearby with plates piled with delicacies and trays of brimming cups. But neither Robert not his guest seemed interested in refreshment.

'It is I who is honoured by your attendance,' said Robert. 'I must congratulate you on your victories in the Khorasan, Highness. You have put down the rebel enemy with great resolution and safeguarded the Ulus from the terrible scourge of chaos.'

'It was bloody butcher's work,' said Tolui, grimacing, 'but it had to be done. People expect it of we Mongols nowadays. I gave them the Great Khan's Choice and they refused to yield. You know how it goes, *Elchin Baghatur*. I heard you gave them the Choice at Otrar *and* found a way into that well-defended city for my father. I also heard that you rode with Subutai all the way west to the Rus' lands. It is I who must congratulate you on *your* victories, *Baghatur*. But let us speak of other more cheerful things apart from war and bloodshed. More civilised things. How goes the trade of your noble House? You appear to be thriving.'

He made a gesture round the lavishly appointed chamber, at the silk tapestries on the walls, the gloriously patterned carpets and the Uzbek servants in matching livery.

'Oh, it goes fairly well,' said Robert modestly. 'We manage to keep ourselves afloat. Have a cup of wine. It comes all the way from the region of Shiraz in Persia.'

He beckoned a servant and they both took a golden cup from his silver tray.

From other parts of the House of Karacha, they could hear the sounds of revelry. A loud crash of porcelain came from somewhere nearby. The wine from Shiraz was strong, and unmixed with water, and the guests seemed determined to drink deeply.

'If you would care to come to our encampment, over the next few days, I am sure our quartermasters would be eager to trade with you,' said Tolui. 'My three *tumet* are setting-up camp ten miles south of the city between the river and the hills, and we shall be there for the whole winter. The spoils from the Khorasan have been considerable and I'm sure we will have some items that would be of interest to you.'

It was Tolui's turn to be modest. The quantities of loot that the Mongol army had amassed over the course of the summer campaign had been stupendous, or so Robert had heard. Large parts of the Khorasan region beyond the Amu Daria had been stripped bare of all their portable wealth by the victorious Mongol army.

'I shall certainly do that, Highness,' said Robert, 'at the first opportunity.'

'Good. I know my wife Lady Sorkoktani would enjoy seeing you again.' Tolui paused then before saying. 'She – *and all her ladies* – would welcome a visit. And, if you can spare the time, *Baghatur*, we might even sally forth and try a little hunting in the hills. I'm told they are full of game this autumn – goats, deer, even a wild boar or two.'

Robert felt a sense of relief. By his words, it was evident that Tolui knew about his relationship with Sarantuya, and had no objections to their love.

And, an hour later, the lady herself was in his arms.

They were in his bedchamber; she had been summoned discreetly by an Uzbek servant and, as the party raged on downstairs, they kissed passionately, and with febrile urgency tore the clothes from each other's bodies. Their first coupling was brief and savage but, as they lay, sweat cooling, spent in each other's arms, Robert was filled with a sense of the rightness of it all.

He knew he had once again broken his vow of celibacy, and once again sinned with the wife of another, but in that glorious post-coital moment he did not care a jot.

The Church and his Brethren might abhor his sinful actions, but Robert felt whole and happy for the first time in years. Deep in his secret heart, he knew that what they had just done was not only good and right, it even felt, in a mysterious way, holy.

The second coupling was more leisurely, with both Robert and Sarantuya taking turns to give pleasure to the other. When the climactic moment came, he once more felt they had been joined in a miraculous way that was as deeply spiritual as it was deeply human.

They lay for a few moments without speaking, gazing into each other's eyes, kissing gently and marvelling at their mutual bliss, then Sarantuya sat up and said sadly, 'I cannot stay with you, my love, they will be asking where I am downstairs.'

'Stay,' he said. 'To Hell with any who asks for your whereabouts. Why can we not defy them all – make our love public? I will fight Khuyag – man to man – for your hand in marriage – or pay him or whatever he wants and be done with it. I plan to go north to find the army and petition the Great Khan himself to allow us to marry. I know that I cannot go on in this life without you beside me, my dearest love.'

'Do not say that, Robyert, I beg you. And do not go north to see the khan. For us Mongols, marriage is not a private matter.'

She kissed him softly. 'My uncle gave me as a wife to Noyan Khuyag for his services to him and the Mongol nation. We Golden Kin are not free to marry wherever we may choose; we are used as valuable pieces to reward loyal followers and make new alliances. Is it not the same in your land?'

Robert muttered something unintelligible. Among people of his knightly rank, marriage was also rarely a question of personal choice. He knew this well enough.

'If the Great Khan were to take me from Khuyag, and give me to you – which, believe me, my love, is something I desire above all else – he would have to compensate Khuyag in some way. Why should he do that? He has already given Khuyag a fine gift – me. Now you ask the Lord of the Steppe to give Khuyag *another* fine prize?'

'You are not some prize – like a horse or a piece of land – to be *given*.'

Sarantuya was already dressing herself. She slipped the leather thong of the St Christopher medal over her head so that the disc dangled between her small, cherry-tipped breasts, then she stopped and looked over at Robert lying in the bed.

'Am I not?' she said. 'Look at this from out of Khuyag's eyes. He has been humiliated, shamed. He believes he is mocked by all Mongols. He does not want *me*. I would remind him of his shame, every day. I would be a living insult, always in his sight, always in his *ger*. What Khuyag wants is to expunge his shame. And that means a trial before the Great Khan. He wants to demonstrate that I am a faithless whore. Then he can have me publicly executed. His honour will be restored. People will not laugh at him. He will have you killed, too. His shame wiped clean by our deaths.'

'I will slaughter him before I let him lay a finger on you again,' said Robert.

'No need for killing. All we must do is be discreet. We cannot show our love in public; we cannot gift Khuyag a witness. But behind doors…'

She leaned forward, took his face in her soft hands, and kissed him.

So it went, all that autumn and winter. Robert visited the sprawling military camp south of Samarkand, where Sorkoktani Beki had moved her household to be with her husband and his thirty thousand Mongol troopers, and there Robert chastely spent many hours with the noble lady and her companion Sarantuya, and sometimes even with the now-toddling Jalair, in the presence of the *beki*'s many servants.

He met up with Tolui, too, several times and they discovered a shared love of dice games. They played together many times, and neither lost too great a sum to cause the other anger. And when the weather was clear, they put away the dice tray and went out hunting for wild goats and deer in the foothills of the Tajik Mountains.

They found, surprisingly, that both enjoyed the other's company. Tolui was a fine horseman and had the usual Mongol skills with a horn-and-bone recurved bow. However, what the young general excelled at was throwing the javelin and he and Robert, accompanied by Idar and a few huntsmen, would ride down the nimble, curly-horned Markhor goats of that hilly region, and skewer them with their light spears; then feast in the woods when the day's hunting was done on the fresh livers of the beasts, lightly roasted on peeled hazel sticks over a roaring camp fire.

They had a fine time. Tolui, for all his ferocious reputation, was good company, often venturing jokes and other drolleries. He seemed fascinated by the Englishman's travels and asked him several times about the mysterious Western lands beyond the Empire of Khwarazmia, and about the Holy Land, where Jesus Christ had been born.

'You do know that my wife Sorkoktani is a Christian, Robyert?' he said one day after they had returned from the hunt. 'She believes in all that nonsense about the woman who gave birth to a baby without ever sleeping with a man – ha-ha! – what a fool her husband must have been!'

They were back in the Mongol camp and the servants were busy preparing a meal. Hot spiced wine had been served and he and Robert were lounging on the big, silk-covered cushions in the men's side of his large *ger*, drinking and taking their ease after a long day in the saddle. Idar was off somewhere with the servants, and the two men were alone. Robert bit his tongue and decided not to take offence at Tolui's jest about the Blessed Virgin Mary. *Forgive them, Lord, for they know not what they do.*

'I believe the *beki* is what is called a Nestorian – a member of the Church of the East,' said Robert. 'However, I belong to the Holy Roman Catholic Church.'

'But you both believe in the Jesus, the son of an all-powerful God, who was executed as a common criminal, and then miraculously came back to life…'

'Yes, but we Catholics believe Christ was both God and Man in one *unified* person, and the Church of the East says there were two *distinct* persons contained by Christ's being. Hundreds of years ago a number of learnèd bishops – as we call the leaders of our Church – argued for weeks about this. We call them Nestorians because they refused to condemn a man called Nestorius when he suggested this bizarre two-person-in-one doctrine and for this belief he was expelled from the Catholic Church.'

Tolui, who was an intelligent man, looked at Robert blankly. 'It seems a very slight distinction to make. So do you *not* consider my wife a Christian?'

This question took Robert into dangerous waters. 'I, um, I have not studied theology to any great degree myself,' he said. 'I cannot claim to know what the bishops would say, but I do recognise Sorkoktani as a follower of Our Lord and Saviour and I am sure that – eventually, by God's grace, hopefully many years from now – she will be welcomed into Heaven along with all the other righteous souls.'

'What about me? Will I go to Heaven when I die – many years from now?'

'Do you *want* to go to Heaven? To spend eternity only with Christians?'

Tolui burst out laughing then, to Robert's considerable relief.

'I wish to expire *under* the great vault of Heaven – under the Eternal Blue Sky of Tenggri – then be reborn as a baby Mongol on the steppe and grow up straight and strong to do it all over again. Everything – the battles won, the enemies crushed, the women bedded, the animals hunted – I want all that is good in life – all of it again.'

It was a sweet agony to be so often in Sarantuya's company in Tolui's camp and yet to be unable even to touch her. But Robert was fortunate that winter to be fully engaged by the huge volume of business conducted by the House of Karacha. The first train of heavily laden packhorses had arrived from Europe – Ziani had engaged the Rum merchant Suleiman Oktay to bring his goods east along the Silk Roads.

And when all the goods from Christendom were unloaded, Robert and Karacha visited the quartermasters of Tolui's *tumet* and haggled ferociously with them for possession of the vast piles of Khorasan loot they had accumulated – golden chains and silver cups, bolts of best-quality silk and fine Cathay porcelain, precious jewels of all kinds, pearls and chests of silver coins, glowing silk carpets – providing in exchange for these treasures practical items that the ordinary Mongol troopers desired: good steel scimitars made in Damascus, with fine-worked red-leather scabbards; chain-mail hauberks, light and strong, fashioned by the greatest German craftsmen, steel javelin heads, hand axes and all manner of knives and daggers forged in Italy.

And some things that were less practical and aimed more at the Mongol troopers' pleasures: barrels of sweet wine from Trebizond, preserved sweetmeats from Rum, dates packed in honey, baskets of ripe fruit in season, fine silk chemises in bold shades of red, green or lilac made up from bolts of cloth by the nimble-fingered team of tailors that Karacha employed, which were worn under armour or a *deel* to add an extra layer of protection and comfort.

A tidal wave of money was soon pouring into the House of Karacha.

One grey January day in Samarkand, a month after he had celebrated the Feast of the Nativity with Sorkoktani Beki and her fellow Nestorians, as the snow fell, thick as goose-down on the muffled streets outside his tightly closed wooden shutters, Robert was tallying up his astonishing profits in the counting house – a small separate room inside the mansion with no windows and an oak door two inches thick, with a second steel barred door beyond – when one of the Uzbek servants came to him and said quietly that a lone Mongol rider had come calling at the House, asking for him by name, and who was only willing to speak to him.

Mystified, Robert went to the front door and greeted a figure, bundled in a *deel* with a sword hanging by its side, the face concealed by scarfs.

The figure spoke no words, just pulled down one of the scarfs a little, and Robert found himself staring into the tar-black eyes of his darling girl.

He dragged Sarantuya into the house and whisked her up the stairs to his bedchamber in a matter of moments. And they spent the rest of that joyous afternoon and the next morning alone in bed. There was only one awkward moment when Idar came into the room a little after dawn, unannounced, as he often did, holding a broken bridle, and saying something about a horse and its shameful worn-out tack…

He stared at the naked couple entwined in bed, twin red spots appearing on his pale cheeks, before apologising profusely and beating a swift retreat.

Sarantuya was unduly alarmed by the intrusion. 'You must chastise your servant, Robyert,' she said, 'and make sure he never speaks of this to anyone.'

'Have no fear, my love, Idar is a loyal man. I trust him. He would never say anything that might endanger us. He is no gossip, I assure you.'

'But you will speak to him, my love? We are playing with our lives.'

'I will impress upon him the gravity of our situation,' said Robert, 'and tell him to keep his silence on pain of death – but on one condition.'

'What condition?'

'You come to me again at the same time, the same day, next week.'

They laughed, kissed, and began to make love again. But Sarantuya did not come again to his grand house near the China Gate – not the next week, nor the one after.

Chapter Seventeen

'What is a… *kurultai*?' Robert asked. He had heard this Mongol word used before but had never quite fathomed its precise meaning.

'It is the Mongol assembly,' said Tolui, 'but so much more important than that. It is a gathering of all the khans of the Mongol nation, during which a new Great Khan is sometimes elected; but it is also the time when captured cities, new lands and appanages are assigned to successful generals and members of the Golden Kin. Also, it is a time when the Great Khan's justice is done before the sight of the whole nation, when grievances are aired and disagreements settled. Furthermore, it is the gathering in which all the Mongol khans decide where the *tumet* will ride during the coming campaigning season, and which lands will next face their wrath.'

Robert was standing beside the general in his large *ger* and all about them was turmoil. A dozen servants were busy packing up Tolui's many belonging into large, box-like containers made of stiffened felt, and bustling about with armfuls of clothes, blankets, cushions, wall-hangings, weapons and tools, pots and pans. The momentous news that the Great Khan had called a *kurultai* had arrived in camp the previous day.

'And we must all go to this assembly?'

'All men of rank must. To refuse to attend the *kurultai* is to declare that you are in rebellion against the Great Khan, that you do not recognise his authority. As a *baghatur*, you must surely attend. If the House of Karacha wishes to continue trading in Mongol lands, when the Great Khan calls a *kurultai* you must immediately pack up your *ger*, round up your herds and saddle your best horse.'

'And where are we all going?'

Tolui grinned. 'To Mongolia, of course. You will finally have the pleasure of seeing the birthplace of the mighty Mongol nation. Genghis Khan is building a capital for his empire on the Orkhon River, at a place called Karakorum. You know, Robyert, how I envy you all your travels in the West; now I shall have the chance to show you the East.'

'I must speak to… uh, I must pay my respects to Sorkoktani Beki. Do you happen to know if she is at leisure in her *ger* today?'

Tolui shook his head in mock sadness. 'My wife will be too busy to see you today, and will be for several days hence. She will also be getting ready for our departure. If you had a message to give her, it might be better if you gave it to her companion, the Lady Sarantuya. I am sure she will pass on your respects to Sorkoktani, and I happen to know that she is at my saddle-maker's tents today. One of my guards will point the way for you.'

And he winked at Robert.

He found Sarantuya standing beside an open-sided tent filled with busy craftsmen, sweating despite the cold and working on the wooden trees and leather coverings of dozens of dismantled Mongol saddles. The whole establishment of General Tolui, it seemed, wanted to refurbish their horse-gear that morning in preparation for the months-long ride to Mongolia. Robert stood as close to Saran as he dared, but he did not touch her.

'You heard about the *kurultai*?' she said, her words barely audible.

'I have just been with Tolui. He says I must attend this assembly in Karakorum or be declared a rebel against Mongol authority. But I do not give a fig for that. I do not even care if the House of Karacha ceases to trade. I will dare to defy the Great Khan, if you ask it of me. I will abandon all I own in Asia, if you wish me to do so.'

'What do you mean?' she said, her dark eyes larger than usual.

'I mean we could gather our possessions, and as much treasure as we can carry and ride west. I have enough for us to live comfortably in Tana, or Venice – anywhere – you and me and Jalair. We would be safe in Tana.'

'You asked me this once before, and I said no. I am a woman of the steppe. My reasons for staying with my own people have not changed.'

'You know that Khuyag will be at the *kurultai*?' said Robert. 'I do not fear him but he will surely seek a confrontation that will likely end in death for one of us.'

'Genghis Khan will be at the *kurultai*. I will beseech my uncle, on my knees, if necessary, to dissolve the marriage between Khuyag and myself. I will ask the Great Khan to join us in matrimony instead. There is nothing else we can do. We *must* go to the *kurultai*, therefore we must face Khuyag. We must find something that Khuyag wants even more than his revenge upon us – and then we will give it to him.'

'I would give to Khuyag everything I own. Every last silver penny. But it will still be extremely perilous at the *kurultai* for you. Are you willing to risk it all?'

'To end our quarrel with Khuyag and be married to you? Of course. To live as a recognised family with you and Jalair? For that, my love, I would risk a thousand deaths.'

–

'I cannot but observe,' said Wilhelm von Eslarn, 'that you appear to be making no effort to bring the Tartar army to Jerusalem, which you claimed was your aim.'

For a blissful moment, Robert had forgotten where he was. In his mind, he was with his beloved Sarantuya in the noisy, muddy Mongol camp south of Samarkand, with the gently tapping hammers of the saddle-makers tinkling in his ears.

The bleak setting of the court in Vienna Castle crashed in on his consciousness. A farrier was shoeing a horse in the courtyard, the hammer blows jarringly loud.

And now this puffed-up German cockerel was crowing at him.

'Indeed,' Wilhelm continued, 'you seem to be far more interested in telling us salacious tales of your adulterous trysts with this Tartar woman and how you made friends with this other fellow, this General Tolui, the barbarian princeling.'

'I am trying to explain, sir, how I came to travel a thousand miles north and east of Samarkand to come into the august presence of Genghis Khan, the Lord of the Steppe, a monarch of multitudes, who ruled all the lands from the Caspian to the coast of Cathay,' Robert snapped. 'By far the most powerful man, at that time, on the face of the Earth.'

The Englishman tried to keep the impatience out of his voice but his frustration with this pedantic official's fatuous interruptions was getting the better of him.

'I was in love with Sarantuya – I have admitted this – and I will further admit that my love for her influenced my plans. But General Tolui was also a powerful man, as powerful, or even more so, as General Subutai, whom I tried and failed to convince to come to Christendom's aid. For Tolui had *thirty thousand men* under his command, sir, and, more importantly, he was the *youngest son* of Genghis Khan.'

'One of the Tartar king's many sons. Why is it significant?' asked Wilhelm.

'Among the Mongols, the *youngest* son inherits from his father,' said Robert. 'The youngest son is known as the *otchigin* – the Prince of the Fireplace – the son closest to his mother's womb, and so closest to the true bloodline. Tolui was the *heir apparent* to Genghis Khan. If, at the *kurultai* that I travelled so long and so far to attend, the Great Khan were to stand down, or to abdicate, as you might say, or if he were to announce that he was dying from some disease, or if he were just to fall off his horse and break his neck, the most likely successor to his crown would be his son Tolui – the man who, with his wife Sorkoktani Beki, protected both Sarantuya and me from the vengeance of our enemy, Khuyag. You need to understand this, sir, so I will repeat it. I knew at that time that if Genghis Khan were to die, his successor as Khan of Khans, Lord of the Steppe, would most likely be my friend General Tolui.'

There was a muttering from the listening crowds on the benches and Robert heard one burgher saying, 'Youngest son?' in wonder to his neighbour.

The Duke of Austria leaned forward in his throne. 'And did the great Tartar king die? He must have. All this, by your telling, occurred many years ago.'

'He did indeed die, Your Grace,' said Robert.

'So did this Tolui, his youngest son, ascend his throne?' asked Duke Frederick.

'If you allow me to continue my tale, Your Grace, I shall tell you.'

'Continue, then,' said the duke. 'But do not take too long about it, the dinner hour approaches and I confess I am extremely sharp set today. Just give us the barest information, man. Spare us all the frivolous, unimportant details, if you please.'

Ivo of Narbonne leaned forward and whispered in the prisoner's ear, 'What His Grace means, my son, is that you must try to be more succinct!'

In return, the Englishman shot the priest a look of white-hot loathing.

–

Tolui garrisoned Samarkand with three *mingghat* of his own troops, three thousand men, and dispatched six other *mingghat* to half a dozen other cities in the Khorasan, in the region to the west of the Amu Daria. Then, in the first days of February, the general set off north and east with his remaining two *tumet* to attend the *kurultai*.

Robert went with him. He bade farewell to his partner Karacha and to his grand house near the China Gate. Suleiman Oktay's packhorses were already loaded up with boxes and barrels of fine goods and silver coin, ready to depart west, and Robert gave the *gerege* to Arslan, and ordered him with four men of his *arban* to escort the Rum merchant's train all the way to the city of Antioch on the Mediterranean, where Ziani's trading ships would meet them and bear the cargo safely onwards by sea to Tana.

Robert and Ziani had agreed before his departure that it was too dangerous to bring the precious fruits of their trading venture over the high Caucasus – Georgia had descended into bloody chaos after its twin defeats by the Mongols, and the lands north of that great mountain range were still infested by gangs of bandits, mostly leaderless men from the broken Cuman and Kipchak armies. And so, the final leg of the journey would be traversed by sea in Ziani's well-armed fleet of trading vessels.

After their arrival in Tana, Arslan and the four troopers were to seek out Subutai and rejoin the Mongol army, wherever it was at that time. The quarrelsome leader of the *arban* seemed mightily impressed by the distinction of bearing the *gerege* and he swore to guard it, and the House of Karacha's precious goods, with great care.

'You do me great honour by entrusting this to me, *ezen*,' said Arslan. Robert was a little surprised to see the pride shining in the steppe warrior's cold black eyes.

'Do not lose it in the desert,' said Robert. 'Or drop it in the deep sea on the voyage. Or give it to anyone else. Return it only to Subutai with my grateful thanks.'

'*Ezen*,' said Arslan reprovingly, 'I would never lose *this* sacred token.'

'I'm only saying be careful with it. Anything might happen.'

'You are wisely observing, I believe, *ezen*, that the steppe is fat.'

'Wide. The steppe is wide,' said Robert, through gritted teeth.

Arslan bowed and turned to go but Robert caught a glimpse of his face as he turned and could not shake the notion that the man was again silently laughing at him.

Robert's own journey north by land to Karakorum was long, slow and frustratingly chaste. There were too many people in the snail-like Mongol columns to make trysts with Sarantuya; too many eyes on him at all hours of the day and night. Indeed, Robert was rarely alone, even for a single moment, for the next three months.

He visited Sorkoktani's *ger* from time to time, and ate there with Tolui, the *beki* and Sarantuya – and much was made of the new baby boy born to the Lady Töregene, a red-faced little ogre, to Robert's eye, who seemed always to be grizzling.

From time to time, his own son Jalair staggered through the *ger* when Robert was there, still unsteady on his plump little legs, and every time the boy appeared in the tent, Robert's heart gave a great lurch of love.

He could not, of course, pick up the boy, or engage with him in any way except the most perfunctory. He knew that the illusion that this was Khuyag's child must be maintained. But, just sometimes, when he had been discreetly watching Jalair at his play, he turned and looked at Sarantuya, and when their eyes met, she offered him the sweetest, most heartbreaking smile. But these happy meetings were few and far between. Robert and his four remaining men – Idar, young Begter, and the twin brothers Saka and Taka – were very soon engaged by General Tolui to act as far-ranging scouts, loosely attached to the veteran Snow Leopard scouting *mingghan*, commanded by a wily old warrior called Boldog.

Robert knew Boldog slightly. This *noyan* had been helpful in the tracking down of his enemy Father Pietro and, while Boldog had initially been suspicious of the Englishman, he now greeted him as a fellow Mongol officer, indeed almost as his equal.

However, Boldog was seriously ill. He had lost a great deal of weight that winter and could only ride with some difficulty and in a great deal of pain. So, while the enormous Mongol column moved tortuously north through the lands east of the Syr Daria, each rider wrapped warmly against the February cold, Boldog loaded many of his routine command duties on to Robert's broad shoulders, as his most trusted subordinate.

The Englishman gladly assumed them, since it took his mind temporarily off Sarantuya and Jalair. Every morning, in the freezing mists of dawn, Robert would consult Boldog, then issue his orders to the *akhmad* of whichever Snow Leopard *jagghun* had been appointed to reconnoitre the road ahead of Tolui's *tumet* that day.

This company of a hundred men rode out to seek ice-free water and what little grazing they could find, and kept a look out for enemies. The *jagghun* of the day was sometimes accompanied by Robert and his men. And, as the weather grew warmer, and days longer, the Englishman went out more frequently with these advance scouts.

He did not find it an arduous duty. The long column moved so slowly – at the ambling pace of the vast herds of horses, sheep and goats that accompanied the Mongols on the march, feeding as they went – that it was rare that more than ten miles was achieved in a single day's march. It was more a migration than a mission. The *kurultai* would take place in late spring, months away. There was plenty of time.

Some days, Robert and his four men would ride out very far ahead of the Mongol column, sometimes fifty miles in advance of it, and in the warming weather they would camp in the open, returning only the next day to deliver their report.

And there was often little to report. The great steppe stretched for ever in all directions, an empty, tree-less land-ocean, which, as the winter snows melted, became briefly a vast meadow filled with tiny, exquisite flowers and thousands of buzzing insects. It was beautiful, he realised. And, perhaps for the first time, he understood why Sarantuya would never leave the steppe and come to live in a crowded town.

Robert was particularly entranced by the marmots he encountered on his scouting missions; comical, inquisitive little rodents, rather like large squirrels, who would pop out of their holes on the steppe in the morning to feed on grasses and play with their young. These creatures would preen themselves, delicately combing their brown fur with their paws in the chilly sunshine, like noble ladies at their toilet.

He knew Mongol boys would hunt these animals for food with thrown stones – and was impressed. Every time he tried to come close to a marmot, moving as stealthily as he could on foot, the rodent would spot him at a spear's throw away, whistle an alarm to his clan, and whisk down into his hole, disappearing completely.

They reached the western shores of Lake Balkhash around St Patrick's Day in March and rested for five days beside that huge body of blue-green water, allowing their herds to graze freely and put on some weight. The Mongol children, excited to shed the irksome discipline of the march, amused themselves by racing their ponies against each other along the edge of the sprawling encampment, shrieking in joy. One night, over dinner with Tolui, in which Robert was served great slabs of freshly caught lake fish, the general invited him to accompany him on a wild-boar hunt the next day. One of Tolui's huntsmen had seen the fearsome animal's sign.

However, when Robert, Tolui and a dozen others rode out to seek their quarry, and diligently followed its trail for some hours, they found to their disappointment that the animal had simply vanished in the reedy, swampy ground by the lake's edge.

'The boar has swum away,' Tolui joked. 'Or drowned himself in the lake.'

They did manage to bag a few ducks, the younger Mongols in the party using slings and throwing sticks to bring a quartet of them down for the general's evening meal, but Robert killed nothing that day. He was delighted, nonetheless, by the excursion because, a little after noon, he glimpsed a male tiger slinking through the reeds. Just a flash of a long, very large, red-and-black body moving across the line of march a good fifty yards away, but, since he had never set eyes on this noble beast before, it pleased him inordinately.

Tolui declared it a sign of good luck.

'The tiger is a *baghatur*,' he told Robert. 'He recognised you as a fellow hero, and a killer of men, so he retreated, declining to do battle with one of his own kind.'

He also managed to snatch a few words with Sarantuya outside Tolui's *ger* that evening, and he learned that Jalair was beginning to speak actual words. But the next day he was summoned back to his duty by Boldog and the long, dull march resumed.

They trekked for another full month across the steppe, heading north and east, the sheep and goats growing fat on the lush spring grass, and the Mongol herdsmen allowing them to move along at their own pace. Robert was struck, again and again, by the extraordinary loveliness of the rolling landscape. He looked up at the immaculate vault of the heavens as he rode and felt the unmistakable presence of God. No wonder, he thought, the Mongols worshipped the Eternal Blue Sky. They were mistaking His perfect creation for the Almighty Himself, but sometimes he, too, felt as if he were riding inside a huge natural cathedral, in one enormous House of God.

Idar and he continued their prayers, at dawn and dusk, but Robert could feel that a part of him was becoming more Mongol, and less English, with every passing mile. Idar, too, was subtly changing on this journey. The Circassian seemed downcast and appeared to miss his homeland more and more the further he rode from it. And one night Robert raised the issue with him.

'The Caucasus does seem very far away this night, lord,' Idar admitted. They were camping in the valley of the Orkhon

River, some thirty miles ahead of the main Mongol column, lying in their blankets on soft beds of cut grass and looking up at the immense speckle of a thousand, thousand diamond stars. 'But I comfort myself by thinking that my wife, Yula, is looking up at this same heaven from her beach at Goro.'

'You miss her very much, I think,' said Robert.

'I miss her like a limb lost to a warrior in battle,' the Circassian said.

Which made Robert think about Sarantuya, Khuyag and the Great Khan's court, and what kind of battles might lie at the end of this long journey. Perhaps a lethal battle with his enemy Khuyag that would mark the end of all his journeys.

At the beginning of May, Robert saw something on the far horizon, a low dark shape with a flat cloud of grey smoke directly above it, created by many thousands of individual cooking fires. He turned his horse and galloped to the nearest Snow Leopard, ordering him to ride to Boldog and tell him they had reached their destination.

–

Genghis Khan had declared he would build his capital city at Karakorum but the Lord of the Steppe was not a man of cities; he was a man of *gers* and horses, scattered herds and hearths enclosed by soft felt walls, and his new capital reflected this.

It had only one wall of yellow, sun-baked mud bricks, reaching up to about waist height, and enclosing a large, square space – two hundred and fifty paces on each side – that delineated the so-called 'city' of Karakorum. And that was it.

There were, as yet, no buildings, no proper streets, no temples for worship, no workshops, houses, shops or food-sellers' stalls. The four gates at the cardinal points were no more than open sections of the low walls. A great mass of *gers*, thousands of them, both large and small, had been pitched inside and outside the enclosure, grouped in roughly concentric rings around the Great Khan's own enormous *ger* on its wheeled base, which stood at the very centre of it all.

Beyond that conglomeration of *gers* were the vast herds of horses and sheep, camels and goats, spread out over an area at least fifty miles wide. A mile to the west of Karakorum flowed the once-mighty Orkhon River, whose crystal waters were now muddied and much depleted by the gathered multitudes of men and beasts.

Tolui sited his own camp two miles out from the walls of the city, to the north, and Robert was soon busy with Boldog and his men exchanging messages between officials of Genghis Khan's court and Tolui's quartermasters and servants.

He was rather surprised to find that the official to whom he reported Tolui's arrival at Karakorum, in a billowing white linen tent near the Great Khan's *ger*, was the tax collector and chief administrator of Samarkand, Yelu Ahai.

This Chinese official was seated before a large table with several piles of documents before him, weighed down by smooth black river stones. He was writing on a piece of flimsy paper, dipping a quill in a pot of black ink and scribbling what looked like a short letter or a brief note. The paper kept flapping in the breeze, and Yelu was using his left hand to hold it in place.

It seemed he remembered Robert.

'Can you write, *Elchin Baghatur*?' he said, without looking up.

'I can,' said Robert, a little irked by the lack of a polite greeting. 'Latin, Greek, the French tongue. Some Arabic, too. But I am not proficient in that script.'

'Uighur?' Yelu asked, indicating the letter before him. He still did not look up.

'No,' said the Englishman.

'That is a pity. I need clever, reliable men who can write Uighur script.'

Yelu Ahai set down the quill, picked up a silver sander and shook a quantity of fine white sand over the paper, then he gently blew the excess granules away, and weighed the letter down with four small pebbles.

Then he finally looked up at Robert.

He smiled and got to his feet, and Robert only recalled then how extremely tall the Chinese man was. A good four inches taller than Robert. And thin with it, which made him seem even more like a beanpole. Yelu stroked his waist-long wispy grey beard as he came stalking round to the front of the big table like a human crane.

He extended his long right hand in welcome.

'I have only thirty-one men who can write in the Uighur script in my employ, and all the lands that Genghis Khan has conquered to administer. I need more literate men, *Baghatur*. I need them badly. I do not suppose that you would care to come and join my Chancery? I can reward you handsomely, and I believe a man like you would be able to learn the Uighur script very quickly – just as you did the Mongol tongue.'

'I'm more skilled with swords than words,' Robert said, shaking Yelu's hand.

'Yet you embraced the unfamiliar role of merchant without difficulty, did you not? I hear from my people in Samarkand that the House of Karacha has been paying a fortune in tax each quarter to the treasury. I congratulate you on your success.'

Robert had also forgotten how clever and well informed Yelu Ahai was.

He said, 'I thank you for your offer but I did not come to discuss the House of Karacha, nor to learn the Uighur script, but merely report the arrival of Lord Tolui.'

'Indeed,' said Yelu. 'And perhaps to seek an audience with the Great Khan?'

Robert swallowed. It seemed this man knew about all his most private affairs. 'I would speak with the Great Khan, when he is at leisure. On a very delicate matter.'

'I have already arranged for you to be received by Genghis Khan tomorrow at noon. After that meeting, I would be obliged if you would report to me to begin your training in the Uighur script. Do not worry, all the materials will be provided: paper, ink, quills, slate and chalk. My clerks will instruct you.'

'I… I am not… That is, I may have other matters that…'

'You have other business you need to transact in Karakorum? Apart from your delicate discussions with the Great Khan, I mean. No? Then you would oblige me by beginning your studies as soon as possible. I need you. I am a good friend to have in Karakorum, *Elchin Baghatur.* You understand? I *could* be a good friend to you or, well… I see you have grasped my point. Good. Then I will see you here tomorrow.'

Robert understood him. Yelu Ahai could be a good friend. Or a bad enemy.

Chapter Eighteen

Genghis Khan, Lord of the Steppe, monarch of multitudes, the most powerful man on Earth, was seated on a soft pink cushion decorated with flowers at the rear of his enormous *ger*, in the heart of his new capital at Karakorum, with his minsters, generals and servants all around him.

As Robert approached him, washed, brushed, shaved and dressed in his best *deel*, with the sword the great man himself had given to him hanging at his waist, he could not suppress a tremor of fear.

With just a few words, the Great Khan could destroy his entire world.

Genghis Khan was a man of ordinary height and build in his early sixties, with narrow, shrewd eyes, and smooth skin lightly tanned by the sun and winds. Both his ears were pierced and twin gold earrings hung from the rather long lobes. His forehead was very high, creased with fine lines, and he wore a plain fur-lined Mongol hat, though the day was quite warm.

Robert bowed before him, and the khan nodded gravely in reply.

'*Elchin Baghatur*, I am happy to see you again. It has been some years, I believe, since we last met. I trust that the House of Karacha prospers.'

'My House prospers, Great One, and I have you to thank for that. But I have not come to you today to discuss trade. I come on a matter of far higher importance.'

'Is that so?' said the Great Khan, lifting his brows. 'What could possibly be of higher importance to a merchant than trade, I wonder?'

Robert knew then that Genghis Khan knew exactly why he had come to him. Indeed, he knew *how* the man had discovered his mission. For sitting three men along from the Great Khan, to his right, giving Robert a furious stare that would have killed him, if looks alone could achieve that, was Noyan Khuyag.

'I'm a man of flesh and blood as well as a merchant,' said Robert. 'And today I come to petition you as such, and beg that you will hear me.'

The Englishman might have been dismayed to see his rival in love in company with the Great Khan, but his courage was bolstered by the fact that at the khan's left hand was his good friend Lord Tolui, who was now grinning at him.

'Speak, then, *Elchin Baghatur.*'

'I would first remind you, O Great One, of the services I have rendered the Mongol nation. I devised a way for the city of Otrar to be captured; I alone found a secret way in to the fortifications for your horsemen. I fought at the Battle of Ray beside Subutai Baghatur, when the Shah of Khwarazmia stood against us, and we defeated him with our valour. And I fought again at the battle of Kalka River in—'

'Yes, yes,' said Genghis Khan impatiently. 'You have rendered us good service, but you have also been richly rewarded – have you not? – with herds and horses, and the title of *baghatur.* I granted you the treaty with Venice that has made you wealthy. I believe even that gold-adorned sword you wear this day was given from my own hand. Tell me what it is you came here to say and do not squander my precious time.'

Robert swallowed. He had no desire to anger the Great Khan, not today.

'I come to humbly petition you to dissolve the marriage between your niece and Noyan Khuyag, and to allow me to take Sarantuya into my *ger* in marriage.'

'No,' shouted Khuyag. 'No, I shall not allow this. I will never consent. Sarantuya is mine, she is my property, granted in marriage to me by the Great Khan. Never will I relinquish her to this foreign-born snake. Instead, I would see her punished for her animal rutting with this wife-stealing *gadaad khun*. My name has been dragged through the mud, trampled on, shat upon… and *he* did the shitting. He came into my *ger*, as a guest, warmly welcomed under my roof for many, many months; and how did he repay my kindness? He seduced my Sarantuya, my wife, the woman I once loved. And the only son of my *ger* is not my own child – but his vile *gadaad khun* spawn. You only have to look at the boy's ugly face, his cold eyes—'

'Enough!' said Genghis Khan. And Robert was pleased to see that Khuyag immediately stopped his ranting, and obediently fell silent.

'The *noyan* here accuses you of seducing his wife, *Elchin Baghatur*, and of making a boy child with her. What do you say to that?'

Robert thought fast. He did not want to lie to the Great Khan, nor did he want to admit that Khuyag's accusations were substantially true.

'I will say this, Great One. I love Sarantuya with all my heart. I would live with her as a husband and care for her, and the child Jalair. I know Khuyag does not love her. Therefore, I humbly beg you, to think of Sarantuya, think of your niece, of her happiness. It is yours to grant – if you dissolve this unhappy union and give her hand in marriage to me.'

Khuyag's face, swollen red from excessive drinking and much scarred from battle, seemed to writhe with his rage. 'She is a filthy bitch-whore who deserves to die,' he said. 'This devious foreigner, too. He must be punished for his insult to me.'

Robert found his right hand creeping towards the hilt of his sword.

'According to the Great Yasa, the Mongol laws you yourself wrote, Great Khan,' said Khuyag, 'the penalty for a woman who sleeps with one who is not her husband is death. A bloodless death, sure, since she is Golden Kin. But I *demand*—'

'Be silent.' The Great Khan did not raise his voice but Khuyag instantly obeyed.

Genghis Khan looked hard at Robert: an icy, perhaps even contemptuous stare.

'If your finger so much as grazes the golden hilt of that sword,' he said quietly, 'I will have you torn limb from limb by four of my strongest horses.'

Robert immediately withdrew his hand, clasping his fingers together.

'If I were to make enquiries,' said the Great Khan, 'would I find you innocent, *Elchin Baghatur*? I do not think so. And our laws, as set down in the Great Yasa for the governance of all Mongols, are very clear on the penalty for this kind of offence.'

'If we speak of the Great Yasa, father,' said Tolui, interjecting for the first time, 'what about your dictum in the laws that all matters of the *ger* should be decided in the *ger*? You used to say that to all your children often when we were growing up, father. You also said that all matters of the steppe must be decided on the steppe.'

Everyone was now staring at Tolui. 'What I am trying to say,' said the khan's youngest son, 'is this quarrel between two men over a woman is not our concern. Whether the *Elchin Baghatur* is guilty of the crime or not, it all took place in Noyan Khuyag's *ger*. It is a matter of the *ger*, to be decided in the *ger*.'

'I will fight Khuyag, if he desires,' said Robert, 'to decide the matter.'

'No,' said the Great Khan. 'I will not permit a duel. This is a matter of law.'

'Then the solution is obvious,' said Tolui. 'Why do we not ask Sarantuya?'

The Lord of the Steppe gave Robert another chilly stare, then he looked at Tolui and made a noise that might have been a grunt of agreement. He turned back to Robert and with a flick of his hand he dismissed the Englishman from his presence.

As Robert swung up on to the back of Bayard outside the *ger*, watched closely by two soldiers of the *kheshig*, the Great Khan's elite unit of bodyguards, he wondered how close he had just come to death. Mere inches away, he suspected. And the danger was very far from over. Now, everything depended on Sarantuya.

-

Surrounded by half a dozen young Chinese clerks, Robert bent to the slate before him, and wielded his stick of chalk. The official was scratching with his own piece of chalk on a much bigger slate propped up on an easel. He was carefully writing out the twenty-two letters of the Uighur alphabet in several vertical columns.

'*Aleph*, *Beth*, *Gimel*, *Heth*...' he chanted as he made the symbols on the slate, indicating the strokes of the letters. Robert dutifully copied them all down.

It was strange to be writing these unfamiliar letters in a vertical line, rather than horizontally, but Robert was intrigued by this style of writing, fully engaged as he always was with a new language. Not that the tongue was unfamiliar. He was learning to write the Uighur letters for Mongol words he already knew, and found it an oddly satisfying exercise.

'No, *gadaad khun*, not like that, like this. *Gimel* must be written just so.'

The official rubbed out Robert's clumsy chalk mark with his thumb and made a neat new mark in its place on his slate.

'Like that,' he said. 'See? You see the difference now? Write it out again.'

For a brief moment, Robert was a child back in the Kentish village of Hadlow, in the musty little chapel beside his father's big, thatched hall, and Father Thomas was laboriously teaching him his Latin ABCs. However, he mused, in Karakorum, his Chinese teacher was unlikely to hit him on the buttocks with his teacher's wand if he made a mistake. On the other hand, if things went badly tomorrow, he might be torn apart by four of the Great Khan's horses. All depended on the meeting between Sarantuya and Genghis Khan the next morning. Robert tried not to think about it, to block the fear from his mind and concentrate on forming his Uighur letters correctly.

Unsuccessfully.

'No, no, *Heth* is drawn like this!' the official cried, correcting him once again.

Robert found it difficult to get to sleep that night in the *ger* he shared with Idar, Begter, Saka and Taka. He drank too much wine and, when he did finally drop off, he dreamed of Gilly and Adorno; the grossly fat Genoese merchant was walking up and down on Gilly's back in Tana, crushing him with his appalling weight. In the dream he tried to push Adorno's frame off Gilbert's body but the Podestà was far too heavy.

He awoke, dry-mouthed and trembling, at mid-morning, wondering whether he would ever manage to take his revenge on the Genoese monster who was responsible for his brother's death. But, as he splashed his face with cold water, and the dream receded, Tana, Soldaya – and indeed, Genoa – all seemed impossibly distant from this *ger* on the steppe.

He could not help but wonder, too, if he would live out this day. And if he, Sarantuya and Jalair, would ever be allowed to live together and be happy.

He saddled Bayard with a growing sense of dread, and rode the two miles south to the 'city' of Karakorum. Once there, he was made to wait outside the *ger* for a full hour, before the Great Khan would deign to see him. And, for the first time, the *kheshig* bodyguards took his sword from him, which he instinctively knew was a very bad sign.

He prayed to St Christopher for the fortitude to face whatever ordeal lay ahead.

Then, at a nod from the guards, and armed only with his faith, Robert strode into the *ger*, his head high. He was determined to face death like a Christian, like a martyr of old.

He would not show his fear. He would show them how an Englishman dies.

Genghis Khan was standing with Sarantuya on the far side of the *ger*, and the first glimpse of her took his breath away, as it so often did. She was dressed in a green silk gown patterned with yellow storks that accentuated the lean lines of her body and her lustrous hair was gathered above her head in an elaborate arrangement, with sprays of yellow flowers and creamy pearls clustered in her coal-black locks.

She had made up her face with white powder, lined her large eyes with kohl and reddened her lips with some substance. He had never seen her look more enchanting.

The Great Khan also seemed to find her captivating. He smiled and reached out and touched her elbow as they talked. Then he turned to face Robert and his expression changed. The warm smile was gone, his face now a mask of cold rage.

Robert stopped dead, frozen by the force of his savage look. He bowed very low.

'I have many things to say to you this day, *Elchin Baghatur*,' said Genghis Khan. 'The first is that you shall no longer be referred to by that title. You are no longer an envoy from the court of Venice. You have been generously given what you desired and, so long as I am Great Khan, you will no longer represent a foreign land.'

Robert was shocked by his brutal words. But he had nothing to say in reply.

'You should also know that, this morning, in front of the whole court, I declared Sarantuya to be my daughter. I have formally adopted her into my own family.'

Robert nodded, as if he fully understood, which he did not, but had just enough wit to remain silent and simply listen. He glanced over at Sarantuya, who offered him a tiny smile from her red-painted lips. But the Great Khan was still speaking to him.

'You came to our lands, into our Ulus, and were taken in by Noyan Khuyag, who treated you with honour and generosity, welcoming you into his *ger*, inviting you to share his hearth. You repaid his kindness by stealing away the affections of his wife. I say nothing of whether you lay with her, nor do I ask whether the child Jalair is, in truth, yours. Those crimes are punishable with death. Now you ask to marry my daughter Sarantuya and deprive Khuyag of a good wife. And for that you must pay.'

Robert nodded again, his mind awhirl. Yet Sarantuya was still smiling at him.

'You will pay Noyan Khuyag five hundred horses for the grave offences committed against his honour, and to compensate him for the loss of a beautiful wife. You will pay this fine to him within the cycle of one moon and, if you fail to do so, I will have your body pulled apart in front of the whole Mongol army by four horses.'

Robert reeled with relief. He would not be executed *now*, that was the point he grasped. And while five hundred ponies was a steep price, he certainly had the means to pay it.

'I have promoted Noyan Khuyag for his good and faithful service to command one of my finest *tumet*. He is now a general and, in future, should your paths cross again, you will treat him with all the respect and deference that his rank demands.

'I do not wish to see any quarrelling or bloodshed. I shall hold you personally responsible if any trouble does occur. Do you understand me? Good. Now, about this marriage. Were I to grant you the hand of my *daughter*,' the khan leaned on the word, 'what would you offer me in return for this honour – a far greater one than you deserve?'

Robert cleared his throat. His mind was still whirling. 'Anything you ask,' he said. 'Horses, herds, gold, whatever you desire, Great One, I shall gladly render to you.'

'I want service,' said the Great Khan. 'I want your true and faithful service. I want your oath to serve me in all my wars, as a scout, as a soldier, as a commander of my men – even as my envoy, should I choose to appoint you in that role. I want *all of you*, in exchange for the hand of my sweet daughter. You will be mine, not a creature of the Doge of Venice, not a greedy Samarkand merchant, ever grubbing for silver, not a *gadaad khun* with designs on capturing the city of Baghdad. My servant only.'

Robert swallowed. 'For how long?' he asked.

'For the whole of my life, or all of yours,' he said. 'Will you give me that?'

Robert knew he was trapped. He could not refuse the Great Khan. Neither could he flee. He was many thousands of miles from Christendom and his own kind; and he would be hunted down by the *kheshig* riders before he got a hundred miles from here.

On the other hand, he was being offered his heart's desire. His lovely Sarantuya.

'I accept,' he said, 'for the sake of my love, you shall have my sacred oath.'

–

There was shock in the packed hall in Vienna Castle when Robert said these words.

The little Dominican friar, Geoffrey of Beaulieu, leapt up from his chair.

'You claim you were then still a member of the Templar Order,' the friar said, walking towards Robert, 'under secret orders from Jean de Malemort to recruit a Mongol army to ride west to the aid of the Latin kingdoms in Outremer. Yes?'

'That is indeed so,' said Robert.

'Yet, not only did you give your sacred oath to a foreign warlord, a powerful Tartar king, but you also took a heathen to wife? Am I understanding you correctly?'

'That is also correct.'

'How then can you claim you have not betrayed your own Christian Order, and flouted its most sacred laws? How can you continue to insist that you are not, as the provost says, a foresworn turncoat and traitor to all of Christendom?'

'I was given special dispensation,' said Robert, 'by Jean de Malemort. The Seneschal said to me that it might be that, in the pursuit of my holy mission, I should have to lie or make false oaths. He said God would forgive me, since I did His work.'

'And did you then make a *false* oath to this Great Khan? And when you made your marriage oaths to this Mongol woman, were they also false?'

Robert had the grace to look shamed. His thin, pale face flushed red.

'I… I kept my oath to Genghis Khan. I served him loyally until the day he died. And I kept my marriage oath to Sarantuya. I love her, still, to this day, and have never loved another woman. I believe I served the Templar Order faithfully, as well.'

'How do you reconcile serving a heathen lord and serving Christendom at the same time? How can any man have two masters? Two masters who are enemies?'

'I had a plan. A secret plan, which I believed would bring the Mongol strength to bear on the Saracen enemies of Christendom. But I knew it would take much more time to achieve than either I or Jean de Malemort had first foreseen. Many years.'

'What then was this secret plan?' asked Geoffrey de Beaulieu. 'Tell us all.'

Chapter Nineteen

Robert and Sarantuya were married by a Nestorian priest, a solemn young Mongol with his head shaven in the tonsure, who spoke the holy words in the Mongol tongue in front of a plain wooden cross in the round felt tent that served as the Nestorian church in Karakorum. Then, and only to please Sarantuya, their union was blessed by a holy man of the Naiman tribe, who had a reputation for casting powerful spells and making women fertile.

This fellow, an ancient, bald, monkey-like creature, with a garishly painted face, leapt and capered in front of Robert and Sarantuya, uttering high shrieks, which were his form of prayers. He was dressed in a voluminous yak hair cloak adorned with tiny bells and many dried animal bones, and the feathers of ravens and eagles, too, and he danced and capered around a fire, wafting pungent smoke towards the happy couple.

As Robert watched his heathen antics, he knew that this fellow would have been swiftly hanged as a witch at home in England, yet he endured the ceremony, just as he endured his sacred oath to the Great Khan, for love of his wonderful new wife.

He paid his fine to Khuyag the day after taking the oath, dispatching Begter, Saka and Taka to deliver the five hundred ponies, purchased from the khan himself.

Robert decided that he would not meet the former *noyan*; when this bride price was delivered to him, he took Genghis Khan's admonition to avoid bloodshed with Khuyag very seriously and wished to avoid any confrontation. Sarantuya's former husband also seemed eager to stay clear of Robert's path. It seemed that the Great Khan had warned Khuyag, too, not to seek revenge and to let the matter rest.

But since the cost of five hundred steppe ponies meant nothing to Robert, and being wed to Saran meant everything, the Englishman counted himself the winner.

They set up a home together in a spacious new *ger* – a lavish wedding gift from Genghis Khan – near Tolui's hearth two miles north of Karakorum. The new tent was big enough to house Robert, Sarantuya, her maid Anya, as well as Idar, Begter, Saka and Taka, with men and women having different sections to sleep, eat and relax in.

Robert and Sarantuya slept together in the central part of the tent, near the back, and it was bliss to be able to lie with her every night in tranquillity, without fear of discovery, although Robert did rig a curtain up around their bed to give them some privacy in their lovemaking – something Saka and Taka thought hilariously prudish.

For a month, they did little, tending to Sarantuya's herds, which gave them their living, sleeping, making love and idling most of the day. Robert took Jalair out riding in the first week and was astonished to see that the boy was able to sit on his pony unaided and even seemed to relish the gallop. He played with him, hiding games, or with a ball and a stick, and every day his love for his cheerful little son grew stronger.

Then, a month after the marriage ceremony, Genghis Khan summoned Robert to his *ger*, sending one of his *kheshig* men to fetch him. The *kheshig*, the *tumen* of royal bodyguards, was comprised of the Day Guard, called the *turghaut,* and the Night Guard or *kabtaut*. The *turghaut* trooper who came to collect him that morning was a tall, broad-shouldered, good-looking fellow – and very arrogant, as he had the right to be.

These *kheshig* were the finest of Genghis Khan's troops – the bravest, strongest and best trained. Even the lowliest *kheshig* trooper outranked the highest officer of any other unit. So

Robert followed the man meekly as they rode the two miles into the half-built city and up towards the red lacquered door of the Great Khan's tent.

Robert paid special attention that day to the *kheshig* when he arrived at the *ger*, more attention than he had ever paid them before. He had noted that there were two score of them in a loose outer screen a hundred yards away from the khan's *ger*; men whose permission must be sought before anyone could come close to the Great Khan.

There were two more *kheshig* posted outside the door of the royal *ger*, and a dozen others posted round the outside of the massive wheeled tent, all armed with swords, spears and bows. Inside the huge *ger*, Robert noted there were two *turghaut* standing on either side of the Great Khan at all times, always within a couple of paces. He had never truly noticed these grim men before, since they never spoke nor interacted with those granted an audience. However, anyone harbouring hostile intent, Robert reckoned, would have to battle and defeat at least seventy elite warriors before he could even hope to come within striking distance of the Great Khan.

'I see married life is to your liking,' said the khan. 'There is more colour in your face, and more weight on your belly. A new light in your eyes, too. I congratulate you.'

The same could not be said of the Great Khan. Robert had heard the Lord of the Steppe had had a fall from his horse two weeks ago. It seemed that he had not yet fully recovered from the accident. That day, he looked all of his sixty-two years.

'I cannot thank you enough, Great One. Your daughter and I are truly happy at last.'

'Well, do not get too comfortable in your nest, I shall need you very soon.'

'As you command, Great Khan.'

'You will remember that when we last spoke, I said you might no longer call yourself *Elchin Baghatur*, since you were no more an envoy of a foreign power.'

'I remember it,' said Robert, a cold hollow beginning to form in his stomach.

'Therefore, I have chosen a new name and title for you,' said the khan, smiling at the Englishman. 'Henceforth, you shall be called *Noyan* Robyert Baghatur.'

'*Noyan?*'

'Have you not heard? Noyan Boldog is dead. He died two days ago. He is with Tenggri until his rebirth into a healthy Mongol baby, when the great god decrees it.'

'I am sorry to hear it,' said Robert.

'Do not be. The Snow Leopards are now yours. You are their new *noyan*.'

Robert found himself speechless.

'Tomorrow, at the grand assembly, I shall announce in which direction my *tumet* will ride. I am sure you will have heard all the rumours. We march on Cathay. In the autumn, we will throw our full strength at the Tanguts of the Hexi Empire and bring them under my control. And you, Noyan Robyert Baghatur, shall be the iron tip of my fleetest arrow. I want you to take the Snow Leopards in hand and train them up to a high pitch of readiness this summer here in Karakorum. Come the autumn, when it is cooler, the Snow Leopards will scout a route for the whole army through the Gobi. We will fall on the Tanguts from the north and annihilate them. Is that clear, *Noyan*?'

'As you command, Great Khan,' said Robert.

'You have the summer to prepare the Snow Leopards. We march in four months. Now, you have leave to depart. Go and give my beautiful daughter a kiss from me.'

-

'It makes sense, of course,' said Tolui. 'The old man has a long-standing quarrel with the Tangut rulers of Hexi. An unsettled score, you might say. He had an alliance with them going way back and then he asked them to supply troops for the war in Khwarazmia. They refused. Their arrogant Tangut envoy had the temerity to say that if Genghis Khan was not strong enough to go to war against the Khwarazmian Empire alone, then he should not go to war at all. My father was furious but he had no time then to deal with them. Now we hear they are trying to make a treaty with the Jin, their eastern neighbours, until recently their bitter foes. The Jin are our enemies, too; but the Tangut used to be our allies. We cannot have them uniting against us.'

Robert nodded. His knowledge of these eastern lands was vague, just what he had picked up from his fellow Mongol officers. He knew that due south of the wide steppe of the Mongol heartland was a vast desert a thousand miles east to west and five hundred north to south – the Gobi, it was called – and on the other side of the desert there were three different Chinese empires in the region known as Cathay.

The closest Chinese state, to the south of the desert, was the Hexi Empire, which had long been ruled by the ferocious Tangut tribe. To the east of them, was the Jin Empire, ruled by a people called the Jurchen, which stretched to the Eastern Sea. And south of the Jin was yet another Cathay state, which called itself the Song Empire.

'We smashed the Jin armies, oh, more than a dozen years ago,' continued Tolui, 'but some people just do not know when to stay down.' The general was grinning at Robert, a sure sign that a joke was trundling inexorably from his brain to his lips. 'Why is it that people cannot stay conquered, Robyert? It would save us Mongols a lot of sweat. You've heard about the Khorasan, I suppose. Those mad followers of the Prophet down there have rebelled again. You turn your back for a moment and…'

Robert laughed dutifully. He liked Tolui but sometimes he found his clumsy jesting a little wearing. The Englishman had gone to visit his friend immediately after his momentous audience with the Great Khan and they had settled down comfortably in his *ger* with a large bowl of wine each, to be swigged over the rattling dice tray.

'Do you think the Great Khan will now go back west to subdue the Khorasan?'

Tolui took a sip of his wine, thinking. 'He might do, if the Tangut are quickly defeated and the Hexi Empire conquered. I would, if I were him. In truth, I would leave the Tangut alone and turn the whole army round and head back down there.'

He threw the dice and cursed his luck. Then he said, 'Or I would at least send Ogedei or one of the other *orlok* with five or six full *tumet*. I think, ultimately, our future lies in the West.' He grinned at Robert. 'For one, the wine is so much better in Persia. Have you tasted that Chinese piss-water?'

Sorkoktani came to them then with the wine jug, to replenish their bowls.

'You drink too much already, husband,' she said, pouring him more wine. 'But I, too, would like to see us based in Persia and beyond, when it has all been pacified. I would like, of all things, to see the holy city of Jerusalem at least once,' she said, looking directly at Robert. 'To walk in the holy footsteps of Jesus Christ. Would that not be a very fine thing?'

Robert nodded and smiled at her, holding out his bowl for more wine.

'I shall take you, Suki,' said Tolui lovingly, 'wherever this Jerusalem place is.'

'If Tolui ever becomes Great Khan,' said Sorkoktani, 'we will make sure we have the Khorasan and all those intriguing Western lands securely under our control.'

'Why do you say *if*?' asked Robert. 'Lord Tolui is *otchigin* – he is the Prince of the Fireplace; surely he must inherit the Ulus of the Great Khan when he dies?'

'It is very likely,' said Sorkoktani. 'But, by our laws the Great Khan must be elected by the other khans and the Golden Kin. My husband has the best claim as *otchigin*, but if Genghis Khan were to nominate another, or, if the khans were to deem Tolui unfit, someone else might become the khan in his stead. Ogedei, the Great Khan's third son, is very close to his father, for example. They might decide that he was the better choice. But he drinks even more than you do, husband, and Ogedei may have expired from an excess of wine long before Genghis Khan is in his grave – many years from now, of course.'

'Of course,' said Robert.

-

All that summer, Robert trained with the Snow Leopards. He tried to impart to the *akhmad*, the ten captains of his ten *jagghut*, all he knew of scouting and stealth. Which was considerable. But, in truth, there was little to teach these men that they did not already know. They were a scouting *mingghan* and their role had always been to ride ahead of the *tumet* and find a path through whatever dangers lay before them.

Robert took them out many hundreds of miles northwards into the fringes of the forest lands, and they climbed cold, bare mountains and forded white-flecked rushing rivers, all the while getting to know each other well as commander and subordinates.

The Snow Leopards impressed Robert with their speed of movement and their stamina. They obeyed his orders swiftly, too. Idar and the three Mongols from his *arban* became Robert's *de facto* staff, along with Kolgen, the man who had been Boldog's lieutenant, and who had worked with Robert on the march from Samarkand.

When the Snow Leopards returned to Karakorum to rest their tired horses and repair their worn-out kit, Robert had the leisure to resume his Uighur writing lessons with the clerks of the Mongol chief minister, Yelu Ahai. He understood now, why the tall official had forced him to learn this script. He would need to be able to write out messages when he was scouting far ahead, and send them back to the army. In order to do that, he must learn to write a script that a commander, or his clerks, could read.

Robert was, in truth, a diligent scholar. He set his mind to the task and, within a few months, he had mastered this strange, squiggling, vertical script. He had always found languages interesting. And Yelu, once, passing by the little school of Chinese recruits, even praised his penmanship in front of the whole class, saying that he was a born clerk. Which both pleased – and utterly dismayed – the proud Templar knight.

Subutai Baghatur and his two *tumet* arrived at Karakorum in high summer, when the grass was beginning to wither on the steppe. The veteran general had fought several battles with the Volga Bulgars on his way back east from the Rus' lands and, while he had eventually triumphed, he had also lost a large number of men to his foes. General Jebe, Robert discovered, had been killed fighting a heroic rearguard action along with thousands of other Mongols. Robert said a prayer for them all.

Genghis Khan welcomed his returning general with a great feast for a hundred Mongol commanders, to which Robert was also invited, and at that long debauch, the Great Khan decreed that summer games would take place the next week so that the young Mongol riders could demonstrate their prowess in horsemanship, archery and wrestling – the Three Manly Sports, as the Mongols called them – and that the best of them would then be recruited into Subutai's depleted *tumet*. Karakorum resounded that week with stories of Subutai's exploits, of how he had led his men in a great circle around the Sea of Ravens and returned to the Mongol heartlands with knowledge of many strange foreign lands. Rightly was he called *baghatur*, all Mongols agreed.

Subutai greeted Robert with a warm hug, a gust of old wine and congratulations on his promotion to *noyan*. The old general insisted on inspecting the Snow Leopard *mingghan* personally, riding out to their encampment the next day, badly hungover, to perform this task. Nonetheless, Subutai declared them to be superb troops, the finest he had seen in years, which, though he knew it to be flattery, pleased Robert greatly.

'Who would have thought,' Subutai said, 'that you would rise to be a *noyan* of such a fine *mingghan*, and Genghis Khan's son-in-law. Perhaps I should not be surprised, Robyert – the cream of the yak's milk always rises to the top of the bucket.'

With Subutai and his army came three of his troopers, Arslan, Hasar and Khuchar, who had escorted the pack-train safely back to Ziani. The other two members of his old *arban* had sadly been killed in a great battle with the Bulgars.

Arslan had brought Robert a thick and slightly blood-smeared letter from Ziani, and, as Sarantuya and Anya busied themselves making a vat of *shulen* to feed the new arrivals, Robert sat in his place at the rear of his *ger* and opened up the wad of papers.

'*Greetings, my friend,*' the letter began:

> *I dispatch this to you with your trooper Arslan, who has promised faithfully to deliver it to you wherever he may find you, and I pray daily to Almighty God it shall be safely received soon.*
>
> *Alas, I have bad news to impart, Roberto, concerning your enemy and mine: Barisone Adorno. The Podestà of Genoa has neither forgotten nor forgiven the utter destruction of Soldaya by your Mongols, and has placed a reward on your head: ten thousand deniers for the man who kills you or delivers you to his palace in Genoa.*

Sarantuya came over to him and handed him a steaming bowl.

'From your merchant friend in Tana?' she asked. Robert nodded distractedly, as he accepted the hot food.

Ziani's letter continued:

> *It also seems that Adorno has learned through his spies of the routes we have chosen for transporting our goods and valuables between Tana and Samarkand. And he has already taken a measure of revenge against us. In April last, a dozen masked men attacked the warehouse in*

Antioch where I had been storing the valuables I intended to send out by packhorse train to Samarkand.

The unknown attackers murdered two of our night watchmen, broke into the warehouse and set a great fire which raged uncontrollably till dawn. A large quantity of high-quality items belonging to the House of Karacha, including woollen textiles, rare and expensive dyes, a large quantity of fine wine and various other comestibles, weapons and armour, and jewels and precious metals were destroyed in the fire.

Prince Bohemond, the lord of Antioch, has ordered his constable to investigate, but no culprits have so far been identified. However, I have discovered independently from my informants that Barisone Adorno was behind this appalling crime. I include a list of the items destroyed, and the ruinous cost to us, in the attached appendix.

Robert quickly glanced at the last page of the letter and saw a long list of items in Ziani's spidery writing, and an amount written at the bottom of the page. A truly enormous sum. One that might even come close to breaking the House of Karacha.

He took a sip from his bowl of *shulen* and continued reading.

Yet even worse than the loss of the goods and treasures in the warehouse fire, Adorno has sent his agents to visit the Turkish merchant Suleiman Oktay. Adorno's henchmen cornered him and threatened to burn down all his grain-storage silos in Antioch and in Constantinople, which would ruin him; furthermore, these villains threatened to murder his two full-grown sons, and slay his four tiny grandchildren, if Suleiman Oktay has any more dealings with the House of Karacha.

Suleiman told me this himself in Tana, weeping and apologising as he did so. But he said that he no longer dared to transport goods for our House to Samarkand. He knows just how powerful Adorno is – and how ruthless. Even my most extravagant promises to triple his fee could not move him.

So, this is the situation, my friend. We have suffered a set-back and a heavy loss. And while it is true that we may recover from that financial loss in time, I fear that Adorno may still not be content with the revenge he has wrought. I believe he will still seek to harm us and our House again in the future. Far more seriously, we now have no reliable merchant willing to transport our goods and money from Europe to Asia, and back again. And no secure warehouse in which to store them in Antioch, before shipping them on to Tana or anywhere else in Christendom.

It pains me to send you this sad news, Robert, particularly since I know you are fully engaged with important Mongol affairs and your new family. However, I do have a solution that may be a small step towards restoring the fortunes of our House.

Chapter Twenty

'How do you feel, Idar, about crossing the Gobi with me and the Snow Leopards?' asked Robert. 'Do you wish to go south from here and fight in the Great Khan's war against the Hexi Empire? I can guarantee you that there will be a great deal of loot.'

The Circassian looked away to the side, just once and very quickly, but Robert spotted it. Then Idar looked him straight in the eye and said, 'I am at your service, lord. If that is what you require of me, then I am more than willing...'

They were in Robert's *ger* and the rest of his household was preparing for bed. The Englishman and Idar were sitting together by the warm iron stove.

'I have my answer,' said Robert. 'I know you do not like it out here in the Eastern wilderness, Idar, and feel the pull of civilisation. So let me tell you something that I think will make you happy: Signor Ziani has written to me with an interesting proposal, which I am minded to implement, if you are prepared to play your part.'

'I cannot deny it,' said Idar. 'I would like to see my wife Yula and my daughters again, and to sleep in a soft bed. And bathe in a tub filled with near-scalding soapy water. I would eat bread and fried eggs again, vegetables and roast pork...'

So Robert outlined Niccolò Ziani's plan. Idar would return to Samarkand and train with Karacha as his merchant-apprentice for six months, over the autumn and winter, to learn everything he could about their business. While he was doing this, he would also recruit a company of horse-warriors, perhaps as many as a hundred men-at-arms. There were plenty of former cavalrymen from the wars in Khwarazmia in and around Samarkand, and Robert told him that he must use his best judgement as to whether he could trust these masterless men to be true and faithful to their House.

Lord Karacha could help him with his recommendations, but the choice was to be Idar's alone. Once he had learned the rudiments of their trade and recruited the men, he would use these riders to protect the packhorse train that carried their cargo west.

Idar would accompany the train overland the whole way back to Tana, through Khwarazmia, the Khorasan, through Georgia and over the high Caucasus – he should feel free to recruit his own Circassian kin in the hill country, if he chose, and of course he might visit his neglected wife, so long as the valuable cargo was kept safe.

Idar would be well rewarded for this task – paid a one-hundredth part of the value of the cargo, when it reached its destination. Once he reached Tana, after a suitable pause for rest and recuperation, he would make the return journey to Samarkand with his hundred men and whatever cargo Ziani desired him to take back east to Karacha.

'If all goes well,' said Robert, 'after five or six journeys, back and forth, you would become a rich man. Perhaps you might wish to buy a share in our House and become a part-owner of the concern along with Ziani, Karacha and me. Or you could buy that land in the hills you spoke of and settle there and tend sheep with Yula and your girls until God eventually calls you to Him. You would be free to do anything.'

It amused Robert to see Idar trying to hide his joy.

'Two hundred horsemen,' the Circassian said. 'The road west is a long and dangerous one and we will be carrying valuable loads. Bandits will sniff us out like a freshly roasted haunch of lamb. Two hundred men-at-arms will make us far safer. And fighting men are cheap. Many of them now would kill for a decent hot meal.'

'Very well. Two hundred. But you must only hire the best. And you will swear on the Bible that you will complete six journeys, back and forth, before you hang up your sword and take up your sheep pasture in the hills.'

'Five return journeys or five years' of service, whichever is the less,' said Idar.

'Done,' said Robert, and he grasped the Circassian's right hand in his.

–

Robert stood in the bed of an empty ox-wagon, with Jalair on his shoulders and Sarantuya by his side, along with General Tolui, Sorkoktani Beki and Lady Töregene, Ogedei's wife. They were all looking over the heads of the shifting crowds of holiday-making Mongols around them. It gave Robert pleasure simply to stand in public beside Sarantuya as her lawful husband, and not to have to pretend that he was anything but that. And Jalair's excited bouncing on his neck filled his heart with happiness.

It was the first day of the *kurultai* games and a glorious sun beat down on the heads of this multitude of Mongols. The excitement in the crowd, dressed in their best clothes in hues of red, green and blue, was palpable. Many had been drinking *airaq* since dawn and were in fine, boisterous spirits.

Robert's party had watched the archery and the horse races in the morning, and the Englishman had been particularly proud to see his Snow Leopards trounce the Black Falcons in the short-distance relay race. It had been a simple contest, with five picked horsemen from the two competing *mingghat* riding in relays round a ten-foot pole planted two miles away on the steppe, passing a baton to teammates at the run.

His lieutenant, Kolgen, had thundered triumphantly over the finish line just a length ahead of the Black Falcon rider, and he had received raucous cheers and his prize, a pair of silver stirrups, from the generous hand of the Great Khan himself.

Idar had quit Karakorum two days before the games began, travelling with the Blue Yak *mingghan*, part of one of Subutai's *tumet*, which had been ordered down to Burkhara to reinforce the understrength garrison in that city. Prince Jalal al-Din, son of the deceased Shah Muhammad, was said to be raising an army in the Khorasan to rid themselves of Mongol rule in that troubled region. Robert had embraced Idar, thanked him for his service and given him a fat pouch of gold bezants as a payment for his labours, and six letters for Karacha and Ziani. Then he bade him farewell.

Idar made Robert a gift, too, before he departed – his Circassian dagger. He had asked the Mongol saddlers to fashion a kind of holster for it, so that the long, slim weapon could always be carried, upside down under Robert's left arm, well hidden inside his voluminous Mongol *deel.*

'Signor Ziani ordered me to guard your life,' said Idar. 'But since I can no longer perform that duty, I give you my blade. May it preserve you from all harm.'

Robert had been deeply touched. He knew what the dagger meant to Idar.

The sun was high and it was time for the wrestling – the traditional sport known as the *Bökh* to Mongols – and in front of the ox-wagon a large oval space had been marked out on the ground with chalk-whitened ropes. Saka, stripped to the waist, his muscular white torso slathered with mutton grease, had just hurled his meaty, half-naked opponent to the earth, to the gratified roar of many thousands of spectators.

This was Saka's second bout, and while he was nominally a Golden Eagle, he was fighting under the tall, fluttering *sulde* of the Snow Leopards this day, the standard which was planted near the ox-wagon of Robert's party. His twin brother, Taka, had also entered the competition, and while he had done well in the early rounds Taka had been forced to retire from the wrestling oval two bouts ago, with a pulled muscle in his lower back and a ferocious scowl of frustration on his sun-bronzed face.

Saka, though, had won his latest bout convincingly and was duly cheered to the heavens by the crowd, and Robert added his own carrying voice to the tumult of adulation. The Englishman knew very little about the *Bökh*. He had seen troopers grappling with each other, stripped to the waist, to settle petty scores or simply for fun, but he had never been interested enough to learn the rules. It seemed the object was to force your opponent to touch the ground with any part of his body above the waist. Dropping down to one knee was permitted, striking, biting and choking were not, but apart from that, wrestlers were free to do anything to put their enemy down.

As he cheered and watched Saka proudly strut round the perimeter of the large oval enclosure, lifting his arms high in triumph, Robert saw a new contestant enter the square, and make the traditional bird-like flapping motions with his arms. This was to claim the god-like status of an eagle, Tolui had whispered to him earlier, but also so that the new competitor could get the hot blood flowing freely into his arms.

It was Khuyag, stripped to the waist and exposing his powerful white body. The general's muscles were clothed in a thick layer of blubbery fat, and marked with many scars, indents and burn marks here and there – all earned honourably in battle – but there could be no denying that he was an extremely strong man, and in his prime.

General Khuyag stopped in front of the ox-wagon, staring up at the occupants. He flapped his big eagle-arms again, singing the traditional entrance song in a nasal drone – a ditty about subjugating all his cowardly foes and bringing undying honour to his illustrious ancestors. He seemed to be singing directly at Robert, taunting him.

The Englishman stared back at him impassively; their eyes locked in hatred.

Khuyag eventually moved away, strolling round the perimeter of the oval, flapping his thick white arms, singing his song, inviting the crowds to cheer him.

And they duly obliged. The cry of 'Khuyag… Khuyag… Khuyag…' echoed across the broad steppe. Robert had not realised quite how popular the man was.

On the far side of the oval, a small black leather awning had been set up over a wooden dais on which three large chairs had been placed. Genghis Khan sat in the middle chair with General Subutai on his right and Lord Ogedei on his left, the Great Khan's overweight son slouched in his chair, sunk right down, half-asleep, seemingly bored by the day's events. In comparison to his well-padded son, the Lord of the Steppe cut a much slighter figure. He was wrapped up in a heavy woollen *deel*, with a red dragon pattern on the sleeves, although the summer's day was pleasantly warm.

Each wrestler who wished to compete had a second, a friend or comrade, who dressed in a long, formal blue tunic with a special cap topped with a crimson tassel as his badge of office. Robert noticed Khuyag's second going over to the royal dais and bowing before Genghis Khan. Something inaudible was asked, the khan responded with a question, and the second replied. The Great Khan gave the man a brisk nod.

The two seconds conferred briefly in the centre of the oval, agreed on some point of order, bowed politely to each other, then called out to the two combatants.

Khuyag and Saka faced each other in the centre of the combat area.

Khuyag was several inches taller than Saka, and a good deal heavier. The wine he was so fond of had thickened his white belly, barrel chest and bull neck but had also surely dulled his wits. Saka was a stocky fellow, young, strong, eager to fight. They circled each other warily, hands open, ready to grapple. Robert heard a voice to his left call, 'Get him, Saka. Put him down in the dust!' And then recognised it as his brother Taka's voice. Other men echoed the encouragement.

Robert shouted, 'A purse of silver, Saka, if you win this bout.'

Saka looked at Robert and grinned. At that moment Khuyag attacked. He charged forward, seized Saka by his left shoulder and belt on the right side and tried to twist him sideways, off balance, and hurl him to the earth.

But Saka was skilled in this art, he immediately dropped his weight by bending his knees, came up thrusting with all the strength in his powerful thighs and shoved Khuyag away, the general staggering backwards, nearly tripping over his own feet.

But Khuyag did not trip. He regained his balance and came in again, and he and Saka grasped each other and began to heave, both trying to shift the other off his balance. They were locked tight for a dozen heartbeats, a titanic battle taking place with little motion but the twitching of muscles as each tested the other's strength.

Then Saka pulled Khuyag forward, a sudden jerk, twisted his torso and tried to pull the bigger man over. But Khuyag resisted, locking his feet, his right hand came loose, and Saka lost his grip, too, then, as they both tried to re-establish contact, Robert saw it: an illegal move, so swift it was lost in the flurry of reaching, grappling hands.

A slap.

Khuyag slapped Saka's left knee on the inside, a lightning blow, and very hard, disguised as a fumbling grab at his belt. He saw Saka buckle as his knee gave way under him. He faltered, trying to regain his balance, but Khuyag bent low, grabbed his other knee, and simply lifted, pulling the lighter man up in the air and over – and Saka crashed on to the ground, his shoulders raising puffs of dust from the dry dirt.

The crowd was roaring Khuyag's name.

Robert tugged Tolui's sleeve. 'He slapped him,' he said. 'Khuyag struck Saka.'

'What?' said Tolui.

'He cheated. Khuyag cheated.'

Tolui just shrugged. The crowd was still feting a triumphant Khuyag who was walking round the oval perimeter with both his thick white arms lifted in victory.

Saka climbed slowly to his feet, shaking his head ruefully at his defeat. Khuyag came to stand in front of the ox-wagon, his arms still up high.

He looked directly at Robert. Then lowered one arm and pointed at him.

'You, *gadaad khun*,' he said loudly. 'You and me – a bout before everyone.'

Robert felt a touch on his arm. He turned and saw that one of the burly Day Guards was now standing below the wagon reaching up to him to get his attention. The *turghaut* said, 'The Great Khan gives you permission to take part in the *Bökh*, if you desire. But there will be no shame if you refuse, as you do not know our sport.'

Robert understood what the second had been asking before the match with Saka: that if Khuyag won, he would be permitted to challenge Robert.

Robert looked at Khuyag standing there, his chin out-thrust. His big, fleshy torso streaked with sweat and dust, an ugly smirk on his thick purple lips.

'There is great skill to the *Bökh*,' said Tolui. 'You do not possess it. The khan has said there will be no shame. You do not have to fight him.'

'Oh, but I do,' said Robert.

–

Robert faced his opponent in the centre of the oval. He had stripped down to the pair of baggy Turkish trousers he wore tucked into his soft, kidskin boots. Tolui had been correct: he did not possess any skill at the *Bökh*, but his Templar trainers had insisted that he learn all the basics of European grappling. Their philosophy had been that a Templar knight should be able to defend himself with all weapons – and with none.

A few voices were shouting for him by his old title *Elchin Baghatur*, others, mainly the Snow Leopards, were calling out for their Noyan Robyert to triumph. A similar number of voices were calling for Khuyag, who was grinning horribly at him.

They circled each other, hands open, ready to grapple, their fingers flexed.

'I shall snap your skinny neck, *gadaad khun*,' said Khuyag. 'I shall pay you out in full for your treachery when you were a guest in my *ger*.'

Robert said nothing. He had never imagined this would be a friendly bout. He prayed silently to St Christopher. 'Ward me now, O holy one; lend me your strength.'

Khuyag rushed in and gripped him by both shoulders, trying to twist Robert's body to the right. Robert seized him by the left elbow and right shoulder. By God, the Mongol general was strong! Robert could feel Khuyag's weight inexorably rotating his body round. He slipped his grip on Khuyag's elbow, grabbed his neck and pulled his opponent's head down, using all his strength. They strained against each other, grunting softly. Then Robert shifted his weight, extended his right leg, and released Khuyag's neck. Khuyag sprang back involuntarily, tangled with Robert's outstretched leg, and stumbled over it. He reeled backwards, breaking his own grip, and very nearly falling to the ground.

Yet Khuyag quickly recovered his balance and took two steps backwards.

He was panting with exertion, the sweat streaming down his white sides.

'Full of clever tricks, aren't you, you sly wife-stealing ape,' said Khuyag.

Robert did not reply. They circled again and came together fast, arms colliding meatily as they each tried for a hold. Robert had him by the right upper arm and left shoulder. He tried to step past, with his long right leg going across his body and pull Khuyag off balance over his thigh, in a classic hip-throw that was as old as grappling itself. But Khuyag knew the move, too, and countered it, grabbing Robert round the waist, his powerful arms lifting the Englishman up high in the air, right up over the Mongol's head.

Robert could foresee his own death – an instant from now. All Khuyag had to do was fall backwards and their considerable combined weight would crash to the earth.

And the Englishman's head and neck would break their fall.

His spine would be snapped like a piece of campfire kindling. In self-preserving panic, he quickly curled both his knees up tight against his belly and, as they both began to slowly fall backwards, he flicked his long legs out, somersaulting over so that the soles of his kid-skin boots hit the ground before any other part of him.

Both their holds were broken and Khuyag, crashed down on one knee – which was permissible. Robert was stumbling away, dizzy but still on his feet, his wits shaken but his neck unbroken, praise be to Almighty God and holy St Christopher.

Khuyag stood straight. 'It gives me pleasure,' he panted, 'when my enemies try to resist me. It makes the joy of the kill sweeter and last a little longer.'

Robert, too, was breathing hard. He knew just how close death had been.

He knew something else, as well. Khuyag was far too strong for him to try to match, chest to chest, muscle against muscle. It was time to use his superior brain.

'After I've snapped your neck,' Khuyag said, 'I shall slit the bitch-whore's throat, and I will watch and laugh as she drowns in her own blood before my eyes.'

Robert felt a cold rage bloom in his belly. He recalled what Karacha had said about Saran coming to him bloody and beaten after this pig had taken his fists to her.

He allowed an image of Sarantuya's bruised face to feed his growing rage.

They circled each other warily again. The shouts of the huge crowd diminished in his ears, and then stopped. Robert watched Khuyag's grasping hands, the left, the right, as they darted in and feinted. Then he deliberately pushed his left shoulder forward, within reach of Khuyag's fingers. As his opponent's hand shot out and touched his left shoulder, instead of grabbing his opponent's arms or shoulders, Robert's own right hand snaked across his chest and grasped the back of Khuyag's hand. He twisted it violently against the wrist joint, at the same time pulling the arm back across his own chest. Khuyag yelled. The pain in his wrist forcing him to allow his arm to be dragged across. Robert twisted his own body right round, fast as a weasel, so that Khuyag's arm was over his right shoulder, his back to Khuyag's chest. He could feel his foe clawing painfully at his neck, nails digging in, and ignored it.

He simply pulled downwards with all his strength. Khuyag's right arm was levered over his shoulder, the elbow joint pressed into his left clavicle.

Then, Robert yanked downwards, hard and fast. There was a loud, popping crack.

Khuyag screamed. The howl of a man in agony. His broken right arm was now flopping loose at the elbow. Robert turned, stepped in close, grabbed his opponent by the shoulders, put his left heel behind Khuyag's right foot and pushed hard.

The big Mongol crashed to the ground.

Robert stood over his vanquished foe. He lifted his own arms in triumph. He could hear the crowd again, several thousand excited Mongols all chanting his name.

He looked down at Khuyag, who suddenly seemed so much smaller, his dark eyes huge with pain, pathetically cradling his snapped right arm.

Robert said very quietly, 'If you ever come near my wife again, I shall kill you.'

Chapter Twenty-one

A month after his victory in the *Bökh* oval, Robert was summoned by Genghis Khan. They took his sword away from him again, and Robert could not decide if that meant he was no longer trusted, or this was a new requirement for all audiences with the Lord of the Steppe.

He was, however, not entirely unarmed that day. He wore the long Circassian dagger hanging in its well-made leather holster under his left armpit, the ivory handle tapping his waist just above his left hip, but hidden by the voluminous *deel* he wore.

And that blade the *kheshig* guards did not discover.

Robert had taken to wearing the dagger daily, even at home in his *ger*, and it made him feel better to have a weapon on his person at all times. Khuyag's threat to slit Sarantuya's throat chilled his soul. And the big man was angry enough to do it, he reckoned, despite the Great Khan's stern warning to him.

Yet he had not seen even a shadow of Khuyag since their bout. Word had reached him that his enemy had had his arm set and that he was treating the injury, or perhaps dulling the pain of it, by sitting alone in his *ger* and imbibing quantities of the potent Chinese rice wine all day and most of the night.

Genghis Khan also looked as if he might be suffering from a surfeit of wine. His skin was pale and sweaty-looking; he appeared to have lost more weight. Robert believed that if he had wanted to slay the Lord of the Steppe that day, he would not have needed either his Mongol sword or his concealed Circassian dagger. He was fairly sure he could have snapped the old man's neck like an arrow with his bare hands – had it not been for the presence of the two burly *turghaut* guards looming on either side of the Great Khan's cushion.

Robert made his report. His Snow Leopards had been scouting the Gobi for weeks, in small groups carrying much water and identifying the few watering holes they found. They marked them with long, streaming flags of blue silk, easily visible, all along the route the army would take when the Great Khan deemed it time to cross.

'You think there is sufficient water at these holes to supply the whole army – maybe seven or even eight *tumet*?' asked the khan. 'And all our various beasts?'

Robert paused and thought for a moment. The simple answer was no.

'It might be done if the army travelled piecemeal. One *tumen* at a time. There is a big river, five hundred miles south of Karakorum, which the local people call the Hei Shui. If we can cross much of the desert and secure that river, there might be enough water there for the whole army. There is a small lake, too, and the Hei Shui River feeds into it. However, both the lake and the river are guarded by a powerful Tangut fort. The place is called Khara-Khoto – the Black City; my Snow Leopards *arbat* have already scouted out the fortress, but only from a distance.'

'And?'

'I'm told there is a strong garrison in there, several thousand troops of the Hexi Empire. Maybe as many as four thousand men. It is more of a barracks than a city, filled with soldiers but with few women and children. It has high walls, and they have access to the waters of this lake, so a siege would be long and costly. However, if we were to take Khara-Khoto, we would have a foothold deep in the Gobi. It would serve as the mounting block from which a full invasion south could easily be launched.'

'So we cross the desert in smaller numbers and capture the Black City, then follow the course of the Hei Shui to the mountains in the far south. So how many *mingghat* would you need to take Khara-Khoto, Noyan Robyert Baghatur?'

'Me? I understood my task to be the scout, to bring you the intelligence.'

'Your task is to do exactly as I tell you. I want you to capture the Black City.'

Robert thought for a while. 'Three *mingghat*; four would be better – and some of the mountain troops. Then at least our numbers would be equal to theirs…'

'I will give you two – your own Snow Leopards and the Golden Eagles, since they already know you. Two against four. Yes, that seems about right. Two Mongol riders are easily a match for four doltish Chinese spearmen. Leave as soon as you are ready. But understand this: I shall expect news of your glorious victory very soon.'

'Ah, Great One, um, you must know that the Golden Eagles are one tenth part of Noyan Khuyag's *tumen*. It might be a little awkward to take away his—'

'That fellow Khuyag is no longer the commander of any *tumen*. I have removed him from the post. He has a badly broken arm and cannot ride.'

Robert was stunned. 'Surely he will recover, in time, and then—'

'If Tenggri decrees it, then I shall decide what is to be done with him.'

'But… why?'

'You wish to know why I removed him from his post?' said the Great Khan.

Robert nodded.

'He asked me, and I gave him permission to wrestle with you at the *Bökh* – but I gave him two conditions. I told him you must not be forced to fight, since you did not know our rough Mongol games. I sent a *turghaut* to you personally with that message. I also said that Khuyag might wrestle with you as long as no one was seriously injured. Now the man has a broken arm and cannot ride. He showed poor judgement. I cannot have my commanders displaying that degree of poor judgement.'

'But you knew very well of the animosity between us.'

'A Mongol, especially a *noyan*, must be able to control himself. He might hate you – he does hate you – but that should not affect his obedience to me. I gave an order that no one should be injured. He ignored my order and sought to kill you in the *Bökh*. I watched him do it. You snapped his arm, very neatly I may say, to stop him killing you. That is why *you* have the Golden Eagles to command, and I will let Khuyag drink rice wine in his *ger* till he's healed, then decide what to do with him.'

Robert said, 'You are not angry because I rendered the man useless?'

'You did what you had to do,' said the Great Khan. 'That is the Mongol way. To do what is necessary. What*ever* is necessary. Keep these words close to your heart, *Baghatur*. Now go and prepare your two fine *mingghat*. Send word back to me when Khara-Khoto is taken.'

–

Robert crouched in darkness in the sand on the far bank of the river course, which had been reduced to a sluggish trickle by the summer and autumn months, and looked across to the lights of Khara-Khoto, half a mile south. At his right shoulder knelt Taghachat, who commanded the Golden Eagles under his authority, on his left crouched Kolgen, who played the second-in-command role for the Snow Leopards.

All three commanders stared across at the sleeping Black City, at the tiny sentries walking along the summit of the fortifications, the patrolling men passing in and out of the pools of red light formed by the round Chinese lanterns that were hung every seventy paces along the walls at each of the many guard towers.

They were observing the long northern wall of the Black City – five hundred paces of smooth sandstone blocks, rising thirty feet above the desert floor. The walls were all at least twelve feet thick, Robert reckoned. And there was even a wide road running around the four sides of the summit of the fortifications, wide enough for two small wagons to pass each other going in different directions.

There were six, square-built towers, red lanterns lit, along the north wall, and two bigger, much stronger towers, dome-shaped with a pointed spire, at both the western and eastern ends, which were now ablaze with dancing orange firelight.

The three men could just make out the main gatehouse in the darkness; a miniature, thick-walled castle, protruding from the western walls, curled like fingers making a fist, with the narrow entrance on its southern side. And, although they could not see it from their position, Robert knew that there was a similar strongly fortified gatehouse on the eastern side of the city.

These two powerful gatehouses were the only two ways to enter Khara-Khoto.

It was a formidable stronghold. Easily as stalwart as many of the castles Robert had seen in Christendom. And it was filled with thousands of enemy soldiers. Robert had no siege train. Nor did he have the leisure to batter down the walls. But the Great Khan had ordered him to capture this mighty fortress – and capture it quickly.

'Two *mingghat* is not enough,' said Kolgen. 'We would need half a *tumen* – at least – and a full train of marmot-men. And six months. It cannot be done, *ezen*.'

'No, Kolgen, it *can* be done,' said Robert. 'And we are going to do it.'

Robert glanced to his right to see the white of Taghachat's bared teeth grinning at him. 'Do you mean to give them the Great Khan's Choice, *ezen?*' he asked.

'I shall do what is necessary,' said Robert. 'What*ever* is necessary.'

They had ridden for thirty-five days from the familiar comforts of Karakorum to reach this half-dried-out riverbed in the southern part of the Gobi; more than a full month of parched travel through the unforgiving wilderness. A relentless journey through the pale yellows and ochres of the dunes, across vast flat fields of grey gravel and baked brown clay, with deep red sunsets filling the western sky like an enormous bleeding wound to mark the end of another brutal, desiccating day on the march.

They had provisioned themselves well, with each Mongol trooper and his spare horses carrying six full leather water skins, and refilling them at each of the waterholes marked out by the blue silk flags. They had brought with them bags of dried mutton and pouches of mare's milk paste, and sacks of ground millet for the horses. It had still been a gruelling sun-blasted journey – even in the cool of autumn – with every man at its end burned red-raw, thinner and saddle-sore, and half the horses lame.

They had hunted the herds of wild antelope near the foothills of jagged-toothed mountains in the north, and watched hundreds of excitable wild donkeys galloping madly across the desolate sandy plains beyond the softer hill country. They had spotted golden eagles soaring high overhead out in the full, baking desert – which was seen as a good omen by one half of Robert's command, but not by the other.

And, one night, in camp, the Englishman had seen a tiny mouse-like creature with enormously long ears in the firelight, a scurrying thing that watched him eat his *shulen* with huge eyes from the shadows as if it wanted to beg a bowl from him.

Yet for most of that long, terrible, sun-roasting journey they had seen little but their horses' two ears and the endless, rippling, desert emptiness for miles around them, and they had heard nothing but the dry clop-clop-clop of their horses' hooves.

Now they were at their destination and the hard work must truly begin.

Robert rode down the bank and across the riverbed, and up towards the formidable gatehouse on the western side of Khara-Khoto, and behind him came a horde of Mongol riders, spaced well apart and almost filling the horizon. Beyond the high walls of the city, the rim of the yellow disc of the sun could just be seen, making Robert squint. He pulled the brim of his heavy iron helmet down over his eyes.

The helm's brim was rather short for glare-shading, but the helm had long iron sidepieces, and a broad lamellar neck covering – a much better protection against swords than sunlight. For Robert was that morning dressed in his full suit of Mongol armour, the kind worn by the troopers of the heavy cavalry *mingghat*.

This included a small round iron shield, which was surprisingly light and strong, and a long lamellar coat made of thin iron plates sewn on to a leather backing, which fell to below his knees when he was mounted, and which came with oblong armoured shoulder pieces that covered his arms down to his elbows. He had three heavy Mongol spears, with vicious hooks behind the long steel blade, carried in a deep leather bucket at his horse's withers, and his Mongol sword hanging at his left hip.

He was watching the enemy on the ramparts, running and shouting, waving their long-bladed pole arms, a peculiar Chinese weapon like a wide falchion on the end of a long spear, which he knew they called a moon blade. He could hear their trumpets squealing the alarm, and the continuous rumble of his own Mongol drummers behind, as they hammered at the taut goatskins stretched over their big cooking cauldrons.

There was a man in a square black hat with a round, ruby-like jewel on the crown, wearing a yellow-green silk robe standing in the centre of the gatehouse wall and pointing at him, with two attendants each carrying moon blades on either side of him. There were running archers now filling the space around that man. And their trumpets continued to sound, like the calls of some enormous yet invisible beast in torment.

Now, a single arrow arced out from the gatehouse and thudded into the ground a dozen paces in front of Robert's horse.

He immediately reined in and turned in the saddle to beckon Kolgen forward.

The Snow Leopard lieutenant came forward and lifted a huge flag made from a white linen sheet high in the air: the ancient symbol that he wished to parley.

The Mongol advance had stopped, some two hundred yards from the walls. The drums finally fell silent and Robert waited, sitting there, watching the yellow sun inching its way above the city, enjoying the warmth of its first rays. He still felt exhausted, but anxious, too. His whole body gripped by a strange, shivering strength.

He heard the creaking of the wooden gates, and saw a quartet of horsemen come cantering out of the side of the block-like gatehouse. They came barrelling towards him – a young nobleman, dressed in red silks, a crimson plumed helm, a burnished hauberk with shoulder pieces, and a straight Chinese sword at his waist held by a crimson sash; and three lesser-ranked horsemen, in lamellar corselets and greaves, with the moon blades carried over their left shoulders like bizarre, top-heavy spears.

They reined in ten yards from Robert and stared at him in silence.

Then the young man said, in reasonably good Mongol, 'I am Li Shu, son of His Excellency Governor Li of the Black City, cousin to Emperor Xian Zong, lord of the Hexi. Who dares come before our walls arrayed for battle?'

Robert said, 'Since you ask in our Mongol tongue, I believe you know that.'

Li Shu said, 'We have been good and faithful allies of the Great Khan, living in peace with our northern neighbours. Why do you come to our lands garbed for war?'

'Not faithful. My lord the Great Khan knows that you have made a treacherous alliance with his enemy Emperor Ning Jiasu of the Jin. The Great Khan demands that your governor surrender the Black City to us and submit himself for judgement.'

'This is not Mongol land. This is Hexi. We Tangut are not beholden to the Great Khan. Our glorious emperor is free to make alliances with whomever he chooses.'

'I shall say this to you once,' said Robert. 'So I ask you to listen with care to my words. I am the Great Khan's representative; I speak with his voice. Surrender to me now and receive mercy, or I shall annihilate you all and leave not one stone of your city standing upon another. Throw open your gates this day and kneel in the dust before me, and all who are innocent shall be spared; dare to resist me and I shall slay all living things inside your walls. It is time to make the Great Khan's Choice!'

Li Shu glared at Robert. 'We do not fear your threats, Mongol,' he said. 'Be gone. Ride back across the Gobi and come no more to our land. If you dare to come against us, your horsemen will be shattered against our strong walls.'

–

They pulled back, but only to the riverbank, a hundred yards away. There they waited. Robert, oddly, felt a sense of relief. He had delivered the Choice and been rebuffed. Everything had been set in motion and would play out as he had planned. There were no more doubts in his mind.

He could clearly see the defenders on the western wall of the castle, a big knot of them busy about some long black object – no, two long black objects, one on either side of the powerful gatehouse. He turned to his lieutenant Kolgen.

'Get them to dress their ranks. Then form them up in three lines, as if we were about to charge. Then dress the ranks again. I want plenty of motion and activity.'

He pulled his horse round and spurred back to a large sandstone out-cropping on the riverbank. He forced the steppe pony to climb to the summit. He had left Bayard back in Karakorum with Sarantuya – he had not wanted to subject the horse to the rigours of the parched desert crossing – but now he missed the noble animal. At the top of the out-cropping, the frightened pony whinnied, shied and nodded unhappily, jerking his head up and down, but from up here Robert had a fine view of the city, the river, the lake and the surrounding desert, all spread out below him.

At the guard towers all along the walls, the red lanterns of the night had been removed now the sun was up and replaced with long, red-and-black banners. Inside the walls of the city, he could now see that several larger buildings inside had the same proud coloured banners flying from the corners of their shiny green-tiled roofs.

Immediately below him, Kolgen was giving orders to the various *akhmad* of the individual Mongol *jagghut*, ordering them to form lines, three horse-lengths apart, and take their time about it. Up on the western wall of the city, the Hexi soldiers were massing on the ramparts, many hundreds of them. The ramparts thick with bodies. Most of them were staring in awe towards the shifting mass of Mongol horsemen.

'That's right,' muttered Robert, 'you watch us here. Keep looking this way.'

Below him Kolgen was now re-ordering the *jagghut* on the front line, this time putting Snow Leopards companies in line with Golden Eagles, for no particular reason. *Good man*, thought Robert. *Activity, motion. Keep them all looking at us.*

His plan seemed to be working. There were thousands of Khara-Khoto fighting men now on the western wall, all facing towards Robert's formed-up horse *mingghat*.

There was a flash of orange light, a loud crack and a puff of smoke on the walls, and Robert thought he could see something flying through the air towards the ranks of his horsemen.

The men on the walls around the long black object were cheering. Then the second long black object exploded in red-orange flame and smoke, on the other side of the gatehouse.

'What in the name of God is that?' exclaimed Robert.

He looked down at the ranks of his men and saw that one Mongol, no, two of his men, both Snow Leopards, were lying flat on the ground. There was blood all around them on the sand. The nearest dead Mongol trooper seemed to be transfixed right through the chest by a gigantic spear, its shaft twice the length of an ordinary one.

'What devilry is this?'

He squinted into the sun at the summit of the walls of Khara-Khoto, and could make out knots of Chinese soldiers working frantically around the two long black objects – two machines that could, apparently, harness fire to hurl huge spears and kill men some three hundred yards away, well out of ordinary bowshot range.

From his vantage point, he looked beyond the western wall to the far side of the Black City, at the distant eastern wall. He saw that, where the other gatehouse stood, the twin of the one on the western wall, there was a heaving knot of men, who were struggling on its battlements, then – praise God – he saw that the red-and-black banner, which had earlier flown above the gatehouse was gone. In its place a Mongol *sulde* had been erected, a spirit banner fringed with dozens of white horsetails.

'Taghachat,' he said. 'You shall be exalted among all the peoples of the Earth!'

Robert turned his pony and forced it stumbling down the steep, rocky slope at the rear of the outcropping, and once more on the flat, sandy desert floor he cantered towards the patiently waiting lines of his men. As he passed the fallen, blood-soaked Mongol, he snatched a quick glance, and saw that the long spear that transfixed him was made of iron, and it had almost entirely cut the poor man in half. Devilry, indeed.

But he did not stop his running horse to examine his poor comrade more closely.

'Snow Leopards!' he yelled, as he approached their ranks. 'Snow Leopards and Golden Eagles…! With me, all of you. At the charge. Now! We attack now! Attack!'

Chapter Twenty-two

They thundered towards the western wall, fifteen hundred Mongols, as if they meant to hurl themselves uselessly, stupidly at the thirty-foot-high sandstone ramparts. Then, at the last moment, twenty paces from the thick base of the fortifications, Robert stuck out his left arm, and the whole mass of charging horsemen wheeled and swept along the smooth face of the western wall, all of them now heading northwards.

The manoeuvre was beautifully executed, the fruit of many hours of training. There was no confusion. The mass of horses wheeled in perfect precision as if controlled by a single mind, and swept northwards to run parallel with the western ramparts.

Above him Robert could hear the shouts and jeers of the enemy. He sensed the falling of many missiles, spears, arrows and even stones, that cracked and hissed into the thundering pack of horsemen. A falling javelin struck his shoulder armour, and bounced harmlessly away but, by then, he was at the north-western corner of the fortress, beneath the dome and spire of the bigger corner tower. He stuck out his right arm, bellowed an order, and the whole galloping Mongol formation changed direction once again and now began to stream along the northern face of the city's fortifications.

Robert felt the barrage of missiles slacken and fall away almost to nothing, and he smiled under his helm. The madly galloping riders traversed the five-hundred-paces' length of the north wall in a cloud of kicked up desert sand in what seemed like a matter of moments. Then Robert, with his fifteen hundred Mongol troopers hard on his heels, turned the final corner, and the eastern gatehouse came into view.

He felt a surge of hot exhilaration deep in his chest.

'Taghachat – *Baghatur*!' he yelled, urging his steppe pony to greater speed.

There was a scene of carnage outside the base of the eastern gatehouse. Dozens, no scores of dead bodies, both Mongol warriors and Hexi men, were scattered about the desert floor in pools of blood. A few wounded Mongols were sitting propped up with their backs to the city wall, grinning at the arriving horsemen through their pain.

One of the sitting Mongols, Robert saw, was Taghachat himself, a great red stain at his belly and wet blood glistening in his lap. Yet, more important to his mind even than his friend's terrible wound, he saw that the two huge wooden doors of the eastern gatehouse were pushed back wide, and guarded by a dozen Mongols on foot.

The way inside the city of Khara-Khoto was free and clear.

Taghachat had done his duty – and done it magnificently. He had scaled the east wall with five hundred dismounted Golden Eagles, and captured this gate while enemy attention had all been on the massed ranks of Mongols formed up in the west.

Robert wasted no time on congratulations. He did not even slow the pony.

He merely shouted, 'Bravely done!' to Taghachat as he thundered past. His Mongol lieutenant just managed to lift a gory hand to acknowledge his praise. But by then Robert was gone, headed deep into the gloomy darkness of the stone gatehouse, the high walls seeming to swallow him and his galloping pony.

He was aware that Arslan was riding beside him, on his left, scowling horribly and Hasar, Begter and Khuchar, too, were at his right shoulder. He wondered where Saka and Taka were, before remembering they were back in Karakorum, on the other side of the Gobi, guarding Sarantuya and little Jalair.

Then, suddenly, they were in bright sunshine again, inside the Black City in the middle of a full-pitched battle.

There was a mass of Golden Eagles to his left, hundreds of his men on foot, battling a swarm of Hexi soldiers, armed with their distinctive moon-blade polearms, and he knew he had arrived just in time. Ahead of him was a city street and he could see a block of Hexi marching forward, a column of perhaps six hundred spearmen three hundred yards away, stomping along in blue coats and steep caps, likely coming from the regiments that had recently been massed to receive them on the western wall.

He selected a long Mongol spear from the bucket on his horse's withers, couched it under his right arm, and yelled, 'Charge!' He spurred his pony into the wild melee around his beleaguered, dismounted Golden Eagles. And rode at a Hexi foot soldier, who heard him coming, turned and slashed at him with his moon blade.

The blow missed him, slicing air just above his hunched shoulder. An instant later, Robert's spear punched into the man's chest, a solid crunching blow, stopped in its forward movement only by the curved hook behind the point. Robert felt the heavy jarring impact right up his forearm to the elbow, and immediately released the wooden spear-shaft, leaving the long weapon wedged deep in the dying fellow's ribs.

Another footman with a moon blade was striking at him from his left, and he took that hard, clanging blow full on his iron shield. Arslan popped up seemingly out of nowhere and put an arrow deftly through the man's right eye. Arslan's shaft, loosed from only a few yards away, smacked right through the Hexi man's skull and sprayed a hot mess of white and pink matter out the other side of his pierced head.

Robert was in the thick of it now, struggling Hexi footmen all around him, a boiling sea of waving silver moon blades. He was still only about twenty yards from the inner entrance to the gatehouse, and he could feel the Golden Eagles faltering, pulling back, but he had his Mongol sword out now, and was laying about left and right, landing every blow, trying to keep the tide of his foes from overwhelming him.

He chopped at a Chinese man on his right, back handed, slicing his screaming face wide open, and saw Hasar spur forward and club the fellow down with a steel-headed mace. Something clanged against his iron shield. He felt a painful pounding chop against his left thigh, but when he looked down he saw no blood. He was now hammering with his sword at the helm of a man with a spear, a fellow who was poking at him, jabbing, trying to pierce his armpit, shouting in the Chinese tongue.

He leaned sideways and hacked into the spearman's shoulder, cutting through the blue padded coat the man wore and releasing a fountain of blood. Then Khuchar's steppe pony backed into his, throwing him off balance. He nearly lost his seat and as he was recovering, a moon blade hissed towards his face and he was forced to jerk his head back to retain his nose. He hacked at his attacker, once, twice, and driving him away into the screaming, jostling, bone-crunching, terrifying crush of desperate men.

Robert looked around wildly, trying to gauge the situation. And with relief, he saw that more and more horse-borne Mongols were shoving their way through the open gate; there was Kolgen with two *jagghut* of Snow Leopards, piling into the fight around the Golden Eagles, sweeping away the Hexi footmen. There were hundreds of his horsemen now fighting inside the city walls. More streaming in through the gate.

They had their short Mongol bows in hand and were shooting down any Hexi in sight. The shafts whizzed and cracked through the air like a lethal horizontal rain; the screams of the wounded were deafening. Genghis Khan had been right: two mounted Mongol bowmen were easily equal of four Chinese soldiers waving knives on sticks.

Robert sensed the tide of the battle beginning to turn.

The Golden Eagles on foot had by now slaughtered or driven off most of the moon-blade-wielding Hexi. Robert saw that Kolgen still had his two *jagghut* of Snow Leopards under his control and was reforming them in four shaky lines for an attack.

There were no more enemies around him. Many of the Hexi were running away.

Without waiting for Robert's orders, Kolgen shouted a command and launched his horsemen west, straight up the city road towards the oncoming Hexi spearmen. Fifty paces out, at the gallop, they launched their first dark volley of arrows, which pattered down on the stolidly tramping Hexi troops, felling scores of men. A moment later they launched a second volley. Then Kolgen's charging horsemen smashed into the heart of the column, splintering the formation like a glass pane under a hammer.

Robert saw one of his Snow Leopard *akhmad*, gathering his *jagghun* in a loose pack around him. The officer was trying to make them form neat lines. Robert bellowed, 'Don't wait! Get up there! Support Kolgen!' and pointed up the street.

The *akhmad* heard and obeyed, clattering his *jagghun* up the street to join in the brutal street fight. Robert turned his attention to the surges of fresh horsemen still piling through the gatehouse entrance. He quickly wiped and sheathed his sword, then began ordering his incoming *jagghut* to go left and right, in turn, as they came through the dark gatehouse into the light. 'Spread out,' he yelled, 'spread out and hunt them – no quarter – go down every street, every alley. But watch for ambushes!'

Then he saw a fresh squad of enemy running directly towards the gate. Two score Hexi guardsmen with long-handled axes. He pulled a Mongol spear from the leather bucket, drew back his right arm and hurled the long missile, taking the leading man, clearly the officer, in the belly. He shouted, 'On me!' and galloped towards the forty axemen, aware that Arslan was still at his right-hand side, his curved sword drawn again, and half a dozen familiar Mongol faces were rallying to his call, as well.

The Hexi axemen did not wait to receive his charge. They scattered before him, sprinting away into the side streets, some running into houses, barging through the doors and slamming them shut behind them. Trying to survive the Mongol onslaught.

It was then that Robert knew he had won. He reined in, turned his pony, and looked back at the gatehouse. There were still more Mongol troopers flooding in – Golden Eagles now, another two *jagghut* – and no one alive left to oppose them.

The grins of delight on their red, weathered faces told him that victory was his.

–

Two hours later, Robert stood on the wide road that led around the summit of the four walls. To his left was the eastern gatehouse that Taghachat had so valiantly captured. He could still see the iron hooks of the grappling irons and knotted ropes the bold Golden Eagles has used to scale the sandstone ramparts.

The sky had clouded over after a brilliant sunny early morning and dark banks of clouds, in hues of purple-grey, were gathering in the south. Threatening a storm.

Taghachat was dead. He had taken a bad wound to the belly from a moon blade in the initial assault and had bled out his life at the base of the walls his brave men had taken.

Robert had no time to mourn him. He looked at the Black City spread out below him and could not suppress a shudder of horror. Many of the houses were burning, and there were hundreds of bloody corpses littering the streets, and also piled up like trash by doorways. Many of the stacked bodies were lacking their heads.

There was blood freely flowing in the city gutters and splashed over the streets and the walls of the houses. Directly below him was the body of a naked girl, her stomach ripped open to display the guts. Her dead eyes stared up at him accusingly.

All this was his doing. And he accepted that. The two thousand Mongol troops under his command were now ranging freely over the city, slaughtering, raping, burning, pillaging at will – and merrily looting the hoarded wealth of Khara-Khoto.

His troopers had no mercy in them and Robert had little to spare either. His left leg was horribly painful. The thigh bone was not broken, for he could put some of his weight on it, but he had been obliged to lean on a spear to get himself up the stone steps to the summit of these walls.

Arslan was now thrusting a leather skin at him, muttering, 'Drink, *ezen*.' And Robert did so. It was wine. Strong rice wine, acrid like some foul but necessary medicine.

He realised that his mouth was bone dry. He drank again. There were half a dozen of his *arban* around him, and he turned to Khuchar and said, 'Who is in charge of loot collection? Someone honest, I hope?'

'Kolgen chose Akhmad Kushi – he's in the main barracks now, presiding over the piles of booty. Kushi swears that any man who withholds loot will be beheaded.'

'Good,' said Robert. He was dizzy with pain and desperately wanted to sit down, but he felt he could not show weakness in front of his men. He gripped his spear-staff tightly, and lifted his chin to straighten his whole frame. Below him, to his left, in the street, a gang of Mongol warriors was in the process of executing three captured soldiers. The three Hexi prisoners looked so very young, and so frightened. The Mongols spoke of them as if they were animals and dispatched them swiftly without ceremony: three blows that hacked the heads off their necks.

Robert looked away. The city had been given the Great Khan's Choice and it had chosen to defy him. It was God's will, his Templar masters would say. *Deus vult.*

He realised it had been weeks since he last prayed. Since Idar's departure he had abandoned his morning and evening routine; there had never seemed to be the time.

He closed his eyes now and offered up these words, 'Forgive me, Heavenly Father, for the things I must do in the service of my temporal lord. You alone know why I must do this. Help me to harden my heart to the sufferings of others… And take unto your bosom my friend Taghachat, I beg you, who left the earthly realm this day. He was no Christian and a sinful heathen of no real faith but he was a good man, and my friend. I humbly ask this in the name of your son, Our Saviour Jesus Christ.'

When he opened his eyes, he saw that Kolgen was running towards him along the north wall, coming all the way from the western gatehouse.

The young officer saluted and said breathlessly, 'Some of the Hexi are getting away, *ezen*. We did not secure the western gate in time and a large number, mostly women and children, but also a hundred moon-blades, are fleeing south along the bank of the river. Shall I take two Snow Leopard *jagghut* to hunt them down?'

Robert was silent for a little while. 'No,' he said, 'just… just let them go.'

'*Ezen*,' said Kolgen, 'you offered them the Choice, and they defied you…'

'Let them go,' said Robert. 'They will tell all the other cities of Khara-Khoto's fate. Their terror of the Mongols will spread far throughout the enemy lands.'

Kolgen stared at him, clearly baffled. 'As you command, *ezen*,' he said.

'I want you to take charge of the fire teams,' said Robert. 'I want all the fires to be extinguished. This city must be whole, not a burnt-out ruin, as my gift to the Great Khan.'

'As you command,' said Kolgen again, and turned to go.

Robert closed his eyes. 'Almighty God,' he prayed. 'This road before me is so hard, and my heart quails with each step I take. Yet I believe this barbarism is what I must do for the holy cause. If I am on the right path, if what I am doing is Your will, show me a sign, I beg you. Show me a clear sign that my actions are not misguided.'

Robert opened his eyes.

Thunder rolled across the vastness of the sky, the lightning cracked and flashed like veins of white fire across the heavens. The rain began to fall. A cold, hard rain that cascaded down on to the burning houses and streets of the captured city. It was a sign.

Robert was drenched to the bone and shivering in a matter of a few moments.

'*Deus vult*,' he muttered. 'His will be done on Earth, as it is in Heaven.'

Then he hobbled away painfully along the wall to find shelter from the storm.

-

'It is good news, I think,' said Sarantuya, her fingers moving with a practised dexterity, as she teased the clumps of raw wool into strands and kept the spindle rotating, forming a long, fine grey woollen yarn.

'Tolui has been given the heartland: all the lands around Karakorum, the Tula, Orkhon and Onon rivers and up to Lake Baikal. He will hold the central area of all the steppe lands his great father conquered during his lifetime.'

'Why do you only *think*?' asked Robert. 'He has been shown by this generous gift from his father to be the Great Khan's heir. Surely there can be no mistaking it?'

They were in Robert's *ger*, which was pitched outside the walls of Khara-Khoto, on the sandy shore of the lake. It was two months after the fall of the Black City and eight *tumet* of the Great Khan had safely crossed the Gobi and settled in around the former Tangut fortress for the duration of the winter.

Robert, who was tired and hungover after a long drinking bout with Tolui the night before, was idly sharpening and oiling his various weapons by the warm hearth, while Sarantuya spun huge bags of sheared sheep's wool into yarn, an endless task, that demanded little conscious thought. Her fingers moved as if of their own volition.

Saka and Taka were snoozing on the cushions in the men's section of the *ger*. Arslan, Begter, Hasar and Khuchar had gone off into the cool desert in the early morning to hunt gazelle for the household pot.

'His two living brothers have also been given their own Ulus, and four thousand families to be their vassals,' said Saran. 'Ogedei has the Altai region to the west of Karakorum, as far as the Tien Shan mountains; and Chagatai has Lake Balkhash and the lands between the Syr Daria and the Amu Daria.'

'What about the Khorasan beyond the Amu Daria?' Robert asked.

While the Englishman had been crossing the Gobi and capturing Khara-Khoto, in Karakorum the Great Khan had called a grand council at the *kurultai* in the last days of the autumn and announced to the Mongol nation the specific inheritances that his sons would receive after his death.

'That region has not been allocated to anyone as an inheritance,' said Saran. 'Perhaps because it is still in so much turmoil. However, Batu, who is Jochi's son – did you hear that Jochi, the khan's oldest son, died?'

Robert had heard. Jochi had died of sickness somewhere in the North. 'Well, Batu, his son,' continued Sarantuya, 'has been given all the lands north of the Aral Sea, and westward "as far as the hooves of Mongol horses can take him". Those were my uncle's very words. So, I think young Batu will rule the Khorasan, in the years to come, when the Great Khan is dead.'

'Is the succession settled,' Robert asked, 'by this division of his lands?'

'The succession, my love, as I have told you before, will be decided by all the khans *after* Genghis Khan's death. Tolui is the *heir apparent*, as the youngest son, but Ogedei has also been shown great favour and he has begun to attract many of his own supporters, men who have been wronged by his father.'

Sarantuya paused in her spinning and gave Robert a significant look.

'Khuyag is now an enthusiastic supporter of Ogedei. He has pitched his *ger* near Ogedei's, and attends him daily. He has a fine new command, too – he is now *noyan* of the White Foxes *mingghan*; Ogedei gave them to him. His right arm is still weak but I hear he grows stronger daily. His hatred for you, I fear, is not at all diminished.'

'I should just kill that drunken donkey and be done with it,' said Robert.

'You would then surely forfeit any favour the Great Khan might show you,' she said. 'Khuyag is not a threat to us. My father has spoken to him – just leave him be.'

Robert grunted something and continued to run the oiled whetstone lightly along the keen edge of the steel blade of his Mongol sword.

'There is another factor to consider, my love, in the succession,' said his wife. 'Yelu Ahai, the khan's chief minister, wields considerable power. He has control of the Arrow Riders, and the intelligence gathering of the scouting *mingghat*, too, is in his hands, as well you know. He is Master of the Treasury – so all the gold and silver of our conquests is in his safekeeping. Whoever would rule after Genghis Khan will do so with Yelu's blessing. That is something to keep in mind at all times, Robyert.'

'I am to meet with Yelu this day,' said Robert. 'I have been summoned.'

'Then make sure you do not displease him.'

'He probably just wants to criticise my Uighur penmanship,' said Robert.

–

That winter passed in relative idleness. In the long, freezing months of the year, Robert and his men – he had happily retained command of both his victorious *mingghat* – exercised their horses in the desert around the Tangut fortress, and made several long hunting trips for game. However, for much of the time they simply remained snug in their *gers*, drinking, sleeping and telling stories, and venturing out only briefly each day to tend to their horses and their herds.

One evening in late January, Sarantuya and her female friends treated Robert and the officers of the Snow Leopards and Golden Eagles to a performance of Chinese music. They performed for several hours to a packed *ger*, scraping away at their long-necked, two-stringed instruments and singing dozens of very high-pitched songs in the ancient Jin language.

Tsai, the hot, bitter Chinese drink made from dried plant leaves, was served, but most of the Mongol men preferred to stick with *airaq* or wine.

Robert endured his wife's playing with a fixed smile on his face, and with little Jalair sitting on his lap, sucking on a leathery strip of dried mutton. But when the boy grew fretful and tired, Robert carried him out of the *ger* and took him to the maid Anya's tent to be put to bed.

On his return, Robert lingered outside his tent, looking up at the black night sky, cloud-swaddled and starless, deliberately delaying his return to the warmth inside.

He thought about the grim task that lay ahead of him, the rights and the wrongs of it. He dreaded this black deed but knew he must accomplish it anyway. He was almost certain that God willed it. All he had to do was await an opportunity, which the Almighty would surely provide. Then he would strike without hesitation – in His name.

If God did *not* grant him the opportunity, then He clearly did not wish him to act.

So the matter was entirely in God's hands. Then, feeling a little better after this abdication of responsibility, Robert went back inside the warm *ger* to resume his musical ordeal.

In the early part of the year, when the snows had melted, Yelu Ahai dispatched Robert and his two *mingghat* south, following the course of the Hei Shui to scout the city of Suzhou. This was the first of a string of Tangut settlements that ran along a strip of land five hundred miles long and a hundred wide called the Hexi Corridor, between the vastness of the Gobi to the north and the soaring Quilian Mountains in the south, which were the beginning of the Tibetan plateau.

This corridor lay on the ancient path of the Silk Road. The camel and horse caravans of that precious textile, the bales of *tsai*, and straw-padded baskets of Chinese porcelain and other valuables had long been carried eastwards along this narrow corridor between the desert and the mountains to reach the markets of the West. This route was one of the reasons the Great Khan wished to possess the Hexi Empire and its vital corridor. Because to control this ancient trade route was to control all the westward trade of Cathay.

Yet Robert had been very reluctant to go. He wanted to stay with Sarantuya.

It was far too early for her to show, and her belly was still flat and firm as a wooden board, but Saran had missed her monthly bleeding and Robert now endlessly shot her surreptitious glances to make sure she was safe and warm, and constantly asked if she lacked anything, and urged her, infuriatingly, not to unduly exert herself.

'Go, my love, and do your duty to the khan,' said Saran, when Robert had urged her once again to sit down and take a rest from her household tasks. 'The baby will not be here till late autumn. Anya is with me, as well as Jargal and Sorkoktani, and all her women. I shall be well. Go and fight the khan's enemies and leave me in peace.'

Before he left, Robert spoke to Jargal. This leather-tough, middle-aged Mongol woman was Taghachat's widow, and a much-lauded cook, and Robert had generously invited her to live with them in his *ger* after Taghachat's death at the eastern gate.

'Make sure that your mistress does nothing too strenuous, Jargal,' he said.

'Men always fuss too much,' replied Jargal. 'Mongol women are hardy. My little sister had her second baby on the march from Lake Baikal to Yanikant and was back on her pony the very next day. You need have no fear for your wife, *ezen*. She is as strong as a mountain yak. And I will watch over her like a ewe her lamb.'

Robert and his men encountered no resistance from the enemy on the week-long journey south from Khara-Khoto, but when he reached his destination, it was clear to him, as he sat on Bayard's back and looked up at the snow-capped mountains beyond the lights on the walls of Suzhou, that the Hexi had reinforced Suzhou, and filled it with many thousands of soldiers. It would not be as easily taken as Khara-Khoto. Word of the Black City's terrible doom had clearly reached the rest of the Hexi Empire.

'You will need all the siege engines and it will take a lot of time,' he told his master and his minister, Yelu Ahai, when he reported back a week later in Khara-Khoto.

'We do not have time,' said the Great Khan. 'It must be achieved with speed or not at all. My horses need the grasslands of the north or the grain stores in all those Hexi cities. I will give them the Choice. They will have realised the price of defiance by your example here, *Baghatur*.'

However, it seemed that the horrific slaughter of the entire Tangut garrison at Khara-Khoto, and the murder of almost all their women and children, had been in vain.

For the great Hexi city of Suzhou defied the Great Khan.

Chapter Twenty-three

The huge stone-throwing engines of the Jin marmot-men were set up around the walls of Suzhou and began the slow, painstaking task of battering the stone fortifications into rubble. However, Robert did not remain to see the crumbling of their walls under the relentless barrage of the trebuchet balls, nor did he witness the slaughter of every living thing inside them that followed only a month later when the Mongol assault *mingghat* were sent in. He had been dispatched long before to scout the other towns along the Hexi Corridor and report on the state of their defences.

Subutai was also dispatched. The general went north-west with two *tumet* to take the cities of Guazhou and Shazhou at the northern end of the Hexi Corridor, while Robert and his men rode south-east to scout Ganzhou and Xiliang at its other end.

And once Suzhou had been stormed, sacked and razed almost to the ground, and the headless bodies of its inhabitants lay in thick drifts on the blood-soaked streets of the burning city, then Genghis Khan's *tumet* turned south-east to follow in Robert's footsteps.

Robert was diligent. He sent back his written reports almost daily on the strengths and weaknesses of the towns and cities he reconnoitred, using the Uighur script he had now mastered. And, in one of the rare, face-to-face meetings with Yelu Ahai, he was actually praised for his reporting and the precision of his lettering.

'I shall commend you to the Great Khan when I see him next,' said Yelu. 'This is valuable intelligence, very valuable. I know he will be pleased with you, Robyert.'

It was a summer of blood and slaughter. Of burning cites, countless beheadings, with the piteous cries of men, women and children ringing in Robert's ears long after they were dead. The gutters of the towns in the Hexi Corridor ran red with the gore of victims. But Robert hardened his heart to the daily horrors and did his duty to the Great Khan.

Whenever he could, he spent time with Sarantuya, as her fruitful belly swelled, and with Jalair, who was now a fearless toddler, swaggering about the *ger*. Robert found that being with the two people he loved most in the world, in the calm of his own home, allowed him to banish for a while the terrible scenes he had witnessed that day, and in all the days before. He told himself that the appalling carnage he helped the Great Khan to wreak was the price he must pay for his uxorious happiness.

When the whole corridor was subdued, and half a dozen Chinese cities and towns were left as blackened shells, the Mongol army turned north-east and followed the Yellow River to Zhong Xing, the fortified capital of the Hexi state, where Xian Zong, the emperor, cowered behind his walls on the left bank of that great waterway.

Zhong Xing was the first of the Hexi cities to give the Great Khan pause.

With the Yellow River at their backs, the denizens had little fear of running short of drinking water. It was also soon clear they had fully stocked their granaries and armouries, summoned all their soldiers, and were prepared to endure a long siege.

The Hexi had mounted dozens of the machines that spat fire and iron spears on the walls of the capital, but more perilous to Robert's scouting *jagghut* than these devilish devices were the traps and tricks they had employed to injure the Mongol ponies when they approached the capital city by the main riverside road.

Deep, narrow pits had been dug in the main highway and on the verges on either side of the road, cleverly disguised with dry sticks, moss and leaf litter.

Khuchar was the first of Robert's men to fall foul of them: his galloping pony put its right forefoot deep in one of the pits, sank in up to the knee, and the animal screamed in pain as its momentum snapped the foreleg like a dry twig. Poor Khuchar was hurled from his saddle and landed with his full weight on his head and right shoulder, the impact breaking his neck-bones and killing him almost instantly.

At the same time, two other scouts' ponies were badly lamed by an even crueller trick.

Robert immediately halted the advance and ordered his men to dismount.

The Englishman walked slowly forward, raking the ground in front of his boots with the curved blade of his sword. He discovered the earth had been thickly strewn with little twists of sharpened iron – caltrops, or the Devil's thorns, they were called in Christendom. He carefully picked up one of these items and examined it closely.

The caltrop was made of two barbs of iron wire, two or three inches long and sharpened at both ends, which were twisted around each other to make a pyramid shape, so that, no matter how the object fell on the ground, one of the four dagger-like iron spikes was always pointing upward, while the other three points were dug into the earth. It was an ingenious defence against horsemen – horribly ingenious.

Robert tucked the caltrop away in his pouch and went forward on foot, stepping carefully, to see to the injured horses. Khuchar's mount had to be dispatched, its big neck vein sliced open with Robert's long Circassian dagger. The other two ponies were in great distress and only time would tell if their caltrop-pierced hooves would heal.

Robert glared up at the walls of Zhong Xing, half a mile away, and cursed his foes, calling on God to smite them for their wanton cruelty to his men's poor animals.

It took three days of painstaking work – and another three ponies maimed – for the road to Zhong Xing to be fully cleared. Mongols from the Golden Eagles and Snow Leopards crawled on their bellies hour after hour to seek out the caltrops hidden deep in the grass, while others followed with spades to fill in the pit traps.

From time to time, the Hexi on the walls would fire off their fiendish machines and, amid a deluge of fire and stinking smoke, an iron spear would arc down upon them. Mercifully, only one man was killed by these devilish contraptions. And, while it was most alarming for the crawling troopers, they bore the daily perils bravely.

Four days later, when Genghis Khan and his *tumet* approached the high walls of the capital city, Robert was able to report that the road was clear of all hazards.

Genghis Khan surrounded the city on the western side and posted one *tumen* on the eastern bank, too, across the waters of the mighty Yellow River. His engineers, the ingenious marmot-men, set about digging placements of their trebuchet batteries and erecting earthworks all around the Hexi, a physical symbol of the city's besiegement and a protection against Hexi arrows and the iron spears of their fire-spitting machines.

Subutai returned victorious from subduing the northern towns of the corridor and the whole Mongol army settled down before Zhong Xing's walls for a long siege.

Autumn was nearly upon them; and no one was anticipating a swift victory.

The eight *tumet* of Genghis Khan – some eighty thousand men – set up their *ger*, pastured their vast herds, and began systematically stripping the surrounding villages and lands of all that was valuable or fit to eat or drink. Robert found himself busy organising camel trains to transport his portion of the Hexi loot, which had been significant, safely back up the corridor and on to Samarkand, some two thousand miles distant. He wrote letters to Karacha, and to Idar, too, greeting the Circassian as a fellow Christian. He expected his heavily laden trains to arrive by Christmastide.

Then, one day in late August, he was summoned to the Great Khan's huge *ger*.

Robert found the khan sitting on a cushion, drinking Chinese rice wine with his two sons Ogedei and Tolui, and telling stories of the old days on the northern steppe when the man who was now the world's most powerful warlord had been a penniless and hunted fugitive. Tolui gave Robert a friendly nod and a grin when he arrived, but Ogedei ignored him completely, as did their father, who was in full storytelling flow.

Robert accepted a bowl of strong rice wine from a servant, sat down uninvited, and listened to the old story. Just behind the Great Khan loomed two men of the *turghaut*, the Day Guard, leaning on their spears, apparently listening intently, too.

Robert thought, *Even in his own* ger, *with his victorious army all around him, and his two sons at his side, the Great Khan feels the need for armed protection*.

He wondered what this lad Temujin, the raggedy steppe beggar of the story, who dreamed of uniting all the tribes, had truly been like. Probably not all that different to the lively old fellow sitting before him now, telling his tale. As he observed the Great Khan, Robert could also see how aged he had become after all these months of war.

He was much thinner than when Robert had first met him outside the walls of Otrar eight years ago. His face more deeply lined, his hand, as he made a gesture to emphasise part of the story, quivered just a little. He noted the large brown spots that his own father had sported on the backs of his hands in the years before his death. There was a looseness, too, under the khan's jaw, the sagging of an old man's skin.

The story was done and Tolui cried 'Bravo!' Ogedei tossed back his rice wine and called for another bowl, and the Great Khan was now speaking directly to him.

'I am pleased with you Noyan Robyert Baghatur. You have served me well this past summer. Your *mingghat* have smoothed our path and allowed us to ride from victory to victory. These Hexi are all but beaten – all but that stubborn city yonder, which will surely fall before the snows come. The cowardly Tangut emperor will soon grovel in the dust before my throne and his entire Hexi Empire shall be mine.

'However, I have no notion of sitting in my *ger* until then, drinking wine and growing lazy and waiting for the marmot-men to finish their work. My brave sons Tolui and Ogedei can complete the task, with wise old Subutai to guide them. I have decided to make a scouting sweep myself to determine our next campaign. I have chosen you, *Baghatur*, to accompany me, as a reward for your valuable service.'

'I'm honoured, Great Khan,' said Robert. 'But where are we going?'

'South,' said Genghis Khan, his faded brown eyes twinkling. 'South along the Yellow River, back along its course, and up into the high mountains.'

-

If Robert had entertained the notion that the Great Khan would be travelling light on this scouting mission, he was quickly disabused of it. A full *tumen* of the *kheshig*, the royal bodyguard – ten thousand men – would be accompanying the Lord of the Steppe in his southern sweep, under a newly appointed *kheshig* general called Chormaqan, whom Robert knew well since he had been on campaign with Subutai in the Rus' lands. Robert's *mingghat* led the way southward along the river with the *kheshig* and the Great Khan following him.

Robert did indeed feel honoured by the great man's display of favour. He dined with Genghis Khan and Chormaqan and his senior *kheshig* officers most evenings on the march, and was usually lavishly entertained in the royal *ger*. At dawn, when he rode out with his own men to scout the road ahead, he quite often went forth with a thumping head and certain woolliness of thought that only a hard gallop could dispel.

The scouting column of twelve thousand Mongols moved comparatively swiftly, traversing the plain of the Yellow River and heading back the way they had come only a month or so ago. They passed through bleak, burnt-out villages stripped bare and crowds of pitiful villagers begging by the roads for something to keep them alive through the harsh winter ahead, and Robert had to harden his heart once again when he saw naked Chinese children the same age as Jalair, but huge-eyed and skinny as skeletons, held up by desperate mothers seeking food or alms by the side of the roads.

The Mongol column forged on south into grassland, where the sheep and goats grazed, and there they lingered a few days before branching off south-west into the foothills, with the white-topped peaks of the Tibetan plateau clear in the distance.

They crossed the Yellow River at a town called Jishi, with the bare, brown shoulders of the mountains crowding around them, then turned east. They skirted the city of Lanzhou, still held by the Hexi, and came down again into lush grasslands, fed by many streams, the natural home of the Hexi herdsmen and their bountiful flocks.

'This is good land,' said the khan, one evening at their usual meal. 'I could graze my horses here, even in the hardest winter, to make ready for the new campaign.'

They were eating a simple repast – roasted lamb, ewe's cheese and millet bread, washed down with *airaq* – and, unusually, Robert was alone with the Great Khan, apart from two looming *kabtaut* or Night Guards. Robert finished his mouthful and wiped his lips before daring to ask where the khan planned to lead his *tumet* next.

'Tomorrow we shall ride out together, you and I, and I shall show you myself, *Baghatur*,' said the khan. 'But, tonight, you will tell me of your home, of the Christian lands.'

This was not the first time the Englishman had been asked to perform this service by his khan, and each time he attempted it, he tried to make Christendom sound more alluring, more wealthy, more welcoming, and also more intriguingly mysterious.

'You would be greeted as a conquering hero in my country, Great One,' said Robert, 'particularly if you helped our kings to defeat their mortal enemies in the Holy Land. You would be praised by all the great lords, kings and emperors, hailed as a saviour. People would line the streets and sing your praises, calling down God's blessings upon your head. You would be given many fine gifts – treasures, jewels and rich lands, fine horses and teeming herds. We would divide the world between us – you, Great Khan, in the East, and the kings of Europe in the West – and together we would usher in a new era of peace and prosperity, a happy age of wealth and plenty.'

'These mortal enemies of your kings, the ones you urge me to defeat, they are followers of the Prophet, yes? Like the Khwarazmians and the Persians?'

'They are Saracens, Great One, a cruel race who would rule over all mankind.'

'And these cruel people live in the harsh deserts beyond Baghdad, between that ancient trading city and the great blue western sea – what was its name again?'

'We call it the Middle Sea,' said Robert. 'An enormous salt lake more than a thousand miles long, with the great deserts of Africa to the south and the green hills of Europe to the north. It is a body of water that stretches all the way from the Holy Land to the Pillars of Hercules and the beginning of another sea, a mighty ocean even greater than the Middle Sea, which marks the very limits of the known world.'

'I do not care for seas, nor yet for oceans,' said the Great Khan. 'You cannot ride far by sea, I find. Give me land, firm land, wide grassland and high mountains.'

'We have grasslands, too,' said Robert, 'a plain in Hungary that rolls like the steppe across—'

'You offer your Christian lands like a bazaar merchant showing me a fine carpet, Robyert,' said the Great Khan, 'but

I do not think that the destiny of our Mongol nation lies in the West, not, at least, while I live. No, I will not take my people west.'

The Englishman tried his best to hide his disappointment.

'Perhaps the next khan will think differently of this matter,' his host said, 'I could not say. But I would conquer the East before looking west. I will possess all the Chinese lands, and subjugate them to my will. Then look beyond, further eastwards.'

Robert knew he was very likely beaten, yet he struggled on, almost heroically, trying one last time to persuade the Great Khan to change his mind on this matter.

'A single *tumen*, Great One, a single *tumen* of ten thousand Mongols could shift the balance in the Holy Land in favour of Christendom. I would lead this column myself, if you wish it – or one of your generals, your son General Tolui, the *otchigin*, perhaps, might command the westward expedition. We would quash the rebellion in the Khorasan, capture the wealthy city of Baghdad, to the everlasting glory of your name, then ride hard for Jerusalem and a victory that would shake the world...'

'I cannot spare even a single *tumen*,' said the khan. 'You will understand why tomorrow. Have patience, Robyert. Do not trouble yourself: there *will* be plenty of loot, as much as your merchant's heart could ever desire. Now I must go to my bed.'

–

Genghis Khan spurred ahead of Robert on his favourite reddish-grey horse, heading up a tongue of land, a narrow promontory of sandstone just a couple of paces wide, which jutted out east over the huge plain below.

They had left at dawn and stopped, briefly, at a one-donkey town called Hao Shui Chuan, where they had taken their noonday meal and rested the horses. Then, in the late afternoon, after a short nap, Genghis Khan had urged Robert to ride with him alone up to this high vantage point.

It was evident the Great Khan had been here before, and it was indeed an extraordinary place from which to view the world.

The two men, the far-from-home Englishman and the Lord of the Steppe, dismounted at the cliff edge of the promontory, with the massed Golden Eagles and Snow Leopards back down the track a hundred yards behind them, and two *turghaut* Day Guard soldiers leading the horses up the steep slope to join up with their master and his honoured servant.

Genghis Khan was clearly excited to be showing this special place to Robert, and took him firmly by the sleeve of his *deel* and almost dragged him to the edge of the cliff at the end of the protruding tongue of land.

'There,' he said. 'Can you see it, Robyert?' He was pointing at the landscape stretched out below them.

Robert looked. There was a narrow ridge of mountain marching away south-east, over to their right, but, to the east of that spine, there was a plain where two rivers met and wound off into the distance. On the eastern slopes of the ridge, the land had been cut into a series of descending steps, strips of farmland shimmering iridescent green in the afternoon sun, fashioned in that manner, Robert knew, for the cultivation of rice.

Down on the plain below, the land was divided into hundreds of square fields of ripening crops. There were also many grassy pastures further out, and here and there were dotted orchards heavy with autumn fruit. It was a rich land, indeed, a land of peace and plenty. It seemed spread before them like a banquet awaiting their pleasure.

'Why am I looking at this, Great One?' asked Robert. He had never seen the old khan so animated, pacing back and forth. He seemed almost childlike in his joy.

'You are looking, *Baghatur*, at our future,' said Genghis Khan. 'That, down there, my friend, is the land of the Jin Emperor: a wealthy, weak and ill-warded land. We could capture it, just you and I, Robyert, with your two *mingghat*. This plain below us is called the province of Shaanxi, and to the east and south is the Empire of the Song. Another rich, decaying realm beyond the Jin lands, which is also ripe for conquest. Here we are, sitting like two hungry wolves in the mountains, looking down at unguarded folds full of lambs. Is that not magnificent?'

Robert was spared from answering by one of the *turghaut* who came forward and said, 'Be careful of the cliff edge, my khan. It may be treacherous.'

Genghis Khan waved the man away. 'Wait for me below, stupid one. I will not fall off this little cliff. I am showing Robyert Baghatur all the wonders of the East.'

The khan then looked directly at the Englishman. 'This is why I will not go west,' he said. 'From here for a thousand miles eastwards is Cathay, and some of the richest lands on earth. Think of the spoils, Robyert – think of the vast riches that your Venetian friends and you will receive when we have conquered this soft land and its soft peoples, and taken away their wealth, their horses and animals, their women. Their gold, their jade and their jewels. What more could a man desire from life?'

Robert was indeed tempted. He gazed down at the lush lands below him and could imagine himself at the head of the Snow Leopards galloping through a dozen burning villages, standing with a red, dripping sword over a vast pile of looted treasure.

'This is where we will campaign next, Noyan Robyert,' said the khan, still looking intently at the Englishman. 'You asked me for a *tumen* last night, and I will give you one. But not to go west – to go east! East into the Jin lands to the rout and ruin of our foes. I shall make you a great man among the Mongols, Noyan Robyert – I swear it – I will make you a general, an *orlok*, and perhaps even, one day, a khan!'

Robert could think of nothing to say, but this seemed to satisfy the Great Khan, who nodded as if they had agreed upon it, turned and began walking back to his horse.

The Englishman walked with him and, in those brief moments between the cliff edge and the two horses, he considered his decision one last time. Could he really do this deed? Would God forgive him for the terrible thing he planned to do. It was a vile sin, and a terrible crime. But it might also be the salvation of Christendom. Here was the perfect opportunity. Now was the time. And God must surely have arranged it so.

Deus vult.

Robert felt nothing. The decision had been made. No guilt, no shame. No fear. He could hear the Great Khan's own words in his head: 'That is the Mongol way. To do what is necessary. What*ever* is necessary. Keep these words close to your heart!'

He slipped his hand into his belt pouch as he walked, then he stood by the red-grey horse's saddle, on the off side, as the Great Khan found his stirrup on the near side. After a glance down the slope to the two *turghaut*, who were speaking to each other at the base of the promontory, seventy yards away, Robert acted. He quickly shoved the caltrop under the khan's saddle between the leather and the horse's flesh.

The Lord of the Steppe put his left boot in the stirrup, swung his right leg over the horse and thumped down with all his weight in the saddle.

The horse screamed as the sharp barb of the iron caltrop was forced into the soft meat of his back. The animal kicked and bucked and Genghis Khan, who had not yet placed his foot in the right stirrup was hurled from the horse's back, sailed through the air and crunched down on the rocky ground. Robert stayed well clear of the kicking horse. He could hear the *turghaut* below, shouting in alarm and beginning to run up the slope, and knew he had little time. He ran to the prone form of the khan. He knew that God was with him, for the kicking, bucking horse was squarely between him and the two sprinting bodyguards, completely blocking their view.

He reached Genghis Khan and knelt beside him. The old man was still breathing but he had a bloody graze down one side of his face and a soft mushy indentation on the back of his skull on the left, where his head had made an impact with rock. Robert whipped out the Circassian dagger from under his left armpit. He said, 'In the name of God!' and rammed the blade into the wet, bloodied part of the Great Khan's broken skull, sending the thin steel deep into his living brain.

Genghis Khan's eyes flicked up. And, as Robert quickly tucked the blade out of sight again in his *deel*, he thought he saw the khan's lips form the question 'Why?'

He was brutally hurled aside by one of the *turghaut*, and the two bodyguards bent over the body of the most powerful man on earth, loudly calling out his name. Robert got to his feet and went to calm the red-grey horse. As gently as he could, crooning to the animal in soft Norman French, he removed the bloody caltrop from under the saddle and discreetly flicked it over the edge of the cliff.

'He is gone,' said one of the *turghaut*. 'Our father, our Great Khan, is no more.'

Chapter Twenty-four

The court had adjourned for dinner and, at his habitual writing desk in the ground-floor chamber of the castle tower, Father Ivo of Narbonne unrolled the kidskin wallet that contained his writing materials. He set out the ink pot and silver sander, selected a goose feather and began to sharpen it with his little folding knife. After a moment's reflection, he dipped the nib in the ink pot, shook off a few excess drops, and began to write on a large piece of parchment on the sloping table before him.

> *To Géraud de Malemort, by the Grace of God, Bishop of Bordeaux, from Ivo of Narbonne, special enquêteur and humblest of his clerks, a description of the first morning of the trial of Robert of Hadlow at Vienna Castle in the Duchy of Austria.*
>
> *My lord, it is with great joy and profound thanks to Almighty God that I may tell you that the trial of the miscreant Templar is proceeding exactly as we had hoped. I have been accepted by the duke's court to represent Robert as his 'prisoner's friend' and this dull-witted Englishman himself believes that I am acting solely and honestly in his interest, with an earnest desire to see him fully exonerated by the court.*
>
> *Your friend Geoffrey of Beaulieu, the lawyer, has been very helpful in this regard, and in fixing the simple form of this trial. May I congratulate you in persuading him to aid us in this matter. The prisoner will be questioned by the court, then his sentence pronounced, and*

he shall suffer its execution shortly afterwards. He has already admitted to numerous crimes, including the brutal murder of a high king of the Tartars, and I have been assiduous in insisting, from the first, that Robert was induced to commit his crimes at the behest of the leaders of the devil-worshipping Templar cult, and in particular by your sin-blackened brother Jean de Malemort.

Robert of Hadlow himself seems oblivious to the way in which the Templar Order will be damaged by this public exposure of their vile crimes. The world will soon know that their senior Knights consorted with the enemies of Christendom, those minions of Satan called the Tartars, and I am confident that by the end of this trial, the Order will be so tarnished by his testimony that a separate prosecution by your master, His Most Christian Majesty Louis of France, of their Grand Master and his officers will be feasible, and will perhaps even be seen as desirable by the nobility of Christendom and even the Pope himself. If we can rouse a righteous fury in the bosom of Christendom, then we can move to expunge this whole heretical Order from the face of the Earth. How I pray that this blessed result may come to pass…

–

During the dinner hour Robert had been led away from the hall to the guard room across the courtyard, where he was given cold cabbage soup, half a pork sausage, a slice of rye bread and even a mug of sweet, nutty ale. After that hour-long respite, he was led back to the castle ducal hall by his gaolers, where the three judges and the provost, and the various members of the public were all just taking their seats.

As he watched the burghers, clergy and local knights finding places on the benches at both sides of the hall, he saw the tall form of a slender man that looked somehow familiar to him.

The fellow was settling himself on the middle bench on the left side, but since he was wearing a long travelling cloak with a deep hood, and had his back turned to Robert, there was no easy way of identifying him. And when the man sat down on his bench, his face was hidden by the others in the crowd. Yet there was something about the way he moved that struck a chord in Robert's mind.

'You are doing very well, my son,' Father Ivo whispered in his ear, as the priest resumed his stool beside his wooden box. 'I do believe the court is on your side.'

It was the Duke of Austria who called the court to order. And when the magpie-chattering crowd had finally quieted, he said, 'I have some questions to put to the prisoner before we hear any more from him about his activities in the East. Firstly – *why*? Why did you do this terrible thing? Why cause this Genghis Khan fellow to fall from his horse, then dispatch him like some common assassin when he was helpless on the ground? Why this gross *lèse-majesté*? This wanton and murderous act is what I simply cannot understand. Will the prisoner answer me?'

'For the sake of his son Lord Tolui,' said Robert. 'And for Christendom.'

'What in God's name do you mean by that?' said the duke.

It was Geoffrey, the Dominican, who replied.

'The prisoner claims that he murdered this Great Khan of Tartary so that his friend Lord Tolui, the khan's youngest son, could inherit his throne.'

There was a stunned silence in the court.

'Is this true?' said the duke, both astonished and appalled. 'You played the assassin to make this Tolui the next high king of the Tartars?'

'I did,' said Robert. 'Tolui – and his Nestorian Christian wife Sorkoktani – had assured me that if he were to become the next Great Khan, he would turn his attention to the West. If Tolui were to rule, the Mongols would ride to Christendom's aid.

Lady Sorkoktani herself even mentioned that she would like to see the Holy Land with her own eyes, and walk in the blessed footsteps of Our Lord and Saviour Jesus Christ.'

The Provost of Vienna, Wilhelm von Eslarn, seemed more astonished than any man there by the reason given for Robert's lethal actions.

'Do I have this correctly? You admit that you are an assassin? You freely reveal to all that you secretly planned and executed the murder of the Tartar king?'

'Have you not been paying attention, Provost?' said Robert. 'Should I begin my entire tale afresh, starting from the very beginning just for you?'

'There is no call for that: you are condemned out of your own mouth. You admit that you are a vile assassin, a Templar assassin. I put it to His Grace that there is no need to continue this trial. We may now proceed to sentencing without further delay.'

'But he is not on trial for murdering a foreign monarch,' said Heinrich von Leitzdorf, the constable of the castle, 'he is charged as a traitor to Christendom.'

'And let us not forget that the prisoner was, in effect, ordered to do this awful deed by his Templar superior,' said Ivo of Narbonne. 'By Jean de Malemort.'

'I must take responsibility,' said Robert, 'but that is partly true. Jean de Malemort asked me the question in Tana that first put this killing into my mind. He asked me, if the Great Khan were to die, who would succeed him, and if one of his sons might not look more favourably on our struggle. I pondered this question for many months afterwards. That query was the seed from which my plan grew. But, keep in your minds, sirs, that the man I dispatched was *Genghis Khan*.'

'So?' said Wilhelm von Eslarn.

'The Dominican called him the Antichrist,' said Robert. 'The little friar sitting there, Geoffrey de Beaulieu, said he knew that Genghis Khan had caused the deaths of thousands upon thousands of innocent men, women and children, which is true, and that he was evil. *And I killed him*. I killed the man you named as the Antichrist. Surely, I should be praised by all Christians for ridding the world of such a monster.'

There was another stunned silence in the hall then one man in the gallery began to laugh, and soon the mirth was both loud and general.

'He's got you there, Dominican,' said a voice that Robert felt sure he had heard somewhere before. 'Mayhap we should declare him a saint for that killing.'

As the duke called for silence, Wilhelm retreated again to his place and the Dominican rose to his feet. 'Now that we have all enjoyed a good laugh at my expense,' he said, 'may I suggest we resume? I, too, have questions for the prisoner.'

He paused for a beat, then said, 'You claim you killed this khan to make Tolui the next ruler of these Tartars. Did this come to pass? Did Tolui ascend the throne?'

'He did become the new khan, in a manner of speaking,' said Robert.

'Then why did he not lead his mighty army to the rescue of Christendom? You committed murder, you say, to aid the beleaguered Christians of Outremer. Yet I have heard of no aid; and not one Tartar horseman has ridden to the defence of the Holy Land.'

'If you will allow me to resume my tale, Brother Geoffrey, you shall discover why this is indeed the case,' said Robert.

-

It was General Chormaqan who saved Robert's life that black day, as a kind of frenzied madness descended on the Mongol scouting column.

The two men of the *kheshig* who had been tasked with protecting Genghis Khan that afternoon were immediately seized and beheaded by their fellow troopers for so signally failing in their duty, and Robert, too, was grabbed by a knot of furious troopers and forced to kneel down beside their headless bodies, while the weeping *noyan* of that detachment brandished his blood-dripping sword high, ready to strike.

Robert truly believed his life on this Earth was over, and he was mumbling his prayers, when Chormaqan came galloping up, with some of Robert's Snow Leopards. The commander of the *kheshig* brusquely ordered the grief-mad *noyan* to put away his bloody sword and release the Englishman immediately.

Shaken but not much surprised by the tumult he had caused, Robert was soon surrounded by his own men, with Arslan standing beside him with a nocked arrow on the string, and Saka and Taka both with drawn swords, while the sobbing *noyan* and the officers of the *turghaut* began to argue loudly about what was to be done.

'Silence!' roared Chormaqan. 'Be silent, you barking dogs. I will decide what is to be done. First, we must care for the Great Khan's remains. You and you, gather up the body of the Lord of the Steppe, wrap him in your cloaks – treat his corpse as tenderly as you would your own newborn babe.'

Back in camp, an hour or two later, Robert was summoned to Chormaqan's *ger* just as dusk was falling. He was ordered to give a full and accurate account to the general of the tragic events on the promontory that afternoon. Since the two *turghaut* guards were already dead, Robert's was the only testimony to the old khan's demise.

'Something frighted his red-grey horse, General, but I do not know what,' said Robert. 'Perhaps it was a snake. I could not say. But the animal reared up and the Great Khan was thrown from his saddle. He landed badly and, by the time I got to him, he was nearly gone. His skull was completely stove in on the left-hand side. And the Great Khan could not speak. He tried to say something to me but he failed, and then he was gone. That is all I know.'

'Tell me, *Baghatur*, what had you been talking about with the Great Khan in the hours before his death. Did you two quarrel? Were there any harsh words?'

Robert looked the general directly in the eye.

'Indeed not,' he said. 'The Great Khan had just promised me a great honour. He told me he would make me a khan, an *orlok* of his troops, and give me my own *tumen* to take on campaign into the Jin lands. And I accepted his offer with gratitude.'

'Hmm,' said Chormaqan. 'As it happens, I believe you. The Great Khan discussed this very matter with me in the days before his demise. He asked me if you could be trusted, and I said I thought you could. On the other hand, Subutai told me once that it was your fervent desire to take the army west to Baghdad. Is this true?'

'Yes, General,' said Robert. 'It is true I would see Baghdad in Mongol hands, and all the lands between Khwarazmia and the Middle Sea, as well. But I was loyal to the Great Khan and, when he offered me a *tumen*, I perceived it the greater honour.'

Sarantuya wept bitter tears when she heard the news. And Robert knew then that he could never admit what he had done. He felt deep remorse, as well, for his actions.

The Great Khan had been kind to him, in his way, and had given him many gifts. And Robert had repaid that kindness with an assassin's blade. He prayed a great deal in the days after the Great Khan's death, asking God for a sign that he had indeed been serving Christendom by striking him down. *Am I yet a Christian*, he asked himself, *if I murder such a great man by stealth? Did I do wrong, Lord?* He begged for divine forgiveness and actually felt a little better after spending so many hours on his knees. He also begged the Almighty to grant that his actions bore the desired fruit.

He recalled the stirring words of Jean de Malemort's letter to him: '*The cause of Christ that we serve is paramount – nothing else matters, not our lives, nor even the lives of our comrades. Only the cause should be your guiding light.*'

And Robert knew that he had indeed killed his khan to serve that cause.

The reconnaissance of the south was abandoned and the dejected column made its way slowly back north to the city of Zhong Xing, bearing the corpse of the Great Khan on a golden palanquin in their midst. Once there, on the banks of the Yellow River, they discovered that Subutai and Tolui had already broken through the high walls and their victorious men were even now looting and sacking the Chinese city.

The Hexi emperor and his family were captured, ritually humiliated and refused the mercy they begged for. They were dispatched by Subutai's men, never knowing that the khan who caused their downfall had already gone on to the Great Hereafter.

Indeed, Chormaqan tried to keep the news of the Great Khan's death a secret for as long as possible within the Mongol ranks. The campaign was over, and Subutai, who knew the truth of the matter, ordered all the *tumet* to return north to Mongolia.

'Will they make you the next Great Khan?' Robert asked Tolui, as they rested the men in the Black City once again before making the harsh crossing of the Gobi. He had not admitted the deed to his friend but Tolui seemed to sense that Robert had played some part in his father's unexpected death. Sorkoktani greeted him as a hero, beaming at him, lavishing him with praise, offering him treats of fine foods and wine whenever he was their guest in Tolui's *ger*, which made Robert feel deeply uncomfortable.

'It is not yet certain,' said Tolui, 'but I think I have the support of most of the generals and the Golden Kin. Subutai says he is privately with me but he cannot make his support public yet, as he must be seen to be impartial as the senior *orlok*. And my nephew Batu Khan, the son of my dead brother Jochi, has written to me to say that he is loyal to me, too.'

Tolui went on to list a dozen other khans and senior officers who were pledged to him and his glorious rule. However, there was one great name, one member of the Golden Kin, that Tolui seemed reluctant even to mention to the Englishman.

The Mongol army had split into two rival factions by the time they reached the Black City. They formed two separate encampments around the lake. Every few days, another officer would come to Tolui's *ger*, drink a cup of *airaq* and make his oath to the Prince of the Fireplace, promising to serve him faithfully as the next Great Khan.

Yet the other faction of the Mongol army, which was almost as large as Tolui's, supported a different candidate – Genghis Khan's third son, Ogedei. And Chagatai, the oldest living son, had sent word from the north that he supported Ogedei's claim.

'It will be decided at Karakorum,' Sarantuya informed Robert one night. 'But Ogedei is spreading rumours that Genghis Khan promised *him* the throne at the last *kurultai*. Ogedei claims the succession was decided, in secret, more than a year ago.'

The Great Khan's body was carefully washed and wrapped in swathes of perfumed felt and placed in a sweet-smelling sandalwood coffin, with two polished recurved bows and four quivers of arrows, a fine sword and many precious objects of jade, silver and gold – all at Subutai's direction – and an honour guard of a thousand *kheshig* carried the body of their khan reverentially across the Gobi, beyond Karakorum and north, far north into the furthest reaches of Mongolia.

The location of the burial was designed to be kept secret for all eternity; but Robert was told privately by Tolui that they took his sandalwood coffin to a mountain called Burkhan Khaldun, near where the boy Temujin was born, and there they buried him deep in an unmarked grave in the wilderness, never to be defiled by his enemies.

A thousand white horses were killed at his grave, so that their spirits could travel with him to the heavens; and Subutai ordered the fifty Chinese labourers who dug the grave to be slaughtered, too, so that none might reveal its location. They said Genghis Khan's spirit would be reborn into a baby boy, when the Eternal Blue Sky decreed it, and he would rise again to bring even greater glory to his beloved Mongol nation.

That autumn in Karakorum, as the nation mourned the Great Khan's death with horse races, archery contests and *Bökh* bouts in his honour, the two factions of the Mongol world existed in a barely veiled state of hostility. Indeed, there were many incidents of actual hostility, even violence, when groups of supporters of the two rival khans met each other on the steppe and fought in the name of their preferred candidate.

While both Ogedei and Tolui blamed each other for encouraging the fighting and called for peace and harmony among all Mongols, in truth, Robert knew the rival brothers were testing their strength and he braced himself for full-scale civil war to break out on the steppe.

As well as Arslan, Begter, Hasar, Saka and Taka living in his *ger*, he posted a dozen Snow Leopards outside his door, day and night, for his own peace of mind. Sarantuya was very large now, since the baby was only a few weeks away, and Robert, who had very little experience of childbirth, was perpetually anxious about her well-being.

Two months after the return of the victorious *tumet* to Karakorum, a grand council was called, to be held in what had been the Great Khan's travelling *ger* with Yelu Ahai presiding, to settle the vexed matter of the succession. Robert was a little surprised to be invited to attend this most Mongol of events.

'You are a *noyan* and a *baghatur*,' said Sarantuya, as she helped him to dress in his best *deel* for the occasion and to hang the sword from his belt just so, 'of course you would be invited to the council. All senior commanders and khans will be there.'

'Have you been invited, Saran – you are one of the Golden Kin?'

'No women. This is men's work. I will visit Sorkoktani, who is very anxious about the outcome. She cannot sleep. She fears that her husband will be dispossessed by the grand council in favour of that worthless drunkard Ogedei.'

'Tell her not to be concerned,' said Robert. 'Tolui is certain to be chosen.'

Chapter Twenty-five

As befitted the pretence of a meeting of equals, about a hundred thick silk-covered cushions had been laid out in a large semi-circle in the centre of the Great Khan's *ger*, with Yelu Ahai sitting cross-legged in the centre at the rear of the tent, in the position the late Lord of the Steppe had occupied. There was no objection to Yelu occupying this crucial position since there was no possibility of Yelu becoming the new khan.

He was a Chinese man from the Jin lands, once a senior envoy of the Jin Emperor, but who, as legend had it, had been so impressed with Genghis Khan on their first meeting that he offered him his lifelong service. He had risen over more than twenty years of diligent labour from a humble clerk to become the Great Khan's chief minister. Tolui had once said to Robert that Yelu Ahai had more power than the Great Khan, and he was only half-joking. However, as a Jin foreigner, he could never challenge the authority of a member of the Golden Kin, and so both sides were content for Yelu to play the important role of arbitrator at the council.

General Subutai sat to the left of Yelu Ahai and General Chormaqan sat to his right; they represented the most senior commanders of the army and the small part of the Mongol nation that was not aligned with either faction. Then the two rival khans took up their places on the left or right side of the semicircle. Lord Tolui took his place halfway around to the left, and Batu Khan, Jochi's son, a handsome warrior in his twenties, sat down next to him, indicating his support. Robert took a place a few cushions along from Tolui, next to an older *noyan*, whom he knew only slightly.

On the right side, Ogedei sat opposite Tolui, his supporters all around him, and Robert could not help but notice that Khuyag was not among them. He wondered where the wretched man was. This was an important day for Ogedei, and indeed for the nation, and Khuyag was an experienced *noyan*. He had been given command of the White Foxes, one of Ogedei's *mingghat*. It was odd that Khuyag was not here.

Yelu Ahai began the proceedings. 'We all know why we are gathered here,' he said. 'Our Mongol nation is divided and this makes us weak. We cannot afford to allow our enemies to enjoy our weakness for much longer. The Jin have seen what occurred in the Hexi lands and are already massing their legions and preparing to make war with us. Our spies also say that the Jin are making plans with the Song to combine and attack us jointly. In the south-west, the remnants of the Khwarazmian forces roam unchecked in the Khorasan, threatening a full-scale rebellion. Even the Bulgars of the Volga are gathering their strength to challenge us in the West. We must settle this matter today and all unite behind whomsoever is chosen as Great Khan.'

Yelu Ahai paused there. 'Are all men here agreed on that?'

There was a chorus of assent. Both Tolui and Ogedei nodded their heads to acknowledge they would abide by the decision of the grand council.

Yelu went on, 'Therefore I ask both men who claim the honour of the title of Great Khan to stand now and make their claim. Lord Tolui, would you begin?'

Tolui got to his feet. He was dressed elegantly, in a robe of heavy black silk that fell to his goat-hide boots, with a wide cloth-of-gold belt wrapped around his slim middle. A chain of heavy golden links hung around his neck. His hair had been freshly shaved in the traditional Mongol pattern: bald on the top, with a fringe across the brows and around the back of his head, and four long, plaited pigtails, two hanging behind his ears, two in front.

He looked rather magnificent, Robert thought.

Like a Great Khan already.

'You all know me,' said Tolui. 'Many of you have fought beside me, against the Jin in the north, south in the Khorasan, and along the Hexi Corridor. You know I am a fearless leader. I am ruthless to my enemies and generous to my friends. My *tumet* are ever victorious. The Great Khan himself praised me for my conduct in war and always showed me his favour. I am of the Golden Kin. The warrior blood of the Great Khan runs in my veins. I am the *otchigin* – the Prince of the Fireplace – the youngest son of Genghis Khan, who is closest to his mother's womb, closest to the bloodline.'

Tolui paused and looked round the semicircle. 'Therefore, I am the man who should be the next Great Khan by right of blood and ancient steppe custom. And I am more than ready for the great task Tenggri has set before me. And I vow to lead the whole Mongol nation onwards to even greater glory.'

His supporters began cheering and clapping their hands. Tolui gave a stiff bow, walked back to his place and sat down. The left side of the semicircle were chanting, 'Tolui… Tolui… Tolui…' And Robert joined in the chant. Yelu Ahai watched this calmly, but Robert could tell that Subutai was angry.

The greatest of all Mongol generals surged to his feet.

'Enough. That is enough,' Subutai shouted, his face red. 'This is not some horse race – nor the *Bökh*. We meet here in solemn council to choose our next khan, not cheer the winner across the finishing line. Be silent, all of you.'

A shamefaced quiet fell over the semicircle.

'Lord Tolui has spoken,' said Yelu. 'It is time for Lord Ogedei to speak.'

Ogedei got to his feet, stumbling a little. Robert could see that he was drunk.

'Well,' Ogedei said, 'that was a pretty speech from my little brother. Very pretty. But know this, all of you: I, too, am of the Great Khan's blood. Not the *otchigin*, that is for sure. I am not the *runt* of the litter. I am the *leader* of the herd.'

There were cries of disapproval at this discourtesy. Tolui said nothing.

'My little brother Tolui claims that his *tumet* are ever victorious, and yet the chief minister has just told us that the Jin are preparing to attack us with their Song allies. How much of a victory did my little brother achieve over the Jin that they are coming back again now, stronger than ever? And he was in the Khorasan, too, he boasts. That region has thrown off Mongol rule with a shrug of its shoulders. What kind of victory did he achieve that they, too, still have the strength to resist us?'

Robert was watching Ogedei walking back and forth before his side of the semicircle, slightly unsteady, but his voice full of fire. He noticed a man come in and join that side of the semicircle, taking his place and sitting down behind Ogedei's cushion. It was Khuyag, and as he sat down, he caught Robert's eye and bared his yellow teeth at him in a kind of silent snarl.

Robert looked away; he could feel his hatred of Khuyag as a glowing coal in his belly. Ogedei was still in full flood, the wine in his veins giving him a fine fluency.

'My runty little brother claims the Great Khan praised him for his leadership in war – but I never heard him do so. Indeed, the Great Khan once told me, in confidence, he thought Tolui was a weak and vain fellow, that he was more interested in rutting with his beautiful wife than riding to war like a man—'

'Lies,' shouted Tolui. 'Those are barefaced lies—'

'Lord Tolui,' said Yelu, 'you have had your chance to speak. It is Lord Ogedei's turn. However, I must say to you, Lord Ogedei, that your insults demean this gathering. And I will hear no more of them. Tell us why *you* should be elected Great Khan, and then we will all make our choice.'

'Forgive me, Lord Yelu, but I think the commanders gathered here should know what my illustrious father thought of his youngest son – but, since you ask, I shall tell you why I should be the next Great Khan. It is simply this: Genghis Khan himself told me that I was his chosen successor. I swear this on my life, and many Mongols here can also attest to it, too. I am of the Golden Kin, the blood of the Lord of the Steppes flows in my veins, and the Great Khan himself *chose* me as his heir. Genghis Khan stated that I should rule the Ulus he won after he was gone.'

Ogedei went back to his place and plumped down on his cushion in front of Khuyag. His supporters began to cheer and call out his name, but Yelu quickly stopped them. The chief minister looked round the semicircle and said, 'It is time to choose. All those who would have Lord Tolui as our Great Khan will please stand up.'

Robert got to his feet along with all the men on the left side of the semicircle; he noticed that Subutai also got to his feet. Yelu was counting Mongols as they stood, as was one of his Chinese officials. They conferred briefly.

'You may all now sit,' said Yelu, and turned to his right. 'All Mongols who would have Lord Ogedei as their Khan of Khans, please stand up.'

It was too close to tell, Robert thought. A similar number of men seemed to be standing on the right side of the semicircle.

Yelu conferred again with his officials.

'Hear this, all you Mongols and listen to my judgement,' Yelu said. 'I have made a count of sixty-two men for Lord Tolui, and fifty-nine for Lord Ogedei, and therefore, by public acclaim, I now pronounce—'

'No,' shouted Ogedei, jumping to his feet, 'this cannot be. Not all the Mongol nation are present. Some of my supporters are still in the Hexi lands. More of my men are in the north. We must hold a full *kurultai* to decide. I do not accept the decision.'

'Do *not* interrupt, Lord Ogedei,' said the chief minister, his voice cracking like a whip. 'Sit down. I remind all present that you agreed to abide by the will of this council. You may not change your mind because you do not like the outcome.'

There was an uneasy silence in the *ger.* And when Ogedei had seated himself again, Yelu said, 'Yet, we must all be united

– that is vital. A war between brothers would be a catastrophe. It cannot be permitted. Therefore, this is my decision.'

Yelu looked round the semicircle, daring anyone to gainsay him.

'Give us your decision, chief minister,' said Tolui. 'I will abide by it.'

Ogedei glowered at Yelu Ahai from his cushion, then he nodded briskly.

'The support for each of the two candidates is roughly equal,' said Yelu, 'although Lord Tolui has the greater number – by three men. Ogedei has called for a full *kurultai* to decide the matter, therefore my decision is this: Lord Tolui shall be declared the Regent of the Mongol nation, and he shall rule as if he were the Great Khan, with all his power and authority… until such time as a full *kurultai* can be called for all our scattered people to gather in Karakorum and decide, once and for all, who shall be the next Great Khan.'

-

As Robert rode back to his *ger*, he reflected that Yelu Ahai was a wise man. Had Tolui been declared Great Khan outright, there was a genuine danger that Ogedei would have rebelled. Half the Mongol nation would have fought the other half and, in the years of bloody carnage that resulted, all that had been achieved under Genghis Khan's unifying rule would be undone.

By giving Ogedei the hope that he might one day be chosen as Great Khan, Yelu had averted an all-consuming civil war. Furthermore, Robert thought, who would be the man to decide *when* this full *kurultai* would be called? Who was the one who would give the order to summon all the people of the Mongol nation to gather in Karakorum?

That would be Lord Tolui, the new Regent.

So Robert was full of hope as he made his way to his home, looking forward to relating what had occurred in the council to Sarantuya.

Tolui had won a great victory, he was now the Great Khan, in all but name. And with God's blessing he would remain so.

Robert reined in his horse. Something was wrong. There was a noisy knot of Mongols outside his *ger*, a dozen men arguing, shoving each other. Snow Leopards, mostly. But Arslan was there, and he was shaking Taka hard by his *deel*, shouting into his face. Robert jumped off Bayard and ran. He sprinted towards the door of the *ger*, burst through the men outside, shoving them aside, flung open the red lacquered door and hurled himself inside.

The first thing that struck him was the metallic stench of blood; the second was the sight of Sarantuya lying on a mound of bloody cushions on the bedding area that she and Robert shared. Her face was red, black and purple and covered in dried blood and swollen out of all recognition.

She was partially naked, stripped to a thin silk shift that she wore underneath her outside clothes, and it was horribly torn and bloodied. She seemed to be unconscious but she was still moving her head slightly, back and forth, and murmuring, 'No, I beg you, no more!' and Anya, her maid, and Sorkoktani were sponging her half-naked body, wiping away the clotted gore that seemed to cover her face, arms and particularly her legs.

'What… what has happened?' Robert could barely speak. He fell to his knees beside her, his eye drawn to the great puddle of dark blood between her legs. He took her limp, blood-smeared hand in his.

It felt as icy as death itself.

'Saran, my love,' he said, 'I am here.' Then he said again, looking around, 'What has happened to her? Will someone please tell me.'

The women did not answer, they continued wiping up the blood with wet rags, rinsing them in a bowl of water and wiping again. Robert looked around and saw Arslan, standing by the *ger* door. The Mongol's weathered face looked pale, his head hanging in shame, and Robert shot up and stalked over to him.

He grabbed Arslan by the *deel* and roughly dragged him outside.

'Tell me!' he said.

'Hasar is dead,' said Arslan. 'He died bravely trying to defend her.'

'Tell me what happened to my wife, God damn you.'

'She went out on foot to visit her friend, Lady Sorkoktani, with Hasar as her only guard and companion. She was attacked on the way to there. They were waiting for her behind a *ger*, near the area of the Blue Lynxes. Five masked men came out from behind the tent and they jumped her. They had wooden clubs. Hasar fought with them but they knocked him down from behind. They dragged her between two empty *ger* and they beat her badly. They forced her. All of them. Hasar saw it. His skull was broken but he saw it, and told me, as best he could, before he died. Everyone was at the council, or near the Great Khan's *ger*, all waiting to hear the result.

'Blue Lynxes found her half-dead and then they went to find me. We all brought her back here, and then we called for Lady Sorkoktani's aid.'

'What kind of masks?'

'Ordinary cloth. Wrapped round the lower part of the face. The kind boys wear when they ride behind herds to keep the dust out their mouths.'

'They all raped her?'

'Yes, *ezen*.'

'Who were they?'

Arslan shrugged.

Robert gripped Arslan fiercely by the shoulder. 'Find them,' he said. 'Go to the Blue Lynxes – who commands them, is it still Noyan Tuguldur?'

'Yes, *ezen*.'

'Go to Tuguldur and ask for his help in my name. He knows me. Tell him to ask his men who was in their area today – any men at all from other *mingghat*.'

Robert remembered he had seen Tuguldur earlier that day, sitting on the cushions in the semicircle at the council – he had been sitting with Ogedei's faction.

'Find them, Arslan. Take Taka and Saka. Take as many men as you need. But do not kill them. Not yet. I want them brought to me alive.'

'Yes, *ezen*.'

Robert released Arslan and turned and went back into the *ger*. He stood looking down at Sarantuya's battered body, the rage grinding his bowels. He knew who was behind this attack. He knew in his belly, his loins, his heart. It was Khuyag – who had been late to the council. Khuyag who had bared his teeth like a wolf at Robert when he saw him.

Khuyag.

Anya got up and carried the bloody basin of water out of the *ger*, slopping a little of the red liquid as she walked. Sorkoktani looked up at Robert. She was trying to cover Saran with a coverlet of soft lambskins.

'The baby?' said Robert.

Sorkoktani dropped her eyes. Then she slowly shook her head.

'Saran was delivered of it an hour ago. It was a tiny girl. But…'

Robert sank to his knees beside Sarantuya's still form. She was breathing, just. He pulled the lambskin up around her neck, leaned down and kissed her forehead, and smoothed the strands of wet hair from her face.

'You are safe here, my love,' he said. 'No one can hurt you now.'

Then he closed his eyes, put his two hands together and began to pray.

Chapter Twenty-six

'I want his head on a spear,' said Robert. 'I want to seize his warm living guts in my two bare hands and slowly pull them from his body, I want—'

'You have no proof Khuyag was responsible, Robyert, none at all,' said Tolui. 'Masked men, unknown attackers, and the only witness is dead.'

'It was Khuyag – I know it. I know it deep in the marrow of my bones.'

'Nevertheless, my friend, I cannot have the *noyan* of the White Foxes taken up and put to death simply because of the feelings in your bones.'

Sarantuya was still sleeping and, after a night and a day of sitting beside her, Sorkoktani had told Robert to take himself out of the *ger* and go and do something else. She, Anya and Jargal would watch over her. Peace and quiet, time to heal, that was what Sarantuya needed more than her fretting, hovering husband at this time.

Robert had ordered an entire *jagghun* of Snow Leopards to surround the *ger*, and had taken himself off to see his friend Tolui, the Regent. Once there, he found all his rage, sorrow and frustration spilling out uncontrollably.

'You can do anything you like – you are the Regent, with full authority.'

'You were at the council, Robyert. You know how close the count was. Khuyag is Ogedei's man. If I arrested him, it would be interpreted as a move against Ogedei, just when we have established a kind of peace between us.'

'I'll kill him myself. I'll cut his fat head clean off his body—'

'No, Robyert, you will not. I forbid it. If you attack Khuyag, his White Foxes will defend him and, if you bring your Snow Leopards and Golden Eagles to the fight, we will have three *mingghat* fighting each other. No, you will not kill Khuyag. If you do so, you will forfeit my friendship. And I would be forced to punish you severely. I am serious. I'll not have you starting a war between the two factions.'

'What then? Khuyag killed my trooper and my unborn child, and his men raped my wife. They defiled Sarantuya – who is your friend, too. Your own wife is in my *ger* this very hour.'

'Find me something, *Baghatur*. Find me something that points the finger of blame at Khuyag and I swear I will act. A witness, perhaps. Until then, tend to your poor wife. She needs you now more than you need your revenge.'

When Robert returned to his own *ger*, he found Jalair sitting beside Sarantuya's sleeping form. The boy was white-faced and shaking. It was obvious he had been crying. Jalair tried to wipe away his unmanly tears with dirty hands and managed to smear his little face all the more. Robert was hit then with a powerful wave of raw, almost painful love for his son.

'Will *Eejee* die?' he asked Robert, staring up with his huge eyes.

'Your mother is hurt,' said Robert. 'But she will not die. She just needs to rest. Come, wash your face and let us go for a ride, you and I. We might see gazelle.'

This was, in truth, unlikely. All the game on the steppe near Karakorum had long been hunted down or driven away by the tens of thousands of hungry Mongols encamped there, but Robert wanted to be alone with Jalair in the clean, pure wild.

He glanced at Anya, as he left the *ger* with the boy, and she gave him a sad little smile. 'I'll watch over her, *ezen*,' she said. 'Fear not, your lady is very strong.'

They rode out on the wide steppe, both man and boy wrapped up warmly against the freezing winter winds, and galloped half a dozen miles northwards, beyond the furthest camping places of the lowliest Mongol families.

Robert was impressed with the boy's seat – he rode his pony as if he had been born in the saddle, easily able to keep up with his hard-galloping father. They took no guards with them – for some reason, Robert wished only to be with his son, no one else. He did have a couple of javelins in the socket at Bayard's withers, his Mongol sword and the Circassian dagger under his armpit and, if he thought about it at all, he relished the idea that Khuyag's troopers, even the *noyan* himself, might try to attack him. He longed for action, for a bloodletting, a chance to carve Khuyag into chunks of offal.

They reined in after an hour or so, in the lee of a small cove at the base of a low series of barren hills, and sheltered there from the bone-chilling wind. Robert built a small fire of dried yak dung and they sat beside its flaring warmth and chewed strips of dried mutton and sipped *airaq* straight from a leather flask.

After they had warmed themselves a little, Robert began to tell Jalair stories of the lives of the Christian saints, as well as tales of his homeland, including some of the more fanciful tales of King Arthur and his brave knights, and the dragons and evil monsters they defeated.

When Jalair asked him how these dread creatures had been killed, Robert drew his curved sword and began to show Jalair, who could barely hold the blade up, the basic cuts and blocks that were the underpinnings of all good swordsmanship.

Robert had been about the boy's age when he had first begun his training, and he did not see why Jalair should be neglected in this essential element of his education.

The boy loved it, although, he wielded the heavy sword in a wild, jerky and slightly alarming way. Robert took one of his javelins and gently fenced with the boy, blocking his swishing cuts and slashes with the long wooden shaft.

And when the boy had had enough of sword play, they took turns in throwing the two javelins at a mark in the earth a dozen yards away.

They both laughed and crowed their victory when they hit their mark, and wailed in exaggerated disappointment when they missed. And, for an hour or so, they were the only creatures in the whole world. Just a boy and his father and a simple game of hand-and-eye skill. Then, as the afternoon sky began to darken, and the clouds in the west to thicken and menace, they remounted their horses and rode slowly back towards Karakorum.

After a half mile of chatter about inconsequential things – the comic antics of the marmots who had come out to feed in the evening light, the sad lack of any gazelles to observe – Jalair blurted out, 'How did *Eejee* get hurt, *Aavaa*? Did she fall off her horse like the Great Khan?'

And Robert realised with a jolt of guilt that he had not thought once about his poor wife's suffering during the past two hours or more.

'Bad men hurt her, Jalair,' he said, not knowing what else to say.

'But you will punish them, *Aavaa*, won't you? You will kill all the bad men for hurting *Eejee*, like the Christian knights of King Arthur killed the evil dragons?'

Robert looked across at his boy, so unspoiled and perfect. Then he imagined Khuyag or his men attacking Jalair, hurting him, and his belly clenched tight.

'Yes, son, I will kill them. One day. I swear it. I do not know how I will do it, nor when, but I will kill them all for what they did to *Eejee*.'

–

Over the next few days, Sarantuya began to regain her strength. After a week, she had recovered sufficiently to be able to sit up and drink mutton broth in her bed, but she resolutely refused to talk about any aspects of the brutal attack on her, mutely shaking her dark head when Robert tentatively asked if she could identify any of the culprits.

She also wept, from time to time, and Robert did not know if it was from the pain of her injuries or the knowledge that she had lost her unborn daughter. Perhaps both.

He tried to comfort her as best he could, bringing her bowls of hot broth and warmed wine, trying to tempt her with sweetmeats from his stores, and keeping the whole *ger* uncomfortably warm all day and all night.

He summoned the witch-man of the Naiman tribe, the one who had blessed their wedding, and when this ancient, bald, garishly painted creature arrived at the *ger*, Robert watched him suspiciously as he capered and shrieked around Sarantuya's bed, scattering rancid *airaq* droplets over her and shaking his big shaggy yak-hair cloak, which made the tiny bells tinkle and all the animal bones rattle.

Then he gave the fellow a silver coin, bundled him out of the *ger*, and knelt beside his wife, closed his eyes and prayed to the Blessed Virgin for her intercession.

Three days later, an Arrow Rider called at the *ger* with a letter from Samarkand.

Robert had been instructing a group of Mongol boys in sword-craft outside the *ger*, as soft flakes of snow gently fell upon them. The boys practised not with real swords but wooden facsimiles, and when the Arrow Rider arrived, clearly on the edge of exhaustion, Robert dismissed his pupils and took the letter inside his *ger* to read by the light of his hearth.

Sarantuya had a little colour in her cheeks that day and was able to get up and move slowly about the *ger*, and even tend to her own business in the latrines.

Robert kissed her in a distracted way, and refused the offer of hot food, turning the letter over and over in his hands.

Then he went over to sit beside the hearth, looking closely at the spiky black handwriting by the red light of the flames. It was written in unfamiliar and, in truth, not very accomplished Persian. And, on opening it, he realised why.

The letter had not been dispatched by his partner Karacha but by Idar.

> *To my good friend and companion in Christ, Robert of Hadlow, Greetings!*
>
> *I write this missive with a heavy heart and the sense of undertaking a grave, unwelcome duty, which must be performed. For I must tell you, my friend, that your esteemed partner Lord Karacha is dead. It grieves me to send you these tidings, and more so to inform you the sad manner of his passing, which was at the hands of low thieves and murderers.*
>
> *It occurred thus. In the late autumn, on All Souls' Day – shortly after we had received your camel trains from the Hexi Empire – Karacha had spent a pleasant evening in a wine emporium in the centre of Samarkand, enjoying a performance of poetry and dance, as was his monthly habit, and on his way home by palanquin after the show, he was set upon in the dark streets by a gang of evil men – Samarkand, alas, is rife with them at this time of uncertainty and rebellion – who attacked and slaughtered all his six Uzbek palanquin bearers and bodyguards, and poor Karacha himself, and made away into the dark night with his purse of coins and a few items of his jewellery. O how tragic that a few paltry baubles should prove to be the price of a man's life!*
>
> *I have written to Lord Ziani in Tana, a missive also dispatched by Arrow Rider, and have discussed the matter with the Mongol governor of Samarkand, Noyan Jamuga. His Excellency says he will investigate using all the resources at his disposal but he doubts he will be successful in identifying and apprehending the miscreants.*

Robert looked up from the letter, and sighed heavily.

'Is it bad news, my love?' asked Sarantuya.

'Karacha is dead,' he said. 'Murdered in the streets of Samarkand.'

'I am so sorry,' she said. 'He was such a good man, and so kind to me when he took me into his house for refuge. I can hardly believe that he is gone.'

Robert did not believe it either. There was something wrong with Idar's story. Six tough Uzbek fighters murdered, and Karacha, too, who was no weakling – he had fought bravely at Otrar during the long siege – and all for a purse of silver coin, a ruby brooch, perhaps, and a few gold rings. Seven good men dead for an insignificant amount that the House of Karacha might take in one day. No, something was not right about this story. He bent to the letter again, tilting the sheets to catch the firelight.

> *Governor Jamuga tells me companies of bandits roam the streets of Samarkand and other cities in the Ulus at night – and he says some of them are allies of the rebel prince Jalal al-Din, son of the late Shah of Khwarazmia, and are obedient to his orders.*
>
> *Jamuga proposes to scour the poorer parts of the city with his men and round up a hundred or so of the beggarly criminal types who infest these stinking stews, and hang them high from trees in the lake-park to serve as a grim warning to others who might contemplate similar crimes. Whether this will be efficacious or not, I cannot say. But I do know that it is not justice. I also have a secret suspicion, one that I scarcely dare to mention to you, as to the identity of the true culprit, or at least the mind behind this terrible outrage. For, in recent months, as well as outbreaks of banditry in the city, Samarkand has also received half a dozen merchant trains from as far afield as the Sultanate of Rum, and even the great city of Constantinople on the shores of the Bosphorus. In short,*

I suspect the hidden hand of Barisone Adorno, who is well represented in Constantinople. Could it be that Adorno was secretly behind the murder of our poor friend? You may scold me for indulging in fanciful conspiracy, but I feel honour bound to mention this to you. We know that the Podestà has a long and vengeful reach. Could it extend even as far as Samarkand?

'Adorno,' muttered Robert, 'that God-cursed turd-mountain!'

The House of Karacha continues to flourish, for which I give thanks daily to God, and our profits have been better than ever, and Lord Ziani and I are working together to repair our fortunes after the disasters in Antioch last year. I have doubled the number of guards in the House and I must also tell you that, in the absence of poor Lord Karacha, I have assumed his mantle in Samarkand, and shouldered his burdens, even going so far as to issue orders as a partner in the House and to dispense the monies from his strong room, and pay the taxes when they are due. I continue to buy and dispatch goods and money back to Tana – well guarded by my two hundred riders, whom I have named the Swords of Karacha in honour of our dear friend. Their captain is a brave man, a former soldier of the shah, called Captain Mir, and I deem him wholly trustworthy – and not only because his wife and children reside in Samarkand, under my eye. Were Mir to play us false, they would pay the reckoning.

Robert winced at the notion that women and children should be punished for a man's crimes – it was a little too close to home for comfort. He continued reading.

I am aware that I have grossly exceeded my authority and am in no sense a partner in this noble enterprise, nor worthy to be one. However, I plan to continue in this role in Samarkand, in all of our mutual interests, and in the absence of another suitable candidate, until you return to your House and arrange matters here to your satisfaction. Which I urge you to do with all speed.

Yours with deep affection, and in deep sorrow, Idar

'What does it say, Robyert?' asked Sarantuya.

'Idar has taken the reins of the House of Karacha but urges me to come there to calm things in the wake of Karacha's sad death. I must go to see Tolui.'

–

'If you have come to shout at me about Khuyag, then I have not the time today, nor the inclination, to listen to any more of your rantings,' said the Regent, when he greeted Robert in the huge, wheeled *ger* that had once been his illustrious father's.

'This is not about the foul creature who attacked my wife,' said Robert. 'I know your mind is set and I have no further proofs yet to offer you.'

Arslan had discovered very little from Noyan Tuguldur. He had been to see the commander and had asked to speak to his Blue Lynxes, but even after several weeks of questioning hundreds of Mongol troopers, all he had discovered was that five unfamiliar men had indeed been spotted on the day when Sarantuya was attacked. The only description he had of the attackers was that one of the men was missing an eye, and another had a horizontal scar from a sword cut across the bridge of his nose. Without visiting the White Foxes camp and looking at the faces of each of the thousand or so riders of the *mingghan*, Arslan, could take his enquiry no further.

'A man with one eye – and another with a scarred nose?' said Robert. 'There must be a thousand men like that in Karakorum. Do you think these Blue Lynxes could identify them if they were brought before them?'

Arslan shrugged. 'The steppe is—'

Robert held up a hand. 'I am in no mood for jokes, Arslan,' he said. 'If you say the steppe is long, or fat, or high, then I will make you pay for it.'

Arslan nodded. 'I cannot say, *ezen*, if the Blue Lynxes would be able to pick them out of a group. They are a donkey-headed lot, those Lynxes – all of them.'

'You have no proof of Khuyag's guilt then?' said the Regent. 'I am sorry to hear it. So, have you come to play dice with me today, *Baghatur*? If that is the case I must also disappoint you. I am far too busy this day for games of chance. Although winning more of your merchant's silver would be a simple and delightful affair.'

'I'm not here to play dice, either,' said Robert. 'I have had a letter from my Circassian servant in Samarkand and the news, I am distressed to tell you, is bad.'

Then Robert related Idar's tidings, ending it with a request, 'I would like to leave your side, Highness, to quit Karakorum for a few months and return to Samarkand. I must bring order to this perilous situation in the House of Karacha myself.'

'Hmm,' said Tolui. 'It will grieve me to see you go, Robyert, you are one of the few people I can trust in this pit of vipers we call the city of Karakorum. But we can make the best of this, I think, if you are willing. You will have heard that Prince Jalal al-Din is raising troops in the Khorasan; I am told he has already attracted thousands to his banner.'

Robert had heard. A new hope began to stir in his heart.

'Do you mean, Great One, to launch the full might of the Mongol army against the Khorasan?' he asked. He dared not say the name of Baghdad to Tolui, not now, not yet, nor to mention the Holy Land and Sorkoktani's desire to walk in the footsteps of Jesus. But warm excitement was slowly seeping into his mind.

'Not the full might, Robyert. I have Jin columns marching at me from the east, and the Song are also restive in the south. Since the Hexi campaign, they are both allied against us. And

Yelu Ahai is badgering me to announce when the next *kurultai* will be held. I do, however, propose to send a significant force south to the former Khwarazmian lands to deal with this rascal Jalal al-Din. And I further propose to send you and your two excellent *mingghat* with it, Noyan Robyert Baghatur!'

At last, exulted Robert. *At last, the* tumet *would be marching in the right direction.*

Chapter Twenty-seven

'One *tumen*,' said Robert scornfully, 'one miserly little *tumen*, that is all Tolui proposes to send south to fight this rebel prince. He has more than two dozen at his command and all he sends is one *tumen* – just ten *mingghat*, ten thousand Mongol riders – barely an army at all, and all of Persia and beyond to conquer.'

It was the evening after the audience with the Regent and Robert was back at his own hearth, chatting with his wife. Her spirits had steadily improved in the weeks after the attack, and while they had not enjoyed congress, she *was* speaking to him.

'Your Snow Leopards and Golden Eagles will ride with the *tumen*,' said Sarantuya. 'That is another two thousand, and when we get to Samarkand there is a garrison there, and garrisons in all the conquered cities, who can lend you more riders.'

'Hmmpf,' said Robert. 'I had hoped for more, that's all. I hoped for four or five *tumet* at least, given the size of the territory we must attempt to control.'

'This man Guchlug, the new commander of the *tumen*, has a fine reputation as a fighter,' said Sarantuya. 'They say he's as brave as a lion – as two lions – even though he is young; not yet thirty. Handsome, too, or so I've been told by Sorkoktani.'

Robert gave her a look out of the side of his eye. 'He is one of Ogedei's most loyal supporters,' he said. 'That's one of the reasons Tolui is sending him away south. He wants to weaken Ogedei and strip him of as many of his loyal people as possible.'

'Did Tolui say when he would call the *kurultai*?' asked his wife.

'He did not. I got the impression he has no intention of calling one soon – or *ever.* Why roll the dice to decide the next khan, when Tolui has all the power now?'

Arslan poked his head round the door of the *ger.* 'Messenger, *ezen.*'

'What message?' asked Robert. He was comfortable on his cushions, with his lovely wife, and a cup of *airaq*, by his side. He resented the intrusion.

'You are summoned,' said Arslan, 'by Lord Ogedei. Summoned to his *ger.* The Regent's brother wants to speak with you on an urgent matter.'

–

Lord Ogedei, prince of the Golden Kin, commander of six *tumet*, son of the mighty Conqueror of the World, was only moderately drunk that evening.

'Ah, the *elchin said* is here at last,' said Ogedei, hardly slurring his words at all. 'I beg your pardon – Noyan Robyert Baghatur, I must call you. That is a far greater title. I honour you for it.' He lifted the goblet in his hand in salute and drank deeply.

'Bring wine for Noyan Robyert Baghatur,' Ogedei said to a servant.

'Not necessary, Highness,' said Robert. 'But I thank you for your kindness.'

'Nonsense, *Baghatur*, you need a drink on a cold night like this. Bring him wine!'

Robert accepted a cup of sweet red wine and sipped a little, waiting for his host to come to the point of this meeting. He had wondered if this heavy-set Mongol prince lolling in his silk cushions meant to have him killed. If that were the case, there would be very little he could do.

There were armed guards all round the huge *ger*, a dozen of them. He would fight for his life, of course, his sword was at his side, but he would surely go down eventually.

'We have not spent much time in each other's company, *Baghatur*,' said Ogedei, 'but I know my father esteemed you. The Regent, too, finds you invaluable. And if I may speak plainly, I would be your good friend, as well.'

Robert was surprised by these words. He had always held the impression that Ogedei despised him as a foreigner, a worthless *gadaad khun*. Now he hoped to be his good friend? What did this wine-sodden oaf really want from him?

'I have, of course, long admired your skill at arms – the way you took Khara-Khoto was the talk of the whole army; General Subutai speaks well of you, too.'

'I'm honoured, Highness, that you should know of my insignificant deeds.'

'Of course I know them. You cleverly delivered up Otrar to us, too, didn't you?'

Robert ducked his head in acknowledgement and sipped his sweet wine.

Why is he being so uncharacteristically civil? Robert wondered.

Ogedei stared at him blankly, seemingly lost for words, then drained his cup, waved it in the air to indicate that he wanted it to be refilled, and said, 'I should like to reward you for your service to the Mongol nation. Therefore, tell me, friend, what is it you most desire? What would make your heart glad? Do you want land? Horses? Herds? Gold and silver?'

Robert was astonished by this shameless offer of a bribe.

He said carefully, 'What I desire more than anything, Highness, is justice. You may know that my wife Sarantuya, who is of the Golden Kin, was attacked more than two months past. I believe the attackers were acting under the orders of one of your *noyan* – Sarantuya's former husband Noyan Khuyag. What I desire is his head, and the heads of those five men who attacked her.'

Ogedei sat up in his cushions. 'Khuyag? You want Khuyag's head?'

'That is what I desire. More than lands or herds, or gold and silver.'

'I cannot give you Khuyag. He has been loyal to me. I heard about this business with Sarantuya – she is my cousin, after all. I even asked Khuyag all about it; I put the accusation to him, as she was his unfaithful wife. But he denied it. I cannot give you him. Ask something else. I'll give you a hundred horses.'

'I do not require horses, Highness. If you will not give me Khuyag's head, allow me to challenge him, and fight him with swords to the death.'

'No, I need Khuyag alive. I heard you alone killed five *gadaad khun* who ambushed you by the river at Otrar. I cannot let you slaughter Khuyag. Put that thought from your mind. If you think your wife has been befouled, and no longer desire her, I will give you a new wife. Three pretty young wives, if you so wish.'

Robert clenched his teeth. 'I do not need any more wives, nor any more horses. I seek justice. If you cannot give me it, I will accept no other gifts.'

'I will not give you Khuyag,' said Ogedei. His face was flushed with anger.

Robert set down his cup and got to his feet.

'If that is so, Highness, with your permission, I shall take my leave. I thank you for the wine and your generous offers.'

'Go,' said Ogedei, 'if you do not wish to be my friend. Go, *gadaad khun*!'

Robert bowed despite the insult, turned and began to walk out of the *ger*. At any moment, he expected to hear Ogedei order his bodyguards to fall on him, and his left hand brushed his scabbard, as he walked away, ready to grasp it and draw the blade.

But all he heard was Ogedei calling loudly for more wine.

–

Robert rode out of Karakorum in the first days of spring with the Snow Leopards, the Golden Eagles and his full household in a column behind him.

He was pleased that Sarantuya had elected to ride at least part of the way south to Samarkand. She was a superb horsewoman and this decision meant that, only three months after the horrific attack, she was mostly healed – in her body, at least.

He was also pleased that little Jalair rode out beside her – that was the plan, anyway. In truth the boy was so excited by the exodus from Karakorum that he spent the first few days of the long journey riding up and down the marching column, hallooing and cheering on the troops, and exhausting one steppe pony after another.

On the fourth day, Sarantuya took the boy in her arms, wrapped him in her *deel*, and they rode together on her horse. Robert had brought along a horse-palanquin that could have carried them both easily, but Sarantuya refused.

'I want to feel the wind in my hair, my love, the sun on my cheeks,' she said.

Robert spent most of his time either scouting far head of the column, or with the *tumen* commander Guchlug. He was indeed handsome, even Robert was obliged to admit this, with his high cheekbones, large jet-dark eyes and thick hair, as glossy as a raven's wing. And while everybody praised his fine looks, nobody had a higher opinion of his excellent qualities than General Guchlug himself.

'We will destroy these cowardly rebels in a single glorious season,' he informed Robert on the eve of the march, 'and, if great Tenggri allows, we will be back here in Karakorum for winter to claim a rich reward from the Regent.'

'Tolui promised you a reward?' asked Robert.

'He promised me wide lands in the Jin Empire once they are defeated.'

This promise seemed to Robert to be premature, but it indicated where Tolui's mind was trained – eastwards towards Cathay. Robert tried very hard to like Guchlug, since he knew they would be thrown together a great deal in the coming months, but it was not easy. The young general was used to victory, having fought various fractious, ill-disciplined tribesmen in the far north, but he was bored by the finer military details of the march. He liked to give grand, sweeping orders, such as telling Robert to take them to good grazing and sweet water, without indicating any route.

In truth, this casual, devil-may-care style of leadership suited Robert, since it gave him complete freedom to choose the path this small army would take. Therefore, he did not complain but just smiled, saluted and rode away to fulfil Guchlug's orders.

He rode out ahead of the column most mornings, with the scouting *jagghut* of the Golden Eagles and Snow Leopards, and when he returned to the army at the end of the day, once he had made his report, he spent his time with Sarantuya and Jalair.

As the *tumen* made its way south and west, Robert felt for the most part content, even happy, except for the one very sharp stone in his boot, which was, of course, Khuyag. It irked him that he had yet to punish the *noyan* for his attack on Sarantuya, but he had been unable to think of a way to bring him to justice, and any move on Khuyag would have resulted in hundreds of deaths, with his two *mingghat* fighting Khuyag's men. And Tolui would surely shun him if he instigated a bloodbath.

Since Ogedei and his part of the Mongol army, which included Khuyag's White Foxes, had been dispatched east to confront the advancing Jin, there would have been no point in remaining in Karakorum. Certainly, he would have had no chance of taking his revenge on Khuyag. And he knew deep in his heart that he simply had to grit his teeth, bide his time and wait for the right moment to strike against the man.

And when he accepted this, the ghost of Genghis Khan rose up in his mind.

He had liked the old khan, and respected him, and he felt a full measure of guilt and shame at his own treacherous actions, but he had done what was necessary – whatever was necessary – regardless of his own feelings. He had done what he saw as his duty, in order to bring about the outcome he desired. That was the Mongol way.

Equally, he knew he would kill Khuyag – one day – he knew it in his bones. But it irked him, nonetheless, that Khuyag still breathed the cold, clean air of the steppe.

One day, when Sarantuya and he were riding together in the foothills of the Altai Mountains, out for an afternoon hunt, he tried rather clumsily to apologise for failing to protect her against her former husband, and failing to avenge the hurt done to her.

Sarantuya turned in the saddle and gazed lovingly at him. 'Have you ever thought, my good, sweet man, that perhaps that terrible day was the price I had to pay for my happiness? Perhaps great Tenggri was punishing me for the crime of infidelity against Khuyag – for betraying him when he was my husband. I sometimes think this may be true. For I know that nothing good in life ever comes without sacrifice.'

Robert often believed *he* was being punished by God for his sins; yet it had not occurred to him she might also feel the same weight of divine judgement.

'You are not to blame for this,' he said. 'It is my doing, and mine alone. If I had not met you, nor fallen in love with you, then perhaps…'

'Then I would still be with Khuyag, childless, unhappy, beaten every night when the wine was strong in him,' she finished. 'I would have taken my own life or killed him in his sleep and been trampled to death as a husband-murderer.'

They walked their horses a few steps before Robert replied to her.

'Khuyag deserves to die. I should have had the courage to kill him long ago. And I will do it, one day, I will kill him. I swear this to you now, my dearest love.'

'I believe you think you will, Robyert,' said Sarantuya. 'But what if you are killed in battle by the rebels? What if you fall off your horse one day like my poor father and break your neck?'

'Then God will surely punish Khuyag in my stead,' said Robert.

'Or maybe I shall kill him,' said Sarantuya. She smiled at Robert. 'Maybe I will put some Chinese poison in his wine. Or plunge a big dagger into his black heart!'

They spoke no more of Khuyag, and, a month later, when they hunted together on the shores of Lake Balkhash, with Jalair rousting out the ducks from the reeds with his boyish cries, Robert watched Sarantuya, riding at the gallop, draw her bow and bring down a flying mallard with a single shaft. He knew two things in that moment, as he looked at her victory-flushed face: Sarantuya had recovered fully from the assault; and he would love her with all his heart till the day he died.

That night, for the first time since the brutal attack, they made love together.

–

The *tumen* made its camp to the south of Samarkand, in the same grazing lands that Tolui had occupied previously, and while Guchlug and his officers went off to see Noyan Jamuga, the governor of the city, and officially announce their presence, Robert escorted Sarantuya to the House of Karacha, where she was to stay while he and his *mingghat* were in the region.

Their lovemaking had now become frequent, always tenderly at first and then with a growing passion. They both hoped to put another child in her belly that year.

Sarantuya had said she would accompany Robert on the campaign against Jalal al-Din, but Robert wanted her far from all the inevitable hardships and dangers. He wanted to put his seed in her and keep her safe in Samarkand while the baby grew.

Idar welcomed them effusively, showing Sarantuya, Jalair and her maid Anya to the lavish master's quarters in the house, which he had been occupying since Karacha's death. He gave Robert a pair of thick letters from Niccolò Ziani, and when Robert had read them, Idar took them both into the dining room. While they ate the feast the Uzbek servants had prepared, he retold the terrible story of the robbery in the dark streets of Samarkand that had claimed Karacha's life.

'The governor, alas, has no further information for us,' Idar said, 'but Ziani wrote to me recently and said he had heard Adorno's minions were boasting of a great victory over a Venetian House in the East. I think there can be no doubt that the vengeful Podestà was the driving force behind the murderous attack on our poor dear friend.'

Robert delegated a whole *jagghun* of Golden Eagles to remain permanently in Samarkand and guard the house while he was on campaign, quartering them in the stables at the back of the huge building. He gave them instructions that no one should ever leave the house without a strong guard of at least two dozen armed men. Idar wholeheartedly agreed with his decision and also vowed to ward Sarantuya and Jalair with his life – and when Robert remembered what a competent man-at-arms Idar was, he felt reassured. Twenty men of the Swords of Karacha also remained in the house to guard its occupants, while the rest of the hired men under Captain Mir were *en route* back to Tana with a shipment of silk, carpets and jade, including many precious items that Robert had dispatched the previous autumn from the Hexi lands.

After dinner, Robert took a look at the ledgers of the House of Karacha. He was pleased and rather surprised at how well Idar had managed after Karacha's death. The strong room, also, displayed a charmingly large quantity of gold and silver coin and many other valuables. Indeed, he soon realised, the House of Karacha was thriving under Idar's control.

'What are your plans?' Robert asked the Circassian, later that night, over a jug of wine. Sarantuya had gone to bed and Robert was yawning and contemplating the long dark ride back to the Mongol camp. He had orders to report to Guchlug at dawn, but he was greatly tempted to ignore them and spend the night here with Saran.

'As you know, lord, I long to see my wife and my daughters. And, now that you are here, I would very much like to embark on the long journey back to the Caucasus. I could transport some of our goods, and your letters, of course, to Signor Ziani.'

'How about staying on? I depart on campaign in a day or two. I would much prefer you to continue to see to our affairs here in Samarkand while I am away. The letter you gave me from Ziani suggested that we make you a full partner in the House of Karacha, with a one-fifth share of the company. You would, in essence, step into Karacha's shoes permanently. You have already demonstrated that you can fulfil his difficult role here. You have shown your quality and Ziani and I are grateful. What do you say?'

'What about Yula in Goro and… and my two girls?'

'Ziani suggests you bring them out here, warded by the Swords of Karacha on the return journey. Would your wife not enjoy living here in this fine house?'

Idar appeared to be stunned by the idea. His pale, handsome face seemed to turn even paler. But, while Robert waited for his reply, he looked at his friend and noted that the Circassian had subtly changed, too, in their time apart: his austere soldier's garb had evolved into a richly patterned long silk robe and his normally booted feet were encased this evening in delicate silk slippers adorned with pearls and rubies. Indeed, he looked as if he had been born and raised a merchant prince of Samarkand.

'Yes,' said Idar. 'Yes, I accept. I do not know how I can thank you, lord.'

'You can start by not calling me "lord",' said Robert. 'Now that we are equals.'

Chapter Twenty-eight

That summer, General Guchlug pursued the rebel Jalal al-Din with all his youthful vigour. The *tumen*, guided by Robert and his two *mingghat*, rode south from Samarkand through the blistering desert and crossed the Amu Daria near the ancient city of Balkh, where their small force was joined by another *mingghan* of heavy cavalry from that city's Mongol garrison.

However, from then on, they were in the Khorasan, a huge territory that, apart from a few of the cities, the Mongols no longer controlled. As they pushed on west, they were beset almost daily by attacks from the enemy.

And Robert's two thousand horsemen bore the brunt of it.

The tactics of the Prince Jalal's riders were hallowed by time and practice; indeed Robert himself had been taught similar manoeuvres by his tutors in the Templar precincts of Europe. Sting and fly, the tactic was called, or strike and ride.

As the army advanced deeper into enemy territory, small groups of enemy riders, usually no more than a hundred men, would gallop out of hidden places – a rocky ravine, say, or in greener parts of the land, wooded hollows – and attack sections of the long, slow-moving column. They would engage Robert's men, since his riders were usually posted on the flanks of the column, shooting arrows at them or launching javelin showers, killing a few men, and then swiftly galloping away.

The enraged Mongols would very often charge after the attackers – only to find themselves suddenly ambushed.

This was a similar tactic to one the Mongols themselves often used. However, sometimes there was no cunning ambush prepared in a hidden defile, and the enemy riders would simply disperse, like campfire smoke on the wind, each individual man of the hundred or so attackers scattering to find his own path into the wilderness.

The enemy knew the ground intimately and, while Robert had also campaigned in the Khorasan, his knowledge was no match for these sheep-herders turned rebels who were bred here and spent their lives among these bare hills and hidden valleys.

His pursuing Mongols frequently got lost, and many of them never returned to the column after chasing the perpetrators of these sting-and-fly attacks. So he ordered his men to cease their pursuits of the attackers, and only to defend the column itself.

However, Guchlug swiftly countermanded his orders. 'I want you to kill these filthy animals, not cower in safety by your slower comrades. They must learn to fear us. Give chase, *Baghatur*, catch them. Bring me their maggoty heads by the sackful.'

This was sheer madness, and Robert knew it. Yet he obeyed, and every few days a dozen of his men were killed, and his two exhausted *mingghat* shrank a little more.

Occasionally, they would manage to capture a party of the rebels they were chasing, and would indeed bring half a dozen heads in a blood-dripping sack to tip out at Guchlug's feet. And when that happened, the general was lavish in his praise and jovial about the victory, crowing that it would not be long before the foe were comprehensively beaten.

Yet Robert knew this was the wrong strategy and he quietly ordered his captains to ensure their men stayed within a mile of the column, no matter the provocation.

These stinging rebel attacks often favoured the baggage column, as well as any Mongol stragglers who became detached from the main body, and after some weeks of daily carnage, Guchlug ordered one of Robert's *mingghat* – the Golden Eagles – to the rear to guard their food and supplies. The other depleted *mingghan* was to remain in its position – but it was now charged with guarding both flanks.

Robert formed half his men around the camel carts and pack mules, and posted individual *jagghun* around the horses and flocks, repeating his orders not to pursue the fleeing enemy beyond a distance of a mile. He also told his men to be vigilant and stay together. The next day they managed to catch one attacking group between two *jagghut* and gleefully decimated their rebel foes before the survivors managed to flee.

However, the enemy learned quickly from that massacre and henceforth they ignored the vulnerable baggage train and switched their attacks to the vanguard of the column some five miles ahead. After a week of this, Guchlug called a halt and the army made itself a strong camp, guarded with an encircling thorn-tree fence.

'We must find Jalal al-Din,' said Guchlug to his assembled officers that same evening. 'Find the prince, we find his army. Once we find his army, we will crush it.'

Robert was very tired, having been in the saddle almost constantly for several weeks. He had a wound on his forearm, a long shallow cut from a passing arrow, that was not life-threatening and, indeed, was healing well given his constant activity, but was still painful and it consequently made him irritable.

'You, Noyan Robyert Baghatur, you are the commander of the scouts and also the chief intelligencer,' said Guchlug. 'You must go and find me the rebel prince.'

'With respect, General, my men are all exhausted. We cannot guard the baggage at the rear, and both flanks from attack, and also ride ahead and seek out the enemy. Give us one task, and we will do it to the best of our ability. We cannot do them all.'

There was a shocked silence. Guchlug enjoyed a great deal of sycophancy from his hand-picked *tumen* officers. He was not used to being gainsaid.

'Go ahead then, *Baghatur*,' said Guchlug, 'go deep into the Khorasan and get me some good intelligence as to the whereabouts of Jalal and his rebel army.'

Robert did as he was ordered. But he left his two battered *mingghat* behind in the thorn-fenced camp to rest and recuperate, with Kolgen in overall command.

He rode out at dawn the next morning on Bayard with only Arslan, Saka and Taka, on one pony each, for company.

The four men took off their *deel* and distinctive Mongol hats, and wore dirty Persian woollen robes and rusty helms or raggedy turbans. Robert hoped, if they were spotted by any of the local people, they would pass for common Khorasan bandits.

They travelled north up into the hills around Sabzavar, to the places which were cool in the summer heat, and there they encountered shepherds and wild-goat hunters and wrinkled old men from no-name villages, and joined their campfires at night eating their mutton stew and millet flatbreads under the vast canopy of stars.

Robert spoke Persian to them, and claimed to be from Herat, and told them wonderful stories about his time as a merchant on the roads to the West, when he had travelled with a camel train of Jews from Arabia. He also handed out small gifts to his hosts: good steel knives and simple pieces of jewellery – a silver bangle, perhaps, or a thin silver ring. Several times he parted with a coin for information about the local area.

Robert found he was actually enjoying himself on this holiday-like excursion into a world of lies and subterfuge – he felt like a lad again playing a dangerous but exciting game in the woods around Hadlow – and when he was asked about the three silent, grim-faced men who accompanied him, he said they were Kirghiz tribesmen on the run from their Mongol enemies, who spoke no civilised tongue. He parted from his various hosts with words of thanks and praise for the One God, whose prophet is Mohammed. And, when these gifts were exchanged, he was often invited to visit again. After two weeks, he returned to the Mongol camp in the lowlands.

'Damghan,' he said to the astonished officers of Guchlug's *tumet*. 'Prince Jalal al-Din is at a town called Damghan, a hundred miles south-east of the shores of the Sea of Ravens. He has an army with him, numbering perhaps twenty thousand men.'

'Do you know this place?' asked Guchlug.

'I do,' Robert admitted. 'It is halfway between Nishapur and Ray. I was with Subutai when we took the town eight years ago. We gave the people of Damghan the Choice, then stormed their walls and slew all the inhabitants.'

'That is what we shall also do,' said Guchlug. 'And you shall lead us there, *Baghatur*.'

–

Six days later, Robert topped a rise and looked down at a brown empty plain that stretched out endlessly before the ancient town of Damghan.

It was a low, dismal place, with thick mud walls twice the height of a man – some of them still blackened by soot from the conflagration caused by the Mongols' last visit. The walls had several stubby guard towers set into them, and a big square gatehouse in the centre of the east wall, facing towards the plain and the main road.

Damghan, in truth, was almost as large as a city, and it squatted on the flat, sun-browned expanse of land like an enormous, angry toad guarding his dwindling watering hole. There was a range of green hills to the north, to Robert's right, which he remembered formed the barrier to the blue Sea of Ravens beyond, and more hills past the town in the west, and also some smaller yellowish ridges to the south.

From his position, Robert could see the tiny black heads of hundreds of Damghan's people on the battlements, and it was clear, despite the mass slaughter that followed Subutai's conquest and catastrophic sack, the town had been at least partially repopulated since then. It was also clear that the arrival of a Mongol army came as no great surprise to the defenders.

Guchlug wasted no time on manoeuvres – or even basic reconnaissance. 'We will show them our full strength – and let them fear us – then give them the Great Khan's Choice,' he said to Robert after he had made his report.

Three hours later, the whole *tumet* was arrayed before their mud walls.

The day was baking hot, and the sweat ran in rivers down Robert's ribs as he sat on Bayard at the rear of the army's massive formation. He had taken the time that morning to don full armour, even though it seemed likely there would be no battle that day. He was fairly sure the people of Damghan would open their gates and surrender the rebel prince to Guchlug. They surely remembered Subutai's wrath and would be most unwilling to risk another annihilating massacre from a Mongol army.

He also knew that, for the Great Khan's Choice to be successful, the Mongol force needed to look as intimidating as possible, and so Robert put on his coat of iron lamellar plates, with shoulder guards and a red-plumed iron helm, and ordered his officers to wear all the armour they possessed.

The Golden Eagles and the Snow Leopards, since they were light cavalry, generally eschewed heavy armour, preferring speed to strength, and most of the troopers wore no more protection than a padded *deel*, thick reindeer-skin boots and a soft fur-lined Mongol hat in battle.

Some of his men had scraps of mail, and a few possessed decent helms, but, if they faced heavy, iron-clad knights in open battle they must flee. Which was why Guchlug had placed Robert's men at the rear of his great horse-borne array.

And it did look impressive, Robert knew that. The frightened men on the walls would be looking down at almost nine thousand battle-hardened Mongol warriors, spaced two horse-lengths apart, and sitting immobile like an ocean of foes out on the plain.

They must appear very fearsome indeed, to any Damghan onlooker.

The Englishman was, of course, too far away to hear Guchlug give them the Great Khan's Choice, but standing up in Bayard's stirrups he watched the young general, and half a dozen of his officers, ride forward towards the gates. He could see Guchlug raising his fist and gesticulating at the gatehouse from only fifty paces away.

Robert wondered where Guchlug had found another Persian speaker to translate his words. Then realised it did not matter. These people had heard the Choice before, and they knew they must surrender to Guchlug immediately or face utter destruction.

Then something very strange happened. Robert saw all the men who were visible on the walls rise up and stand tall on the battlements, some hundreds of them.

He saw that they were all armed with bows and had quivers full of arrows at their waists. Then he watched in helpless astonishment as a dark flock of their arrows sailed up into the cloud-dotted sky and fell like a black rain upon Guchlug and the half-dozen mounted Mongol officers around him in front of their closed gates.

There were shouts of outrage and the immobile ranks of Mongol troopers began to ripple and shake. A lone Mongol horseman was now galloping along the side of the massed formation, speeding towards the gatehouse, shouting a warning as he came.

Still standing in his stirrups, Robert could see that three of the six Mongol envoys were now on the ground, skewered by arrows, another man was limp and lolling in his saddle. Some atavistic instinct caused him to whip his head right, looking north towards the low, green mountain barrier between Damghan and the Sea of Ravens. And that was when he became aware of the danger they faced. He could see a mass of horsemen coming at them, thousands of them.

A fast-moving line of men, beasts and billowing dust, only a half mile away.

He bellowed to his troops, 'Right wheel!' – then to Kolgen, who was beside him, 'Get them turned – that way! Prepare to engage the enemy.'

He could feel the disaster growing, swelling, rearing up like some fell monster in his mind. While his Golden Eagles and Snow Leopards were rearranging their ranks, lining up to face the threat from the right flank, the horses whinnying and shying as they were spurred into their places, Robert walked Bayard forward so he was ahead of the first rank of his repositioning men.

As he rode to his place, he glanced very quickly back at the gates of the town.

The two great doors of Damghan were swinging open, and he thought *What?* and then *Why?* But now he could see a mass of horsemen *inside* the gates, filling the space, and moving forward in packed rows out of the gloom, coming out towards the first ranks of the Mongol *tumen*. He almost turned fully round in the saddle, and there, far away behind him, there was more bad news – another great mass of horse coming from a hiding place behind the walls and swinging up on the Mongol left flank.

It was a trap. A well-laid trap. And there was now nothing for it but to fight.

He faced forward again, plucked a javelin from the leather socket on his horse's withers, and pointed it one-handed, like a staff, towards the oncoming enemy host on the right.

'Golden Eagles!' he shouted, and was rewarded with a roar from the ranks behind. 'Snow Leopards!' he bellowed, and received another proud bellow at his back.

'Advance to battle!' And he dug his spurs hard into Bayard's ribs.

They charged, his two *mingghat* going almost immediately up to the full gallop.

The two opposing sides met only a few moments later in a great deafening crash of splintering wood, ringing metal and the screaming of men and animals.

Robert picked his target, waited until the last moment, and hurled his javelin into the chest of a Persian horseman who was galloping towards him, skewering the man right through his mailed chest, and killing him instantly. The Persian horse carried on past Robert, who stared at the flopping, unconscious man in the saddle as he went by.

Then the Englishman was hurled into the mad, jostling, heaving crush of men and horses, and found himself fighting for his existence. He whipped out his sword and lashed the blade across the face of a snarling Khwarazmian knight to his right. He saw his blade drawing blood but also heard it clanging against the nasal guard of the man's helm. The knight disappeared shouting his hatred into the churning mass of dusty, sword-swinging, screaming warriors and barging, braying, out-kicking horses.

Out of the dust on his left, a horsemen came straight at him, a long spear aimed at his chest. Robert took the glancing blow on his round iron shield and shrugged the spearpoint off past his left shoulder. The two horses crashed bodily into each other, Bayard's powerful shoulder hitting the other horse squarely in the middle of its chest.

The smaller animal bounced away and Bayard whipped his head out towards the Persian beast, to bite it with his big yellow teeth, just as he had been trained to do.

Robert cut once, twice, at the rider with his sword, wounding him on the left arm and the neck, and the man, bleeding, yelled a curse and tried to haul his horse away.

The Englishman spurred forward and lunged hard, jamming the sword into his enemy's back, and through into his chest cavity. He heard the dying man's gurgle.

An oasis of space suddenly opened up all around Robert. He put the bloody sword in his left hand, with the shield, and seized a javelin. As he looked around for a target, he saw that the main Mongol army was now besieged on three sides. The *tumen* was being assailed from the front by the hundreds of horsemen who had erupted astonishingly from the open gate – and there seemed to be more of them, even now, streaming out of the gates – and over on the far left, another army, perhaps five thousand armoured horsemen, was furiously chewing its way steadily into the Mongol left flank. His own charge had connected only with the left wing of the huge Persian force coming in from the north, and while they had stopped hundreds of their opponents dead in their tracks, the bulk of that rebel force had carried on straight past his two *mingghat* and smashed deep in the main Mongol formation.

Two blocks of Persian horsemen at either flank were burrowing into the Mongol ranks, surging forward on a narrow front, like an iron awl punching into soft leather.

Their strategy was suddenly crystal clear to Robert. They meant to drive their left and right wings straight through the Mongol formation until they met in the middle.

They meant to divide the Mongol army into two halves.

Yet the *tumen* seemed to be doing nothing to stop them. That great mass of Mongol horsemen was hemmed from the front and on both sides – yet the majority of his comrades had no opponents to fight. They were being crushed as if trapped in a gigantic vice.

'Break out,' Robert yelled, 'break away, you fools!'

What was Guchlug thinking!?

Then Robert realised the arrogant young commander and his favoured *noyan* had likely been cut down in the first perfidious arrow storm from the gatehouse – or moments later were overwhelmed by the unexpected enemy charge from out of the open gate. The Mongols were now leaderless. He could see some horsemen in the rear of the army, those not engaged by the three enemy attacks, were beginning to shift and turn their ponies, their heads turning left and right as they looked for ways to escape.

These leaderless Mongols were making ready to flee the field.

Robert hauled back his right arm and hurled the javelin at a passing Persian. The point hit him above the left hip and sank in. The force knocking him from the saddle.

Robert snatched his last javelin and, spurring Bayard, he forced the horse to charge into the backs of a mass of Persians who were engaging the Mongol lines.

He found he was yelling, 'On me, on me, everyone to me!' and realised he was shouting in Norman French, so he repeated his rallying cry louder in Mongolian.

He saw Arslan, scowling like an ogre, making his way towards him, slashing at passing Persians as he drove onwards. There was Saka, and Taka, behind him. And a group of Golden Eagles. And a hundred Snow Leopards, too, coming on with them.

Robert crashed into the rear ranks of the enemy, and hurled his last javelin into the mailed side of a rider. Such was the force of the throw – from ten paces away and delivered from the back of a galloping horse – that it punched straight through the man's mail and stuck there, protruding out like some weird skeletal limb.

He was once again in the storm of the melee, hacking and slashing on both sides with his Mongol blade, while fending off sword blows and spear thrusts with his iron shield. The steel clanged and clashed, and he felt every enemy blow shiver deep in the bones of his battered left arm. Yet, somehow, by God's mercy, he kept the enemy blades away from his flesh. And dealt hard blows to match those he received.

His plan, if it could be called such, was to break through the attacking enemy, get right through to the Mongol *tumen* and then rally the panicked horsemen. He hoped he might yet salvage something from this swift-growing catastrophe. He could see the tightly packed, jostling ranks of Mongol troopers only a few yards ahead of him.

He shouted, 'For Genghis Khan! Fight, men, as if the old khan were watching!'

A few of the Mongols heard him; one shouted back, '*Baghatur! Baghatur!*'

Robert did not feel like a hero. He exchanged vicious cuts with a Persian with trailing moustaches – crack, crack – their steel blades spitting sparks. The man struck at his helm, a glancing blow but Robert felt the jolt right through to his neck-bones.

The Persian attempted another swipe at Robert's head. But the Englishman was ready for him. He ducked the fast-hissing blow, lunged forward and drove his sword into the Persian knight's neck, stabbing the blade in just below his oiled black beard.

Dozens of Mongols were shouting '*Baghatur! Baghatur!*' and Robert saw there was only one man between him and the Mongol ranks, a fellow half-turned away. Arslan came thundering up on Robert's left side, drew his bow-cord, loosed and punched an arrow in his enemy's ribs. The man was swept out of his saddle, hurled to the ground to be trampled into ragged gore by a hundred milling hooves.

Robert found himself surrounded by a sea of grinning Mongol faces. But Saka and Taka were alongside him, and shoving Mongol horsemen away, putting their mounts between him and the other soldiers and telling them to show proper respect to their *noyan*.

He stood tall in the stirrups once more to look over the heads of the troopers, and he saw with dismay that the two flank attacks from the rebel horse had now joined in the middle of the Mongol army and the *tumen* formation had been neatly cut in half.

Close by the gatehouse and the eastern walls of Damghan, three thousand Mongols were encircled by perhaps as many as fifteen thousand Persian warriors.

The Englishman saw a man dressed in a shimmering green-and-gold robe, a slim gold crown on his elaborate helm, point his shining scimitar at the encircled Mongols and shout a command, and the prince's rebel army surged forward with cries of savage joy.

The slaughter of the Mongols began.

Robert hesitated, but only for a scant moment. Then he did the correct thing. He lifted his own sword in the air and shouted, '*Tumen*, at my command, you will follow me. We will retreat, in good order. Now. Retreat. At the trot. All of you, follow me!'

He turned Bayard away from the encircled half of the Mongol army – away from thousands of his comrades who were surrounded by a shrieking mass of Persians, their bloody swords hacking furiously – and led his surviving men west and to safety.

Chapter Twenty-nine

'Too many mistakes,' said Robert. 'Guchlug made too many – as did I, I freely admit it. We were all at fault. But our main failure was bringing too few men to the battle.'

Robert was dining with the governor of Samarkand, Noyan Jamuga, in his grand palace in the city. It was three weeks after the bloody disaster at Damghan.

'He was always an arrogant puppy – and too pretty by half,' said Jamuga. 'I never liked him. But you know the Regent will be angry. A whole *tumen* chewed to pieces – ten thousand good men humiliated and more than half of them slaughtered on the plain. He is a good friend of yours, isn't he? The Regent? So *you* will probably be all right. But I wager somebody is sure to lose their head over this fine, bloody fiasco.'

'Guchlug has already lost his. Unless he is a prisoner of Jalal al-Din, in which case he will dearly wish he had already lost it,' said Robert.

The Englishman had managed to extricate only three thousand Mongol horsemen from the catastrophe at Damghan, and they had retreated fast for ten miles in fairly good order until he felt they could safely pause and assess the situation.

It was bad. None of the grey-beards in the ranks could remember a Mongol defeat as heavy as this one. While only a few hundred of his three thousand had been wounded, all were low in spirits, and bewildered by the inaction of their officers in the face of the rampaging enemy. This was not how Mongols were supposed to fight. It would never have happened if Genghis Khan were alive, they muttered. The only thing

Robert could do was lead them all out of the Khorasan and back to Samarkand.

'Yes. Not enough men – only one *tumen*,' said Noyan Jamuga. 'What was Lord Tolui thinking to give you so few horsemen to take on Jalal and his rebel army?'

Robert remembered that when Guchlug had requested a contribution of two *mingghat* from the Samarkand garrison, this same Noyan Jamuga had refused him. But there seemed no point in reminding his host of this. And he was right. Tolui's meanness had been the cause of the disaster. That and Guchlug's arrogant stupidity.

Back in the House of Karacha later that night, with Sarantuya cleaning his wounded left arm again with hot wine and herb-infused goose fat, Robert told her of a more serious result of the battle even than the loss of half a *tumen* of fine troopers.

'All the lands west of the Amu Daria are now in rebel hands,' he said, wincing as she dabbed his cut. 'The Mongol garrisons in a dozen towns will now be waiting for the rebels to overrun them. I doubt any Mongol will be allowed to surrender.'

'We will soon retake the Khorasan, my love, do not fret. I am quite certain that Tolui will send us some more *tumet*.'

Robert was not so sure.

–

The Englishman remained in Samarkand all that autumn, working with Idar to fill the coffers of the House of Karacha, and indeed, their business was fruitful. However, they had suspended all shipments of goods west through enemy territory and there had been no news for months from Niccolò Ziani. Robert feared that the Swords of Karacha had been attacked on the road and killed, and the valuable goods they carried lost.

He was also concerned, although he did not admit this to his new partner, that Idar's wife and daughters might also have been killed with the Swords' convoy. And there was a further disappointment in this troubled time – while he and Sarantuya made love as often as they could spare the time and summon the desire, there was no sign of another baby ripening in her womb. The Englishman wondered if something had been broken inside when the five attackers ravished her so brutally.

He took Jalair out hunting in the hills north of Samarkand, with only a small party of Snow Leopards to protect them, and was delighted to see the boy, wielding a bow with all his mother's skill, take down a young buck – his first kill.

Father and son built a campfire and feasted together on its roasted liver under the stars.

In late autumn, he received a letter from Yelu Ahai, written in elegant Uighur script. After the usual flowery pleasantries, the letter said:

> *I am sorry to inform you, Robyert, that the disaster at Damghan has had serious repercussions here in Karakorum. A large faction of the army, mainly those who support Lord Ogedei, is claiming that the Regent is unfit to lead the Mongol nation. They say that if – and I use their own ugly words – Tolui is too weak to be able to quell a small rebellion of raggedy sheep-fuckers that have already been subdued twice under the Great Khan's rule, then he must step down. The pressure on Tolui has grown to such a pitch in recent weeks, with some senior Mongols insulting him to his face, that the Regent has been forced to call a kurultai in the spring of the new year.*
>
> *The Regent therefore summons all noyan, generals and members of the Golden Kin to make their way to Karakorum, so the matter of the succession can finally be decided. Consider yourself and the Lady Sarantuya hereby summoned. Come north and support your friend. I look forward to seeing you both again soon. However, I must warn you to be prepared to defend yourself and all your actions at Damghan.*

'We could just take all the money in the strong room and run west,' said Robert, when he broke this news to Sarantuya, but his wife just laughed.

'You would not do that, even if I asked you to,' she said. 'I know you too well, my love. I know you will go north to stand beside your friend in his hour of need.'

In the last dregs of winter, as Robert and Sarantuya were making their final preparations to travel north to Karakorum, they received some good news at long last.

A cavalcade of just over a hundred travel-worn riders appeared one snowy evening outside the House of Karacha, and Idar, whooping loudly with joy, rushed down the steps to welcome the Swords of Karacha home after their long, gruelling journey – and to greet his plump wife Yula and their two lovely twin daughters.

Robert had never seen his Circassian partner so happy.

Captain Mir, the leader of the Sword of Karacha, dined with them that night, and told them of the terrible journey he had endured to reach Samarkand.

He was a short, wide man with a head of grey stubble and cold blue eyes. Both his thick arms were marked by many ancient scars, and he was missing two fingers from his left hand; Robert recognised immediately that he would be a formidable man to face in battle. Yet his tale of the long, harsh journey was laconic, and his report of the many perils he and his men had faced brief in the extreme.

'Hit by bandits near Tabriz. Georgians. Great bearded Christian oafs with long swords. But we beat them off. Only lost five men there. We were again beset, near Nishapur. That fight was more serious. They were Jalal al-Din's men and they chased us into the hills, a thousand of his horsemen hard on our tails. We had to hide while they hunted us. Thought we were done for. But we found some caves and waited them out. Took over a month but they got bored, eventually. Attacked again at a caravanserai near Herat, too, while we were sleeping. Afghan bastard gave me this.'

Here the captain lifted the hem of his grubby chemise to show a raw wound curling under his ribs, which had been crudely stitched up with black horsehair.

'The rest was easy. Only two men drowned crossing the Amu Daria.'

After this terse recital, Captain Mir fell silent and concentrated on shovelling down as much food as was humanly possible. Later in the meal, Robert said to him, 'Are you prepared to make the same perilous journey back to Tana?'

Captain Mir looked Robert square in the eye. 'Give me a day to rest the horses and my surviving men, then yes. I'll head back to Tana.'

'No, no, I meant in a month's time, or even two. In the spring.'

Mir shrugged. 'May I recruit more riders? To fill the empty saddles?'

'Certainly,' said Robert. 'Idar will arrange the money with you. Work it all out between you. I regret that I must leave for the north in two days' time. But I salute your bravery, Captain. There will be a large bonus in silver for you and all your men.'

–

For many leagues all around them, the steppe was a brilliant multicoloured carpet of spring wildflowers that released their perfume when they were crushed beneath the hooves of their horses. However, as they came within ten miles of Karakorum, the delicate blooms became sparser, then vanished entirely to be replaced by hoof-scuffed bare earth and barren mud, and the fragrances they had enjoyed were overwhelmed by the musty odour of horse dung. Therefore, it came as no surprise at all to Robert, more than two months after their departure from Samarkand, when he caught the first glimpse of the dark shape of Karakorum low on the eastern horizon.

The city had expanded in the year they had been away. As they came close, they could see that there were even a few houses built of mud-bricks among the many *ger* pitched inside the low perimeter wall that marked the boundary of the town; even the beginnings of two paved streets that crossed each other in the centre of Karakorum.

The Regent had gone so far as to build himself a palace, of sorts, next to the central crossroads. A huge, square building, three times the height of a man and painted a buttercup yellow on the outside, and with a Chinese-style roof of dark green lacquered tiles, including four fearsome stone dragons at the corners.

A pair of muscular *turghaut* Day Guards stood as sentries outside the blood-red lacquered double doors, leaning on their Mongol spears and glaring at anyone who dared to approach them without an invitation. But, when Robert presented himself at the scarlet portal the next day, they saluted smartly and immediately stepped aside.

Lord Tolui was seated in the centre of the main room on a large cushion, with Yelu Ahai beside him and a mound of papers and scrolls in front of them both. Two more grim Day Guards stood behind the Regent, spears in their hands, swords at their waists, and there were several more *turghaut* sentries posted around the interior walls.

As Robert entered, a servant approached the two men and, kneeling down before them, he gave them small porcelain cups of some hot, steaming drink, which Robert strongly suspected was that filthy boiled Jin concoction known as *tsai*.

A servant went forward to announce him and the next thing he knew he was bowing to his friend and expressing sincere joy to be in his presence once again.

'Never mind that, Robyert, sit down and help us tally the numbers here,' said Tolui. A cushion was brought, and Robert sat beside them while they pored over the various sheets of paper. Yelu gave him one quick glance and a grin of friendship, then handed the Regent a slip of paper, murmuring, 'These are all Subutai's *noyan*… you will see Noyan Bunchuk is listed among them.'

He handed Tolui another sheet of paper. 'And see here, Highness, Bunchuk is also listed with Ogedei's men.'

Tolui looked at Robert. 'Subutai is loyal to me, Robyert, is he not?'

'I believe so, Highness,' said Robert, 'but I could not say for certain since I have not seen him for more than a year.'

'Yes, of course, he has been in the East fighting the Jin. But he's back now. When you see him, make sure he knows who to support at the grand council. Tell him I will reward his loyalty when I am confirmed as the Great Khan. Tell him, Robyert.'

'I will, Highness,' he said. 'When does the grand council meet?'

'A week from today,' said Yelu. 'Almost everyone is here now.'

'How do the numbers look?' asked Robert.

Yelu responded with a meaningless little grunt.

Tolui said, 'If my calculations are correct, I have just enough votes to win, I believe. But it will be close, very close indeed. But I am the Prince of the Fireplace, and all true Mongols will know it. The problem with these lists is Mongols are such liars – all of them. At least I know I can count on you, Noyan Robyert Baghatur!'

'You can, Highness,' said Robert. He had never seen his friend Tolui like this – so nervous, so unsure of himself.

'Let us count them again,' said Tolui, 'maybe I have missed some. Here Robert you take this pile and tally the totals for me – and for Ogedei, may he rot.'

The Regent handed Robert a sheaf of papers and Robert bent his head to the long lists of Mongol names. After an hour, in which it became clear to Robert that Tolui's victory was by no means certain and, indeed, unlikely, the Regent was called away by one of the servants to deal with another matter. Yelu and Robert were left alone together.

'Will he win?' asked Robert.

'He might,' said Yelu. 'It is quite *possible* he will be chosen as Great Khan.'

Robert nodded, comprehending Yelu's careful words.

'Tell me all about Damghan,' said the chief minister. 'Tell me all the small details that you did not include in your reports.'

So Robert gave him a fuller account of the disaster, and his assessment of why it had occurred. He spoke the truth unflinchingly and, when he finished, Yelu nodded.

'Damghan might prove the end of Tolui. The feeling in Karakorum is that he did not send enough of a force to quell the rebels and so wasted the lives of half a *tumen*. Five thousand Mongol lives lost.'

'I have to say, in all truth, I think that assessment is correct,' said Robert. 'What will happen to Tolui if he loses the vote at the grand council next week?'

'Ogedei will want him gone. He will be exiled, probably, sent somewhere remote. Tell me, if you were to recapture the Khorasan and put down the rebels, how many troops would you need? The minimum. What numbers would *you* require, *Baghatur*, to do this work?'

Robert thought for a while, then said, 'Five *tumet*, that would be the minimum, and authority to order the local governors to lend me additional troops. I would need a competent commander, too, someone like Subutai, or maybe even Chormaqan.'

'Thank you, Robyert,' said Yelu, 'you have been very helpful to me as always.'

Chapter Thirty

When it came, the decision was taken quickly. Robert knew Tolui had lost the moment he sat down beside him on his large silk cushion in the semicircle in the Regent's palace a week later. Because, looking over at Ogedei's side, he saw that General Subutai was sitting beside Tolui's older brother.

The council went through the same ritual as before, with Yelu Ahai presiding, flanked by two of his senior clerks. Tolui stood and made his case briefly, essentially that he was the Prince of the Fireplace, and tradition demanded he be elected Great Khan. He made no mention of Damghan, but insisted he had won a victory against the Jin the summer before, and had thus proved his value to the nation as a battle commander.

Ogedei stood and repeated his claim that Genghis Khan had privately told him he was his chosen successor. Then he spent an hour criticising Tolui for his weakness and incompetence – the disaster at Damghan was mentioned five times.

General Subutai, the greatest Mongol battle commander, did not speak, but every man knew whom he favoured, and the vote, when it came, was not even close.

As the two rivals spoke and made their claims, Robert watched his enemy Khuyag on the cushions opposite, placed further away, this time, from Ogedei. He minutely examined the creature who had defiled his wife. He had not seen the *noyan* for nearly two years, yet he found that his hatred was as fierce as ever. He was more than ready to take his revenge on this man, no matter the consequences.

Khuyag had walked the Earth long enough. It was time to act.

Yelu Ahai announced the result to loud cheers from Ogedei's side, then the new Great Khan lumbered to his feet once again.

'My father, Genghis Khan, is surely smiling down upon us this day. After the feeble rule of a weakling and a coward, our long nightmare is over at last. A new era begins. I swear to you all that I shall lead the proud Mongol nation to victory after victory, to greater glory, and greater conquests even than my sacred father. Onwards to glory!'

When the cheering had subsided, Ogedei said, 'My first decree as your elected Great Khan is that there shall be a full month of games. We will celebrate the glorious new epoch here in my capital Karakorum with the Three Manly Sports – and all Mongols who would show their valour to the nation and their new khan will compete in either the archery, the horse racing or the *Bökh*. The worthy winners of each of these three noble competitions shall receive a lavish reward from their khan's hand.'

Ogedei paused, now looking directly at Tolui. 'My second decree is this. That my brother Tolui is henceforth exiled from Karakorum and, indeed, from all the Mongol heartlands for the rest of his life. There has been too much rancour and discord in our great nation, fomented by him, and allowed to continue for far too long.

'I shall not allow that disruption, that confusion, that *weakness* to continue a moment longer. Lord Tolui is banished to the lands of the Forest People in the far north, where he may quietly live out his days in peace. Your Great Khan has spoken.'

–

Tolui Khan, erstwhile Regent of the Mongol nation, packed up his *ger* and his family, all his horses and herds, his wife Sorkoktani and his sons Mönke, Kublai, Hulagu and Ariq Boke, and was on the road north before the week was out, with only a token *mingghan* of personal guards to accompany the man who had once ruled an empire.

Almost all his followers, who had once numbered in their tens of thousands, deserted the former Regent, his *noyan* all rushing to pledge their loyalty to Ogedei.

Robert had no opportunity to say goodbye to his friend, but he did speak to the turncoat General Subutai some weeks later, when the *orlok* summoned him to his *ger*, just outside Karakorum, to interrogate him personally about the disaster at Damghan.

Robert was, by now, heartily sick of speaking about the catastrophe in the Khorasan but he decided to indulge the *orlok* for the sake of their long acquaintance.

Subutai gave him wine and a warm greeting, begging him to take his ease.

After a few limp pleasantries, Subutai said, 'The Great Khan has ordered me to go east again, Robyert, as I expect you have heard. The Jin are holding fast at a city they call Kaifeng, and Ogedei wants me to go east and capture it for him. I wondered if you would care to come with me. I will give you a *tumen* of scouts to command, including your own Snow Leopards and Golden Eagles, of course, and another eight *mingghat* to lead as well. What do you say, *Baghatur*? I could surely use your skills.'

'You don't want to talk about Damghan?' asked Robert.

'What more is there to say about it? You had too few men, that was perfectly obvious even before you left Karakorum, and Guchlug was always an arrogant idiot.'

Robert pondered Subutai's offer for a few moments. In truth, he had no plans to do anything, except somehow to arrange the painful death of Khuyag. That one idea had been dominant in his mind for weeks now. The *noyan* was still in Karakorum, but he was surrounded by his White Foxes, and Robert had not yet thought of a way to get at him. But to go off and fight again in Cathay? That was unexpected. The offer of a *tumen* was tempting, and he knew Sarantuya would be pleased by this promotion.

'You know what I desire, General,' he said. 'I want the Mongol army to turn west. I want to retake the Khorasan, then capture Baghdad, and go on even further. And, if Ogedei Khan's eye is turned eastwards – if he, like his father, has his mind fixed on the conquest of the Jin, and then the Song – there is no point offering him my sword. So I must say no, but I thank you. I will give up command of my two *mingghat* and take my family back to Samarkand; then I will find a way to return to my people in Europe and draw my sword against Christendom's foes.'

'Your mind is made up?'

'It is. I will go west.'

Subutai regarded him for a long while with his odd, leonine eyes, slowly sipping his wine. 'Do you remember, my friend, when we first met, you and I, some ten years ago, I think, outside the walls of Otrar?' the general asked.

'Vividly,' said Robert. 'You suspected me of being a Khwarazmian spy.'

'Not for long,' said Subutai, grinning. 'I saw your quality shining through and knew you were no spy. But, more than that, I had a feeling about you – I saw a man who needs to belong – to belong to something, to a clan, an army or even to a person. You were like a stray dog, eager to please. Hoping to be taken in and fed. Loved. And we took you in, we Mongols, did we not? We gave you your trade treaty, and your woman. We even gave you *mingghat* to command. You belong to us, Robyert. You *are* one of us. You cannot give up the fight and go home. You are a Mongol now.'

'You liken me to a dog?'

'Do not pretend to be angry, Robyert. You know that I hold you in the highest esteem. Besides, dogs are fine creatures – dogs are fierce, dogs are strong, dogs are loyal. Loyal to their pack. This is my point. Your pack is the Mongol nation.'

Robert thought about that for a while. He was not, in truth, angry with Subutai. He also held the general in high esteem.

However, he did not trust the wily *orlok* – not as far as he could throw the man in the *Bökh* oval.

'Why did you side with Ogedei?' he asked. 'We all thought you were a supporter of Tolui. If you had sat beside Tolui, he might have won the vote.'

'Maybe. Maybe not. But, if Tolui had won, Ogedei would never have stayed quiet. The quarrel over the succession would have rumbled on for as long as Tolui and Ogedei both remained alive. If Tolui had had any sense, he would have had Ogedei quietly murdered when he was Regent. He did not. That means Tolui is weak. And a weak leader is a disaster for the Mongol nation. So I decided to support the stronger candidate. The old khan used to have a favourite saying, which I am sure you must also have heard: a Mongol must be prepared to do what is necessary. What*ever* is necessary. I did what was necessary. I abandoned Tolui, who is a good man but a weak one, and I threw my full support behind Ogedei, who is neither.'

'I, too, must do what is necessary,' said Robert. 'I must return home.'

'Think about my offer. You are a Mongol dog. This is your pack.'

'I'll take my leave, *Orlok*. I thank you for the wine and your candour.'

'One more thing,' said Subutai. 'I have a message to you from Ogedei Khan. He invites you to come before him this day, to formally acknowledge him as Great Khan and Lord of the Steppe, and humbly make the proper submission to his throne.'

–

Robert did not attempt to drive Bayard hard that day. He was heading north, following the tracks of more than a thousand horses and an even greater number of sheep, camels and goats. He allowed the horse to go at a fairly leisurely ambling pace, since he was in no hurry. However, the steppe was so inviting for that noble beast, so lush with spring grass, flat and empty, that Bayard soon chose to gallop just for the sheer joy of it.

Robert's feelings, on the other hand, were the very opposite of joyful.

When he stopped for the night in the lee of a small range of hills and made his camp, he sat for some hours simply staring up at the black sky, the blanket of cloud obscuring all but a few feebly winking stars, with Bayard munching millet contentedly beside him from his nosebag.

Robert was thinking about what he had set out to do. And what consequences there might be, not least for his immortal soul. He was also thinking about what kind of man he was – was he a good man, as he had always believed? Or an evil one? His actions would indicate one kind of man; his beliefs another. Eventually, he got on his knees and began to pray. 'Lord, I cannot know Your plan,' he said, 'but You know the course on which I'm set. If what I must do offends, I beg You to show me a sign.'

When he had finished his prayers, he sat again, with his back to the flames of the fire, and looked out at the silent blackness all around him.

He realised he had not been alone, with only his horse for company, for a long time. He had always had companions. And he did not dislike the feeling at all; he felt no loneliness in that hour. Sarantuya was safe in Karakorum, with Arslan, Taka, Saka, Begter and a dozen Snow Leopards sleeping in the *ger* to keep her and Jalair safe from Khuyag and his men, and another full *jagghun* of Golden Eagles was posted round their tent.

He missed Idar, then, and wondered what advice he would have offered about the task he planned to undertake. Then he realised he had already received Idar's sage advice on matters very much like this. Then, suddenly very tired, he rolled himself up in his warm blankets and fell into a short, and much troubled sleep.

He rode due north for a week, and the weather grew chilly. He had to stop and shelter from a thunderstorm on the seventh day, and wondered if it could be the sign he sought from God. No, he realised, it was just a commonplace summer downpour.

On the ninth day, he saw trees and knew he was at the beginning of the forest lands. He stopped and tied Bayard to a tall spruce tree, feeling the fat globules of resin from the rough bark sticky on his fingers. That night he made a great campfire of fallen pine branches, and cooked a hot meal of *shulen*, to bolster his courage.

The next day he turned west, riding along the tree line, with the great steppe stretching away on his left, and the northern arboreal realm on his right. Two days later, he came across a few scattered sheep and goats and the red-cheeked Mongol boys who tended them, astonished to see him in this wilderness.

Then he came to the horse herds and armed Mongol riders, who were wary of him.

That night he dined in Tolui's ger, with Sorkoktani and her maids and the former Regent's four sons. It was a jolly meal, with plenty of hot spiced wine and with Tolui ludicrously pretending his loss of immense power was what he had secretly wanted all along.

'You have no idea how irksome it is to rule a nation composed of donkey-headed Mongols,' he told Robert. 'Each man thinks he knows better than you, and only does your bidding if you threaten to cut off his stupid donkey head. I am much happier up here, Robyert, truly, I am, with my family, and not a care in the world but to keep my flocks on good, sweet grass and keep the forest wolves at bay.'

They drank a lot more wine, and when Tolui grew loud and red-faced and suggested a game of dice to Robert, an epic battle over the tray, his wife suggested that they take their dice and their wine and go off to a smaller, separate *ger*, so that their drinking and clattering and stupid man-talk would not keep the children awake.

As Robert and Tolui collected flasks of wine and the dice tray and went out to the other *ger*, Tolui grumbled that he was no longer master even in his own *ger*. But his mood improved as the wine flowed once more and the dice merrily rattled in the wooden tray, and he managed to win a goodly amount in silver from Robert's purse.

'I am so happy that you came up here to join me, Robyert,' said Tolui. 'All my other friends have abandoned me since the… since the grand council.'

They were entirely alone. Tolui was lolling drunk, his *deel* was pulled half-open. His words were slurred and he had, it seemed, entered the tiresome maudlin stage.

Robert rose and gathered up the dice and the tray. He walked behind Tolui, carrying the tray, and set it down on a shelf by the wall. Then he reached inside his own *deel* and pulled out the Circassian blade from its sheath under his armpit.

He had nothing in his mind in that moment. It was empty of all thought and feeling; empty but for the bare mechanics of the deed he must now accomplish.

Tolui was still speaking. 'I did not know, at first, if you were truly my friend, my brother… I thought, perhaps, you only sought to befriend me because… I might one day be the Great Khan, and it would be to your… advantage. Now all that has come… and gone. I know you truly love me… your coming here to be at my side when I have nothing proves it. And I am very sorry for ever doubting you.'

'I am sorry, too,' said Robert, and he dropped to his knees behind Tolui's back. He quickly reached his left hand around Tolui's head and clamped his mouth shut.

Robert put the point of the long blade in the open top of his *deel*, in the soft pit of Tolui's shoulder between the muscle and the left clavicle, then with one swift movement, he shoved the steel down, deep into Tolui's chest, the thin blade's point reaching, then rupturing his beating heart.

Tolui struggled feebly in Robert's grip as his heart was ripped and torn apart by the questing blade. Then he slumped back against Robert's body, as if he was resting. His right leg kicked out once, he made a muffled moaning sound. Then he was still.

'I beg you to forgive me,' whispered Robert. 'But I am required to do this for the cause. The holy cause. I *was* your friend, despite everything. Farewell, brother.'

He pulled a silk scarf from his neck, pressed it around the buried steel blade of the Circassian knife, and pulled the steel out, free of Tolui's dead body.

The entry wound was a tiny slit, weeping just a few drops of scarlet blood, which he carefully wiped away with the silk scarf. Then, keeping the corpse sitting upright with his knee in the small of Tolui's back, he tucked the long dagger away, and reaching into an inside pocket, he produced a lump of amber-coloured resin, taken from a spruce tree. He moulded the resin in his fingers until it was warm and pliable and pyramidal in shape, and then he used it as a plug to seal up the small wound, like a wooden stopper in the neck of a bottle of fine Persian perfume.

He pulled the former Regent's *deel* tightly closed, and laid his body back on the cushions, pausing to close his friend's unseeing eyes. He covered him with a warm bearskin. With luck, he thought, he might get a couple of days' start on his pursuers.

'Goodbye, my friend,' he said quietly. 'I pray that God will forgive you your sins and, of his boundless mercy, welcome you into Paradise.'

Then he walked out of the *ger* into the dark, cold night.

Outside, he stopped to speak to the two guards at the entrance to Tolui's tent. 'Your lord is sleeping,' he said. 'Do not disturb him.'

He made his way to where Bayard was hitched, saddled him as quickly as his clumsy fingers could work the buckles, mounted and rode into the night, feeling the hot tears flowing freely down his cold cheeks.

–

‘Where have you been?’ asked Sarantuya. It was more than a week later and Robert was back at his *ger* in Karakorum, saddle-sore and very tired. There had been no pursuit from Tolui’s *mingghan*, as far as he knew, but he had not lingered to find out if the former Regent’s men had sought to avenge their leader.

He had fled south as fast as Bayard could carry him.

‘I told you,’ he said to his wife. ‘I had something to attend to.’

‘I did not think you would be gone the best part of a month. I thought Khuyag had killed you, or you had suffered a thousand other fates. Where were you? What were you doing?’

‘I cannot tell you. Neither do I wish to lie to you. Do not ask me again.’

Sarantuya stared at him. She said, ‘Are you hungry? Do you want food?’

‘Yes,’ said Robert, trying to smile. ‘And a very large bowl of wine.’

There was a commotion outside the *ger* and Taka came tumbling in. ‘*Ezen*,’ he said, ‘they’re all here. Ogedei is outside. The Great Khan is here!’

Chapter Thirty-one

Robert got slowly to his feet and took a moment to adjust the belt around his *deel* and sling the Mongol sword at his left side. Then he went out of the *ger*.

It was a bright summer morning and, looking up into the harsh sunshine, Robert could see Ogedei Khan outlined on his horse with a dozen mounted men around him. He bowed before the Lord of the Steppe. He knew that Sarantuya was behind him in the doorway, and that young Jalair was also peering round the jamb of the red door.

'Noyan Robyert Baghatur,' said Ogedei, who for once sounded sober. 'In recognition of the great service you have rendered me, I have a gift for you.'

Robert could now see that Subutai was one of the riders with the Great Khan, and that the old general was grinning broadly at him.

Ogedei made an expansive gesture with his right hand and the horsemen parted to allow a dozen Mongols on foot to come rushing forward, hustling a number of prisoners who were trussed up as tight as hogs on market day. The six terrified prisoners were hurled to the turf before the *ger*, and Robert stared intently at their faces.

One of them had lost an eye, another had a long scar across his nose, which looked like it had come from a sabre slash. In the middle was a larger figure, a man with a much-scarred face, purple and swollen from years of dedicated wine-drinking.

It was Khuyag.

'I honour my bargains,' said Ogedei, 'just as you have honoured yours. When you have settled the score with these filth-eating pigs, you will report to Chormaqan. He is expecting you. You and your new *tumen* will ride in three days. Be ready.'

Robert's mind leapt back to the last time he had seen Ogedei, in the Great Khan's enormous *ger*, shortly after his meeting with General Subutai.

Ogedei Khan had greeted him civilly, invited him to sit and then had dismissed all his servants, and even his two *turghaut* guards, and he had sat down on the cushions next to Robert; the two men alone, their two heads very close together.

'I do not want this conversation to be caught by any other ears,' Ogedei said quietly. 'Furthermore, I want your sacred oath, by whatever God you follow, that you will never speak of this day to any other Mongol. Do I have that sacred oath from you?'

Robert, mystified, gave his word that he would remain silent.

Then Ogedei said, 'General Subutai tells me that you wish to go west, to retake the Khorasan for us from the rebels. And then to go further yet, even as far as the city of Baghdad, and beyond. Is this true?'

'It is true, Great One,' said Robert. 'That is what I most devoutly wish to do.'

Ogedei nodded at him. 'Good. Now, when we spoke before, you asked me for the head of Noyan Khuyag, my loyal supporter, whom you said had sent his men to assault your lady wife – Lady Sarantuya. This is still your heart's desire?'

'You will give me Khuyag? Or allow me to fight him?'

'Slowly, slowly, *Baghatur*,' said Ogedei. 'Do you want some wine?'

'No, Great Khan, no wine. I thank you.'

'I would like some, but my doctors tell me I drink too much of it. So, no wine.'

'You were speaking of Khuyag,' said Robert.

'Indeed, I will return to him in a moment. You were close to my younger brother the Regent, were you not? I saw you sit with him at the grand council – both times.'

'He is my friend.'

'Then it pains me to tell you that I cannot allow him to live.'

Robert reared back in surprise.

'Slowly, slowly, *Baghatur*,' said Ogedei once again. 'I cannot let him live because there are many important men among us, *noyan*, generals, *orlok* – perhaps even you, *Baghatur* – who love him and wish that he were the Great Khan and not I. They might profess their undying loyalty to me but, in their hearts, they hope Tolui will rise again and challenge me. That is bad for me, and bad for the whole Mongol nation. Therefore my younger brother must die.'

'Great One, Lord Tolui has accepted his fate. He is content that you should rule. You were the choice of the council. Tolui knows this and he is at peace with it.'

'Nevertheless…'

'Great Khan, I cannot keep my oath. I must warn my friend of your intention.'

'If you do so, I will take your head, *Baghatur*. But if you go north for me and remove Tolui from this Earth, I swear I shall give you Khuyag's.'

Robert sat back, his mouth open, stunned by Ogedei's murderous offer.

'Furthermore, I shall give you a *tumen* to command, under General Chormaqan, and orders to ride to the Khorasan and finally crush this running sore of a rebellion. Once you have done that, I will consider your request to take the army further west – even unto Baghdad. I have allocated five *tumet* to Chormaqan – and one of them shall be yours. I swear this. This is the bargain I would make with you, General Robyert Baghatur. A *tumen*, and the freedom to subdue the Khorasan. And Khuyag's head – and the lives of all those men who defiled your wife.'

Robert's mind was a maelstrom. He knew he was in the presence of great evil. This plan was despicable and yet… and yet if he agreed to it, he would be able finally to bring a Mongol army west to save the whole of Christendom.

Five *tumet*. Fifty thousand men under Chormaqan. And Khuyag's head.

And, if he refused, the Englishman knew his time with the Mongols was over, as was his life. Ogedei Khan would not allow him to live to speak of this day.

'I accept the bargain,' said Robert.

–

Ogedei made a gesture to his horsemen. They turned their mounts and cantered away, leaving the six bound prisoners in a line kneeling before the door of Robert's *ger*.

Robert drew his Mongol sword and walked over to the first prisoner.

He was the man with only one eye, and he stared up at Robert angrily with it. The Englishman said, 'Tell me who ordered you to assault my wife? Tell me this instant and I may even spare your miserable life.'

The one-eyed man shook his head, his teeth gritted. Robert lifted the sword and, without another word, he hacked at the man's neck, once, twice, until the one-eyed head rolled free on the ground amid a hot, pumping jet of blood.

Robert went along to the next man in the line. 'Tell me who ordered you to attack my wife, Lady Sarantuya. Tell me this instant—'

The man cried out, shrieking piteously, 'It was the *noyan* – it was Noyan Khuyag! He promised us five horses each if we would do the deed…'

The other bound men were all squirming in their ropes. Robert looked over at Arslan. 'Hold them fast,' he said.

Arslan, Begter, Taka and Saka rushed forward and seized the remaining bound men. Then Robert hacked the head from the man who had admitted the crime; it took him three hard blows before the head finally rolled free.

The Englishman asked no more questions. He simply walked up to the three bound men and methodically hacked their heads free of their bodies. His loyal men, who held them steady, were liberally spattered with the blood, as was Robert. He cared not.

Finally, he stood, breathing heavily, his clothing painted with fresh gore, before Khuyag, his curved sword dripping red in his right hand.

'Wait!' said Khuyag. 'Wait, Robyert, I beg you. Remember I was your friend. Remember how I took you into my *ger* when you were a *gadaad khun*. Was I not generous to you? Did I not treat you like my own brother?'

'You ordered my wife to be defiled. My unborn child is dead because of it.'

Robert lifted the sword. Sunlight sparkled on the glistening blade.

'Stop!' said a voice from behind him. 'I cannot allow you to do this.'

Robert lowered the sword, frowned and turned to look at Sarantuya, who was still standing in the doorway of the *ger*.

'I cannot let him live,' said Robert. 'He deserves to die for his crime.'

'The crime was against me,' said his wife. 'You were not harmed.'

Robert stared at her.

'I am the one he wronged,' said Sarantuya. 'He was my husband; he shared my *ger* for many years. It must be I who decides Khuyag's punishment—'

'Sarantuya,' said Khuyag, 'I was a good husband to you, I loved you—'

'—and I who carries out that same punishment,' said Sarantuya.

She lifted the recurved Mongol bow from her side and plucked an arrow from the full quiver at her waist. Without another word, she nocked the arrow to the string, drew the cord and shot Khuyag through the belly. The black shaft sank in deep, almost to the fletchings. Khuyag's whole body shivered and he let out a low groan.

Sarantuya nocked another arrow and loosed again, this time the shaft smacked into the centre of Khuyag's chest. He twitched and sagged, gasping for breath. She drew the bow once more, nocking a third arrow and whacked the last shaft home, deep into her former husband's bull neck.

Khuyag toppled over, gasping and choking on his own blood.

He tried to say something, gargling his own precious life fluids, then he died.

–

'Another one?' said Wilhelm von Eslarn, crashing into the flow of Robert's tale.

'My lord?' asked the prisoner, his face as pale as his white penitent's garb.

'You murdered another one,' said the provost. 'You assassinated another of these Tartar lords – this one that you claimed had been your friend.'

'If you speak of Lord Tolui, the former Regent,' said Robert, 'then yes, I did kill him. And he was my friend, and I wept bitter tears that I was forced to do that deed.'

The courtroom was deathly quiet.

'You were not forced; you chose to murder the poor man in cold blood.'

'My mission was always to bring the armies of the Mongol nation to the aid of Christendom,' said Robert. 'When Ogedei Khan asked me to do that terrible deed he promised me that I would be able to bring the *tumet* closer to the Latin kingdoms. If I refused, I would have been killed. So I *was* forced to kill Tolui. I had no other choice. And, I must tell you, that Ogedei was as good as his word. I did indeed ride west that summer with five full *tumet* under the command of a fine Mongol general.'

'Yet no help for the beleaguered Latin kingdoms was forthcoming,' sneered Wilhelm. 'Another way of looking at this is that you murdered this Tartar lord in cold blood to better your own circumstances – you were made a commander, were you not? – and to take revenge on this other brute, the one who had attacked your wife.'

'I was promoted to general of a *tumen*, this is true. And I was also revenged on Khuyag, but I swear that my true motive was to bring the Mongol army westwards.'

'I can attest to this,' said Ivo of Narbonne. 'The prisoner has always said his reason for joining this heathen army was to bring them west. Furthermore, he was acting under orders from his superior – and so he bears no responsibility for whatever foul deeds he was forced to do. His masters ordered him east, therefore they are to blame for anything that occurred. Robert was only part of a wider Templar scheme.'

'So you have claimed… several times,' said Wilhelm. 'But I think—'

The Dominican, Geoffrey of Beaulieu, interrupted the provost. 'You claim, do you not, that the Seneschal of the Order, Jean de Malemort, was your superior in this secret mission, that Malemort himself ordered you to join the Mongol horde?'

'That is so,' said Robert.

'Then would it not be helpful to call Jean de Malemort before the court to hear his testimony?' asked Geoffrey. 'He may well exonerate you.'

'Would that it were possible,' said Robert. 'But Jean de Malemort is dead.'

'How do you know this?' asked the Dominican.

'This man here, Ivo of Narbonne, told me so himself,' said Robert. 'He said that his master, Géraud de Malemort, the Bishop of Bordeaux, who was brother to Jean de Malemort, had attended his sibling's deathbed. My friend Jean de Malemort, alas, is no more.'

'That is a lie,' said a loud voice from the public benches, and a tall man with a deep hood pulled forward over his face stood up.

'What is this?' exclaimed the Duke of Austria, seeming to go instantly from fast sleep to full battle alertness. 'Who are you to interrupt the proceedings of my court?'

The man pushed back his hood to reveal an angular face with sharp cheekbones. He was an older man in his middle-sixties, bald but with a magnificent grey beard.

Robert gasped in surprise.

'Who are you, sir?' said the duke, rising from his throne. 'Speak up quickly or I shall have my guards eject you from the court.'

'I'm Malemort,' the man said. 'I have the honour to hold the rank of Seneschal in the Order of the Poor Fellow-Soldiers of Christ and of the Temple of Solomon.'

He came out from the packed benches, the other people moving quickly aside to let him pass, and stepped out on to the floor of the court.

'I am Jean de Malemort,' he said, 'and I come here this day to accuse… You!'

He turned fast and pointed directly at Ivo of Narbonne, who seemed to be trying to shrink into his stool beside the dock.

'That lying, cringing wretch who now cowers beside Sir Robert of Hadlow,' thundered Malemort, 'is not fit to lick his boots. This false fellow who claims to be the prisoner's friend is no such thing at all. This vile slithering worm, this Ivo of Narbonne, is a former heretic of the Paterinian sect, outlawed by His Holiness the Pope, and he is employed as a secret informer for the Church, a dirty spy, working for the Bishop of Bordeaux, my misguided brother, and *his* mission is nothing less than the ruin of the Templar Order.'

'What?' said the duke. 'What? Can this be true? Speak up Father Ivo?'

'I… er, I am, ah… It is true that I am in the employ of His Grace, the Bishop of Bordeaux, but I am not and nor have I ever been a—'

'Do not believe a word that comes from this liar's mouth,' said Malemort. 'He told Sir Robert, when this poor man had been tortured for a month and deprived of food, water and light, that I was in my grave. Father Ivo told the prisoner this cruel lie to remove from this Christian knight his last hope, and to force the prisoner to reveal his secrets. Father Ivo lies. He lies as he breathes. He seeks only to blacken the reputation of the Templar Order on behalf of his master. You are not the prisoner's friend, wretch, you are the prisoner's enemy. As you are mine!'

There was uproar in the court, with many people shouting out from the benches. The duke called for silence and threatened to order the court cleared by force.

When the tumult had subsided, the duke said, 'Can any man verify the identity of the fellow here who claims to be the Templar Seneschal Jean de Malemort?'

'He can,' said Malemort, turning back towards the dais and pointing directly at Geoffrey de Beaulieu. 'The Dominican friar knows me well enough.'

The Dominican stood up and slowly nodded his tonsured head. 'I do know him,' he said. 'He is, indeed, Jean de Malemort, Seneschal of the Templar Order.'

There was another storm of noise, cheering, jeering and general laughter.

'Silence,' bellowed the duke, 'I will have silence in my court.'

When quiet was eventually achieved, he said, 'The hour grows late, and I have had enough nonsense for one day. We will adjourn this trial until the morrow when we will examine the matter further, and I swear by Almighty God we shall finally get to the truth of it. The prisoner will be returned to his cell and proceedings will resume in the morning. This day's deliberations are over. You are, all of you, dismissed.'

Robert looked to his right at the stool where Ivo of Narbonne had been sitting. But the priest had gone. He looked up and his heart soared to see his old friend and mentor Jean de Malemort striding long-legged towards him across the crowded hall.

'My lord,' said Robert. 'You came for me… Praise God. You came in my hour of need. Is it truly you?' He reached out and clutched Malemort's wiry right arm.

'It's me, Robert. I am here for you. Put your trust in me and we'll find a way out of this mess together, one way or another. Remember: God is with us. All will be well.'

–

An hour later, alone, and back in his cold, dank prison cell beneath the stone keep of Vienna Castle, Robert fell to his knees in the chilly darkness and began to pray.

First, he gave thanks to God for the arrival of Jean de Malemort. All would be well, his mentor had said. And, for the first time in many weeks, he felt a glimmer of hope in the dark swamp of his despair. Malemort, his friend, his Templar Brother was here to save him.

Then, examining his conscience, he prayed again, 'Forgive me, Father, for my many sins. Forgive me for the blood that stains my hands, for the deaths for which I am responsible. For the murder of the Great Khan, who was my lord, and for the killing of Tolui, who was my friend. You alone know why I did these terrible deeds, and You know that I committed the crimes in Your service and in the service of Christendom.

'If my actions do indeed merit death at the hands of these men who hold me captive, then grant me the grace to die with honour and the courage to accept my fate without fear. But if it is Your will to grant me life, to remove me from the Valley of the Shadow of Death, then, Lord, show me a sign. Give me an indication that my life will be spared, my sins forgiven. I ask in the name of Your son, Our Lord and Saviour Jesus Christ.'

At that very moment, he heard the sound of footsteps outside his cell door, and the gaoler Gutto's reedy voice protesting, 'This is most irregular, my lord, I have received orders from Father Ivo that no man may visit the prisoner save him—'

'I am countermanding those orders,' said Jean de Malemort's strong voice. 'I have spoken to Heinrich von Leitzdorf, the constable of the castle, spoken to him this very hour, and he has granted me permission to visit the prisoner this same night. Unlock this door, man, do it swiftly, or you shall feel the force of my wrath.'

The door creaked open, filling the cell with an orange light, and there was Jean de Malemort, with a heavy bundle under one arm and a candle-lantern in his right hand.

They sat together on the floor of the cell and shared the cornucopia of food that Malemort had brought – a venison pie, a whole ham, a wedge of cheese, two fresh loaves of bread and a pat of butter. A small cask of wine, too. Enough to keep a man for days.

'I do not have much time,' said Malemort. 'Ivo of Narbonne fled the castle earlier tonight – the gate guards saw him slip out. I mean to go after him, to apprehend him and bring him back to Vienna to answer questions in the presence of the duke.'

'Why would Ivo flee?' Robert asked, indistinctly, since his mouth was full.

'He is part of a plot with my wicked brother Géraud of Bordeaux and other great lords of France to bring the Templars to ruin,' said Malemort. 'I do not know all the details yet, Robert, but I do know that you are a mere pawn in a much greater scheme. They are using you to bring down our Order, and I'll not allow it. Together we shall foil their vile plot against our Brethren.'

'You would leave me in here?' said Robert, hating how weak he must sound.

'Forgive me but I must. I ride out after Ivo of Narbonne within the hour. If I am to catch the wretch, I must go now.

Stay strong, and keep the faith. I'll be back before long and we will put an end to this wickedness together. Can you do that? Can you hold on here a little longer?'

Robert swallowed his mouthful. 'I can do that, lord,' he said. 'Your presence has given me the strength I needed. God grant that I can hold fast until you return.'

A little while later, alone in the dark, but with a full belly for the first time in weeks, wrapped up tight in the warm cloak that Malemort had left for him, and comforted by this sign from a loving and merciful God, Robert lay down on the floor and fell into a peaceful sleep.

Historical Note

The Englishman who rode with Genghis Khan in the thirteenth century was a real person. He was captured with a party of Mongol scouts outside Vienna Castle in the summer of 1241 and tried as a traitor to Christendom by his captor Frederick II, Duke of Austria.

We know this because his story is recorded in the *Chronica Majora* of Matthew Paris, a medieval Benedictine monk of St Albans. Further research has been done by the Hungarian historian Gabriel Ronay in his fascinating book *The Tartar Khan's Englishman* (Cassell, 1978). Ronay identifies him as Robert, an English Templar, who was adept at foreign languages. In an appendix to his book, Ronay includes a letter written by Ivo of Narbonne, Robert's interrogator in Vienna, to his boss Géraud de Malemort, the Bishop of Bordeaux, describing his capture and outlining the Englishman's story.

I have used these sources and the work of half a dozen other historians to create a *fictional* story of Robert's life and deeds. I put the emphasis on fictional because this is my task as a novelist. I take the raw clay of history and mould it into a (hopefully) gripping historical adventure. Since what we know for sure about the Englishman's movements is scant, I have invented the majority of his story based on the activities of his Mongol hosts. However, I suspect I may have bent the bounds of history more than I usually do in this novel by having a foreign secret agent murder Genghis Khan.

Did Robert really assassinate the Great Khan? To be honest, I think it extremely unlikely. However, there are so many different, conflicting stories swirling around the great man's death, which the Mongol high command tried to cover up for as long as possible, that my version is *not* the most outlandish. Most historians agree that the Great Khan fell off his horse and was badly injured at some point at the end of the summer of 1227, just before the fall of the Hexi capital on the Yellow River, although others suggest that he died of a fever, or possibly from typhoid. Some claim he was struck by lightning or felled by septicaemia from an arrow wound in the leg gone bad.

My favourite legend is that Genghis Khan took a captured Tangut beauty to his bed but she, a patriot, had hidden a piece of glass or a steel blade in her vagina and this gave him a mortal wound to the genitals. The truth is, we don't know how he died, so I felt I had the right as a creator of fiction to add a Templar assassin to the list of possible causes for his demise.

The great cavalry raid

Subutai Baghatur is one of those men who jump out at you from the pages of history. He was Genghis Khan's ablest commander and a genuine military genius. Subutai's finest exploit, among many, was the great cavalry raid that took place between 1220 and 1223 in which Subutai and General Jebe circumnavigated the Caspian Sea (aka the Sea of Ravens), something which had never been done before, nor has been done since.

Subutai took an army of about twenty thousand Mongols from Azerbaijan into Georgia, where he beat the Christian Georgians in two pitched battles six months apart – ending Georgian hopes of joining the Fifth Crusade – before crossing the Caucasus, led by local guides, one of whom he had beheaded for leading him the wrong way.

When he descended from the mountain passes on to the plain of Terek, Subutai was confronted by a huge combined enemy force of Cumans, Kipchaks, Bulgars, Alans and other local tribes. Using a combination of diplomacy, trickery and bribery, he persuaded the rebel Cumans to abandon their allies on the field of battle and then he destroyed all his enemies piecemeal, one after the other.

The Mongols had negotiated a lucrative trade treaty with the Venetians of Tana, which formed much of the plot of the first novel in this trilogy, *Templar Traitor*, and so in 1222, to aid the Venetian Republic, Subutai sent a strong contingent of his Mongols to sack and burn the port of Soldaya, which was a trading outpost of Venice's bitter rivals Genoa.

The next year, pursuing Cuman rebels under Khan Köten, Subutai invaded the Rus' lands west of the Dnieper (modern-day Ukraine), looting and burning as he went, and had to flee from a massive army raised from the Rus' principalities, which was said to be some eighty thousand strong. He retreated before them to the banks of the River Kalka, where in the spring of 1223, he fought a great battle against this combined Cuman and Rus' army and comprehensively defeated them. Fire-pots to create smoke and confusion and whistling arrows to direct Mongol cavalry movements were used as described in this book.

Subutai then marched east to destroy the Bulgars in their homeland on the Volga River, before returning as a hero to Genghis Khan's domains east of the Aral Sea.

This 'reconnaissance in force', as we might call it today, garnered vital intelligence for the full-scale Mongol invasion of Eastern Europe, which took place fourteen years later during Ogedei Khan's reign, and which will be covered in the final novel in this Mongol Knight trilogy.

Mongol politics and law

The conquests of Genghis Khan and his successors were on a global scale: at the height of the Mongol Empire, an Arrow Rider, bearing a silver or gold *gerege* (the equivalent of a diplomatic passport), could ride from the Carpathian Mountains to the coast of Korea, stopping at way stations every fifteen to forty miles for fresh horses, food and shelter, without ever leaving territory controlled by the Great Khan. But the greatest Mongol leader's achievements were much more than mass slaughter and continent-wide subjugation.

Beginning his life as a raggedy nobody on the fringes of steppe society, Genghis Khan went from being a hunted, starving fugitive to uniting all the various tribes under his banner, turning them all into Mongols, and becoming the most powerful warlord in the world. He created a set of laws to govern his new people called the Great Yasa, which really did include such dictums as 'Matters of the steppe should be decided on the steppe; and matters of the *ger* should be decided in the *ger*'.

Genghis Khan was also a surprisingly tolerant leader when it came to religious matters. In an age when the Catholic Church was busy hunting down heretics and burning them at the stake for their beliefs, the Great Khan allowed complete religious freedom in his domains. His subjects could worship any god they chose, just as long as they did not question his temporal authority. And, indeed, his subjects included Muslims, Buddhists, Taoists, animists – and Christians, of the Eastern (or Nestorian) Church. Sorkoktani Beki, for example, wife of his youngest son Tolui, the Prince of the Fireplace, was a Christian. And she taught her father-in-law's principles of tolerance to her four sons – Mönke, Kublai, Hulagu and Ariq Boke – all of whom became khans in due course. Sorkoktani herself gave alms to both Christians and Muslims, and paid for a new madrassa (an Islamic school) to be built in Burkhara.

The selection of a new Great Khan was also governed by a kind of election. A *kurultai* was called, which every Mongol man of rank was obliged to attend, and a new khan was elected by a vote. In the *kurultai* of 1227, after the death of Genghis Khan, Tolui might have expected to be chosen as the next Great Khan, but such was the support for Ogedei that he was only made Regent, a role he played for two years until he was forced to call another *kurultai* in 1229, at which his hard-drinking older brother was elected to the ultimate position of power.

And here I must confess another crime against historical accuracy.

Tolui Khan lived on for another two years after Ogedei's succession to the throne, and while he was sidelined and much diminished in his military power, he still participated in the campaign against the Jin Empire. Like his father, Tolui's death is cloaked in mystery. One story goes that, after Ogedei was cursed by a Jin sorcerer, Tolui, his loyal brother, voluntarily sacrificed his own life in a shamanic ritual to save his khan. But there are other darker rumours that Ogedei had Tolui quietly murdered, which I think is more likely given their intense rivalry for power. Anyway, I must admit that I latched on to that murder story, since I had an English assassin to hand, and the idea of Tolui killing himself to save his brother did not seem plausible.

The point is, this is historical fiction, not fact, and I think it made for a better story to have Robert doing these dreadful deeds to further his plan to save Christendom. And Robert's story is not yet over. The Englishman's adventures with the Mongol army will continue, and his trial in Vienna will come to its conclusion, in the final book of the trilogy, which is scheduled to be published in the summer of 2027.

Angus Donald
Tonbridge, 24 February 2026